I0576201

Frederik E. A. Schiern, James Hepburn

Life of James Hepburn

Earl of Bothwell

Frederik E. A. Schiern, James Hepburn

Life of James Hepburn
Earl of Bothwell

ISBN/EAN: 9783337094881

Printed in Europe, USA, Canada, Australia, Japan

Cover: Foto ©Raphael Reischuk / pixelio.de

More available books at **www.hansebooks.com**

Life of James Hepburn
Earl of Bothwell

BY FREDERIK SCHIERN

PROFESSOR OF HISTORY IN THE UNIVERSITY OF COPENHAGEN

Translated from the Danish by the Rev. David Berry,

F.S.A. Scot.

EDINBURGH: DAVID DOUGLAS

1880.

TRANSLATOR'S PREFACE.

PROFESSOR SCHIERN first published his work on Bothwell in 1863. Another edition of it, with considerable alterations, was issued by him in 1875. The present translation has been made from this edition, with such changes and additions by the author as more recent information enabled him to make. To adapt the work for publication in this country a few other alterations have been introduced, but in no instance affecting the integrity of the text. The original Danish title has been altered in order to express more adequately the contents of the volume. These, as the reader will find, embrace much more than an account of Bothwell's detention in Norway and imprisonment in Denmark (which was the only thing stated in the original title), and in reality trace his career from the beginning, besides discussing at length his relations to Queen Mary. As far as possible, all the authorities appealed to by the author have been carefully verified, and where extracts from English or Scottish writers rendered into Danish were given in the text within inverted commas, these have invariably been replaced by the words of the original authority. One or two notes correcting or explaining certain statements of the author have been added. A few of the longer notes that were put at the foot of the page have been thrown into an Appendix, in which is also printed for the first time the copy of Bothwell's so-called "Testament," presented by Drummond to the University of Edinburgh, that had for a long time gone amissing, but was recently recovered by Mr. Small, the Librarian. To facilitate reference a table of contents and a copious index have also been added.

Acknowledgments are due to various gentlemen for valuable assistance and suggestions in bringing out this work. To the author I am indebted, not only for kindly granting me liberty to translate his book into English, but for notes and communications sent me while engaged in its translation. I would also take this opportunity of expressing my obligations to Mr. John Robson of George Watson's College Schools, and especially to Mr. Joseph Anderson, keeper of the National Museum of the Society of Antiquaries, Edinburgh. Other gentlemen have kindly supplied me with information in reference to some matters stated in this work whose names I have mentioned elsewhere. Thanks are also due to the Senatus Academicus of the University of Edinburgh for allowing a copy to be taken of the MSS. of Bothwell's Testament in their possession.

Professor Schiern has won for himself a distinguished name as an historical investigator. His *Nyere Historiske Studier*, though hardly known in this country, hold a high place on the Continent. The largest of these, his Monograph on Bothwell, is represented by R. Pauli in a recent article of his on Mary (*Historische Zeitschrift*, herausg. von H. v. Sybel, Neue Folge vi. 213), along with Dr. Hill Burton's *History of Scotland*, "as bringing no less honour on the science of history in our day by its trustworthy researches." It is equally favourably noticed by Professor Gaedeke of Heidelberg in a work on the same subject. In its English form it is hoped that it may be no less acceptable as a valuable contribution to the illustration of a most interesting period of Scottish History.

AIRDRIE, 27th *November* 1879.

CONTENTS.

CHAPTER I.

CHAPTER II.

CHAPTER IV.

CHAPTER V.

CHAPTER VI.

CHAPTER VII.

CHAPTER VIII.

CHAPTER XI.

JAMES HEPBURN EARL OF BOTHWELL.

CHAPTER I.

CHAP.
I.

1536.

IN going southward from Glasgow by railway, one of the first stations which is reached is Uddingston. From this point is seen in the horizon the church spire rising over the village of Bothwell, and as the traveller advances towards the latter, and is within a fourth part of the way from Uddingston, he has on his right hand the mansion-house of Bothwell, which for two days a week is open to visitors. Entering the policies he passes the new castle of Bothwell, for what attracts his attention here are the ruins of the old—the once famous castle of Bothwell, the most magnificent of the kind which have been preserved from Scotland's middle ages. In these ruins he meets with a noble relic of the so-called Norman style. They form a rectangle, which extends to two hundred and thirty-two feet in length and ninety-nine in breadth, and is flanked on both sides by two lofty round towers. Up the walls, which are fourteen feet thick and sixty high, climb the ivy, the wild rose, and wallflower. The bank whereon the ruins stand slopes down towards the noisy brown Clyde, which at this point sweeps

A

suddenly round in a semicircular course, and sometimes, as an inscription here tells us, rises to a great
height. This bank, like the one on the opposite side
of the river, from which the ruins of the priory of
Blantyre present themselves to view, is covered with
wood, and, as "Bothwell Bank," became early celebrated in Scottish song, though more from the
melancholy than the cheerful interest attached to it,
and has ever since retained its place in the Scottish
mind. An English traveller, who was in Palestine
in the sixteenth century, happening to pass through
a village not far from Jerusalem, heard there a
woman, who sat at the door of her house, and
rocked her babe, humming to herself the words,
" Bothwell Bank, thou bloomest fair." On address-
ing her, he learned that she was a Scottish woman
whom a romantic destiny had joined in marriage
to a native of Turkey, and who now in the distant
East sought to soothe her home-sickness with the
national songs of her own dear Scotland.[1]

Bothwell Castle, where Scotland's oppressor,
King Edward III., had for a long time his residence
during his invasion of the country, now belongs
to the Countess of Home, and this, with many
other possessions, she has inherited as the eldest
daughter of Lady Montague, sister to the last
Lord Douglas, who died in 1857 without issue.
The renowned race of the Douglases owned Bothwell Castle in the middle ages; but during the
period which elapsed after their forfeiture in the
reign of James II., it, along with other posses-

---

[1] *The Songs of Scotland before
Burns.* By J. C. Shairp. *Mac-
millan's Magazine* for March 1861.

[See also Verstegan, *Restitution of
Decayed Intelligence.* Amsterdam,
1605.—*Translator.*]

sions, had devolved upon the then existing family CHAP.
of Hepburn—the Hepburns of Hales. Lord Patrick I.
Hepburn was in 1481 created Earl of Bothwell by 1536.
James IV., who also bestowed upon him the hereditary office of Lord High Admiral of Scotland,
along with many other dignities and extensive
possessions. His grandson became the best known
Lord of Bothwell, but at the fall of the latter his
possessions were confiscated, and after having in
the reign of James VI. been made over to his
nearest relative, only to be in a short time taken
away from him again, the castle of Bothwell re-
verted once more to the Douglas family.

James Earl of Bothwell, or as he himself writes
his own name, James Erle Boithuille, was born
in the year 1536 or 1537.[1] In the battle of
Flodden, which cut down the flower of Scotland's
nobility, Adam, the second Earl of Bothwell, was
slain by the English, leaving his son Patrick in
his minority, who later, as third Earl of Bothwell,
played an important part in Scottish history. By
his contemporaries he has been described as "the
fair Earl," but an English statesman, who, if not
quite an impartial witness, had a long acquaintance with the country, at a time when he was
associated with the enemies of England, gives him
the character of the proudest and haughtiest man
in all Scotland.[2] In the year 1535 he married
Agnes Sinclair, who belonged to one of the most
renowned of the families of Norman extraction in

[1] Robert Douglas, *The Peerage of Scotland.* Edinburgh, 1764, fol. i. 229.
[2] "I think him the most vain and insolent man in the world, full of pride and folly, and here, I assure, nothing at all esteemed."—*State Papers and Letters of Sir Ralph Sadler;* edited by A. Clifford. Edinburgh, 1809, 4to, i. 184.

CHAP.
I.

1543.

Scotland,—a family which has acquired additional fame especially in the Scandinavian north, alike from Colonel George Sinclair who fell in Guldbrandsdal in Norway, during the Kalmark war; from Andrew Sinclair of Sinclairsholm, the highly-trusted counsellor of Christian IV., King of Denmark, who also, in the same war, fought on the Danish side; and from Major Malcolm Sinclair, who was murdered by the Russians in his homeward journey from Turkey to Sweden, during the so-called "time of freedom."[1] Agnes Sinclair, during her union with Earl Patrick Hepburn, bore him a daughter Jane and a son James, latterly so famous and so often confounded by historians with his father. So early as 1543 their marriage seems to have been dissolved by a divorce, and Earl Patrick remained unmarried until his death in 1556. His divorced wife, or, as she is now commonly called from the usual place of her residence, "the Lady of Morham," however, survived him until the year 1573, and thus became a witness both of her son's exaltation and overthrow.

An attempt is commonly made to account for the divorce between Earl Patrick Bothwell and Agnes Sinclair on the ground of too near relationship, but the real ground of it was certainly something else. It has been remarked of both the

[1 This is the name usually given in Swedish history to the period lasting from 1720 to 1772. During this period, owing to the weakness of the reigning sovereigns, the power in a great measure fell into the hands of the nobles, who ruled the country through the Council and States of the kingdom. They were divided into two leading parties, named respectively the "hats" and the "caps," and, by their constant struggles with each other for the supremacy, gave rise to an amount of licence and anarchy that caused the nation gladly to welcome relief from such freedom through the measures taken by Gustavus III.—*Translator*.]

grandfather and father of the first of the Hepburns
who became Earl of Bothwell, namely, Lord Patrick
Hepburn of Hales, and Adam Hepburn of Hales,
that they had already ventured to court the regard
of Queen dowagers of Scotland—the former that of
the beautiful Jane Beaufort, widow of James I., and
the latter that of Mary of Gueldres, widow of James
II. We have the assurance of Patrick Hepburn,
third Earl of Bothwell, given not long after his
divorce from Agnes Sinclair, and bearing his own
signature, that the widow of James V., Mary of Guise,
mother of Mary Stuart, "promest faithfullie, be hir
hand writ, at twa sindre tymis, to tak the said
Erle in mariage."[1] When his son at a later period
ventured his all to be united in marriage with the
reigning Queen of Scotland, he could thus see in
retrospect among his ancestors examples of those
who had lifted their eyes almost as high.

The only information we have about the childhood of Bothwell, or about his fortunes during
those years while he was known simply as James
Hepburn, occurs in a polemical tract against Mary
Stuart, which enjoyed no small celebrity in his time.
Its substance is to the effect that he had received a bad training in Spynie Castle, near Elgin,
with his grand-uncle, Patrick Hepburn, Bishop of
Moray, who seems to have been one of many in-
vested with the clerical office, who, in the period

---

[1] See "Deeds connected with
the Hepburns, Earls of Bothwell,
and the Hepburns of Waughton,"
and "Letters of Patrick, Earl of
Bothwell," in the *Bannatyne Miscellany*, containing original papers
and tracts, chiefly relating to the
history and literature of Scotland.
Edinburgh, 1827-55, 4to, iii. 273-
312, 403-423. Also the preface of
Joseph Robertson to the edition
issued under his care for the Bannatyne Club of *Inuentaires de la
Royne Descosse, Douairiere de
France*. Edinburgh, 1863, 4to, pp.
84-95.

anterior to the Reformation of the sixteenth century, and especially when occupying remote situations in places screened from active superintendence, entirely devoted themselves to the acquisition of lands, riches, and worldly influence.[1] Could we warrantably assume that some of the books, which at a later period belonged to Bothwell, had been employed in his early tuition, we should have reason to expect that they would be highly advantageous in moulding the future commander of his country's army. Of the books which once were his, two finely bound volumes with his arms stamped upon them are still extant. One of these is a work by two mathematical authors;[2] the other, which embraces two works bound together, consists partly of a tractate by Robert Valturin on military matters,[3] and partly of a translation of some treatises concerning the military art by classical authors.[4]

[1] Quæ virtutes ab eo expectari poterant? ab homine scilicet, in aula Moraviensis Episcopi, hoc est longe corruptissima educato, in vino et stupris, inter vilissima solutæ illius disciplinæ ministeria. Buchanan, *De Maria Scotorum Regina.* Londini, 1571, p. 54. That the often unreliable charges of Buchanan are not in this instance without foundation, is shown by the unusually large number of children for a Scottish prelate in the Reformation time, which later became legitimised as the Bishop of Moray's. They are to be found mentioned in one of the notes to the *History of the Reformation in Scotland* by John Knox; edited by David Laing. Edinburgh, 1856, i. 41.

[2] *Larismetique & Geometrie de maistre Estienne de la Roche dict Ville Franche, Nouuellement Imprimée & des faultes corrigée, a la* qvelle sont adioustées les Tables de diuers comptes, auec leurs Canons, calculées par Gilles Huguetan, natif de Lyon. 1538, fol. This volume now stands by the side of one of Mary Stuart's books in the beautiful library belonging to Mr. J. T. Gibson-Craig, Edinburgh.

[3] *Les Dovze Livres de Robert Valtvrin touchant la Discipline Militaire translatez de langve Latin en Francoyse par Loys Meignet, Lyonnois.* A Paris, 1555, fol.

[4] *Flaue Vegece Rene homme noble et illustre du fait de Guerre et fleur de cheualerie quatre liures : Sexte Jule homme consulaire des Stratagemes especes et subtilitez de guerre quatre liures : Aelian de l'ordre et instruction des batailles vng liure : Modeste des Vocables du fait de guerre vng livre : Pareillement cxx. histoires concernans le faite guerre ioinctes a Vegece. Tra-*

That these works are wholly in the French tongue is in accordance with the influence which France still exercised at that time on all matters in Scotland, and this fact taken together with another obscure announcement from Scotland, which at a later date speaks of the young lord's "first entrance into this kingdom immediately after his father's death," may also possibly point to his having been early sent over to visit France.[1] In any case James Hepburn could hardly have had many years' instruction in his youth, for he was still in his nineteenth or twentieth year when his father died, and when he not only succeeded him as Lord of Bothwell Castle; but also came into possession of the hereditary offices of Lord High Admiral of Scotland, Sheriff in the counties of Berwick, Haddington, and Edinburgh, and of Bailiff in Lauderdale, with Hales and Crichton Castles as his fortresses.[2] If we except only the head of the Hamiltons—the then Lord James Hamilton, who, by his descent from

duicts fidellement de Latin en Francois : et collationnez (par le polygraphe humble secretaire et historien du parc d'honneur) aux liures anciens tant a ceulx de Bude que Beroalde et Bade. A Paris, 1536, fol. The volume containing this work and the other before-mentioned treatise, is now in the Library of the University of Edinburgh.

[1] "Begynand from his verie zouth, and first entres to this realme, immediatelie efter the deceis of his fadir." These words occur in Mary Stuart's instruction in 1567 to the Bishop of Dunblane, who was appointed to notify her marriage with Bothwell to the Court of France, contained in Lettres, instructions et mémoires de Maria Stuart, publiées sur les originaux et les manuscrits du State Paper

Office de Londres et des principales archives et bibliothèques de l'Europe, par le Prince Alexandre Labanoff. Londres et Paris, 1844, ii. 33. It is Chalmers in his Caledonia, an account, historical and topographical, of North Britain, London, 1810, 4to, ii. 453, who has made the observation about the intimation which seems to be implied by the words above cited.

[2] That these offices were not conferred by Mary Stuart as marks of favour, but simply inherited by Bothwell, Chalmers shows in his disquisition, "Of the several grants which were said to be made by the Scottish Queen, to James Erle Bothwell," contained in his work, Life of Mary Queen of Scots, drawn from the State Papers. London, 1818, 4to, ii. 248-55.

Mary, daughter of James II., had become the nearest heir to the crown, and had also received from the King of France in 1554 the dukedom of Châtel-herault[1]—young Bothwell was now the most powerful nobleman with the greatest number of vassals in the whole south of Scotland.

While still in early youth we find him thus in high positions taking an active part in public affairs. In the year 1557 we meet with him as a member of the Scottish Parliament, by which, on the 14th December, Commissioners for Scotland were appointed to be present on the 24th of April following, in the Church of Notre Dame, in Paris, at the solemn betrothal of their Queen Mary Stuart, who had hitherto been brought up in a nunnery in France, and was now, in her sixteenth year, affianced to the Dauphin, afterwards Francis II.[2] When Bothwell succeeded his father, the dispute about Naples had already given occasion to the war between Spain and France, in which the marriage of Philip II. with Queen Mary Tudor had very naturally placed England on the Spanish side, just as Queen Mary Stuart's union to the Dauphin placed Scotland on the side of the French. This war called forth Bothwell's earliest martial exploits. In the end of the year 1557, Mary Stuart's mother, the widow of James V., Mary of Guise, who, in the name of her young absent daughter, acted as Regent of Scotland,

---

[1] Labanne, *Histoire de Chatel-leraud et du Chatelleraudais Cha-telleraut.* 1859, vols. i. ii. The representative of the ducal house of Hamilton, in respect of this inheritance in France, still bears the title of Duke of Chatelherault. Consult Teulet's *Mémoire justifi-catif du droit qui appartient à Mr. le duc d'Hamilton de porter le titre de duc de Châtelheraulte.* Paris, 1864.

[2] *The Acts of the Parliaments of Scotland.* London, 1814-1844, vol. ii. p. 514.

had ordered the Scottish troops assembled at Kelso CHAP.
to make a raid into England; but the most powerful leaders among the nobles being dissatisfied with 1558.
the way in which she had assigned the chief offices
of the government in Scotland to Frenchmen alone,
after mutual consultation jointly refused to obey,
asserting that it would be sufficient to defend the
country against attack from the south. Bothwell,
however, who, in spite of his youth, was in the following year appointed Lieutenant-General of the
southerly Scottish frontier—the so-called marches
or Borders[1]—and keeper of Hermitage Castle in
the remote and inaccessible wilds of the Scottish
border toward England, readily marched across the
frontiers; and having made a destructive inroad
upon the English,[2] again took his place in Parliament on the 29th November 1558, when it met
anew in Edinburgh.[3] Thus from his first entrance
on public life Bothwell showed himself an enemy to
the English government, and to the English party
in Scotland, and we shall ever find him the same
during his whole subsequent career.

The death of Queen Mary Tudor on the 17th
November 1558, and the accession of her half-sister
Elizabeth to the throne, having dissolved the Eng-

---

[1] About this appointment Mary
Stuart, at a later period, thus expresses herself in her instruction to
the Bishop of Dunblane :—" Notwithstanding he wes yan of verie
young aige, yit wes he chosin out
as maist fit of the haill nobilitie to
be oure Lieutenant-Generall upoun
the bordouris, having the haill
charge alsweill to defend as to
assayle." Labanoff, *Lettres, instructions et mémoires de Marie
Stuart*, vol. ii. p. 34.

[2] In an account of the events in
Scotland, from 1559 to 1568,
written by Bothwell, given in
Teulet, *Lettres de Marie Stuart*,
Paris, 1859, p. 162, he expresses
himself later about this expedition
to the following effect : " J'avois
faict des dommages irréparables
sur les frontières, et mesmement à
ceux qui y demeurent."

[3] *The Acts of the Parliaments of
Scotland*, vol. ii. p. 503.

CHAP. lish league with Spain, the war carried on by Spain
I.   and England with France and Scotland was termin-
1559. ated by the conclusion of peace at Cateau-Cambresis
on the 2d of April 1559.[1] In this treaty a special
article stipulated that the new fortresses which had
been built on the Scottish side of the borders should
be demolished, and that in like manner all the castles
and forts reared by the English on their side should
also be razed. On this occasion it was arranged that
commissioners from both kingdoms should meet on
the frontiers, and, along with Sir Richard Maitland
and Sir Walter Ker, the Earl of Bothwell was appointed a member of the Scottish commission which,
acting in concert with the English guardians, made
a full settlement of these points.

But neither the treaty of Cateau-Cambresis, nor
any other, brought lasting peace to Scotland so long
as Queen Elizabeth did not wish it. It was her
constant endeavour to extend the English influence
in Scotland, and to weaken the independence of the
country [2] by the invariable support which she gave,
during almost the whole of her reign, to any Scots
party that happened to be in opposition to the
government. A few months after the conclusion of
the peace of Cateau-Cambresis the fiery eloquence
of Knox gave an impetus to the Reformation struggle
which, like a hurricane, tore down the images from

---

[1] In Danish, as well as in many
German historical and geographical
hand-books and school-books, this
name is written Chateau-Cam-
bresis, not Cateau-Cambresis as
above. The latter form, which is
alone used by Frenchmen themselves, is however the more correct
one.

[2] Consult Chalmers' treatise " Of
the Project of the English Government for the Subduction of Scotland, under Henry VIII., Edward
VI., and Elizabeth," in his *Life of
Mary Queen of Scots*, vol. ii. pp.
401-414.

the Romish cathedrals, overthrew the monasteries, CHAP. and levelled so many ancient ecclesiastical monu- <u>I.</u> ments with the ground. At the time when in Scot- 1559. land the adherents of the Reformation were gathered together in open rebellion, and the Regent was plainly declared to be deposed, the death of Henry II. (on the 7th July 1559), unexpectedly caused by a wound which he had received in one of his tourna- ments, suddenly placed his son the Dauphin, a weak-minded youth, as Francis II. on the French throne. In consequence of the young King's de- pendence on his wife, the royal power fell chiefly into the hands of two of the most influential of Mary Stuart's uncles, the zealous Catholic brothers —Duke Francis the elder of Guise, and the Cardinal of Lorraine : the former of whom, by his successful defence of Metz, in the reign of Henry II., against the Emperor Charles V., and by his recent capture of Calais, after it had been held for two centuries by England, had already become the favourite of the French people, while the latter had attained to a degree of political influence in the Court of Henry not enjoyed by any other. The Guises now sought first, and chiefly, to employ the power of France in sending over money and troops to their high-spirited sister the Regent in Scotland, who was striving to put down the rebellion raised by the adherents of the Reformation. During a crisis like that through which Europe was then passing, it was hardly possible to hold the balance between the contending parties. But even partial opponents have been obliged so to acknowledge the discern- ment and fairness of the Scottish Regent, that they have not charged to her but to her brothers the

blame of the faults from whose consequences she
did not wholly escape.[1] She saw the cause of the
Scottish rebellion to be already tottering. But
at this stage Elizabeth stepped in. The English
Queen gradually became a partisan of the rebellion
in Scotland, to which, at first, her support was
given secretly, but, latterly, quite openly ; and
although her letters to Mary of Guise are full of
asseverations that she had not the slightest share
in what was going on, yet in reality her assistance
very soon more than counterbalanced the aid received by the Regent from the Continent.

During the whole of this contest the Earl of
Bothwell, though he was one of those who had
embraced, and always continued to profess the
Reformed doctrine, nevertheless stood with constancy on the side of the Regent. In account-
ing at a later period to others abroad for this
seemingly inconsistent conduct, Bothwell maintained that the Scottish aristocracy were actuated
in the contest by no purely religious motive, but
simply by a desire to set the lower classes of the
people, or, as he calls them, "the simple folk," in
agitation, making use of religion only as a pretext.[2]
Bothwell took not a few of the Regent's enemies
prisoners during the war.[3] Having, by her com-

[1] Erat enim singulari ingenio
prædita, et animo ad æquitatem
admodum propenso. *Rerum Scoticarum Historia,* Auctore Georgio
Buchanano. Edinburgi, 1582, fol.
p. 197.

[2] "Du prétexte de la religion."
Bothwell's representation as given
in Teulet, *Lettres,* p. 158. The same
expression is used by one of Bothwell's contemporaries, who speaks
of the nobles as making their ap-

pearance "under pretext of religion."—*The Memoirs of Sir James
Melvil of Hal-hill;* now first
published from the original manuscript by George Scott. London,
1683, fol. p. 64.

[3] "Je prins," he writes, "selon
le droict des armes, plusieurs Escos-
sois et Anglois, et en toutes choses
faisois de mon mieulx, me compor-
tois comme de debvoir le requéroit."
Teulet, *Lettres,* p. 160.

mand, in the autumn of the year 1559, placed himself in ambush with some French troops, at Dun-
pender Law in East Lothian, he was so fortunate as
to surprise and take prisoner one of the leaders of
the rebellion, who at the time was charged with an
important mission. John Cockburn, laird of Ormiston, had been secretly sent in the latter days of
October to Berwick, in England, for the purpose
of receiving from the accredited agents of Elizabeth, Sir Ralph Sadler and Sir James Croftes, a
thousand pounds sterling, as part of the sums which
Elizabeth had destined to fan the flame of the
rebellion. Carrying the treasure intrusted to him
he had got safely past Dunbar, with its French
garrison, where Mary of Guise had once sought
refuge. On the evening of the 31st October in the
neighbourhood of Haddington, he was suddenly set
upon by Bothwell, and, sorely wounded, fell into
the Earl's hands,[1] along with the treasure which
he carried. The leaders of the rebellion keenly
felt this blow, which they never forgot nor forgave. Bothwell is said, only three days before
he executed his successful surprise, to have sent
one of his servants, Michael Balfour, to Edinburgh,
which they had then occupied, in order to request
a safe-conduct for the Earl, that he might be able
to come and treat with them. The partisans of
the rebellion, therefore, flattered themselves with
the hope that now the Earl of Bothwell also
wished to join their cause, and since, as Knox

[1] *La Vigille de Toussainctz.*
Letter, dated Leith, 12th November 1559, from Henry Clutin
d'Oysel, French ambassador and
commander of the French troops in
Scotland, contained in Teulet,
*Papiers d'état, pièces et documents
inédits ou peu connus, relatifs à
l'histoire de l'Ecosse au 16me siècle.*
Paris, 1852. 4to, i. 379. *Miscellany of the Wodrow Society.*
Edinburgh, 1844, i. 70.

states, they had agreed to grant him the safe-
conduct only on the supposition that he on his
side was pledged not to do them any injury
in the meanwhile, they were consequently led to
deem it an act of treachery that Bothwell had
complied with the Regent's command in the way
just described.[1]   Elizabeth's agents advised the
confederate lords to deny that the money had come
from the English Queen, and to say that it was
their own.[2]   Two leaders among the lords forthwith hastened from Edinburgh at the head of two
thousand horsemen after Bothwell, in order to recover the lost treasure, which was to provide a
supply for their pecuniary distress.   One of the two
was the illegitimate son of King James v., Lord
James Stuart, prior of St. Andrews,[3] and afterwards
Earl of Murray.   Having been born in 1531, he
was now eleven years older than Mary Stuart, and
he had already laid his powerful hand on the helm

[1] Knox's *History of the Reformation in Scotland*, i. 456.

[2] Account of 4th November
1559, from Sir Ralph Sadler and
Sir James Croftes to Thomas Randolph, contained in *Calendar of the
State Papers relating to Scotland*,
preserved in the State Department
of Her Majesty's Public Record
Office. By Markham John Thorpe,
Esq. London, 1858, i. 120. The
circumstance that d'Oysel's already
cited letter of 12th November expressly says that "la somme
n'estoit que de mil ponds sterling,"
while other contemporaries, on the
contrary, have stated the whole
sum with which Elizabeth had
secretly sought to support the rebellion, in one case at "xiiii. mille
livres" (*Teulet*, i. 382), and in
another at "tre tusind Pund sterling" (*The State Papers of Sir

Ralph Sadler*, i. 391), has led
Teulet to the supposition that
Bothwell must have surreptitiously
employed for his own advantage a
portion of the money which he had
seized. But the sum seized by
Bothwell was only a part of the
amount which Elizabeth had designed for the Scottish lords, and
Sadler and Croftes give the sum
itself just as d'Oysel does.

[3] Properly the Commendator of
St. Andrews. This Scottish title,
which frequently occurs in the
history of the Reformation, is thus
explained in Anderson's list of ancient Scottish words—"Commendator, who enjoys the rents of an
abbey or other benefice." Anderson's *Collections relating to the
History of Mary Queen of Scotland*. Edinburgh, 1727, 4to, i. 154.

of the State, and quickly became the principal
leader of the Reformed party, by whose means
he was afterwards to bring such utter ruin upon
his half-sister.[1] The other leader on this occasion
was the impetuous Lord James Hamilton, Earl of
Arran, a son of the Duke of Châtelherault. He had
recently held the command of the Scottish Guard
in France, but had lost this post in consequence of
having embraced the Reformed doctrine, and finding his liberty in danger on the Continent, he had
secretly returned home with a zeal for the new
order of things, which led him to express a wish
that he might see all the Papists in Scotland
hanged, and which had now enabled him to gain
over his father, the powerful duke, to the cause
of the rebellion. Bothwell, with his booty, had
sought refuge in one of his hereditary fortresses on
the banks of the water of Tyne—the now ruined
Crichton Castle, which in its present state has been
so well described by Sir Walter Scott in *Marmion.*
The castle was speedily taken by the Reformed
party, but not before Bothwell had succeeded in
escaping from it with the money, which at that
moment was of so great importance to both parties.
His possessions were spared by his enemies until
they had summoned him to deliver up his booty,
and this Bothwell having refused to do, the
lords caused Crichton Castle to be completely
sacked. Bothwell looked upon the Earl of Arran
as the real author of this act of devastation, and

---

[1] He was, in consequence of the
Bishop of Glasgow's report at a
later period, called by the Spanish
ambassador "grande herege y en-
nemigo capital de su Reyna y her-
mana." Don Frances de Alava's
letter to Philip II., dated Paris,
17th July 1567.—Teulet, *Papiers
d'état,* iii. 36.

accordingly sent him a challenge to single combat, in which he professed his willingness to meet him openly before "French and Scots," and in whatever way he pleased, either "on horseback or on foot." The challenge was scornfully rejected. "First when ye," so ran the Earl of Arran's answer to him, "may have again won back the name of an honest man, which by your last exploit you have lost, I shall be ready to give you the satisfaction which is meet, but not before Frenchmen, to whom you assign the precedence over Scotsmen, for there is no Frenchman in this kingdom with whose judgment I will have anything to do." But this taunt was by no means unpunished. When the Scottish lords, after Edinburgh had fallen into their hands, attempted also to seize the port of Leith, which the Regent had caused to be fortified, and which was defended by a part of the French troops sent her, they were repulsed, and, by the 8th November, the French were again enabled to occupy Edinburgh, which the Protestant nobles had evacuated during the night. In December 1559, the Queen Regent saw herself even in a position to give over to the hitherto successful Bothwell the command of eight hundred French and Scottish soldiers, with whom he was sent from Edinburgh to Stirling to secure its famous fortress.[1]

Meanwhile a decisive turning-point drew near with the commencement of the new year 1560. Although Elizabeth, in her communications to Mary of Guise, still continued to protest that she was striving only for peace and all that was good,

[1] *The State Papers of Sir Ralph Sadler*, i. 667.

yet the moment had now come when she in her CHAP. I. actions dared wholly to throw off the mask. On the 27th February 1560, she caused the Duke of 1560. Norfolk to conclude, in her behalf, at Berwick, a formal treaty of alliance with the rebellious subjects of the neighbouring kingdom—a treaty whose ostensible aim was to expel the French troops from Scotland. Circumstances had then arranged themselves so strangely that she could boldly venture on this step. She was now induced to interfere in behalf of the Reformation contest in Scotland, with a zeal which was quickened even by the most Catholic of all princes, Philip II. of Spain. For, on the one hand, the latter saw the union between Spain and England dissolved in consequence of the recent death of its Popish queen, his second consort, Mary Tudor ; and, on the other hand, he now beheld the alliance between France and Scotland so strengthened by the almost contemporary decease of Henry II., that at this peculiar juncture he was easily predisposed to listen to the representations of his half-sister, Margaret of Parma, who, ruling the Netherlands in her brother's name, found reason to fear that if the gigantic policy of the Guises once became supreme both in Britain and France, the Netherlands would also be subjected to their all-powerful influence.[1] Amid these externally tranquillising

[1] In Ranke's representation of the Scottish relations it is strikingly remarked—" Für alles, was in der Welt zu Stande kommen soll, bedarf es der rechten Zeit und Stunde. Wer sollte es glauben ? Der Vorfechter des strengsten Katholicismus, der König von Spanien, war in diesem Augenblick nicht allein dafür, dass den Schotten Hülfe zu Theil würde, sondern er drang darauf ; seine Minister beklagten sich nicht, dass die Königin einschritt, sondern darüber dass sie dies nicht schleuniger that."—*Englische Geschichte vornemlich im sechszehnten und siebzehnten Jahrhundert.* Berlin und Leipzig, 1859-1868, i. 330.

events, Elizabeth, on the 30th March, caused an English army of 8000 men, commanded by William Lord Grey de Wilton, to cross the river Tweed and enter Scotland. At Preston it was joined by an equally large contingent of the Scottish confederate army, under the command of the Duke of Châtelherault and Lord James Stuart. Sometime previously, about the middle of winter, she had also sent an English fleet, under Admiral William Winter, up the Firth of Forth, where the English ships safely anchored. Nearly about the same time—just as happened afterwards on a still more famous occasion most propitiously for Elizabeth—the storms out in the North Sea drove back two "Armadas" which had been fitted out on the French coast, and destined for strengthening Mary of Guise, causing the loss of many ships and over three thousand soldiers.

The Regent, with unabated heroism, although suffering from sickness, had now betaken herself to the castle of Edinburgh, but the real contest concentrated itself again around Leith, which was blockaded by the English ships in the Firth, and besieged on the land side by the greatly superior force of the combined army. At daybreak on the 7th May, Leith was assaulted by 10,000 English and Scottish troops, but the Frenchmen were prepared for the assault, and with great bloodshed drove back the assailants at all points. That was a proud day for France, when a handful of her sons, cut off from all connection with their country and exhausted with hunger, triumphed over the combined military forces of Scotland and England. Mary of Guise herself had sat during the fight on the battlements of Edinburgh Castle, and thence CHAP. had followed the course of the struggle; and it may well be believed, though Knox relates it as 1560. worthy of reprobation, that, after having been a witness to the victory of her countrymen, when she saw their standard again flying over the ramparts of Leith, she instantly went to mass.[1] But in spite of this victory, and notwithstanding the brave sallies of the beleaguered Frenchmen, the Regent of Scotland could not anticipate, during the existing complications, any successful issue to the contest, and accordingly, in the month of May, she charged the Earl of Bothwell to hasten over to her daughter's Court, anew to urge the sending of greater assistance.[2] After having received this commission, Bothwell betook himself to the north of Scotland,[3] and we are informed that he thence proceeded to Denmark,[4] but it is matter of doubt whether he really did so under the impression that thus he would more easily reach France, the goal of his journey, or whether he at that time possibly had

[1] And quhen sche perceivit the overthraw of us, and that the ensenyeis of the Frenche war agane displayit upoun the wallis, sche gaif ane gafwe of lauchter, and said— "Now will I go to the messe, and prayse God for that quhilk my eyes have sene."—Knox, *History of the Reformation in Scotland*, ii. 67.

[2] Bothwell's letter to the Regent, dated Crichton, 15th May 1560, contained in Chalmers, *Life of Mary Queen of Scots*, ii. 217.

[3] "It is very certain that Earl Bothwell has his despatch into France, and is now in the north parts to search passage; he was with the Earl of Athol and divers gentlemen; his train is very small,

he rides only with five horses, and is uncertain to all where he comes or how long he tarries in one place."—Letter of the English Minister, Thomas Randolph, to the Duke of Norfolk, dated Holyrood-house, 7th June 1560, contained in *Calendar of State Papers, Foreign Series, of the Reign of Elizabeth.* 1560-1561, p. 108. London, 1865-1871.

[4] "Earl Bothwell has arrived out of Denmark into Flanders, and is daily looked for here."—Letter from the English Ambassador, Sir Nicholas Throckmorton, to Cecil, dated Pau, 12th September 1560, contained in *Calendar of State Papers, Foreign Series*, 1560-1561, p. 293.

had also an alleged political errand in Denmark. The latter supposition seems to receive support from the circumstance that the English minister in Copenhagen, in the summer of 1560, communicated to Queen Elizabeth that the French ambassador in Denmark urgently desired Frederick II. to lend the French his fleet to assist them against the Scots.[1] In Resen's *Annals of Frederick II.* for the month of June 1560, the information is added, that "at the same time came Lord James Earl Boudevill, high admiral of Scotland, into Denmark to the King, and was well received, and as he wished to travel further into Germany, he was conducted through Jutland and the duchy, both by the King and the Duke of Holstein."[2] In France, where subsequently in the year 1560, we for the first time meet with Bothwell, he was rewarded, after completing his mission, with an appointment at court as the King's "Gentilhomme de la Chambre," and received a personal gift of six hundred crowns,[3] but was unable to accomplish anything essential for the cause of the Regent in Scotland. Only a short time before his arrival, the discovery of the plot of Amboise, which threatened the outbreak also in France of a dangerous conflict with the adherents of the Reformation, had compelled the Duke of Guise and the Cardinal of Lorraine to think only of their own defence.

During Bothwell's first sojourn in France, one

---

[1] Letter from the English Minister, Johannes Spithovius Monasteriensis, to Cecil, dated Copenhagen, 20th June 1560, contained in *Calendar of State Papers, Foreign Series,* 1560-1561, p. 132.

[2] Resen, *Kong Frederichs den*

Andens Krönicke. Kjöbenhavn, 1680, fol. S. 42. "Boudevild" we take here to be a slip of the pen or a misprint for Boudevill.

[3] Hardwick, *Miscellaneous State Papers.* London, 1778, 4to, i. p. 143.

messenger after another brought him from Scotland
nothing but news of the victory of that party against
which he had given his aid. Shortly after his
departure from Scotland, the sickness of the Regent
had taken such a turn that she herself could foresee
that death was at hand. She then caused the
Scottish leaders of the rebellion to be summoned
to meet her in Edinburgh Castle, prayed their
forgiveness for that wherein she had erred, or if
she had happened to wrong any one, and recommended to their hearty regard her young and inex-
perienced daughter. The dying princess's magnani-
mous and gentle words were not without their
impression on the rugged leaders of the Reformed
party, and when they wished on their side to show
their attachment by asking her to receive one of
their favourite pastors, John Willock, she also displayed her superiority to the prejudices of the times
by yielding to their request in this matter. The
wish which Mary of Guise specially impressed on
the minds of the lords of the Reformed party,
that they ought to save Scotland from being the
battle-field of foreigners, was almost immediately
fulfilled after her death on the 10th of June, inasmuch as the country, by a treaty concluded at
Edinburgh 6th July 1560, was evacuated by the
French troops, and thereafter was likewise abandoned by the English. But to this result their
respect for her death-bed wishes was wholly confined. The hope which Mary of Guise had cherished,
that the old alliance between France and Scotland
would be revived with new strength, was never
realised, for as the cause of the Reformation
had no success in France, while its victory in

England was followed by its victory in Scotland ; so also that intimate union which earlier in the century bound Scotland to France came to an end, and in its stead was planted the germ of that new development which soon would place both crowns on one head, and thus make the two kingdoms one. After the treaty of Edinburgh had been concluded, and had indicated the wane of the French influence, William Cecil, who especially had prompted the intervention in Scotland, with the clear glance of the genuine statesman, wrote to Elizabeth that "it would finally procure that conquest of Scotland which none of her progenitors with all their battles ever obtained, namely, the whole hearts and goodwills of the nobility and people."[1]   The provisional government which was formed in Scotland, and which after the Regent's death acquired the ascendency, among other illegal measures, took upon it, without royal authority, to call together the Parliament which abolished the episcopal jurisdiction, prohibited the Romish mass, and, on the whole, laid the foundation of the edifice of Protestantism in Scotland.   Mary Stuart said with truth, in the month of November 1560, to Sir Nicholas Throckmorton, the English ambassador in Paris :—"My subjects in Scotland do their duty in nothing, nor have they performed one point that belongeth unto them.   I am their Queen, and so they call me ; but they use me not so."[2]   The English statesman just named, in his communications to his govern-

[1] Letter of Sir William Cecil and Sir Nicholas Wotton to Queen Elizabeth, dated Edinburgh, 8th July 1560.   Tytler, *History of Scotland.*   Edinburgh, 1841-43, vi. 170.

[2] Letter of Sir Nicholas Throckmorton to Queen Elizabeth, dated Paris, 17th November 1560, contained in Tytler's *History of Scotland,* vi. 193.

ment, could not help at that time praising the young CHAP.
Queen "for the great wisdom for her years, modesty, I
and also great judgment" she displayed in these 1560.
difficult circumstances,[1] but with these qualities it
was only very little she was able to accomplish in
her remote kingdom.   To bring back her turbulent
subjects to obedience she sent a number of Scottish Lords from Paris to Edinburgh, for the purpose of forming in her name a legal government.
But this project they were unable to carry out.
Equally fruitless proved the Queen's desire to get
the illegal parliament, assembled without royal
authority, dissolved by one opened in a lawful
manner.   This object she could not in the present
case overlook, because of the position she had
therein reserved for Bothwell.   For the Queen
had designated him as one of the commissioners
empowered to call together a new Parliament, and
accordingly the Earl having suddenly left Paris in
November, hastened through Flanders to Scotland,[2]
where, meanwhile, he soon found that under present
circumstances he could have no opportunity of
effecting anything in the service of the Queen.
He was thus induced to return again to the Continent, where, by the sudden death of the young
King Francis II. at Orleans on the 5th December
1560, Mary Stuart had in the meantime become
a widow at the age of eighteen.   Bothwell in the
spring of 1561 again got an opportunity at Joinville

[1] Throckmorton's letter contained in Tytler's *History of Scotland*, vi. 199.
[2] Throckmorton describes him
on this occasion to Queen Elizabeth
as "a vainglorious, rash and
hazardous young man ; and therefore it were meet for his adversaries
to have an eye to him, and also to
keep him short."   Throckmorton's
letter of 2d November 1560, contained in Hardwicke's *Miscellaneous State Papers*, i. 149.

of saluting the Queen, and remained at her court in France until she herself, in the month of August 1561, was obliged with deep regret to bid farewell to the land of her youth.[1]

Devoted subjects had called upon her to return. To the master-spirits of the period, the real rulers in Scotland as well as in England, on the contrary, the idea of her return was anything but welcome, for we now know how the thought had already begun to be entertained of despoiling her of her crown, and how in her native land while she still stood on French soil it was announced that "wonderful tragedies" would not fail to happen when she set her foot on Scottish ground. But if her crown was not to be utterly lost no choice was left her. Followed by three of her six uncles, Claude Duke d'Aumale, René Marquis d'Elbeuf, and their brother Francis of Guise, Knight of Malta, renowned for his naval engagements against the Turks, along with a multitude of other French gentlemen, and again attended by her "four Maries," who, when little girls, had accompanied the Queen, also a girl, on her journey to France, Mary Stuart embarked at Calais 14th August 1561, and a few days afterwards the squadron, bearing the mourning-clad Queen, who was returning after thirteen years' absence, lay at the mouth of the Firth of Forth. A Scottish fog, which made it impossible to see from stem to stern, and forced the ships con-

[1] Languet writes from Paris 13th July 1561, about the two elder of the Guisean brothers :— "Ipse cardinalis et frater prosequuntur jam in Normanniam Reginam Scotiæ redeuntem in patriam. Misera juvencula noctes et dies flere dicitur."—*Huberti Langueti Epistolæ secretae ad principem suum Augustum Sax. ducem et S. R. I. Septemvirum.* Ed. I. P. Ludovicus. Halae, 1699, 4to, p. 127.

tinually either to take soundings or to anchor, met
her there as the first greeting from home, and in
the opinion of many of her attendants as a bad
omen. Twenty-four hours elapsed ere the fog
lifted; Scotland showed her rugged coasts, the port
of Leith came in sight, and Mary's eyes rested on
Arthur's Seat and the castle of Edinburgh.

After Mary had on the 19th August set foot on
her native land and put herself at the head of the
Government, Bothwell received his reward. His
father, Earl Patrick, had had in his time a place
in the privy council, and when the Queen on the
6th September formed her privy council the new
Earl of Bothwell, although still absent on the
Continent, also became a member of the same.[1] On
his return home, the Queen, to prevent disturbances
of the peace of the country, caused, on the 11th
November 1561, some of his chief enemies, particularly her half-brother Lord James Stuart, whom
she had made her first minister of state, and John
Cockburn, laird of Ormiston, to enter, after the
fashion of the times, their recognisances not to make
war on Bothwell, who in turn was also obliged to
pledge himself not to attack them. Friends and
foes could not but praise the young Queen's whole
conduct, commend the attention with which, when
called to consider business of importance in the
Council, she listened to the suggestions made
for disposing of it, and asked for good advice, and
the tact she also showed in choosing the proper
method of disposing of legal matters. But she was

---

[1] Keith, *History of the Affairs of Church and State in Scotland, from the beginning of the Reforma-* tion to the retreat of Queen Mary into England. Edinburgh, 1734, fol. p. 187.

nevertheless unable to prevent the violent and often bloody feuds which were in such a high degree characteristic of the Scottish nobles; they must still longer continue to weaken the country to the advantage of its neighbours. At the close of the fifteenth century the power of the feudal barons in many of the western countries of Europe showed a marked decay; what in this respect took place in France or Spain through the rise of commerce and the increase of towns was, in England, for the most part, the consequence of the long-continued and destructive contests in which the nobles were divided between the houses of York and Lancaster. But in Scotland there was, as yet, no corresponding development of this kind; its nobility was not like that of England, weakened through wars occasioned by any contested right of succession; its towns had, as yet, not reached any special political importance. In England, during the reigns of Henry VIII., Edward VI., Mary Tudor, and Elizabeth, the power of the sovereign over the nobles, and the influence of the crown, were infinitely greater than in Scotland, where Sir Ralph Sadler then found only what in one of his letters home he calls "a beastly liberty."[1] Mary Stuart was soon compelled to witness with her own eyes its manifestation. The Earl of Arran, owing to the border wars waged in the reign of the Queen Dowager, had become one of the most notorious of the enemies of Bothwell, and had hitherto resisted all overtures for reconciliation with

[1] The different modes of thought prevailing among the nobles of the two countries are also brought strongly into view in a letter from Mr. Thomas Martyn to Queen Mary Tudor of England, dated Carlisle, June 11, 1557, given in Tytler's *History*, vi. 380-81.

him. Accordingly in the winter, when Bothwell CHAP.
resided in Edinburgh, where he lived on terms of ‾L‾
the most intimate friendship with the Queen's 1562.
uncle, the Marquis d'Elbeuf, who had not yet returned to his own country, it needed only a frivolous
occasion, a contest about a respectable merchant's
daughter who passed for the Earl of Arran's mistress, but whose favour the Marquis d'Elbeuf was
supposed to have gained, to make Edinburgh become
the scene of the violent street riots or causeway
fights between the Hamiltons and the Hepburns,
which remind us of the bloody street brawls between
the factions of the Italian cities, and which the
Queen's government only succeeded with no little
trouble in finally preventing.[1] The Queen issued a
proclamation which, in severe language, reprobated
these disturbances ; and the Earl of Bothwell was,
by her command, obliged for a time to leave Edinburgh. But no sooner had the Earl obeyed this
order than similar outrages recurred in another
place, for we next hear of a new conflict between the
Earl and John Cockburn, laird of Ormiston, in
East Lothian. The latter having, with his wife and
eldest son, ventured too far out hunting, was surprised by Bothwell, who actually took prisoner his
son, Alexander Cockburn, and carried him away to
Crichton Castle.[2]

[1] A complaint from a now for-
midable body, from the Protestant
clergy (the Assembly of the Kirk),
in which punishment was demanded for these riots, and especially
upon the Queen's uncle, is given in
Knox's *History of the Reformation
in Scotland*, vol. ii. 316-17. The
Queen excused her uncle, the Marquis d'Elbeuf—of whom it is said
in Knox's description of the riots,

that " he starte to ane halbart, and
ten men were skarse able to hald
him " — inasmuch as he was a
foreigner, but promised for the
future that such scenes should be
prevented. At last, in February,
the Marquis d'Elbeuf left Scotland
where he had a bastard son " de
Marguerite Chrestien, demoiselle
Ecossoise."

[2] Thomas Randolph's letter to

CHAP.
I.

1562.

However little Bothwell's character in itself seems to have been able to awaken any very deep sympathy among his countrymen, there yet occurs a moment in which even Scotland's famous Reformer, John Knox, appears to have shown special interest in him. Bothwell set at liberty young Cockburn, who had been a follower of Knox, and caused him to entreat the latter to employ his great influence to bring about a reconciliation between him and his enemies. Bothwell himself belonged to the Reformed Kirk ; and Knox, in whose eyes the contest between the Lords of the Reformed party was a scandal to the cause, readily fell in with the Earl's wish for a meeting. This took place in what is still held as a relic by the Scottish Church—the undisturbed and carefully preserved house in the High Street of Edinburgh, where Knox resided from the year 1560 until his death in 1572. Here, in the room occupied as a study, sat the Earl one night right over against the Reformer, expressing regret for his past life,[1] and complaining of his powerful foes,

Cecil of the 31st March 1562— Fr. v. Raumer's *Die Königinnen Elizabeth und Maria Stuart nach den Quellen im britischen Museum und Reichsarchive*, Leipzig, 1836, p. 18. Randolph's statements, which are always directly unfavourable to Bothwell, become different as soon as Mary Stuart, contrary to the wish of the English government, united herself to Darnley, the respect and good-will with which they speak of the returned Queen changed to the keenest opposition. They have become a chief source of the severe statements of Raumer and so many others against Mary Stuart ; and by the intriguing Randolph's despatches one may very often be

reminded of what a well-known German author has said of the despatches of an English statesman of a more recent date : " Die ganze misère der Depechen wird mir wieder recht deutlich ; was für elende Nachrichten geben diese in den meisten Fällen ! und jede Lüge, jede Albernheit, jeder Irrthum ist durch das Geheimnis gedeckt. Wehe dem, der aus Depechen vorzugsweise die Geschichte schöpfen will." — *Tagebücher von K. A. Varnhagen von Ense*, Leipzig, 1861, ii. 406.

[1] " The said Earle lamented his formare inordinate lyef."—Knox, *History of the Reformation in Scotland*, ii. 323.

and of the circumstance that, for the sake of his own safety, he was obliged to keep so many wild and expensive men about his person, while otherwise a single page and a couple of servants could suffice for his attendance at court.[1] Knox, who has left on record the words which he then uttered to the Earl prayed him, first of all, to be reconciled to God, so should reconciliation with men certainly follow, as God would, beyond doubt, incline their hearts to him. Even he himself, in the first place as a minister of the Gospel, and next also as one, many of whose ancestors had fought, and some fallen, under the banner of the Earls of Bothwell, would labour to help him to peace.[2] Knox at length succeeded both in getting Cockburn and Bothwell to submit themselves to the arbitration of the Earl of Arran, and subsequently, on the 25th March 1562, in bringing about a meeting between Arran and Bothwell. In Hamilton's lodging of the so-called Kirk-of-Field in Edinburgh, Knox saw the two Earls meet. As Bothwell entered, and was about to pay the marks of respect agreed upon by those mutual friends, Gawin Hamilton, prior of Kilwinning, and Henry Drummond, laird of Riccarton, the Earl of

---

[1] "I wald await upoun the Court with a page and few servandis, to spair my expensis, whare now I am compelled to keap, for my awin saifty, a number of wicked and unprofitable men to the utter destruction of my living that is left."—Knox, *History of the Reformation in Scotland*, ii. 323.

[2] "For albeit that to this hour it hath nott chaunsed me to speik with your Lordship face to face, yit have I borne a good mynd to your house ; and have bene sorry at my heart of the trubles that I have heard you to be involved in. For, my Lord, my grandfather, goodsher, and father have served your Lordshipe's predecessoris, and some of thame have died under their standartis ; and this is a part of the obligatioun of our Scotishe kyndnes."—Knox, *History of the Reformation in Scotland*, ii. 323. This passage in Knox's History is remarkable as furnishing the only information we have about his kinsmen.

Arran hastened up to him and embraced him.
Thereupon Knox gave them a lengthened exhorta-
tion. Afterwards the two Earls were seen at a
window talking together in a friendly manner, and
the following morning the Earl of Bothwell came
again, and went with the Earl of Arran to church,
"whereat many rejoiced."

"But God," says Knox, "had another work to
do than the eyes of men could espy." The meeting,
which was intended to effect the reconciliation of
the Earls of Arran and Bothwell, took place on the
25th March 1562. A few days later the Earl of
Arran, whose ambition had led him at an earlier
period to dream of winning the hand of either
Elizabeth or Mary, was seized with mental disease,
which never left him; and no sooner had Bothwell
ridden to Kinneil House to pay a visit to his father,
the Duke of Châtelherault—the castle still belongs
to the Dukes of Hamilton—than the Earl of Arran
fled by night from the castle, and presented himself
on the 29th March in the palace of Falkland before
the Queen and Bothwell's implacable enemy, her
half-brother, James Stuart, with the accusation that
Bothwell, along with his father, the old duke, and
Gawin Hamilton, had formed a plot to surprise the
Queen during her stay at Falkland, when she was
hunting deer in the neighbouring woods,[1] to carry
her off to Dumbarton Castle, and to remove her
powerful half-brother, and others of her too influential counsellors, out of the way. Subsequent
events might seem to add confirmation to this

[1] "Modica in propinquo silva est,
in qua platycerotes cervini generis
—quas vulgo damas falso appellant
—aluntur." — Buchanan, *Rerum
Scoticarum Historia.*

accusation, if there were not the weighty words of CHAP. Knox to furnish proof against it. To him the Earl I. of Arran, in a very bewildered state of mind, had 1562. addressed himself before coming forward with his charge, and in his presence had stated that every-thing would be reported by Bothwell to the Queen, and that it was only calculated to ruin himself. Knox therefore immediately warned the govern-ment that the Earl of Arran had become insane, and that consequently much weight was not to be attached to his words.[1] Meanwhile James Stuart seized this opportunity to cause, on the 31st of March, both the Earl of Bothwell, who had come to Falkland, and Gawin Hamilton, to be imprisoned in the castle of St. Andrews. That Knox was nevertheless right was soon very plainly seen, when Bothwell and the Prior of Kilwinning were there confronted with the Earl of Arran in presence of the Queen and the privy council,—the Earl's malady having now increased to such a degree that he spoke altogether wildly and confusedly, and it was found necessary to take him into custody. His father, the old Duke of Châtelherault, had himself ventured to come to St. Andrews, and in presence of the Queen begged, with tears in his eyes, that he should not be made a sacrifice to the accusation of a demented son. With respect to him the Council contented itself with resolving, on the 18th April, that, as a security for the future, he should give up to the Queen's government Dumbarton Castle, of which he had been appointed keeper

[1] " He did planelie foirwarne the Erle of Murray that he espyed the Erle of Arrane to be stricken with phrenesy, and thairfoir willed not oure great credytt to be gevin unto his wordis and inventionis."— Knox, *History of the Reformation in Scotland*, ii. 328.

CHAP.
I.

1562.

during the rule of Mary of Guise, but on the under-standing that this post of great trust could be at any time withdrawn at the pleasure of the Crown.[1] And although even the English ambassador in Scotland at that time himself owned that there was no sufficient evidence on which to raise any accusation against Bothwell,[2] yet the examination, which had thrown light upon the recklessness of the Earl of Arran's charge, produced no other result either for him or for Gawin Hamilton than to cause their removal under the custody of a troop of horsemen to Edinburgh castle, after they had lain for six weeks in the castle of St. Andrews.

It was while Bothwell still lay imprisoned there that he received intelligence of the outbreak of the first important conflict in Scotland since the return home of Mary Stuart. If her now very powerful half-brother had attributed greater weight to the reckless charges of the Earl of Arran than they deserved, he was hardly wrong when he regarded the most of Scotland's magnates as envious of the power which he possessed, and which he was prepared to let them feel.[3] Especially had he at this time his enemy in the representative of the power-

[1] Buchanan, *Rerum Scoticarum Historia*, p. 204.

[2] Sir Thomas Randolph's letter to Sir William Cecil, dated St. Andrews, the 25th April 1562. Chalmers, *Life of Mary Queen of Scots*, ii. 213, and *Calendar of State Papers relating to Scotland*, i. 180.

[3] John Lesley, Catholic Bishop of Ross, thus writes of James Stuart in his *History of Scotland :* " Jacobus, quum nobilium omnium in se animos probe agnosceret, quoscumque vel infensos, vel in-festos sibi putant, maxime autem eos, qui prudentia ac potentia ex-cellerent—etsi sub imagine iustitiæ et Regiæ auctoritatis velo, cuncta se gerere ab omnibus dignosci cu-peret—legis alicujus violationem prætexens aut carcere, aut capite, aut certo exilio damnari provide curavit."—*De origine moribus et rebus gestis, Scotorum libri decem, auctore Ioanne Leslæo, Episcopo, Rossensi*, 4to, p. 552. Romæ, 1578.

ful families of the north, George Gordon, Earl of CHAP. I. Huntly. The latter had become chancellor of the kingdom. He was also the head of the party of 1562. the nobles who still retained their preference for Catholicism, and along with other adherents of the old church, he had formerly made the proposal to Mary Stuart, that, on her return to Scotland, she should land at Aberdeen, where twenty thousand soldiers would be at her command—a proposal obviously intended to induce her to strike yet a great blow for the old religion. Mary nevertheless chose, as we have seen, to land at Leith, and in her new council the Earl of Huntly did not succeed in occupying the first place, as she found it most prudent to admit to it a majority of the reforming nobles. A new street brawl, of which Edinburgh was witness on a summer evening in the year 1562, furnished not indeed the cause, but became at length sufficient occasion, for the previously anticipated conflict in the north. John Gordon, a younger son of the Earl of Huntly, had formerly had a quarrel with Lord Ogilvie: they met each other in Edinburgh; both were attended by an armed band of followers; swords were drawn, and Lord Ogilvie was dangerously wounded by his antagonist. To avoid the punishment with which James Stuart, at the demand of the authorities, and as representative of the Queen's government, showed himself very ready to avenge this new violation of law and order, young Gordon sought and found opportunity to escape to his powerful father, and now ensued an open breach between the latter and the existing rule in Scotland. On learning this the Earl of Bothwell could no longer bear to remain

C

inactive, and accordingly, on the 28th of August 1562, he broke one of the iron bars of his prison window, and by means of a rope boldly let himself down from the castle rock during the night.[1] Bothwell sought refuge in Hermitage Castle, in Liddesdale, and was about to fortify it.[2] But at this stage disheartening news reached him from the north. The Earl of Huntly, with his Highlanders, was speedily overthrown. On the 28th October 1562, he fell at Corrichie, in an action with the Queen's troops, led by her half-brother; his young son, who had given the immediate occasion to the breach, was a few days afterwards beheaded at Aberdeen; his eldest son, George Gordon, who at a later period was to be related by marriage to Bothwell, was indeed spared the infliction of the fatal penalty to which he had also been doomed, but this favour only subjected him to a life-long imprisonment in the castle of Dunbar; the possessions of the Gordons were confiscated, and at their cost James Stuart

[1] Eisdem forte diebus, Bothuelius, per funem e fenestra demissus, ex arce Edinburgensi evasit.—Buchanan, *Rerum Scoticarum Historia,* p. 205. Some say that he brack the stancheour of the wyndo; utheris whispered that he gat easye passage by the yettis.—Knox, *History of the Reformation in Scotland,* ii. 347. When Knox adds here, "one thing is certane, to wit, the Quene was litill offended at his eschaiping," there seems some discrepancy with what he afterward (ii. 351) states: that he himself, shortly after Bothwell's escape, had, through a friend, Sir John Maxwell of Terregles, written him to keep himself quiet, so as not to increase the Queen's displeasure. Bothwell himself, at a later date, asserted that before his escape from prison, he had considered "par quelz moyens je pourrois au vray sçavoir, quelle velonté la dicte Royne me portoit, et fiz tant qu'il me fust dict qu'elle cognoissoit bien que j'avois esté accusé par hayne et envye, mais que, pour lors, elle ne me pouvoit aulcunement ayder ne secourir pour n'auoir elle mesme autorité quelconque ; mais que je fisse, du mieulx que je pourrois."—Bothwell's *Representation;* Teulet, *Lettres,* p. 162.

[2] Thomas Randolph's letter to Sir William Cecil, written in Spynie Castle, 18th September 1567.—*Calendar of the State Papers relating to Scotland,* i. 184.

was now created Earl of Murray, the title by which CHAP. I. he was afterwards most frequently designated. Murray was now more powerful than ever; his 1563 position in the government seemed so firm that the Earl of Bothwell no longer saw any prospect of security for himself in Scotland. Finding it advisable to return to France, he embarked in the winter at North Berwick, and was once more out upon the stormy North Sea.

His voyage proved far from successful. Tempestuous weather drove the ship that carried him into the Holy Island, on the coast of Durham, and here he was detained and placed in custody.[1] Bothwell immediately wrote to the nearest of Elizabeth's commanding officers, the Earl of Northumberland, that it was only a winter storm which drove him into the Holy Island; at the same time he did not conceal his apprehension of being sent back to Scotland, and prayed the English earl to desire his Queen to grant him protection.[2] But hardly had the tidings of the disastrous issue of his journey reached Scotland ere Thomas Randolph, the English ambassador in Edinburgh, at the request of Murray and his friends, hastened to remind Elizabeth's government of Bothwell's bad disposition towards England, and how desirable it was that England's enemy should be made incapable of doing harm.[3]

[1] The Erle of Bothwell fleing out of Scotland, was taken besyde Tynmouth, where he is in prison in the castle. — William Cecil's letter to Sir Thomas Smith, dated Westminster, 7th February 1563, given in Thomas Wright's *Queen Elizabeth and Her Times : A series of Original Letters.* London, 1838, i. 123.

[2] Bothwell's letter of 7th January 1563, to the Earl of Northumberland.—*Calendar of the State Papers relating to Scotland,* i. 187.

[3] Thomas Randolph's letter to Sir William Cecil, dated Edinburgh, the 22d January 1563.— *Calendar of the State Papers relating to Scotland,* i. 187.

Queen Elizabeth did not hesitate at this time to
cause a Scottish peer, who in time of peace had
sought refuge on the English coast, to be kept in
custody as a prisoner for more than a year,[1] until
Mary Stuart, in the beginning of 1564, after urgent
requests by Bothwell's mother and his other relatives, herself interceded with her good sister in
England, in favour of her hitherto highly trusted
servant, and at length succeeded in getting permission for him to continue his journey to France.[2]
Here letters of recommendation from Mary Stuart
to the King of France and the good word of the
latter procured for him also an appointment in the
Scottish guard, which from the time of Lewis XI.
had become a hereditary part of the French king's
military force,[3] and which had lately had Bothwell's
Scottish antagonist, the Earl of Arran, for its commander.

Bothwell was nevertheless far too restless a man
to be able long to submit to an inactive life in
France. When his impatience had found vent for
itself—if we dare believe one of his bitterest
enemies,—not only in complaints against Elizabeth,
but also in injurious words about Mary Stuart,[4] it

[1] An order to bring Bothwell to
London was issued by Elizabeth,
18th March 1563 (*Calendar of
State Papers*, 1563, p. 127), but
must have afterwards been recalled,
a fact which has not been noticed
by Chalmers (*Life of Mary*, ii.213).

[2] Mary Stuart's letter to Elizabeth, dated Holyrood, 5th February 1564.—*Calendar of the State
Papers relating to Scotland*, i. 195.
Knox also (*History of the Reformation in Scotland*, ii. 361) has made
the remark about Bothwell's arrival in England :—" He was stayed

and was offered to have been rendered by the Quene of England.
But our Quene's answer was : That
he was no rebell, and thairfoir she
requeasted that he should have
libertie to pas whair it pleiseth
him."

[3] " Je fuz faict capitaine de la
garde Escossoise," says Bothwell
himself.—Teulet, *Lettres*, p. 163.

[4] Randolph's despatches from
Edinburgh to Cecil, of 19th
and 30th March 1565, and to
Throckmorton, of 31st March
1565.—*Calendar of State Papers,*

drove him, in the month of March 1565, in spite of
the risks he thereby ran, after two years' absence,
back again to his native land, where he first visited
his mother; but afterwards, roaming restlessly about,
was eagerly sought for on the Borders by the English officials, who were stirred up by requisitions
from the authorities in Scotland to take action
against him, and there also was keenly pursued by
Murray himself, who still continued his deadly
enemy. On receiving tidings of Bothwell's return,
Murray had immediately gone to his sister and had
demanded how far it was according to her will and
advice that Bothwell had come home, adding that
either he himself or Bothwell would require to quit
the country. The Queen answered that the Earl of
Bothwell was a nobleman who had formerly done
her so good service that she could not hate him, but
that she would not do anything prejudicial to her
brother, although she would rather see the matter
dropped.[1] A few days afterwards, Bothwell was
again summoned in the Queen's name to defend
himself as to his connection with the insane Earl
of Arran's alleged conspiracy, and also for having
thereafter broken out of his prison. In the end of
March 1565, Bothwell still remained in Hermitage
Castle, where he showed himself surrounded by a
large retinue of his vassals in Liddesdale, and thence
he gave, at the Queen's citation, a promise of his

Foreign Series, 1564-5, pp. 315, 325. Randolph also writes at the same time to Cecil about Mary Stuart, that "she hath sworn upon her honour, that he shall never re-ceive favours at her hands," and he also explains that these new accus-ations against Bothwell originated with Murray, and that Bothwell subsequently "complained of the evil opinion conceived of the Queen of England against him, and de-clared that he never spoke but honourably of her."—*Calendar of State Papers, Foreign Series*, 1566-8, p. 28.
  [1] Knox, *History of the Reforma-tion in Scotland*, ii. 473.

willingness to appear before the court of justice
which was to be held in Edinburgh on 2d May
following.   But when Murray and his brother-in-
law, Archibald Campbell, Earl of Argyll and Justi-
ciary of the Court, made their entrance into Edinburgh on the 1st May, at the head of five or six
hundred men, Bothwell at length despaired of being
able, in any manner, to enter the lists against such
opponents.   Accordingly he let the matter rest for
the present by getting his kinsman, Alexander Hepburn of Whitsum, to appear before the court with
the assurance of his innocence, and protest against
the Earl's absence being interpreted otherwise than
as arising from a natural reluctance to present himself before so powerful antagonists.[1]   He had already
embarked anew at North Berwick, and this time he
escaped without impediment to the Continent, convinced that he could not venture on any new step
so long as he found no firm support from either of
the two rival queens.[2]

At this time occurred that important change in
Scotland which was also to bring about for Bothwell
a season of exaltation.   Bothwell was as yet not far
away from the coasts of Scotland, when the Queen
expressed herself dissatisfied at the keenness with
which Murray continued to persecute him, and,
after sentence, on the ground of Bothwell's non-
appearance on the occasion mentioned above, had
gone against him, she interposed and forbade the
court to take any further proceedings.

At length the breach between Mary Stuart and
her half-brother had become complete, for " she

---

[1] Bedford's letter to Cecil.—Tytler, *History of Scotland*, vi. 325.

[2] Chalmers, *Life of Mary Queen
of Scots*, ii. 215.

saw," she said, "whereabout he went, and that he would set the crown upon his own head."[1] We venture here upon a brief statement in reference to this matter. After the death of the Catholic Queen Mary Tudor, the throne of England fell to her half-sister Elizabeth, although by an act of the English Parliament, passed in the reign and at the wish of Henry VIII., his daughter by Anne Boleyn was declared illegitimate. On the other hand, Mary Stuart had, after the death of Queen Mary Tudor, and during her stay in France, been induced, along with the Dauphin, to assume in her seal the arms of England, for the purpose of indicating the hereditary rights which she claimed as a grand-daughter of Margaret Tudor, the eldest sister of Henry VIII., who had married James IV. of Scotland. "Franciscus et Maria, Dei gratia rex et regina Franciæ, Scotiæ, Angliæ et Hiberniæ,"—so Mary Stuart and Francis II. designated themselves during the short time that the sovereigns of Scotland and France were united in marriage. Although this conduct of itself was not more particularly offensive than that of Elizabeth continuing to call herself, just as many of her successors have done, sovereign not only of England but also of France, yet to her such rivalry was intolerable. In accordance therefore with her wish, one of the articles of the Treaty made in Edinburgh 6th July 1560, had expressly acknowledged that the crown of England belonged to her, and stipulated that Mary Stuart should lay aside the use of the English title and the English arms. But Mary refused unconditionally to ratify

CHAP.
I.

1565.

[1] Thomas Randolph's account of 3d May 1565, given in Tytler,   *History of Scotland*, vi. 325-331.

this treaty,[1] and Elizabeth then again manifested her unchanged disposition when Mary Stuart was on the point of returning from France; for the latter through d'Oysel, the brave defender of Leith, whom she had sent to London, having requested a letter of safe-conduct in case she might be obliged to touch on the English coasts, or come in contact with English ships on her journey, Elizabeth refused to grant it, alleging the Treaty of Edinburgh as her reason; her English counsellors being afraid lest Mary Stuart might now come to take part with those of her religion in the north of England, while Mary's Scottish friends were still more anxious, because she would not turn back, but would venture over the sea, close past the English ships that were then in the German Ocean to search whether any of the vessels sailing there had not "pirates" on board. Through the sheltering mist, however, Mary Stuart got safely to land in her own kingdom, and for a long time flattered herself with the hope that now by friendly concession on her part an end would be put to the strife between them. "When Elizabeth," so she expressed herself at this time to Thomas Randolph, "shall treat me as if I were her sister or daughter, then will I, according as she wishes, demean myself either as the one or the other, and will not show less readiness to obey and honour her than I would towards a sister or mother."[2] Of the festive entertainments and per-

---

[1] To the ratification of the Treaty of Edinburgh Mary Stuart and Francis II. added this proviso:— "N'entendant toutefois, par ceste ratification, quicter ne renoncer aucune chose des droicts qui nous peuvent comporter et appartenir es dits royaulmes, et aultres nos droicts."—De la Barre Duparcq, *Histoire de François II.* Paris, 1867, p. 191.

[2] Randolph's account, Raumer, S. 33.

formances of which Holyrood was the scene after CHAP.
I.
Mary's home-coming, a pageant during Shrovetide
is noted as especially magnificent, in which, while 1565
the nobles appeared in the same costumes as did
Mary and her Court ladies, there might have been
heard a choir singing various pieces in verse, and
among these pieces still extant of February 1564,
which Randolph, who was present on the occasion,
sent to Elizabeth, were also stanzas which Mary
had at the same time caused to be composed by
Buchanan, and which openly announced that Scotland's Queen would always love England's Queen,
the English Queen always the Scottish.[1] Mary
Stuart wished now only to see herself recognised
by her relative on the mother's side as nearest
heir to England, and for this purpose she would
have prepared for Europe the unwonted spectacle
of an interview between Britain's two reigning
Queens, but Elizabeth who never desired to show
herself by the side of her younger and more
beautiful rival, after having promised Mary a
meeting first at Nottingham and next at York,
finally terminated her many delays with altogether
refusing to meet her. Mary then, since it was
wished in Scotland to see her again married, had
at last, to evince her willingness to respect Elizabeth's admonition not to unite one of the crowns of

[1] Randolph's statement to Cecil
of 21st February 1564.—Keith's
*History of Church and State in
Scotland*, p. 249 ; *Georgii Buchanani Poemata quae extant*, Lug-
duni Batavorum, 1628, p. 417.
Of Buchanan's Stanzas for the
festival in the year 1564, which
have in the collection the heading
"Mutuus amor," the following are

the concluding ones :—

" Durabit usque posteris
Intaminata sæculis
Sincera quæ Britannidas
Nectit fides Heroidas.

Rerum supremus terminus
Ut astra terris misceat
Regina Scota diliget
Anglam, Angla Scotam diliget. '

Britain to any of those of the Catholic princes on the
Continent, listened to her wish to the effect that as
a security against future dispeace she would rather
prefer one of England's nobles, and when to the
astonishment of most Elizabeth bethought herself
of recommending her own favourite, Lord Robert
Dudley, Earl of Leicester, she did not absolutely
refuse him, and accordingly the latter had actually
begun to correspond with her. By such means she
strove to remove the main scruple which had arisen
on Elizabeth's side, and which proceeded from a
fear lest an express acknowledgment of Mary Stuart
as England's nearest heir might one day become
dangerous to her own and her Protestant kingdom's
security, should Mary afterwards be united in marriage to a Catholic prince. But Elizabeth after
having for a long time laboured with apparent zeal
in behalf of the person proposed by her had allowed
her jealousy again to end the matter by refusing
the condition constantly put forth on Mary's side,
that before any such marriage took place her right
of succession to the English throne must be assured
to her by a formal Act of Parliament.

At length Scotland's young Queen impatiently
fastened her eyes upon a relative of her own, her
still younger cousin, who at this time also resided
in England as one of Elizabeth's subjects. Mary
Stuart's grandmother, Margaret Tudor, sister to
Henry VIII. of England and consort of James IV. of
Scotland, after seeing her royal husband fall in the
fight at Flodden against her brother's army, had at
a later period married the Earl of Angus, Archibald
Douglas, who for a length of time ruled Scotland
until James V. her royal son attained his majority,

and drove him as an enemy of the State into exile CHAP.
in England. Margaret Douglas, a daughter of I.
Archibald and the widowed Queen, married the 1565.
Scottish Earl of Lennox, Matthew Stuart, who
having been also driven at a subsequent period
out of the northern kingdom had likewise betaken
himself to England, and by him, five years after
the birth of Mary Stuart in Scotland, she there
became the mother of Henry Stuart Lord Darnley.
His ambitious father, who himself was collaterally
related to the royal race of the Stuarts, had at one
time before Mary Stuart was born been led by
James v. to entertain the hope, on the ground of
the King's dislike to the Hamiltons, that he might
be preferred as his successor, and although Mary
Stuart's birth caused the dream to vanish, yet
the Earl of Lennox never forgot it. Lady Margaret
Lennox always recollected on her part that she was
descended from the sister of Henry VIII., and that
his daughter, Queen Mary of England, had even
favoured her at her half-sister Elizabeth's cost,
and from a mother who was at once Elizabeth's
cousin and Mary Stuart's aunt, young Darnley
could hardly fail early to hear accounts of his
exalted descent, and receive encouragement to win
a dignity to which he was said by his birth to
be called. While the Earl of Lennox himself remained not disinclined to the Reformed doctrine,
his wife, who was zealously devoted to the old
religion, took care that their castle in Yorkshire
should resemble a little Catholic court, she deeming
it to be so much the more important to have her
son trained up in all the Catholic ceremonies, since
a union between him and his royal relative in

Scotland was the hope she had long cherished.[1] When Mary Stuart returned from France she had, at the news of her happy arrival in Scotland, joyfully fallen upon her knees, and with uplifted hands had thanked God because the Queen had so successfully escaped Elizabeth's cruisers. At a later period she had addressed herself in writing to Mary Stuart in reference to her project, and at length in the year 1564 she saw it on the eve of being realised. The Earl of Lennox sought and received at this time from Queen Elizabeth, who as yet did not suspect any mischief, six months' leave of absence in order with Mary Stuart's permission to appear again in Scotland, whence for more than twenty years he had been exiled, and which he had not visited since the time he had carried arms against his native land along with an English host. He was graciously received by Mary, got his formerly forfeited estates restored to him, and in the beginning of the year 1565 was followed to the north by his son Darnley, who also had obtained permission to make a half-year's visit to Scotland. It was at Wemyss Castle, on a weather-beaten rock rising from the Forth, that Darnley for the first time had an opportunity of saluting the Scottish Queen. Her eyes rested with pleasure on her handsome cousin, then in his nineteenth year, who did not long hesitate to present himself as her

[1] In a statement of the reasons which Mary Stuart gives for resolving upon marriage with Darnley, she points out in the year 1565 that he was "de mesme religion que moy." — Labanoff, *Lettres, instructions et mémoires de Marie Stuart,* i. 295-99. And even so early as the year 1562 Knox (*History of the Reformation in Scotland,* ii. 336) makes the remark that "the Erle of Levenax and his wyff war committed to the Towre of London for trafiquin with Papistis."

suitor; and though Mary at first refused the ring CHAP.
which Darnley offered her, yet she speedily resolved I.
on a union which seemed to combine with it the 1565.
advantage that it would give double weight to
her claim in England. In the spring of 1565 the
Scottish Queen declared to the assembled nobles of
her kingdom that she intended to marry Lord
Darnley her near kinsman, whose main recommendation in her esteem was that he bore the
name of Stuart, so dear to Scotland.

At the meeting of the Scottish nobles in Stirling
not a single voice raised itself against this marriage,
but how much ill-will broke out ere long against it
both from Elizabeth and her ministers in England,
and from Murray and his followers in Scotland!
The English Queen in vain sent Sir Nicholas
Throckmorton to Mary to induce her to give up
her intention. Mary only replied by expressing
astonishment at this request at the very moment
when she was in reality complying with her wish
to prefer a nobleman born in England. Equally in
vain Elizabeth reminded Lennox and his son of
their limited leave of absence, and ordered them
as her vassals to return, and when they would not
obey but still remained in Scotland, her irritation
was turned upon Lady Lennox, who, as she was
staying behind in England, was with her younger
son Charles Stuart committed to prison, while the
English possessions of the family were confiscated.
In Scotland Murray had, at least according to the
words of Mary, at that time fancied the possibility
of one day being able to reach the throne of the
childless Queen; at all events he perceived that his
hitherto all-predominant influence would be at an

end after her union with the Lennox family.
Young Darnley had unwarily, when a map of
Scotland one day lay before him, let fall the remark that the possessions of the Earl of Murray
were too great.[1]

Regard for religion was once more put forth as
a reason for opposing the marriage with Darnley;
it would, so it was now again said, bring "the
Evangel" into danger.   But while Mary had never
concealed that "she believed in the Church of Rome
as God's true church," she had also early declared
that "albeit she did not belong to those who every
year changed their religion, and though she could
wish that all her subjects were herein agreed with
her, yet she did not think of compelling any of
them."   And these had not been empty words.   So
far is it from being true, as older and more recent
authors have reiterated, that Mary Stuart had
joined the league against the Reformation, which
after her return to Scotland was entered into by
the mighty Catholic powers on the Continent, that,
on the contrary, it has been matter of bitter complaint on their side that she remained deaf to all
the ambassadors secretly sent to her on this errand.[2]
But for herself she had claimed the same religious liberty as she conceded in the case of her
Protestant subjects; she had on her return to
Scotland been openly attended by the Catholic

[1] Thomas Randolph's letter to Cecil, written in Edinburgh the 20th March 1565.—Keith's *History of Church and State in Scotland,* p. 274.

[2] *Ma ella non l'ha voluto mai intendere,* non ostante che siano stati mandati alla Maestà Sua Mon-signor Damblanen et il padre Edmondo per persuaderla ad abbracciar questa savissima im-presa.—Letter from the Bishop of Mondovi, the Papal Nuncio in France, to Cosmo I., Grand Duke of Tuscany, dated Paris, 16th March 1567. *Labanoff,* vii. 107.

priest, René Benoist, who, during his stay in Edin- CHAP.
burgh, challenged Knox to a public disputation,
and afterwards became confessor to Henry IV. of ⎰1565.
France, to whose conversion to Romanism he is said
to have essentially contributed.[1] For so far as concerned the Queen, that intolerant Parliament had
also agreed to make an exception to the strictness
with which, in the case of every other, it had forbidden all Catholic ceremonies in Scotland. Nor
could it be doubted that when the nuptials of the
Queen and Darnley took place on the 29th July
1565, there would also be on their part an endeavour
made not to cause offence. The marriage was
celebrated in the chapel of Holyrood—the single remaining relic of the old church of Holyrood Monastery
—where so many of Mary's ancestors were crowned
and married; Darnley put three rings on the
Queen's finger, they kneeled side by side, and
when the marriage ceremony had been performed
by John Sinclair, Bishop of Brechin, Darnley kissed
the Queen, and went back to his apartments
in the palace, leaving her alone in the chapel to
hear her Catholic mass. Nor did Darnley neglect
to visit the Kirk of St. Giles, where John Knox
preached; but neither this nor any similar con-
ciliatory act was able to disarm the dictatorial
Reformer, in whose opinion the Bishop of Brechin
was only "an arrant hypocrite,"[2] and who with
regard to the Queen's own religious service, had

[1] Niceron, *Mémoires pour servir
à l'histoire des hommes illustres
dans la république des lettres.*
Paris, 1729-45, xli. 1-49.
[2] Knox assails John Sinclair
more severely as follows:—" No
goodly man did creditt him; for

not only ganesaid he the doctrin
of justificatioun and of prayer
which befoir he had tawght, but
also he sett up and manteaned the
Papistrie to the uttermost prick."
—*History of the Reformation in
Scotland,* i. 266.

CHAP. long before declared in a voice of thunder, that "he
I.   would rather see ten thousand Frenchmen in Scot-
1565. land than one single mass." It was also, at the
time, believed by some in Scotland, that a secret
Catholic marriage had already, before the public
nuptials, united the Queen to her cousin.[1] And
when the latter after the wedding, on the 19th
August, attended to hear Knox, the Reformer spoke
with such vehement words about the "regiment"
of women and boys, that young Darnley in just
displeasure hurried out of St. Giles' Kirk.[2] By his
union with the Queen, occasion had now been taken
to make the assertion that she also should give up
her Catholic mass, and when Mary refused to do
so, there were from this denial only a few steps to
open insurrection.

This new insurrection, in which Murray, secretly
supported by Elizabeth, took the lead, had as its
aim to get Darnley put out of the way, or to deliver
him and his father up to England, to imprison the
Queen in Scotland, and to have Murray himself
placed as Regent at the head of the kingdom. But
this insurrectionary movement was subdued with
vigour and success by Mary. She herself accompanied her army during the campaign. Like an
Amazon, the young Queen was to be seen on horseback crossing over Scotland's rivers, or advancing
against the foe. Again she issued a proclamation, assuring her dear subjects that she had

[1] In an Italian account of the events in Scotland furnished in the year 1566, after David Riccio's murder, to Cosmo I., Grand Duke of Tuscany (*Labanoff*, vii. 67), it is said regarding Mary Stuart and Darnley :—" Fossero da un capellano catolicamente sposati in camera di esso David."

[2] Knox, *History of the Reformation in Scotland*, ii. 497.

never thought, nor would at any time think, of CHAP.
forcing a single one's conscience. While she repaired I.
to the contest, she had also taken care to collect all 1565.
Murray's enemies about her; she released young
Gordon, the Earl of Huntly, who since his father's
defeat and fall in the year 1562, still remained a
prisoner in Dunbar Castle, and now amongst others
she recalled from France—the Earl of Bothwell.

The summons was not given him in vain. But
just as formerly, so also at this time his enemies
sought to prevent his return to Scotland by again
applying to the representative of Elizabeth there.
" Yt is saide," so writes the latter to Cecil, "that
the Earle of Bothewell and Lord Seaton are sente
for, which hathe appearance of trothe, and are
knowne to be feet men to serve in thys worlde. Yt
is wyshed if theie do arryve in Englande that theie
myghte be putte in good suerty for a tyme, [to] passe
their tyme ther."[1] Meanwhile, Bothwell having
left France, struck out another path for himself, and
thus in the autumn, Queen Elizabeth could, with
bitterness, complain to the Spanish ambassador in
England, that at Flushing in the Spanish Netherlands, the Scottish Earl had been permitted to equip
a couple of ships of war.[2] A few days after Elizabeth had made this complaint in London, Bothwell
arrived in Scotland. An English harbour-master,
Charles Wilson, who had been commissioned to prevent the arrival of the Scots who were returning from Flanders, happened to detain the Earl of

[1] Randolph's letter to Cecil of
4th July 1565.—Keith, *History of*
the Affairs of Church and State in
Scotland, p. 295.

[2] Paul de Foix's account to
Catherine de Medici, dated
London, 18th September 1565.
—Teulet, *Papiers d'état*, ii. 78.

D

Sutherland,[1] but was not able to stop either Lord
Seton or the Earl of Bothwell, the latter having, by
the immediate use of the oars, taken his two small
vessels out of the reach of Wilson's cannon.[2]   On
the 17th of September 1565, Bothwell landed at
Eyemouth,[3] and immediately betook himself to the
Court, which by an act of oblivion of the 5th of
August, had already pardoned him "his breaking out
of the castle of Edinburgh without permission;" and
on the 20th September he was graciously received
by Mary at Holyrood, who restored to him all his
former dignities and offices, especially his place in
the privy council, where his influence speedily
became conspicuous.[4]   In conjunction with the Earl
of Lennox, he was appointed commander-in-chief of
the army which Mary Stuart and Darnley personally
accompanied.   He had come in sufficient time to

[1] Wilson, having been in wait for Bothwell and others returning from Flanders, chanced to hit upon the Earl of Sutherland.—Letter of the Earl of Bedford to Cecil, dated Berwick, 11th November 1565.—*Calendar of State Papers, Foreign Series*, 1564-5, p. 516. The Earl of Sutherland, like Bothwell formerly, was now for a long time imprisoned in England, and was first set at liberty on the 19th February 1566. — *Calendar of State Papers, Foreign Series*, 1566-8, p. 19.

[2] The escape of Bothwell happened in this sort. He had two small boats with oars, and getting under sail with the help of their oars, went his way, albeit Wilson shot at him, but did no harm. He landed at Eyemouth, and brought with him six or eight men, certain pistolets and jerne armour. . . . Lord Seton comes home with armour, and his ship is very well

furnished ; Wilson shall not be able to encounter with him.— Letter of the Earl of Bedford to Cecil, dated Berwick, the 19th September 1565. — *Calendar of State Papers, Foreign Series*, 1564-5, p. 464.

[3] "Upoun the samin XVII day James erle Bothuill arryvit in Scotland out of France," is said under 17th September 1565, in a *Diurnal of Remarkable Occurrents that passed within the country of Scotland, from the death of King James IV. till the year 1575.* From a manuscript of the sixteenth century in the possession of Sir John Maxwell of Pollok, Baronet. Edinburgh, 1833, 4to, p. 83.

[4] In October 1565, Randolph, with his usual sarcastic bitterness, writes to Cecil :—"My Lord Bothwell, *for his great virtue*, doth now all, next to the Earl of Athole." Chalmers, *Life of Mary Queen of Scots*, ii. 217.

take part in the consultation held by the Queen on CHAP.
the 10th October 1565, at Castlehill, on the way I.
to Dumfries, and to see the fate which he had 1565.
long endured now befall the man who had prepared it for him. Murray himself was now sent
into exile along with his friends, and accordingly,
on the 14th September, they escaped from Dumfries
over the Borders. Here, where the Government of
Mary appeared stronger than ever, fear might well
be entertained lest the Scottish feudal army, which
had grown to 18,000 men, would follow after them :
it was even reported that the Scottish Queen would
now seriously enforce her claims, and intended to
lead her forces to London, and hence, for the sake
of precaution, the suspicious Elizabeth took occasion,
under some pretext or another, to summon the
Catholic Earls in the North of England to her
Court. The Queen of Scotland did not go over the
Borders, but while she herself went back to Edinburgh, she left as Warden the recently returned
Earl of Bothwell, on whom, in · particular, devolved
the task of watching with two "·bands" of footmen
and two "bands" of horsemen, so that no emissaries
from the rebels who had fled into England should
stir up new disturbances on the Scottish side. And
although Francis Earl of Bedford, commander on
the English frontiers, hated Bothwell personally, and
continually complained of him, yet Mary would not
be induced to supersede him. "I told the Queen
of Scots," writes Randolph at that time to Cecil,
" that Bothwell was a person hated by the English
Queen, and known not to incline to peace. So
that if bad consequence followed upon her choice,
she had herself to blame. She answered that she

also could make exceptions against Bedford, and so
would not name another in the place of Bothwell."[1]
The history of Bothwell very much resembles
that of Scotland. His political life had been stormy,
nor had his private life known greater quietness.
The latter reflected Scotland's unruliness combined
with an impréss of the characteristics of France in
the sixteenth century. The new Presbyterian strictness had, after the Queen's return to Scotland,
already pronounced judgment upon him, since, during her uncle's visit to Edinburgh, he had as the
Marquis d'Elbeuf's companion also taken part in the
French wantonness of the latter. At a later period,
while Bothwell was so long kept a prisoner in England, Randolph, who specially had occasioned his
detention, thus writes to Cecil—"I beseech your
Grace, send him where you will, only not to Dover
Castle, not so much for fear of my aged mother, but
my sister is young and has many daughters."[2] In
spite of this and similar utterances, we must not
overlook the fact that in this direction we have now
only the traits of his early life drawn by his bitterest
enemies, who do not hesitate to paint them in the
darkest colours,[3] and whose accusations must by no

[1] *Diurnal of Remarkable Occurrents*, p. 85. Letter of Randolph
to Cecil of 24th January 1566.
—Keith, *History of Church and
State in Scotland*, Appendix, p.
166.

[2] Randolph's despatch to Cecil,
dated Edinburgh, 3d June 1563.
*Calendar of State Papers, Foreign
Series*, 1563, p. 383.

[3] Ubi adolevit, in alea et scortis
ita patrimonium amplissimum pro-
degit ut etiam, (uti poeta quidam
ait) deesset egenti æs, laquei pre-
tium. — Buchanan, *De Maria*

Stuarta Regina, p. 54. " Is enim,
luxuriosa adolescentia inter scorta
et popinas acta, eo reductus erat,
ut aut civile bellum ei foret exci-
tandum, aut audaci aliquo facinore
extremæ inopiæ metus propel-
lendus.—Buchanan, *Rerum Scoticarum Historia*, p. 204. In a
letter from the Earl of Bedford to
Cecil, dated Berwick, 6th April
1566, these words occur in reference to Bothwell :—" I assure you
he is as naughty a man as liveth
and much given to that vile and
detestable vice of sodomy" (*Calen-

means be received here without qualification.[1] He
seems at least not to have had any other issue than
one illegitimate son, for to this son, born of some
unknown union, his mother Agnes Sinclair left by
her testament all that she possessed.[2] That Lady
Margaret Reres, one of the Beaton family, so called
after her marriage with Arthur Forbes of Reres,
and who was one of Mary Stuart's court ladies, and
the nurse of her son, was at an earlier period one
of Bothwell's mistresses, rests entirely upon Buchanan's unreliable statement.[3] Of her sister, Janet
Beaton, widow after her last marriage with Sir
Walter Scott of Branksome and Buccleuch, it was
likewise maintained, during a legal process in the
year 1559, that she either stood in an illicit relation,
or, at all events, was by betrothment bound to
the Sheriff of Edinburghshire,[4] and that, therefore,
the latter, who was none other than Bothwell himself, was not qualified to be judge in her cause.
But betrothment, or "hand-fasting" as it was

dar of State Papers, Foreign
Series, 1564-5, p. 301). Also in a
letter from Sir William Drury to
Cecil, on the 13th March 1567,
mention is again made about
Bothwell's "inordinateness towards
women" (Calendar of State Papers,
Foreign Series, p. 229).

[1] At the same time, while Randolph so bitterly persecuted Bothwell, one of the young Earl's
keepers in England, Sir Henry
Percy, recommended him to Cecil,
with the testimony that "he is
very wise, and not the man he was
reported to be." "His behaviour has
been courteous and honourable,
keeping his promise."—Calendar of
State Papers, Foreign Series, 1563,
p. 129 ; 1564-5, p. 83. Sir John
Forster also writes at that time to

Cecil, that Bothwell "all time of
his abode here behaved himself as
to him appertained."—Calendar of
State Papers, Foreign Series, 1564-
1565, p. 75.

[2] Item, the said nobill Lady left
hir hail gudis, the saidis dettis
beand payit, to William Hepburn,
son natural to James Erle Bothuel.
—Testamentet of 21 March 1572 in
the Bannatyne Miscellany, iii. 304.

[3] Quæ inter pellices Bothuelli
fuerat.—De Maria Stuarta Regina,
p. 7.

[4] Queytly mariit or handfast.—
Riddell, Inquiry into the Law and
Practice of the Scottish Peerage.
Edinburgh, 1842, i. 427. Robert-
son, Preface to Inventaires de la
Royne Descosse, pp. xcii. xciii.

CHAP.
I.

1560-6.

called in Scotland, would not involve any engagement that constituted a valid marriage,[1] and while the Lady of Branksome was not ashamed openly to attribute to herself earlier blame in another instance,[2] yet she has not in the least owned to any guilty connection with young Bothwell. On the other hand, it appears quite a different thing with Anne, a daughter of the Norwegian nobleman, Christopher Throndssön, of the Rustung family, who, after an eventful career, had become one of the admirals of Christian III., and of his wife, Karine, a daughter of Knud Pedersson Skanke, deacon of the Chapter in Throndhjem.[3] She latterly complained that Bothwell "had taken her from her fatherland and paternal home, and led her into a foreign country away from her parents, and would not hold her as his lawful wife, which he with hand and mouth and letters had promised both them and her to do."[4] As to the time at which this must have happened, we may certainly connect it with the already mentioned journey of Bothwell in the year

[1] Bothwell's sister, Jane Hepburn, was on the 24th July 1556 bound by hand-fasting to Robert Lauder of Bass, but on 1st September in the same year this engagement was again broken off.—*Bannatyne Miscellany*, iii. 279.

[2] *Liber Officialis Sancti Andreæ, curiæ metropolitanæ Sancti Andreæ in Scotia Sententiarum in causis consistorialibus quæ extant.* Edinburgi, 1845, p. 86. The Lady of Branksome is the same person who at a later period came to be designated as "Lady Buccleuch," and who in one of the many vague reports about Bothwell—it is contained in one of the anonymous placards in Anderson's

Collections, ii. 156—as late as the year 1567, was branded as the individual believed to have helped him by witchcraft to fascinate the Queen.

[3] "L. Daae, Christopher Throndssön Rustung, his son Enno and his daughter the Scottish wife," *Historisk Tidsskrift*, published by the Norse Historical Society, vol. ii. Christiania, 1872, p. 116.

[4] *Absalon Pederssöns Dagbog over Begivenhederne, især i Bergen*, 1552-1572. *Udgiven efter offentlig Foranstaltning med Anmærkninger og Tillæg af N. Nicolaysen.* Christiania, 1860 p. 148.

1560, when it was falsely rumoured in Scotland
that he had contrived during his stay in Denmark
to make a rich match.[1] In as far as the complaint
of Anne Throndssön affirms that Bothwell had taken
her with him from her "ancestral home," it may
also be remarked that her father in the year 1556, in
presence of Christian III., who at this time made
over to him some landed property in Norway, had
pledged himself "during his lifetime to reside in
Denmark, and not in any other place." Christopher Throndssön had here in the year 1544 been
enfeoffed in the monastery of Ebelholk on Zealand,
which, in 1560, he exchanged for the fief of Tryg-
gevælde, but he certainly had also his home in
Copenhagen, where his daughter Anne thus seems
to have resided in the year 1559.[2] After having
accompanied the young Scottish Earl from Denmark
to the Netherlands, Anne was there abandoned by
Bothwell, and being left by his friends among
strangers, was obliged to dispose of her jewels and
dowry.[3] She seems afterwards for a time to have
taken up her abode in Scotland itself, so far as one
may infer from a passport which was issued by

[1] It is said that the Earl of
Bothwell is married in Denmark
to a wife, with whom he has 40,000
yoendallers. The author of this
tale is Lady Buccleugh, his old
friend and lover.—Randolph's
letter to Cecil, dated Edinburgh,
23d September 1560. *Calendar
of State Papers, Foreign Series,*
1560-1561, p. 311. "Yoensdallers"
means doubtless Jochims or Joa-
chimsdollars, so called from the silver mine Joachimshab in Bohemia.

[2] A letter from Anne Throndssön preserved in the Privy Archives of Denmark, in which during her father's absence she answers

an order come to the former to
send Duke John the elder a ship-
builder, is dated Copenhagen, 11th
March 1559.

[3] " Ein schottischer Graf, Borth-
uil geheissen, welcher in unser
Behaftung gerathen und vor etzlich
jharen unsers Herrn Vaters Admirall Christoffer Thrundtheim
Töchter einer die Ehe zugesagt und
mit ihme hinweg gefhuret, aber ihm
in Niederlandt sitzen lassen" is
stated latterly in a letter from
Frederick II. to the Elector Augustus of Saxony, dated Engelholm,
22d June 1568. (*Ausländische Re-
gistranter in Privy Archives.*)

CHAP. Mary Stuart in the year 1563, to this "Anne
  I.
~~~~~ Trundtze, a daughter of Christopher Trundtze,"
1560-6. formerly naval commander of the King of Denmark,
and which assigns as the occasion of its being given,
the desire of Anne to sail to Norway.[1] Another
daughter of Christopher Throndssön appears to have
been married to one John Stuart in Shetland,[2] and
perhaps Anne resided some time there with her
sister. Perhaps too it is Anne Throndssön to whom
allusion is made in one of Randolph's letters of the
year 1563, which speaks of a gift that Bothwell
still retained in remembrance of a union with a distinguished lady in "the north country"—phraseology which may possibly be intended as a circum-
locution for Shetland.[3] This, or other like unions,
had, however, not left any permanent impression
with him,[4] since after his last return to the land
of his birth, he seems at some moments to have
thought of beginning a quieter life.[5] A few years
previously he had seen his sister marry the half-
brother of Mary Stuart, John Stuart, prior of Coldingham, also one of the many illegitimate children

[1] Note A, Appendix.
[2] Compare the genealogical table
of Christopher Throndssön's children in *Samlinger til det norske
Folks Sprog og Historie;* Christiania, 1833-38, 4to, vi. 253.
[3] A Portugal piece which he
received for a token out of the
North from a gentlewoman, that if
ever she be a widow, shall never
be my wife.—Randolph's letter to
Cecil, dated Edinburgh, 3d June
1563.—*Calendar of State Papers,
Foreign Series,* 1563, p. 383.
[4] The above-mentioned betrothals
are nevertheless represented as
marriages by Buchanan, who in his
highly-coloured descriptions says

—"*duas* uxores nondum dimissas
Bothuelium habuisse, tertiam nec
legitimo nuptam, nec rite dimis-
sam."—*De Maria Stuarta Regina,*
p. 91. In like manner it is said in
his *History of Scotland,* that Bothwell, before his marriage with the
Queen, "duas uxores adhuc vivas,
habuit, tertiam ipse nuper suum
fassus adulterium dimisisset."—
Rerum ScoticarumHistoria, p. 357.
[5] "Je délibéray," he himself
has written about this period, "de
me reposer et vivre paisiblement,
après les emprissonnements et exil
que j'avois soufferts."—Bothwell's
Representation; Teulet, *Lettres,* p.
167.

of James V., Lady Jane Hepburn's marriage having CHAP.
then taken place on Sunday, 11th January 1562, I.
"with much good sport and many pastimes,"[1] in the 1566.
Queen's own presence at Crichton Castle. Wishing
now to follow his sister's example, the Earl of
Bothwell determined to marry, and, accordingly, at
the age of thirty, he espoused "a good, modest, and
virtuous woman,"[2] Lady Jane Gordon, then in her
twentieth year, the daughter of the powerful
Catholic Earl in the North, who fell in 1562 at
Corrichie, in the battle against Murray, and sister
to the young Earl George of Huntly, and his own
relative in the fourth degree.[3] A likeness of her
taken in her advanced years, and still preserved in
Dunrobin Castle, displays large but well-formed
features, with a thoughtful expression.[4] In this
painting she holds a cross and a rosary, she having
like her ancestors, and in contrast to her brother,
who had gone over to Protestantism, adhered until
her death to the Catholic faith, to which she also
belonged when her marriage-contract with Bothwell
was subscribed on the 9th February 1565-6. In it
the bridegroom settles on the bride the lands and

[1] Note B, Appendix.
[2] The Earl of Bothwell had to
his vyffe a good, modest, and vertuous woman, sister to ye Earle of
Huntley.—The Diarey of Robert
Birrel, burges of Edinburghe, in
Fragments of Scottish History,
Edinburgh, 1798, 4to, p. 9. In an
English account (given by *Raumer*,
p. 99), sent 16th February 1566
from Berwick by Sir William
Drury, it is said, on the contrary,
in reference to Bothwell's approaching marriage, that the Earl of
Huntly's sister, whom he was
about to marry, was a vaga-

bond woman (a prole), and that
his future brother-in-law had on
that account dissuaded him from
uniting himself with her. Such a
statement shows very conspicuously how one in general must be
cautious in regard to all English
reports which concern Bothwell.

[3] See the genealogical table in
the *Bannatyne Miscellany*, iii. 308.

[4] [The above-mentioned painting
has been engraved for Dr. John
Stuart's *Lost Chapter in Queen
Mary's History;* Edin. 4to, 1874.
—*Translator.*]

castle of Crichton, etc.   But they are heavily mort-
gaged ; and the bride's dowry of twelve thousand
merks is to be applied to the redemption of the
mortgages.   The contract is signed by the Queen,
with whose "aduiss and express counsale" the
marriage is contracted ; by the Earl of Huntly, the
bride's brother, who undertakes to pay her dowry ;
by the Countess Dowager of Huntly, who, as she
cannot write, subscribes " with my hand led on the
pen by the Lord Bischope of Galloway ;" by the
bride, "Jane Gordoun with my hand ;" by the
bridegroom, " James Erle Boithuille ;" . . . and
by George Lord Seton, Alexander Lord Hume,
David Lord Drummond, and Laurence Master of
Oliphant, who are sureties for payment of the
bride's dowry.   The witnesses to the contract are
the Earl of Atholl, the Earl Marischal, the Bishop
of Galloway, the Commendator of Lindores (John
Lesley, afterwards Bishop of Ross), Mr. James
Balfour, parson of Flisk (afterwards Sir James
Balfour, Lord President of the Court of Session), and
Mr. David Chalmers, Chancellor of Ross.[1]   Although
the Queen had also at this time a Popish husband,
yet Bothwell, like others of the nobility, and in
opposition to those of them whom the example
of Darnley had drawn over to the Romish Church,
refused to be married according to its rites.   "The
Queene desired," says Knox, who in this instance
is an unexceptionable witness, "that the marriage
might be made in the Chappell at the Masse, which
the Earle Bothwell would in no wise grant."[2]   But

---

[1] Joseph Robertson's Preface to *Inuentaires de la Royne Descosse*, p. xciii.

[2] Knox, *History of the Reformation in Scotland*, ii. 520.   In a letter to Cecil written two weeks

this refusal on his part did not hinder Mary Stuart from herself celebrating right royally the wedding of one who had proved himself such a servant to her kingdom as the Earl; and who, in this service, had never yet betrayed the motto—*Keip Trest*—which he bore on his arms.[1] The marriage ceremony took place in the royal chapel of Holyrood the 24th February 1566, and was performed by the bride's uncle, Alexander Gordon, Bishop of Galloway, and titular Archbishop of Athens, who had abandoned the old faith; the wedding feast, which was kept "with great splendour," lasting with its tournaments and chivalrous sports for five days.[2]

before the Earl's wedding, or on the 7th February, Randolph names Bothwell as likewise among the Scottish Lords who would not be present at any mass, while, even on this occasion, he cannot forget to add: "And of them all Bothwell is stoutest but worst thought of." — Thomas Wright's *Queen Elizabeth and her Times*, i. 220.

[1] Bothwell's coat-of-arms, which is found preserved in the seal attached to one of his writings in the Danish Archives, has been restored in *Les Affaires du Conte de Boduel*, Edinburgh, 1829, after an impression on his copy of *Les dovze Livres de Robert Valtvrin*.

[2] *Diurnal of Remarkable Occurrents*, p. 88. Lindsay of Pitscottie, *History of Scotland*. Glasgow, 1749, p. 394.

CHAPTER II.

DARNLEY was also present by the side of Mary Stuart at this splendid entertainment which sealed the union between the chiefs of the two families that had especially supported his cause. But the relation betwixt him and the Queen had become cold even when the Earl's wedding was being celebrated, and there elapsed only a space of fourteen days between it and the ruinous catastrophe to which that coldness at last beguiled Darnley.

Mary had been warned by her own relatives on the Continent against choosing Darnley;[1] and he was not long in showing how ill fitted he was to bear his sudden exaltation. Ere even his marriage with the Queen he had been knighted by her, created Earl of Ross, and Lord of Ardmanach, later also Duke of Albany. At the festive repast in Holyrood, which followed the nuptial ceremony, and during which the Queen was served by the Earl of Atholl as master of ceremonies, the Earl of Morton as carver, and the Earl of Crawford as cupbearer ; Darnley was likewise waited upon by the

[1] The Cardinal of Lorraine asked her to remember that he was only "a young pretty fool." Letter given in Teulet, *Papiers d'état,* ii. 42.

Earls of Eglinton, Cassilis, and Glencairn, with hat in hand.[1] During the evening there was a dance in Holyrood which lasted until the exalted pair with- drew to their apartments ; at the same time one of the proclamations put forth by the Queen publicly notified that Darnley should in future be entitled King, and all letters issued hereafter should be made out in both names jointly.[2] There can scarcely be a doubt that the bestowment of the royal title previously required the assent of parliament, but Mary's mild rule caused at that time so unusual an exercise of the Crown's authority to pass without opposition. Certainly the royal title did by no means make Darnley really sovereign of the realm, yet one saw, nevertheless, his name by the side of, and in some instances even before that of Mary on Scottish coins from the year 1565, and in Scottish state papers from the same date.[3]

Even in foreign countries, with the single excep- tion of England, the same respect was shown him as to crowned kings. During the winter that the Queen and Darnley continued to reside in Holy- rood, a deputation reached him from the King of France, headed by Jacques d'Augennes, Lord

[1] According to a letter from Randolph to the Earl of Leicester, dated Edinburgh the last day of July 1565; Wright, *Queen Elizabeth and her Times*, i. 203. Randolph remarks in the same letter : " I was sent for to have been at the supper, but like a churlisch or uncourteous carle I re- fused to be there."

[2] " The Proclamation, which is dated the day before the marriage, the 28th of July 1565, is printed in Anderson's *Collections*, i. 33.

[3] As an instance of this there is

in the Danish Privy Archives a letter to Frederick II., which begins : " Henricus et Maria, Dei gratia Scotorum Rex et Regina," and which concludes : " Datum ex regia nostra Edinburgensi, Cal. Octobris, Anno 1565, et regnorum nostrorum annis primo et vicesimo tertio." In the subscription the order is on the contrary reversed, the first signature, being : "S[ere- nitatis] T[uae] Soror et consan- guinea Maria R. ;" and immedi- ately following it : " S. T. Frater et consanguineus Henry R."

de Rambouillet, who was charged to confer on
him the order of St. Michael,[1] — the same distinguished order as another deputation of French
nobles, " with white cloaks on," had some time previously, in Flensborg, presented to the young King
of Denmark and Norway, Frederick II.[2] When the
investiture, preceded by the celebration of the
Catholic mass, had taken place in the royal chapel,
this new mark of honour was again followed by a
splendid banquet in the Palace, and in the evening
by a masquerade, in which the Queen, along with
all her " Maries " and the rest of her ladies, appeared
clad in male attire, as usual to the great scandal of
the Protestant party.[3] But Darnley aimed at something higher ; he wished not merely to be king
in name, but to rule as an actual king, and obtain
what, in the language of the times was designated
" the crown matrimonial ; " that is, the right to the
crown after the Queen's death. Mary's affection
for him did not, however, extend so far. This
he lost at the same time as he deprived himself of
the favour with which a part of the people in spite
of his popish leanings welcomed him at first. Mary
had, before the marriage, with great tenderness,
nursed Darnley during his illness ; she had doubtless
thought to give not merely her hand, but also her
heart, to the noble, handsome youth, but this he
speedily lost by his exaggerated notions of himself,
which so little accorded with his puerile abilities,
and by his immature rawness, which made this

---

[1] Usually called the Cockle
Order, from the golden cockle-
shells of which the chain of the
Order was composed. It was instituted by Louis XI.

[2] Resen, *Kong Frederichs den
Andens Krönike*, p. 60.

[3] Note C, Appendix.

pride still môre intolerable to her. At this time
Mary Stuart ordered Thomas Randolph to leave the
country within fourteen days, because it had come
to light how he, after having held the rebels
together, and supported them with money, still
served as a bond of union between the exiles in
England and their friends remaining in Scotland,
and instead, therefore, of his letters from the capital,
where he had done his best to fan the dangerous
flame,[1] the English Government continued at this
critical juncture to receive communications from the
border town of Berwick, giving intelligence of what
was doing in Scotland, and these could now indicate
how much addicted Darnley was to the besetting
sin of the times—intemperance in drinking bouts.
One instance was especially detailed which occurred
at a social party in the house of a merchant in
Edinburgh, at which the Queen, advanced in pregnancy, had been present, and where Darnley, in
reply to her request not to drink too much himself,
nor to entice others to do so, answered with such
words, that she left the place in tears.[2] Also,
on another occasion, he had pained his wife still
more keenly, so that it is impossible to restrain the
thought of what a different direction the life of Mary
and of her people might have taken by a union with a
better man than Darnley. Elizabeth's agents, who

---

[1] *A Diurnal of Remarkable Occurrents*, p. 88. What Sir James Melvill (*Memoirs*, p. 109) writes in respect of Randolph's renewed activity in Scotland at a later period, may well in part be applied to it on this occasion :— "Now as Nero stood upon a high part of Rome to see the town burning, which he had caused to be set on fire, so Mr. Randolph delighted to see such fire by his craft kindled in Scotland, which was in all probability like to burn it up."

[2] Sir William Drury's account from Berwick of 16th February 1566. Keith, *History of Church and State in Scotland*, p. 329.

had in strong language described the passionate
fondness of the honeymoon, quickly came to the
unanimous conclusion that the Queen of Scotland
was tired of Darnley, and frequently avoided his
company. She no longer permitted, as she had
done at the beginning of their married life, his
name to stand before hers in state papers or on
coins.[1] She also endeavoured from this period to
reserve to herself alone the actual authority in
the management of the state, and she would by no
means allow that Darnley, to the injury of the
Hamiltons, should like her first husband also
acquire " the crown matrimonial."

The fiery passionate youth did not regard his
own conduct as the cause of this alienation, but
made the breach wider by laying the blame of it on
the Queen's favourite companions. Above all, his
hatred directed itself upon one amongst them who
had lately laboured successfully for his own ad-
vancement, the Queen's gifted and highly trusted
secretary for foreign correspondence, David Riccio,
an Italian, who had in December 1564 attained to
this position on the decease of the Frenchman
Raulet, and whose services were so richly recompensed, that the citizen-born foreigner could
maintain a degree of magnificence which cast into
the shade that of many a Scottish nobleman.[2] As

---

[1] He was wont in all writing to
be first named, but now he is
placed second. Lately pieces of
money were coined with both
their faces, " Hen. et Maria";
these are called in, and others
framed.—Randolph to Cecil, Edinburgh, the 25th December 1565.
*Calendar of State Papers, Foreign
Series,* 1564-5, p. 541.

[2] Riccio, who had come in the
year 1562 to Scotland in the
retinue of the Savoyard Ambassador, Count Morreta, and was at
that time a " huomi di 28 anni
in circa, accorto, savio et virtuoso "
(*Labanoff,* vii. 86), got for the
times special gifts from the Queen,
who likewise at her marriage with
Darnley, which he had contributed

Riccio's duty was to lay before the Queen whatever required her signature, he was among those who had their residence in the palace, and had at all times easy access to her. He was likewise in another capacity often welcome to her; for Mary, who had inherited her father's fondness for unconstrained sociality, was renowned for her singing and playing,[1] and the Italian was—according to the words of Sir James Melvil, who himself warned him not to allow the Queen to thrust him forward so much[2] —also "a lively companion and good musician," and

so much to bring about, gave him for a festive garb ten ells of black velvet brocaded with gold (*Inventaires de la Royne Descosse*, p. 155). But how he, according to the general impression of the Scottish nobles, was able to attain his position, and to gather his fortune, was, notwithstanding, for a long time an enigma which was first solved by one of the papers in Teulet, *Papiers d'état*. In this is found the so-called "Estat des gaiges des dames, damoiselles,gentilzhommes et autres officiers domesticques de la Royne Escosse, Douairière de France, pour une année commençant le premier jour de janvier 1566 et finissant le dernier jour de décembre ensuivant." The document which is signed in Edinburgh 13th February 1567, by Mary Stuart and Riccio's successor and younger brother, Joseph Riccio, was designed to serve as an assignment in France for the benefit of the persons therein named. The whole amount of the rewards and pensions which were to be paid out of Mary Stuart's income as Queen Dowager of France exceeds £1000—an immense sum in those days. It may be added in passing, that Bothwell's name does not occur in the long list.

[1] Ad cantus excellentiam multum ei profuit natura quædam non adscita vocis inflexio; testudinem lyram et clauicymbalum quod vocant, apte pulsabat.—Georgius Conæus, *Vita Mariæ Stuartæ*. Jebb, *De vita et rebus gestis Mariæ, Scotorum Reginæ*, ii. 15.

[2] "I told him that strangers were commonly envied when they meddled too much in the affairs of other countries. He said he being secretary to her Majesty in the French tongue, had occasion thereby to be frequently in her Majesty's company, as her former secretary used to do. . . . I remembered her Majesty's command lately laid upon me, when she particularly injoined me, to forewarn her of any circumstance to be observed in her carriage which I thought could tend to her prejudice. . . . I told her Majesty very freely what advice I had given Rixio. She answered me that he medled no further than in her French writings and affairs, as her other French secretary had done formerly. And that whoever found fault therewith, she would not be so far restrained, but that she might dispence her favours to such as she pleased. . . . And she gave me her hand, that she would take all in good part

E

could, at her musical entertainments, supply a part
in which she might be wanting. Recently it had
been Murray who would gladly have seen Riccio
hanged, because the latter promoted Darnley's
marriage; now it was Darnley himself, who was
instigated by the enemies of the foreigner not only
to see in the influential Italian his political
antagonist who caused his highest wish to miscarry with Mary, but under the blinding influence
of jealousy, to regard his intercourse generally
with the Queen as intolerable, and to find in his
person, although Riccio was ugly,[1] what he might
thank for the Queen's coldness.[2] In a fit of silly
passion, Darnley (if we may credit one of Randolph's
earlier accounts),[3] once when the Court Secretary
brought him the intelligence that the drawing up
of the patent of his elevation to the dukedom must
be postponed for some time, wished to strike him
down with his poniard. With like temper he now
resolved, in order to get rid of Riccio, to enter into
union with his foes, and stretch out his hand to
the enemies of the Queen and her government, who
found in the facile king a ready instrument for
carrying out their plans.

On the 10th of February, Darnley, whose
mother was a Douglas, had sent his kinsman, George

whatever I did speak, as proceeding from a loving and faithful
servant.   Desiring me also to
befriend Rixio, who was hated
without a cause." — *Memoirs of
Sir James Melvil*, pp. 54, 55, 56,
58.

[1] For Riccio's ugliness we have
Buchanan's own testimony in his
Rerum Scoticarum Historia, p. 209.

[2] An idea is obtained of the
mode in which the enemies of

Riccio were inflamed against him,
when in a letter to the Earl of
Leicester from Randolph, after his
expulsion from Scotland, one meets
with words like these :—" Woe is
me for you when David's sone shal
be kynge of England."—Randolph
to the Earl of Leicester, Berwick,
29th January 1566.   *Calendar of
State Papers, Foreign Series*, p. 13.

[3] Randolph's Letter to Cecil of
21st May 1565.   *Raumer*, p. 63.

Douglas, to the powerful lord, Patrick Ruthven, CHAP. II. who was united by marriage to the same family, for 1566. the purpose of asking his support against Riccio. Ruthven was then so ill with a distemper which was soon to lay him in the grave, that "he scarce could go to the end of his room;" but he readily promised to help the king to gain his object. The Italian was equally hateful to him—hateful as a papist who might become the Queen's right hand in schemes for the advantage of Catholicism, hateful, too, as a foreigner—just as we afterwards see Concini hated in France—and hateful as a man of humble birth. That the son of a Piedmontese musician should have influence in the government of the kingdom, and even be named, as he already was, as a future peer—nay more, that an Earl like the exiled Murray should now have to stoop so far as to send him a costly diamond to induce him to speak a word in his favour to his sister,—all this was something as intolerable to Scotland's proud nobles, as the favouritism of Christian II. had been to the Danes. Lord Ruthven was closely allied to the exiled Lords as well as to their Protestant friends still remaining in the country, and just at this time Parliament was about to meet for the purpose of sanctioning that forfeiture of their rank and possessions to which Mary's government wished to subject them. It was also rumoured that a new proposal in favour of Catholicism was about to be transmitted from the King of France and the Cardinal of Lorraine, who had recently returned from the Council of Trent, and that Riccio was endeavouring to overcome Mary's scruples with respect to it. But what above all was feared was

CHAP.
II.

1566.

the probability of a claim being now put forth by the government for the restoration to the crown of the many estates, which the nobility during the Queen's minority had " under pretence of religion " appropriated to themselves,—there being a Scottish law which empowered the wearer of the crown within four years after having attained his majority to resume all such previous alienations or transfers. Accordingly at this juncture, a league was concluded between the Queen's husband and her systematic enemies. Lord Patrick Lindsay, who, like Lord Ruthven, was allied by marriage to the Douglas family, and James Douglas, Earl of Morton, who was a cousin of Lady Lennox, and the most powerful member of the Douglas family, along with many others in Scotland, were won over to lend it their support, while the ungrateful Earl of Lennox himself hastened into England, where his wife and youngest son then lay in prison, for the purpose of acquainting the exiles with the plan of the proposed *coup d'état*. According to it they were to be prepared, as soon as it was effected, to rush from the Borders to Edinburgh. There Riccio was to be put out of the way, the other opponents of the party in the government in like manner either killed, imprisoned, or in some other mode made harmless, the parliament again dissolved ; the judicial prosecution, already begun, was to be quashed, and the Queen put in confinement. On the part of the exiles it was also stipulated that Murray and his friends should meanwhile do their utmost to get Darnley's mother and brother released by the English government, and in Scotland to help their tool to " the matrimonial crown,"so that " if the Queen remained childless," Darnley should be

upheld as King of Scotland in preference to any
of the Hamiltons. Murray's accession to the conspiracy is placed beyond question by his subscription
to the bond, in which the conspirators oblige themselves " to extirpe out of the realme of Scotland, or
tak or slay " every person whom the King " sall
pleis to command " as opposing his right of succession to the Scottish crown in default of the Queen's
issue.[1] Darnley took upon himself the responsibility
of the whole matter, and promised in writing on his
honour as a prince that the participators in this
conspiracy, to which Elizabeth was also made privy,
should be defended by him against all and sundry.

The 7th of March was a great day in Edinburgh. Darnley alone was absent, being unwilling
to make his appearance on this occasion in company
with Mary, and accordingly, he rode with a small
retinue down to Leith. But the Queen herself,
as yet suspecting no mischief, went on horseback,
and richly attired, in solemn procession from Holyrood up to Edinburgh to open the new Parliament that was to assemble there, and in which
she had at length secured to the Scottish prelates
their former places among the other estates of the
kingdom, of which under the revolution they were
deprived, and this with the hope, as she herself
has owned, of thereby once more being able to
obtain some relief for the still down-trodden Catholic
Church.[2] The so-called " Lords of Articles," or

[1] The bond, dated eight days
before Riccio's murder, is printed
in the *Miscellany of the Maitland Club*, Edinburgh and Glasgow, 1833-1850, iii. 188-191, from
the original in the Charter-room
of the Earl of Leven and Melville.

It was Murray who first signed the
bond.

[2] Letter of Mary Stuart to the
Archbishop of Glasgow, dated 2d
April 1566. Labanoff, *Lettres de
Marie Stuart,* i. 341.

members of that important committee, upon whose
proposal every measure rested in the old Scottish
Parliament, were appointed, and the choice, for the
most part, fell on such persons that the motion
of the government for the punishment of the
exiles assumed a still more threatening aspect.
Among the members chosen were Bothwell and
Huntly. The friends of the exiles had now no
time to lose. The intention of striking the blow
while Riccio was in attendance on Mary Stuart
during a visit she paid at Seton, had at an
earlier period been frustrated through the vigilance
which Sir George Seton, always a devoted friend
of the Queen, had shown on this occasion in protecting her. Another plan, according to which it
was proposed to strike down Riccio while playing
balls with Darnley, had likewise to be given up,
because one of the conspirators said that the Queen
ought not to be altogether exempted from the
shadow of suspicion which might fall upon her if it
should afterwards be reported that Riccio was seized
by her side.[1] At all events it was to her royal
palace that on Saturday evening, 9th March 1566,
the conspiring Lords might have been seen passing
down through the Canongate at the head of five
hundred armed men without any resistance being
offered to them. How this happened, whether from
the smallness of the royal guard, or because its presence had been prevented on this occasion by the
interference of Darnley, is uncertain; for though
the powerful Scottish nobles, who were themselves
always attended by crowds of vassals, would not
allow their sovereigns to maintain household troops

---

[1] The Italian account given by Labanoff, vii. 72.

like the princes on the Continent; yet we cannot
well admit with later, and even Scottish authors,
that Mary Stuart was entirely without a royal
guard, since the original authorities very often
make mention of a " garde " which usually attended
her.[1] While certain detachments of the conspirators were ordered to watch the environs of the
palace, and Morton and Lindsay with a hundred
and sixty men occupied the chief entrance to the
palace and the palace garden, Ruthven and some
others of the leaders were able to ascend to
Darnley's rooms where "the king" awaited their
coming.

How many wanderers from the regions of the
old and new worlds have visited the palace of
Holyrood and the picturesque remains of its beautiful old chapel, and who amongst them, at all acquainted with Scotland's history or its poetry, has
really been able to look upon the double towers
which ornament its front, without being reminded
of the sad fortunes of the Scottish monarchy, so
stormy and so continually threatened with dangers;
or to tread those silent and yet eloquent rooms
without being affected with emotions of sadness
and sympathy? If Mary Stuart's French attendants,
as well as herself, were struck with the sight of so
much poverty and rudeness in Scotland, yet in one
respect they made an exception, for even in their
eyes, though accustomed to behold what the riches
of France and the revived art of Italy had already
created in Amboise and Fontainebleau, Holyrood

---

[1] About his stay at Holyrood, in the beginning of the following year, Bothwell writes thus : — " Aussi j'estois logé dans le circuit, où l'on asséoit ordinairement la garde, qui estoit de cinquante hommes." Teu-let, *Lettres*, p. 168.

seemed a beautiful building.[1] The external form
which Holyrood then presented was altered after it
was burned during its occupation by Cromwell's
soldiers, and its subsequent rebuilding in the reign
of Charles II.; but one still sees, in the old part of
the palace, and in its lowest range of apartments,
Darnley's bedroom and audience-chamber, and in
that right above it, those in which Mary Stuart
resided, and in which everything, as far as possible,
is retained in its ancient condition. Through the
first of these apartments, which is usually called
" Queen Mary's audience-room," one enters " Queen
Mary's bed-chamber," in the north side of which a
small door, half hidden by tapestry, leads to a little
stair which, alongside the main stair, leads up from
Darnley's apartments. At the south-west corner
of the bed-chamber, a narrow door opens into the
Queen's " little dressing-room," while at the north-
easterly corner is an entrance to a corresponding
room, which also contains a space of twelve feet
square, but as " Queen Mary's supping-room" has
become specially famous in Scottish history. Here
on that Saturday evening sat the young Queen at
one of the small social parties of which she was
so fond. At the table where she was, sat her
half-sister Lady Jane Stuart, who, a couple of
years previously, had been divorced from Archibald
Campbell, Earl of Argyll. There were also present
with her, her half-brother Lord Robert Stuart,
Prior of Holyrood-house, her High-Steward Robert
Beaton the laird of Creich, who likewise was

---

[1] Est certes un beau bastiment
et ne tient rien du pays.—Brantôme, *Vies des Dames illustres*, in
Œuvres du Seigneur de Brantôme.
A la Haye, 1740, i. 143.

"keeper" of her palace at Falkland, her Master of the Horse the young Arthur Erskine of Black- grange, younger brother to the Earl of Mar, and in Knox's eyes "the most pestilent papist within the realm," and lastly, her secretary David Riccio. Suddenly the curtain which concealed the secret entrance to the bed-chamber from Darnley's apartments was lifted aside, and the king entered the little room where Mary sat, and as she turned herself kindly towards him he took his place by her side, putting, in an affectionate manner, his arm round her waist.[1] In another instant the arras in the adjoining room was again lifted, and Lord Ruthven now stalked into the midst of the company with helmet on his head, and his lofty form clad in armour, and with his countenance marked alike by the pallor of sickness, and the wildness of unbridled frenzy, while he ordered Riccio to take himself away from a spot which was no place for him. Disturbed by so strange and menacing an apparition the Queen sprang up, and commanded Ruthven, with a severity which she could assume when necessary, to leave her royal apartments, adding that if Riccio had incurred any blame, she would get him punished by the Parliament.[2] At the same moment after these words were uttered, as Robert Stuart, Arthur Erskine, Beaton of Creich, and some of the servants were about to lay hold of Lord Ruthven, and as the latter with drawn dagger

[1] "With his hand about her waste."—Lord Ruthven's account of the murder written at Berwick, 30th April 1566. Keith, *History of Church and State in Scotland*, Appendix, p. 123.
[2] Declaring we should exhibite the said David before the Lords of Parliament, to be punisht, if any sorte he had offended. — Mary Stuart's letter to the Archbishop of Glasgow, of 2d April 1566. Labanoff, *Lettres de Marie Stuart*, i. 344.

threateningly exclaimed, "Lay no hands on me, for I will not be handled," the noise was heard of many persons rushing up the secret stair, then the tramping of heavy feet in the adjoining bed-chamber, and the next moment there rushed, amid the glare of torches borne after them, George Douglas, Andrew Ker of Faldonside, Patrick Bellenden of Stanehouse, and some others into the little room, with swords and daggers gleaming in their hands,—"so rudely and irreverently," says a contemporary, "that the table with the candles and dishes upon it was overturned on the floor." The table in its fall struck the Queen, then in the sixth month of her pregnancy, and the Countess of Argyll was obliged to seize one of the candles, as Ruthven brandishing his dagger cried out to the Queen, "No harm is intended to you, madam, but only to that villain." Who does not know the scene which ensued? Who has not pictured to himself the unhappy wretch in his deadly terror springing behind the Queen, clutching her robe with the energy of despair, and drowning the noise itself with his cries, "Madama, io son morto, giustizia, giustizia;" or who has not called up before his mind's eye the scene as the conspirators press on,—Darnley striving to wrest Riccio's hand from the Queen's person, the brutal Ker of Faldonside menacingly presenting a pistol towards her breast, or George Douglas snatching the king's dagger from its sheath, striking Riccio with it over Mary's shoulder, and leaving it in his body? Who has not followed, in imagination, the furious actors as they subsequently dragged away from the Queen, whom Darnley held fast, their trembling victim through the bedroom and the audience-chamber, striking him as they went, until at last on reaching the doorway of the latter, where others of the conspirators, having ascended by the main stair, awaited him, and where alleged traces of his blood are still pointed out—he expired pierced with fifty-six sword and poniard stabs ?

Mary remained behind with Darnley in the little room in which the onslaught had taken place, trembling at the horrid scene which was being enacted a few steps from her, and weeping incessantly. " My poor David," she exclaimed, in words interrupted by sobs, " my good and faithful servant, God have mercy on thy soul !"[1] Describing the murder in a letter to her ambassador in Paris, James Beaton, Archbishop of Glasgow, she writes : —" After this deed immediately the said Lord Ruthven, coming again in our presence, declared how they and their complices foresaids were highly offended with our proceedings and tyranny, which was not to them tolerable ; how we was abused by the said David, whom they had actually put to death, namely, in taking his counsell for maintenance of the ancient religion ; debarring of the lords which were fugitive, and entertaining of amity with foreign princes and nations with whom we were confederate ; putting also upon council the lords Bothwell and Huntly, who were traitors, and with whom he (Riccio) associated himself."[2] When Ruthven also declared that everything was undertaken only in agreement with the king's wish, the

---

[1] " Ah povero Davit, mio buono et fedel servitore, Dio habbi misericordia di vostra anima." — The account from Edinburgh of 8th October 1566, as given by Labanoff, vii. 92.

[2] Mary Stuart's letter to the Archbishop of Glasgow of 2d April 1566. Labanoff, i. 343.

CHAP.
II.

1566.

Queen, deeply moved, turned to Darnley, and vehemently upbraided him for his "Judas-kiss," and for having had the heart so to injure her. "Traitor, son of a traitor," she exclaimed, "thus you requite her who has done you so much good, and conferred on you so great an honour; this is the acknowledgment which you make me for having elevated you to so high a dignity. What injury have I done to you that you have willingly caused me such shame?"[1] Darnley answered by saying how different for a long time past had been her conduct from that at the first period of their married life, by shunning him on every occasion when he wished to approach her, and how he had reason to believe that Riccio had persuaded her to show such coldness towards him.[2] "My Lord," at last replied the Queen, "all the offence that is done me, you have the wite thereof, for the which I shall be your

[1] Allora voltatasi la Reina verso il Re gli disse: "Ha traditore, figliuolo di traditore, questa è la ricompensa che hai dato a colui che t'ha fatto tanto bene et honor cosi grande; questo è il reconoscimento che dai a me per haverti inalzato a dignità cosi alta."—Account communicated to the Grand Duke of Tuscany, dated 8th October 1566. Labanoff, vii. 75.

[2] My lord, why have you caused to do this wicked deed to me; considering that I took you from low estate, and made you my husband? What offence have I given you that you should do me such shame? The king answered, I have good reason for me, for since yonder fellow David came in credit and familiarity with your Majesty, you neither regarded me, entertained me, nor trusted me after your wonted fashion; for

every day before dinner you were wont to come to my chamber, and past the time with me, and this long time you have not done so; and when I came to honour your Majesty's chamber, you bare me little company except David had been the third person; and after supper your Majesty used to sit up at the cards with the said David till one or two after midnight; and this is the entertainment that I have of you this long time. Her Majesty answered, that it was not a gentlewoman's duty to come to her husband's chamber, but rather the husband to come to the wife's. The king answered: How came you to my chamber in the beginning, and ever till within these six months, that David fell into familiarity with you?—Lord Ruthven's account as given in Keith's *History of Church and State in Scotland,* Appendix, pp. 123, 124.

wife no longer, nor ly with you any more, and shall never like well till I cause you have as sorrowful a heart as I have at this present."[1]

The altercation between the Queen and Darnley had reached its height, when a loud knocking was heard at the door of the larger room into which, followed by Ruthven, they had meanwhile entered from the little one where the onslaught had taken place. It was stated that there was fighting in the palace garden, and Lord Ruthven, whose presence had been long intolerable to the Queen, seized the opportunity to get away leaving Darnley behind. On the rumour of what had happened in the Queen's presence getting abroad, the uproar became quickly transferred to other parts of the palace, and divers of the Queen's adherents who had their residence within its precincts, and especially the Earls Bothwell, Huntly, and Atholl, put themselves at the head of some hastily armed men and hurried to the Queen's assistance. When Ruthven arrived they were already driven back to their apartments by their more numerous and better armed opponents,[2] and were being threatened by the Earl of Morton that it should fare badly with them if they ventured again to leave their quarters. Accordingly it only remained for Lord Ruthven to endeavour to quiet them by assuring them in the King's name that their lives were not in any danger. But scarcely was the alarm put an end to within the

---

[1] Lord Ruthven's account. — Keith, *History of the Church and State in Scotland*, Appendix, p. 124.
[2] Comites Huntilææ, Atholiæ et Bothuelii, qui in diversa palatii parte cœnabant, quum prorumpere vellent, ab iis, qui in area adservabant, intra cœnacula sua sine noxa sunt cohibiti.—Buchanan, *Rerum Scoticarum Historia*, p. 211.

palace than it began outside. The report of the
outrage also extended up to the city, and then
"the cry and noyas rais," says a contemporary,
"in sic manner throw the Cannogait, that it was
said that the Quenis grace was haldin in captivitie
and seignour David slane, quhairthrow the common bell rang in sik sort that euerie man past to
armour, and rusheit down with Symon Prestoun
of Craigmillar, thair provest, to Halyrudhous, willing to haue delieverit the Quenis grace and
revengit the caus forsaid."[1] When Mary meanwhile wished to speak to the crowd, she was not
allowed by the murderers, "who," she writes, "in
our face declared, if we desired to have spoken
them, they should cut us to collops and cast us
over the walls."[2] Darnley showed himself in her
stead, and assured the citizens that the Queen was
safe and sound. When the Provost desired that
they might nevertheless hear the Queen herself
speak, he answered him with the words :—" Provest,
know you not that I am king ? I command you to
pass home to your houses."[3] The citizens obeyed,
and in the evening Darnley gave the keys of the
palace gates to the Earl of Morton, who, dismiss-
ing all untrustworthy persons, took upon himself
along with Lord Ruthven to keep all things secure
for the night.

One thing nevertheless happened otherwise than
had been looked for. Bothwell and others of the
Queen's adherents were found in the morning to
be no longer present. In spite of the peaceful

---

[1] *Diurnal of Remarkable Occurrents*, p. 91.
[2] Mary's letter of 2d April 1566, Labanoff, i. 346.
[3] Knox, *History of the Reformation in Scotland*, ii. 522.

assurance given by Lord Ruthven their fears remained, especially as they knew that Murray and
their other enemies were expected to return on the
following day, and although the armed hosts of
the murderers watched the gates of the palace,
yet the darkness made it possible for them to effect
their escape with safety. "If," writes Bothwell
subsequently, after having spoken of the murder
of Riccio, "some noblemen and I myself, in order
to avoid such a peril, had not escaped through a
window in the back of the palace, we should not
have received any better treatment, since they had
so resolved among themselves, or we had at the
least been compelled to approve of an action so
very base and detestable."[1]   Like Bothwell, the
Earl of Huntly, his brother-in-law, also escaped,
as did in other similar modes John Stuart Earl of
Atholl, Lords John Fleming and William Livingston and Sir James Balfour, "against whom," writes
the Queen, "the enterprise was conspired as well
as for David (Riccio); and at whose flight the
conspirators were therefore specially chagrined, and
found themselves much disappointed in their enterprise."

When Mary Stuart, after that sorrowful night,
during which she was so apprehensive of a mis-

---

[1] Et si (pour éviter ce péril)
quelques seigneurs et moy n'eussions passé par une fenestre
derrière le-dict logis, nous n'eussions eu meilleur traictement,
d'aultant qu'il avoit ainsi esté
résolu entre eux, ou pour le moins
eussions esté contraintz de ap-
prouver un si meschant et détest-
able acto.—Bothwell's Representation : Teulet, *Lettres*, p. 164. Sir

James Melvil likewise says that
Bothwell in company with the
Earls Atholl and Huntly escaped
" by leaping over a window toward
the little garden where the Lyons
were lodged."—*Memoirs*, p. 64.
Lastly, Mary Stuart herself remarks :—" Yet, by the providence
of God, the Earls of Huntly and
Bothwell escaped forth of their
chambers in our palace at a back-

carriage that she had a midwife sent for,[1] found
herself on Sunday morning a prisoner in the palace
of her ancestors, she suddenly hit upon a new idea
for effecting her liberation. She saw Sir James
Melvil, who as yet had not fled with her other
adherents, but had now got permission to repair
to the city, going across the palace garden, throw-
ing up a window, she prayed him to call in the aid
of her faithful subjects that she might be delivered
out of the hands of traitors. Wisbet, the steward
of the Earl of Lennox, was sent after him with a
troop of soldiers, but Melvil nevertheless got leave
to proceed, as he pretended that he "was only going
to sermon at St. Giles's Church."[2] He gave the
Provost information as to his errand, but the latter
relying on the contrary orders of Darnley, although
still not unwilling to summon the citizens together,
was so divided in his inclinations between the one
and the other that nothing was done. On the
other hand there were published the same day two
proclamations which were subscribed by Darnley.
In the one it was forbidden, under pain of death,
for any persons to carry weapons in the streets of
Edinburgh. In the other Parliament was dissolved
by Darnley, who as King, in his own name alone
issued in it orders, commanding all members of
Parliament, with the exception of such as he might

window by some cords." The
above-mentioned letter of the
Queen of 2d April 1566 is given
in Labanoff, i. 346.

[1] Account given by Raumer in
his *Die Königinnen Elizabeth
und Maria Stuart*, p. 113. The
nervous timidity of James VI.,
which in Sir Walter Scott's novel,
The Fortunes of Nigel, has

become the subject of a well-
known representation, is still
commonly adduced as an instance
of how the incidental mood of the
mother during pregnancy may
operate on the whole after-life
of the child.—Andrew Combe's
Principles of Physiology.

[2] *Memoirs of Sir James Melvil*,
p. 65.

specially exempt, to leave Edinburgh within three
hours. In the palace the Queen was the whole day
so closely watched, lest she might escape in dis-
guise, that none of her ladies or women were
permitted to leave her apartments wearing veils.[1]
And in the evening the arrival in Edinburgh was
also witnessed of the Earl of Murray and other
gentlemen of the exiled nobility who immediately
rode to Holyrood, where they were welcomed by
Darnley, while the captive Queen was still so ignorant of Murray's complicity in the murder that she,
forgetting the old wrong in the new, threw herself
into his arms, kissed him, and exclaimed :—" If he
had been at home he would not have suffered her
to have been so uncourteously handled."[2]

The account which speaks most fully of these
days so crowded with events, but which as it proceeds from the conspirators themselves has no claim
to implicit confidence, tells that this day or Sunday
did not close without the Queen at last consenting
that Darnley should pass the night with her.[3] She
knew the weakness which was combined with his
roughness, and that she might be able to use her
influence over him for the purpose of separating him

---

[1] So the King commanded him to give attendance thereunto, and put certain to the doors and let no gentlewomen pass forth muffled. —Lord Ruthven's account given in Keith, *History of Church and State in Scotland*, Appendix, p. 127.

[2] *Memoirs of Sir James Melvil*, p. 65.

[3] Lord Ruthven's account.— Keith, *History of Church and State in Scotland*, Appendix, p. 128. A draft of this account dated 30th April 1566, had already on the 2d April been sent from Berwick to William Cecil by Lord Ruthven in conjunction with the Earl of Morton, and in an accompanying letter (Chalmers, *Life of Mary Queen of Scots*, ii. 57 ; *Calendar of State Papers relating to Scotland*, i. 232) they had requested him to correct their draft in order that they might thereupon cause such an account to circulate in Scotland and France.

F

from those guilty of the murder was probably the
wish which sprang up in her trembling heart.
Darnley was himself, certainly to her advantage in
this respect, so overcome by the foregoing events,
that he remained sunk in a deep sleep till the
morning was far advanced, and then betook himself to the room in which the Queen had sought
repose. When Darnley subsequently appeared again
among his confederates his behaviour was altogether
changed. Formerly they had intended to confine
the Queen until by means of a new parliament they
had procured for Darnley the so-called "matrimonial
crown," and full authority as King ; now it was
he himself who represented the needlessness of such
a step, since the Queen was disposed in favour of a
reconciliation. He also himself afterwards led
the Queen by the hand into the large hall where
the conspiring Earls and Lords were assembled,
who knelt to receive her. Having first heard the
Earl of Morton as their spokesman, she reminded
them of her lenity, that she had never shown herself
bloodthirsty, and then ordering them to rise up,
she subsequently passed some time walking up and
down the room with Darnley on one side, and
Murray on the other. When Mary declared herself
prepared to subscribe whatever articles the conspirators might deem necessary for their safety, the
adherents of the King, as they still called themselves, drew up a few. Darnley received them and
found nothing objectionable in them, but, nevertheless, made a request to the effect that the Lords
should forthwith withdraw their retainers, and again
leave the custody of the palace in the hands of the
Queen's guard, since a letter of safety such as they

desired would by no means agree with any appearance of imprisonment on the part of the giver of it.
Lord Ruthven, "quhome (the Queen) wald not thole
to come in hir presens,"[1] and who especially began to
suspect mischief, "protested to Darnley that what
bloodshed and mischief should ensue thereof, should
fall upon his head and his posterity, not upon
theirs."[2]   But because of the expected letter of
safety, and, perhaps also, because Murray did not
show himself so frank towards them as they had
anticipated, the Earl of Morton and the other
leaders were disposed to submit to the request
made by Darnley.   After the revolution had, in all
essential respects, apparently succeeded, they left
the palace on the afternoon of Monday with their
retainers.   In the evening Archibald Douglas was
sent from Morton's house in Edinburgh, where they
had assembled for supper, to Holyrood to ask for
the letter, but the only answer he got from Darnley
was, that the Queen was sick, and that it would be
subscribed the following day.   For meantime the
Queen had exerted her influence more and more
upon the facile King, had in private vividly represented to him what humiliation he had been on the
point of preparing for the kingdom and the Catholic
religion.   In the middle of the same night, after
the custody of the palace had been given over to
Darnley, he and the Queen, with only one of her
ladies, secretly passed out of Holyrood,[3] and having

[1] *Diurnal of Remarkable Occur-*
rents, p. 92.
[2] Lord Ruthven's account given
in Keith's *History*, Appendix, p.
128.
[3] It was thus unnecessary to try
a plan of escape that, in compliance

with the Queen's wish, had been
communicated to her by Bothwell
and Huntly, according to which,
as she herself writes, it was proposed by them, "that we should
have come over the walls of our
palace in the night upon towes and

mounted horses which Sir John Stuart of Traquair and the young Arthur Erskine had in readiness for them outside, after a brisk trot the whole way they arrived on Tuesday morning at the Castle of Dunbar.

From Dunbar Mary Stuart summoned her vassals to arms, and, at the same time, she, who, during the whole of this catastrophe, had shown, for a woman, an admirable bearing, issued a proclamation against the audacious persons that had violated her royal dwelling with bloodshed, and kept herself a prisoner. In a letter sent to France to the Cardinal of Lorraine, immediately after her arrival at Dunbar, she subscribed herself " Vostra Nepote Maria Regina senza regno;"[1] but in a very short time she saw crowds from all quarters hasten to her help, the first to come being led by Bothwell, and Huntly, who, after Riccio's murder, had escaped from Holyrood to Crichton Castle. These were now very graciously received at Dunbar by the Queen, and here she saw her forces so much increased, that Bothwell himself reports the army, with which the Quéen a few days afterwards marched towards Edinburgh, as numbering four thousand men.[2] She understood how to divide her enemies. Accordingly she forgave her half-brother Murray, who deserted his fellow-conspirators, and also the other insurgents that had come back to Scotland, provided they had

chairs, which they had in readiness to that effect." Mary's letter dated 2d April 1566. — Labanoff, i. 348.

[1] Labanoff, vii. 78.

[2] She herself forcibly relates afterwards as to Bothwell's ser-

vices " how suddanlie be his provydence not onlie wer we deliverit out of the pressoun, bot alswa that haill cumpany of conspiratouris dissolvit and we recoverit oure formar obedience."— Labanoff, ii. 35.

not abetted Riccio's murder. The latter, after Mary
Stuart had on the 19th March returned in triumph
to Edinburgh, ventured thither also, either in obedience to the Queen's summons to appear before the
court of justice, or to make some special resistance to
her; but they speedily found, in most cases, that now
their turn had come to flee again to England. Of
those who remained behind, the greater number
were imprisoned, yet the Scottish Queen did not let
her kingdom become the scene of such a series of
executions as those with which Queen Elizabeth, a
few years later, punished the Catholics in the north
of England who rose in defence of Mary Stuart ; for
while Elizabeth, in the county of Durham alone,
caused the impotent insurrection of 1569 to be
followed by three hundred executions,[1] only two
of those guilty of Riccio's murder, Thomas Scott of
Cambusmichael, under-sheriff of Perth, and Henry
Yair, formerly a Catholic priest, were executed.
When William Harlaw and John Mowbray, two
Edinburgh burgesses, who had been condemned
to death the same day as the two others, were
standing at the foot of the gallows, the Earl of
Bothwell appeared " with the Queen's ring," and
announced that the Queen's grace had commuted
the punishment of death to banishment.[2] Among
others who were indebted to Bothwell for the
pardon of their guilty complicity, Knox expressly
names the lairds William Lauder of Halton, John
Sandilands of Calder, and John Cockburn of Ormis-

[1] C. Sharpe, *Memorials of the
Rebellion of* 1569. London, 1840,
p. 140.
  [2] *Diurnal of Remarkable Occurrents*, p. 98. " But the Earl

Bothwell presented the Queen's
ring to the Provost, which then
was justice, for the safety of their
life."—Knox, *History of the Reformation in Scotland*, ii. 527.

CHAP.
II.

1566.

ton, the last of whom will be remembered as Bothwell's former deadly enemy.   Although Murray,
who now took his place again in the Council of
State, and also set his name to its notification of
"sharp punishment" for the murder of Riccio,
certainly did what he could to allow other accomplices in it to remain in Scotland unpunished, yet
one readily catches a glimpse also of Bothwell's
share in this freedom from prosecution, for which
Knox himself had reason to thank him.[1]   During
the Fast week which had been prescribed by the
Reformed Kirk before the onslaught that proved so
fatal to Riccio, the Reformer had made mention
of his unhappy end while discoursing of the Lord's
sudden judgment on His enemies, but when the
hour of judgment came for the authors of that
bloody work, Knox withdrew from Edinburgh,
which he did not see again until after Mary's
deposition from the throne; but he went only to
the west country—he did not leave Scotland.   The
Earl of Lennox was merely forced to keep away
from the Court; while his son stigmatised himself
by a declaration which on the 20th March was
posted up in Edinburgh, and in which he cleared
himself from all blame of the murder.   He owned
indeed that he had so far erred inasmuch as
through the persuasion of the conspirators without the Queen's consent, he let himself be beguiled
into giving his approval of the recall of the exiled
Lords, but to refute the slanderous reports in which
he was charged with having had a share "in the

---

[1] For he (Bothwell) showed
favour to such as liked him . . . .
that by his favour they were
relieved of great trouble.—Knox,
*History of the Reformation in
Scotland,* ii. 527.

horrid murder which was committed in the Queen's CHAP.
presence, and in the criminal detention of her II.
Majesty's exalted person;" it is also stated that 1566.
"His Grace had before her Majesty and in the
presence of the Lords of Council declared upon
his honour, faith, and word as a prince, that he
never had the slightest knowledge of the perfidious
treason whereof he was unrighteously and falsely
accused, and never had either counselled, commanded or approved of it.[1] Darnley went still
further; he not only informed against his late confederates, but was as zealous in getting them brought
to justice as if he had been an absolute stranger to
their proceedings.

To foreigners the Queen made it appear as if she
too admitted Darnley's guilt to be merely second-
ary,[2] but she herself knew better, and was unable to
forget his "Judas-kiss." The accomplices whose
names Darnley revealed had taken ample care to
communicate to her the agreement in which he had
in writing both stipulated for the Crown to himself,
and assumed the responsibility of Riccio's murder.
More and more must her heart have turned away
from him, and less than ever could he be allowed to
take part in the government. Yet it ought not to
be said, as many earlier and more recent authors
have repeated, that Mary Stuart had after Riccio's
murder maintained an implacable disposition towards
him. In the summer, when the period of her confinement approached, she prepared herself for death ;
she drew up at that time a testament, a copy of

---

[1] Darnley's Declaration.—Keith,   [2] Compare her letter dated 2d
History of Church and State in   April 1567 to the Archbishop of
Scotland, Appendix, p. 167.   Glasgow.—Labanoff, i. 349).

which she also sent to her relatives in France, but which is not now extant, or at all events has not hitherto been found, although a contemporary supplement to it came to light by a fortunate discovery, in 1854. This document professes to be a complete inventory of her jewels to the number of two hundred and fifty-three, and on the margin, opposite every number, is a note in the handwriting of Mary Stuart, stating to whom she wished to leave it, if she and the child should die :— "for should the child continue to live," so she concludes, "then shall it be heir to all."[1] The following are her keepsakes to all her relations and friends as marked in this inventory :—A ruby "to my sister," a diamond "to my brother Murray," four other diamonds "to the four Maries;" at one number she has written "to Earl Bothwell," but at three "to Lady Bothwell." No one however is so often remembered as Darnley to whom she bequeaths twenty-six different objects, among which she marks a diamond ring, adding at the same time :—"It is that wherewith I was espoused ; to the king, who gave it me."[2] To her father-in-law she also left a diamond, and two to her mother-in-law. On the other hand, when in the Castle of Edinburgh, on the 19th June 1566, she had been safely delivered of a son, who was to become both Scotland's and England's king, we find that

---

[1] The Inventory was discovered in the Register House in Edinburgh, and is printed by Robertson in *Inuentaires de la Royne Descosse*, pp. 93-115. The concluding words in the Queen's handwriting are :—"Ientands que cestuisai soyt execute au cas que lanfant ne me suruiue mays si il vit ie le foys heritier de tout Marie R."

[2] C'est celui de quoy ie fus espousee. Au Roy qui la me donne.—*Inuentaires de la Royne Descosse*, p. 112.

Darnley himself, with great joy, immediately sent CHAP.
the tidings to the Continent, to her maternal uncle II.
the Cardinal of Lorraine.[1]   Even in the month of 1566.
August strangers still imagined the possibility, after
some days, of more friendly relations arising between
them.[2]

But if Mary Stuart, even after the birth of
James VI., really did perhaps for some moments
cherish a young mother's feelings towards her
husband, these nevertheless procured for him at
all events only a passing regard. In one of her
letters to her aunt the Duchess of Guise, the Queen
complains of the loss of the gay temper of mind of
past times.[3]   In the autumn of the same year her
former lively manner seemed to give way to utter
dejection; she openly fretted. Referring to the
King a contemporary writes :—" That is ane heart-
break for her to think that he sould be hir husband,
and how to be free of him scho sees no outgait."[4]
" She repeats," writes another, "always these words:
—I could wish to be dead."[5]   " So many great sighs

<hr />

[1] The letter dated Edinburgh
the 19th June 1566, is printed in
F. v. Raumer's *Briefe aus Paris
zur Erläuterung der Geschichte
des sechzehnten und siebzehnten
Jahrhunderts* (Leipzig, 1831), ii.
94-95.

[2] " I have heard," it is said in
an account from the Earl of Bedford, dated 12th August 1566
(Raumer, *Die Königinnen Elisabeth und Maria Stuart*, p. 120),
" that since Mauvissière, the
French messenger, was with them,
the King and Queen have slept
together, from which it is thought
that they may come to better terms."
In a list (given by Labanoff, vii.
242-49) of articles belonging to
the imprisoned Mary Stuart, upon

which Queen Elizabeth in the year
1586 unexpectedly laid an arrest
in Chartley, one also meets with a
" petit livret d'or," in which Mary
had miniature likenesses of herself,
Darnley, and their child.

[3] Je layrray ces belles parolles
pour vous dire combien, en peu
de temps, j'ay changé de rolle,
qui est de la plus contente en
soi-mesmes et à son ayse, en
continuels troubles et fascheries.
—Letter of Mary Stuart to the
Duchess Anne of Guise, dated
May 1566.—Labanoff, i. 354.

[4] Maitland's letter of 24th
October 1566 to the Archbishop
of Glasgow.—Laing, *History of
Scotland*, ii. 74.

[5] Letter of the French Am-

she would give," remembered later a third who was
then always with her, "that it was a pity to hear
her."[1] The disagreement had become aggravated
at the time of the young prince's baptism. This
was solemnised on the 17th December 1566 with
great splendour in the Chapel of Stirling Castle.
On this occasion Queen Elizabeth had been invited
to become godmother, but excused herself on the
ground that however willing she was to be present,
she was unable to come to Scotland, and as she
could not well send an English lady so far in winter,
so she caused herself to be represented by Mary's
favourite half-sister, the Countess of Argyll, and
likewise sent the Earl of Bedford as bearer of a
baptismal font of gold to be used in the baptism of
the prince. The ceremony of baptism was performed
according to the ritual of the Romish Church by the
Archbishop of St. Andrews, Lord John Hamilton, a
half-brother of the Duke of Châtelherault, assisted
by three other bishops.[2] The sovereigns of France
and Savoy were also represented on this festal occasion, and after the religious part of the rite was
over the Queen gave a splendid banquet to the
foreigners and the Scottish lords, many of whom,
including Bothwell himself, had refused to be
present in the chapel during the ceremony so
obnoxious to the Reformers.[3] But Darnley, who

bassador Du Croc of 2d December
to the Archbishop of Glasgow.—
Keith, *Church and State in Scotland*, Pref. p. vii.

[1] *The Memoirs of Sir James
Melvil*, p. 74.

[2] Quha was executour officij in
pontificalibus with staf, mytoure,
croce, and the rest.—*A Diurnal of
Remarkable Occurrents*, p. 103.

[3] In reference to this ecclesiastical transaction it is incorrectly
said by Tytler, *History of Scotland*, vii. 54) and by Mignet,
Histoire de Marie Stuart, i. 219, that
although Bothwell was a Protestant, yet he it was who directed
the Popish ceremony. This assertion can hardly be regarded as
warranted by anything in the

was present in the castle, did not make his appear- CHAP.
II.
ance at all during the festive season. Elizabeth, 1566.
who, as long as Darnley lived, would never give her
runaway vassal the royal title, had on this occasion
specially charged the Earl of Bedford and his suite
not to designate him by it,[1] and thus before his own
countrymen also Darnley, who had lately lifted his
head so high, found himself now in an intolerable
position. The French Ambassador, who had ad-
mired the behaviour of Mary Stuart in the presence
of her foreign guests, perceived how much this self-
command had cost her when a couple of days later
she allowed him to pay her a visit, and he found her
resting herself with tearful eyes, and complaining of
a violent pain in her side.[2]

The idea of taking advantage of these feelings,
which could no longer remain any secret, had
about this time been conceived. It originated perhaps with the Macchiavellian but highly-gifted Sir
William Maitland, laird of Lethington, of whose

---

letter of John Forster from
Berwick appealed to, and this
letter is at any rate six days older
than the baptismal ceremony,
about which a contemporary (in
*Diurnal of Remarkable Occur-
rents*, p. 104) expressly remarks :—
" At this tyme my lordis Huntlie,
Murray, Bothwill, nor the Inglis
Ambassador, come nocht within
the said chappell, because it was
done against the poyntis of thair
religioun." The Countess of
Argyll, who had overcome her
scruples, and been present at the
baptismal ceremony, the Reformed
Church found itself called on to
subject to a reprimand.—Keith,
*History of Church and State in
Scotland*, p. 569.

[1] Jussitque expresse, ut nec ille,

nec Angli illum comitati, Darlium
regio titulo dignarentur.—*Annales
rerum Anglicarum et Hibernicarum regnante Elizabetha*, Guillel-
mo Camdeno authore (Londini,
1615), fol. p. 109. When Randolph in the beginning of the
year had got orders to leave
Scotland he would not, as he
himself reports to Cecil from
Edinburgh 25th February 1565,
receive a passport " because it was
subscribed by Lord Darnley."—
*Calendar of State Papers, Foreign
Series*, 1566-68, p. 23.

[2] Letter of Du Croc of 23d
December 1566 to the Archbishop
of Glasgow.—Keith, *History of
Church and State in Scotland*,
Pref. p. vii.

abilities, his contemporaries, both friends and foes, speak with high admiration, as being, in an age so rich in talented men, perhaps the greatest of them all.[1] Some of his retainers had also been present at the murder of Riccio, while he himself had undertaken the part of entertaining the Earl of Atholl until this was accomplished. For such conduct he had been dismissed from his office as Secretary of State and banished to Caithness. This Scottish statesman was one of the first of the conspirators against Riccio that obtained pardon; for the Queen after her confinement had, at the intercession of the Earls Atholl and Murray, but at first much against Bothwell's wish, taken him into favour, and made him again Secretary of State. On the 17th September 1566 he once more took his seat in the Council of State. Recently this man, so fertile in devices, had seen the conspiring nobles supporting Darnley against Mary in order to compass the return of Murray and of the other insurgents who had fled to England; and might it not be possible now by helping Mary against Darnley to obtain from her the same favour for the betrayed accomplices of the latter, Lethington's good friends?[2]

One condition seemed nevertheless inevitable. Scotland had lately seen both Murray's insurrection and the conspiracy to which Riccio became a victim miscarry through the action of the political party

---

[1] Vir inter Scotos maximo rerum usu, et ingenio splendidissimo, si minus versatili.—Camden, *Annales rerum Anglicarum*, p. 241.

[2] Lethingtoun proponet and said that the nerrest and best way till obteine the said Erle of Mourtounis perdoun, was to promeise to the Quenis Majestie, to fynde an moyen to make devorcement betwixt hir Grace and the Kinge hir husband.—Declaration of the Earls Huntly and Argyll. Anderson, *Collections*, iv. 189.

of nobles that supported the Queen, to which CHAP. II. Bothwell adhered. It was therefore necessary on this occasion to win over these old enemies, and 1566. above all Bothwell himself. For though it can hardly be deemed correct to represent his will as all-powerful subsequently to Riccio's death, as has been attempted to be done by the contemporaries of Bothwell and particularly Knox,[1] yet his influence with the Queen had now become greater than ever. The many instances which she had already witnessed both under the government of her deceased mother and her own, of his readiness to venture his life in her cause, convinced her that in him she had found a most trustworthy servant. The behaviour too which he had shown during the last trying occasion had recently drawn from her a fresh proof of her favour, inasmuch as she had rewarded him with the appointment of "Keeper" of the Castle of Dunbar, the strongest of all the Scottish sea-fortresses, which was likewise an arsenal for the whole kingdom in which the most of its gunpowder was kept, and which by its proximity to Bothwell's estates was of special importance to him.[2] Nor was this all; for it

[1] Knox, *History of the Reformation in Scotland*, ii. 527. In opposition to the statement which he there makes, that "the Earl Bothwell had now, of all men, greatest access and familiarity with the Queen," it is sufficient to refer especially to Randolph's letter to Cecil of date 7th June 1566 respecting the relations subsisting in Edinburgh during the Queen's confinement. His words are :—"The Earls of Argyle and Moray lodge in the castle, and keep house together, the Earls of Huntly and Bothwell wished, also, to have lodged there, but were refused." — Chalmers, *Life of Mary*, ii. 264.

[2] Bothwell's own words on this point deserve perhaps to be quoted :—"Ils se floyent bien fort en moy, à cause de la faveur que sa Majesté me portoit et de l'accèz que j'avois auprès d'elle ; ce que j'avois acquis seulement par le fidèle debvoir que je feis tantes ès guerres de feu Madame sa mère, que aussi ès siennes propres, èsquelles je mis plusieurs fois ma vie en hazard, y faisant de grandz fraiz, dont elle m'a très libérale-

has been believed that shortly after the birth of
James VI. the Queen began to show an interest in
the Earl which was of another and more tender
nature than simply political.

The idea just mentioned has been chiefly based
on what took place when the Earl in the autumn of
1566 left Edinburgh and entered upon the charge
of the turbulent Border regions intrusted to him,
and the peace of which happened at this period to
be specially disturbed by the Elliots, the Arm-
strongs, and the Johnstons.   Bothwell had already
laid hold of some of the many lawless foresters in
Liddesdale and put them in custody in Hermitage
Castle in order to have them brought to justice;
when one day—the 7th of October—in a wood
close in front of the castle, he having gone bravely
in advance of his attendants, met face to face with a
notorious outlaw, John Elliot, also known by the
name of John of the Park.   On coming up with him
the latter demanded whether the Earl would spare
his life, to which Bothwell answered that he would
be heartily satisfied should the Court set him at
liberty, but that he must appear before the Queen's
court of justice.   When the outlaw heard these
words he slipped down from his horse, and attempted to run away through the wood; Bothwell
then wounded him with a pistol-shot, and sprang
from his horse to seize him, but while hastily pur-
suing after him he stumbled over the stump of a
tree, and fell so violently upon it that he lay for
some moments completely stunned.   As soon as
Elliot saw the Earl fall he came back to where he

ment recompensé, tant par présens,   quels Sa Majesté m'a honoré."—
que aultres gouvernements, des   Teulet, *Lettres*, p. 167.

lay, and with his sword gave him in return for
the shot by which he himself had been struck
three wounds in succession, one in his body, one
in the head, and one in the hand, until at length
Bothwell, recovering himself, with his dagger stabbed
his adversary twice in the breast, so that he
staggered away mortally wounded.[1] The Earl
had again swooned when his followers reached
him, and his servants bore him back to Hermitage, where the imprisoned bandits had meanwhile been able to effect their liberty and to
take possession of the Castle, so that it was
only after having promised to them in Bothwell's
name that their lives should be spared, and they
themselves allowed to go away, that the Earl
could be brought in and have a resting-place.
During this time the Queen was staying in the
neighbourhood, having, according to the royal Scottish custom of holding Assize-Courts throughout
the country, just arrived for this purpose at Jedburgh, the chief town in Roxburghshire, near the
foot of the Cheviot Hills. Here she immediately
got tidings of the accident the Earl had met with,
and when she afterwards found an opportunity on
the 16th October she rode attended by her half-
brother, the Earl of Murray, and some other lords,
notwithstanding the insecurity of the district, over
to Hermitage to visit the wounded Bothwell. With
him she passed a couple of hours, and immediately
rode back to Jedburgh, having thus accomplished a
distance of about fifty miles in one day. The con-

[1] And the said theif that hurt
my Lord Bothwill, deceissit within ane myle, vpone ane hill, of the
woundis gottin fra my Lord Bothwill of befoir.—*A Diurnal of Remarkable Occurrents*, p. 101.

CHAP.
II.

1566.

sequence of this forced ride was to bring upon herself the next day a fever so severe that, on the 26th October, it was ordered that prayers be made for her life in the churches. During many days she was given up by her physicians. For two whole hours she lay as if she were dead.[1] She also believed herself at this time near death, expressed her readiness either to depart or to live according as her Creator's good pleasure had determined, exhorted, as her mother had done, with impressive words the nobles of the kingdom to peace and unity as the only safety and blessing for the people, charged the French ambassador to carry her last greeting to her relatives in his country, requested the lords present to pray to God for her soul, and declared that she was dying in the Catholic faith.[2]

Like many in later times, contemporaries thought, as the tradition in the district still indicates, when it tells how her white steed sank in a morass, now called "The Queen's Myre," that it was on the wings of love that Mary Stuart flew backwards and forwards. To us the conclusion nevertheless seems more doubtful; for while the reigning princess might well show her faithful vassal such attention, a passionately loving woman would not have easily waited for eight days ere doing so. Bothwell was a man of high rank, and occupied a high position. He had

---

[1] For she lay two hours long cold dead, as it were without breath, or any sign of life; at length she revived, by reason they had bound small cords about her shackle bones, her knees, and great toes.—Knox, *History of the Reformation in Scotland*, ii. 534.

[2] Knox adds: "She said the creed in English, and desired my Lord of Murray, if she should chance to depart, that he would not be over extreme to such as was of her Religion; the Duke and he should have been Regents."—*History of the Reformation in Scotland*, ii. 535.

recently endangered his life in her service, and it CHAP.
II.
was said by himself even from the first that he could
not survive the wounds which he had received.[1] 1566.
The sympathy and anxiety which Mary Stuart
showed by her visit to Hermitage, and at a later
period when the wounded Earl was able, during the
Queen's own sickness, to drive over to Jedburgh,
may therefore be as well explained by solicitude to
preserve the most trustworthy counsellor and support of her government, and this conjecture is all
the more probable since Bothwell is described by
those who must have seen him as quite otherwise
than handsome, and as wanting in those external
advantages which ordinarily help to captivate.[2] The
haste with which the Queen urged her steed forward on the way to Hermitage, and back again to
Jedburgh, may also be sufficiently explained by her
knowledge of the dangerous region through which
she was passing, full of outlaws, who only required
a few hours to enable them to convey the Queen
over the English Border. And just as Mary Stuart,
on the 16th October, even during her flying visit
to Hermitage, did not avoid putting her name
to a state document, so she also, as we find re-

---

[1] For he believed surely to have departed forth of this life, and sent word thereof to the Queen's Majestie.—Knox, *History of the Reformation in Scotland*, ii. 543.

[2] Ce Bothuil estoit le plus laid homme et d'aussi mauvaise grace qu'il se peut voir.—Brantôme, *Vies des dames illustres* in *Œuvres du Seigneur de Brantôme*, i. 147. Quem amorem qui non viderit illum autem viderit, incredibilem fortassis opinabitur. Quid enim erat in eo, quod mulieri paulum honestiori, concupiscendum foret?

Visne eloquentiæ? an formæ dignitas? an virtus animi, quæ rerum fortuitarum accessione commendarentur? At de eloquentia et forma non est opus oratione longa, cum et qui eum viderint, vultus et incessus corporisque totius qui fuerit habitus, meminisse possint; et qui audierint hominis infantiam et hebitudinem non ignorent.— Buchanan, *De Maria Scotorum Regina*, p. 51. In reference to his showy dress Bothwell is described in the same book (p. 41): "Tanquam simius in purpura."

CHAP.
II.
1566.

corded, caused immediately after her return to Jedburgh, "a mass of writings" to be transmitted to Bothwell,[1] which certainly does not look like any love-message or amorous greeting. That the Earl, on the other hand, by the manliness which the Queen trusted to find in him, and for the possession of which he was most anxious to have the reputation,[2] *might* have made a stronger impression upon her than the two husbands to whom she had hitherto been united, each of fewer years than herself, was nevertheless not at all an absurd idea. And at all events, where such a persuasion was entertained, the gaining over of the Earl manifestly became more of a necessity for the political friends of Morton, Lindsay, and the other fugitives. The Scottish communications arriving in England in the year 1566 fully evince how Bothwell, after the murder of Riccio, by the greater influence which now fell to his share, had become more insufferable than ever to his opponents of the former absolutist party,[3] but subsequently this political position sud-

---

[1] "To ane boy passand off Jedburgh with a mass of writings of our Soverane to the Earl Bothwell,"—so we meet under date 17th October 1566, with an item in the abstracts of the Treasurer's accounts, which are given by Chalmers in his *Life of Mary Queen of Scots*, ii. 111. A letter from Mary Stuart to her brother-in-law Charles IX. of France, dated Jedburgh, 16th October 1566, is also found in Labanoff, i. 372, 373.

[2] "Fortitudinis opinionem captavit," says Buchanan, who nevertheless immediately, so as not to attribute to Bothwell any superiority whatever, hastens to add: "Sed inter equites sedens in equo pernicissimo sui securus, alienæ pugnæ spectator."—*De Maria Scotorum Regina*, p. 51.

[3] "I hear," so reports the Earl of Bedford, after these Scottish communications on 12th August 1566 from Berwick, "that there is a plan in contemplation with respect to the Earl of Bothwell, about which I could indeed obtain precise information, but since such things are not addressed to me, I do not wish to hear any more of them. Bothwell has gradually become so detested that matters cannot go on long with him as now." If the Earl of Bedford in this letter (which is here given

denly appears altogether changed.   No one of the
opposite party is seen so completely placed in sharp
antagonism to Bothwell as Maitland, the estate, formerly belonging to a cloister or nunnery in Haddington, having become an apple of discord between them
which increased their ancient enmity,[1] yet now the
wily Laird of Lethington seems to have been the
very one who gained over the potent Earl, and
with him his adherents. He was won over by the
prospect presented to him of perhaps being able to
reach the throne which Darnley had vainly striven
to obtain.   This allurement acted upon Bothwell as
the greeting of the witches on the heath did upon
Macbeth.   Why should the Earls of Bothwell not
bear a resemblance to the Earls of Lennox ?   Had
Bothwell's ancestors not actually lifted their eyes
as high as the latter ?   Had not his own father been
a rival with Darnley's father for the hand of Mary
of Guise when the latter, as Queen Dowager, ruled

after Raumer, p. 120) had communicated the precise particulars
of that "plan," it might perhaps
have thrown much light upon
coming events.

[1] In Haddington, midway between the possessions of the Hepburn family, stood an ancient
nunnery endowed by the same
family, in which Bothwell's father,
Earl Patrick, had, during his time,
got Elizabeth Hepburn, a relative
of his own, appointed abbess. She
died in the year 1563 ; and, during
the time of Bothwell's adversity
and exile, Maitland had contrived
to come into possession of the
landed property of the nunnery ;
but after the participation of the
latter in the assault upon Riccio,
Bothwell had been able, with the
aid of the Queen, to make good his

title to the property—*A Diurnal
of Remarkable Occurrents*, p. 94.
At a subsequent period, on the
re-entrance of Maitland into the
Council of State, he was required
by her as a pledge of peace between
him and Bothwell to relinquish a
part of the apple of discord. According to an anonymous letter
from Alnwick of 3d April 1566
(given by Keith, Appendix, p.
167), the breach between the two
antagonists had in spring been
nevertheless so wide that "one of
Bothwell's servants confessed that
himself and four more of his fellow-
servants had conspired to murther
or poison the said Bothwell, and
that Lethington had engaged them
in that design. The other servants
that were concerned in that design
upon examination confessed the
same."

Scotland during Mary Stuart's minority? Might he not, therefore, with better success follow in his father's footsteps by one day marrying the Queen herself? Both among his contemporaries and in after ages this ambition has been recognised as the passion which would hereafter drive Bothwell onwards in his dark ways. Along with this we can well imagine to have been conjoined, what was equally in accordance with his character, his feeling himself captivated by the almost demoniacal power with which Mary's beauty so often contrived to enforce its sway. She was still in her twenty-fourth year the same beautiful woman whom no one, during her early stay in France, could look upon without losing his heart—according to the assurance of Brantôme, who accompanied Mary on her return voyage to Scotland; the same who, in Highland garb, or, as he describes it, "estant habillée à la sauvage," had transported him with admiration; the same, of whom the recollection caused him at a later period to exclaim: "Ah royaume d'Escosse! je crois que maintenant vos jours sont encore bien plus courts qu'ils n'estoient, et vos nuits plus longues, puisque vous avez perdu cette princesse qui vous illuminoit."[1]

In behalf of the new aristocratic confederacy Maitland had also become spokesman to the Queen. The latter, on her recovery from sickness, and after distributing alms among the poor of the place,[2] had, on the 9th of November, left Jedburgh for the purpose of being present in Stirling at the approaching baptism of her son. Attended by a splendid

[1] Note D, Appendix.

[2] "By the Queenis precept to Maister John Balfour, to gif the pure in Jedburgh £20," remarks the Treasurer under the 31st October in the abstracts of accounts given by Chalmers, II. iii.

retinue of eight hundred horsemen, and the nobles
of the country with their retainers, she then passed
slowly through the picturesque valley of the Tweed
to Berwick, the English Border town, which saluted
her with all its cannon, and outside of which Sir
John Forster, the English commander, paid his
respects to her. Subsequently continuing her journey along the sea-coast, on the 20th November, she
arrived, by way of Dunbar, at Craigmillar Castle,—
its ruins still exist about three miles south from
Edinburgh,—and stayed in this old castle until she
went forward to Stirling. It was during her sojourn
here that Maitland, in presence of the Earls Murray,
Argyll, Huntly, and Bothwell, first ventured to
strike the chord from which it was certainly believed that an echo would be awakened. From
respect to such combined advocacy, she, at that
time, showed herself not at all disinclined to pardon
the Earl of Morton, Lord Lindsay, and the most of
the other exiles, in whose behalf these leaders peti-
tioned her. But though they all subsequently joined
in trying to induce her to separate from a husband
who had caused her so much injury, and the kingdom no less harm, who, as they said, "plagued you
and us all," yet she would only listen to any discourse on the subject under two conditions : first,
that the separation should be brought about in a
legal manner, and, next, that it should not involve
detriment to her son, "for otherwise she would
rather endure all torments and dare all dangers
which might befall her during her whole lifetime."
The Earl of Bothwell replied that he did not in the
least doubt that a divorce could be effected without
any detriment whatever to his Highness the prince,

alleging himself as an example, since he also had,
without the least difficulty, succeeded his father,
although there had been a separation between the
latter and his mother. It was next proposed that
after a dissolution of the marriage the King should
live alone in some part of the country, and the
Queen in another; or that he should retire altogether to another kingdom; but to this the Queen
replied that she would rather go over to France and
remain there for a time until he came to a knowledge of himself and perceived his errors. The Laird
of Lethington still continued: "Madame, fancie ye
not we ar heir of the principall of your Graces Nobilitie and Counsale, that sall fynde the Moyne, that
your Majestie sall be quyte of him without prejudice
of your sone, and albeite that my Lord of Murraye
heir present be lytill les scrupulus for ane Protestant
nor your Grace is for ane Papist, I am assurit he will
looke throw his fingeris thairto, and will behald our
doeings, saying naething to the same. The Quenis
Majestie answerit—I will that ye do nathing quhair-
to any spot may be layit to my honor or conscience,
and thairto I pray you rather let the matter be in
the estait as it is, abyding till God of his goodnes
put remid thairto; that ye beliefing to do me service,
may possibill turne to my hurt and displeasor."[1]

As the Laird of Lethington throughout this remarkable negotiation had merely said that "Her
Grace sall si nathing bot gud, and *approvit by
Parliament*," and as the Earl of Murray at a
later period likewise bore witness that there had
not been proposed at Craigmillar in his presence

---

[1] The declaration of the Earls   at Craigmillar.—Anderson, *Collec-*
Huntly and Argyll of what passed   *tions*, iv. 192.

anything "tending to ony unlawfull or dis- CHAP. honorable end,"[1] we have in all this sufficient cause II. for assuming that it was only intended at that 1566. time to make use of the near relationship in this case also as a ground for divorce, or at all events simply to get Darnley prosecuted by Parliament, because he had himself joined in the plot to hold the Queen a prisoner in her own palace. Only a few days elapsed however after these expressions of the Queen had been heard before a considerable portion of Darnley's enemies found it necessary to take a further step. Darnley certainly stood at this period very much alone ; Sir James Melvil, who first wrote his Memoirs when his son had become king, mentions with special sympathy his being now so greatly deserted ; but contemporaries themselves did not see, as Melvil did, in Darnley only " the good young prince, who failed rather for want of good counsel and experience than from any bad inclinations."[2] In their eyes he also appeared as the poor wretch who not only wished to pass for being more Papistically-inclined than the Queen, but who, while really cherishing a natural horror of the return of his deceived and fugitive accomplices, gave reason to believe that he wanted to assume the government in his infant son's name, and con- sequently they, whom after Riccio's death he had disowned, had as little pity for him as those whom, before his slaughter, he had been able to drive out of the country. Sir James Balfour of Pittendreich drew up the new bond. He had become a member

---

[1] Murray's Declaration, dated London, the 19th January 1569.— Anderson, *Collections,* iv. 194.

[2] *Memoirs of Sir James Melvil,* p. 67.

of the Council of State in the spring of 1565, and afterwards had been one of those whose life had been threatened during the assault at Holyrood, Mary Stuart, in her letter about Riccio's murder, saying even that Darnley's confederates had also at that time intended to hang Balfour.[1] In this bond they engaged, " that sick ane young fool and proud tirrane sould not reign nor bear reull over thame ;" and explained " that for diverse causes, thairfoir that thay all had concludit that he sould be put off by ane way or uther, and quhosoevir sould take the deid in hand or do it, they sould defend and fortifie it as thamselffis, for it sould be every ane of their awin, recknit and halden done be thamselffis."[2] The great probability of murder being the result certainly had not much deterring influence on the subscribers ; the first thing noted in a contemporary diary of a citizen in Edinburgh is significant to this effect: " There hes beine in this kingdome of Scotland ane hundereth and fyve kinges, of quhilk ther wes slaine fyftie sex."[3] Besides the Earl of Bothwell, the Earls of Huntly and Argyll, Maitland the Secretary of State, and Sir James Balfour,[4] as the first subscribers are mentioned, and Lethington, and especially Bothwell, seem after this to have

[1] And namely to have hanged the said Sir James. The Queen's letter to Archbishop Beaton.— Labanoff, i. 346.

[2] This document disappeared afterwards, having been burnt by Maitland, but the words quoted above, "that he sould be putt off by ane way or uther," etc., are taken from a larger fragment of the agreement which James Ormiston, who had read it with Bothwell, had learned by heart, and could still remember at his last confession, the 13th December 1573. It is given in Laing, *History of Scotland*, ii. 291-6.

[3] Robert Birrel's Diary, *Fragments of Scottish History*, p. 3.

[4] Quha lute me sie ane contract subscryvit be four or fyve hand-writtes, quhilk he affirmit to me was the subscription of the Erle of Huntlie, Argyll, the Secretar Maitland, and Sir James Balfour, and

been those who chiefly urged the matter forwards, CHAP.
just as they also, by sending Archibald Douglas to II.
England, already sought helpers among the enemies 1566.
of Darnley there before the latter had yet again set
foot on Scottish ground. This happened in the
close of the year, when Mary, on the 24th December
1566, yielding to the request of almost the whole of
her nobles, as well as to the warmly supported
representations of Elizabeth, granted a full pardon
to the Earl of Morton, Lord Lindsay, and seventy-
six other fugitives,[1]—the same, who six months
later, tore from her the crown.

alleaged that mony mae promisit,
wha wald assist him gif he were
put at.—The Confession of the
laird of Ormiston : Laing, *History
of Scotland*, ii. 293.

[1] The Earl of Bedford writes
thus on 30th December 1566 from
Hallyards, in Fife, about those
pardoned : "The Earl of Murray
hath done very friendly towards
the Queen for them ; (*so have I
according to your advice.*) The
Earls Bothwell, and Athol, and all

other lords helped therein, or else
such pardons could not so soon
have been gotten."—Chalmers,
Life of Mary Queen of Scots, ii.
175. None but Andrew Ker of
Faldonside and George Douglas
were excluded from the amnesty,
the former because he had pointed
his pistol at the Queen herself, the
latter because he had wounded
Riccio in her presence. Lord
Patrick Ruthven had died in New-
castle the 13th May 1566.

CHAPTER III.

MARY STUART has herself commended her name to posterity. She has asked: "Ayez mémoire de l'âme et de l'honneur de celle qui a esté vostre royne," and here accordingly, in the *History of Scotland*, meet us the two questions, which, beyond all others, have been so debated, that one is able to name two long lists of authors who have, during a period of three hundred years, answered them in opposite ways. The first of these questions is: Was Mary Stuart made aware by Bothwell of the murderous design to be carried out against her husband? The other question relates to what extent she already had really thrown herself into the arms of Bothwell before Darnley's death, and her own abduction to Dunbar.

The answer to the first-mentioned question depends especially upon the weight we place on two historical authorities of a very doubtful nature. The one of these is the collection of different writings—autographic letters and sonnets, along with the so-called contracts, or properly promises of marriage—which the Queen is alleged by her enemies to have sent to Bothwell, and to which, in the first instance, we shall confine our attention; afterwards the other authority shall come under review.

In what way the foes of the Queen had been
able to get possession of the writings attributed to
her, and which brought such ruin upon her, they
have themselves told us. A few days after the
rising against Bothwell had finally succeeded in
snatching Mary out of his hands, he sent, as her
opponents have declared, one of his servants, George
Dalgleish, to the commander of Edinburgh Castle,
Sir James Balfour, in whose custody he had left
a silver-gilt casket, not quite a foot long. This
casket, afterwards produced in England, had, as
a distinctive mark in many places, the Roman letter
F beneath a royal crown, and therefore had, in all
likelihood, previously belonged to Mary Stuart, and
been a present to her from her first husband,
Francis II.[1] Sir James Balfour still held Edinburgh
Castle ostensibly in the Queen's name, but had nevertheless been secretly won over some time before by
the Laird of Lethington to the cause of the revolt.
Accordingly he delivered the casket to Dalgleish,
but at the same time gave a hint of the fact to the
confederate lords, so that Dalgleish, on the 20th
June 1567, when on his way to Dunbar bringing
the casket to Bothwell, fell with it into the hands

---

[1] This gilt casket, whose contents have made it a veritable
Pandora's box for Mary Stuart,
has been latterly, since the loss of
its contents, pretended to be again
found in Hamilton Palace, near
Glasgow. But in this instance we
have only another example of the
credulity which everywhere and at
all times habitually distinguishes
relic-hunters. For while Mary
Stuart's contemporary opponents
declared that the casket "in many
places"—or as Buchanan expresses
it, "alleveque" (undique)—was
marked with a Roman F beneath
a royal crown, the casket which in
later times has been taken for it
has this letter marked upon it only
in two places, and no crown above
it. This remark has already been
made by Henry Glassford Bell
(*Life of Mary Queen of Scots*, 1828,
ii. 294), who adds : " Antiquaries
however have investigated subjects
of less curiosity, and have been
willing to believe upon far more
slender data."

CHAP.
III.
1567.

of the Earl of Morton. In the casket was at that time found a collection of writings and sonnets in the French language, penned by the Queen to Bothwell, besides assurances in which she engaged to marry him. These were certainly at first the more precise explanations of her later opponents respecting their alleged discovery,[1] but ere a month after it had taken place, Sir Nicholas Throckmorton, who had now been sent by Queen Elizabeth to Scotland, had nevertheless been able, on the 25th July 1567, to report thus from Edinburgh : "Thirdly, They mean to charge her with the murder of her husband, whereof (they say) they have as apparent proof against her as may be, *as well by the testimony of her own handwriting, which they have recovered*, as also by sufficient witnesses."[2] The catastrophe which caused the fall of Bothwell, and made Mary Stuart a prisoner, recalled at that time her half-brother Murray from France, whither he had betaken himself to await the issue of the crisis, and accordingly there now elapses some time before such papers from the Queen are again mentioned, but on the 4th December 1567, Murray anew produced, in the Scottish Council of Government, " her previe lettres, *written and subscrivit with her awin hand*, and sent by hir to James Erll of Boithwell, cheiffe executor of the said horrible murder."[3] When,

---

[1] Murray's acknowledgment for having received the casket from Morton, given at Edinburgh, 16th September 1568, contained in Walter Goodall's *Examination of the Letters said to be written by Mary Queen of Scots to James Earl of Bothwell*, ii. 90. Edinburgh, 1754.—Buchanan, *Rerum*

Scoticarum Historia, p. 191 ; Knox, *History of the Reformation in Scotland*, i. 562.

[2] Throckmorton's Letter : Keith, *History of the Affairs of Church and State in Scotland*, pp. 424-27.

[3] Goodall's *Examination*, ii. 64.

moreover, a few days afterwards the Scottish Parliament met, which declared Mary Stuart to be deposed, it was also with reference to the same papers that this was done, since the Parliament, on the 15th December 1567, adjudged that " the ground thereof was the Queen's own guilt, in as far as by *diuers of her preuie letteris, written halelie with hir awin hand,* and send be hir to James, sumtyme Erle of Bothwell, chief agent of that horrible murder, as well before as after its execution, it was absolutely certain that she had been privy to and a partaker in it."[1]   About a year later, when Queen Elizabeth offered a mediation which apparently had as its object to reconcile Mary Stuart, who had then escaped from her Scottish prison to England, to the Lords of the opposition party, who, in her name, ruled Scotland, they met on this occasion in a conference which was opened the 4th October 1568 at York, but afterwards removed to London, or more correctly, according to the distinction then made, to Westminster, and here also Murray, after receiving a promise of secrecy, produced before the English commissioners both the silver casket and in it the papers brought from Scotland.   In regard to the letters, said by those authorised to act in behalf of the Scottish Government to have been sent by the Queen to Bothwell, it is expressly stated in the English official account of the proceedings which took place at Westminster in presence of the commissioners empowered by Elizabeth, that " of which lettres the originals, supposed to be written with the Quene of Scott's own hand, were then also presently produced and perused ; and being read,

---

[1] *The Acts of the Parliaments of Scotland*, iii. 27.

CHAP.
III.
1567-8.

were duly conferred and compared, *for the manner of handwriting and fashion of orthography,* with sundry other lettres long since heretofore written and sent by the said Quene of Scotts to the Quene's majesty : And next after these was produced and read a declaration of the Erle Morton, of the manner of the finding of the said lettres, as the same was exhibited upon his oath the 9th of December : In the collation whereof no difference was found."[1] The original papers produced in England are known to have descended from one to another of Scotland's four regents during the minority of James VI., from the Earl of Murray to the Earls of Lennox, Mar, and Morton, and afterwards, in the year 1582, to have belonged to a son of Lord Patrick Ruthven, William Ruthven, Earl of Gowrie, who also had taken part in the murder of Riccio, and who, having latterly been pardoned along with the other conspirators who fled to England, had again joined in the new rebellion that ultimately precipitated Mary Stuart from the throne.   We have still four letters, written in the year 1582 by Robert Bowes of Aske, Elizabeth's ambassador in Scotland, to Sir Francis Walsingham, the English Secretary of State, which show with how much interest even then the possession or preservation of those important papers was sought

[1] Goodall, *The Journal of the Commissioners apud Westminster,* ii. 256. How far this collation, which failed to discover any difference in the things mentioned above, can yet in reality be described as proper and sufficient, every one will be able to judge after what follows in this official English account itself (Goodall, ii. 258) : " It is to be noted, that at the time of the producing, showing, and reading of all these foresaid writings, there was no special choyce nor regard had to the order of the producing thereof : but the whole writings, lying altogether upon the counsel table, the same were one after another shewed *rather by hap, as the same did ly upon the table,* than with any choyce made, as by the natures thereof, if time had so served, might have been."

after.[1] Bowes had in Elizabeth's mission at length CHAP.
been so fortunate as to discover that the papers in   III.
question were in the hands of the Earl of Gowrie at 1582.
Ruthven Castle, and accordingly represented again
and again to him what a valuable gift they would
be to the English Queen, to whom they had been
promised before they came into his possession, and
who was best qualified to defend them against all
foolish objections,[2] while no man who lived in Scotland could secure or possess them without danger to
his person.   The Earl of Gowrie would not at first
admit that he really was in possession of them; next
he asked if Bowes had perhaps got information
about them from the sons of the Earl of Morton;
reminded him that this Earl, like the other preceding regents, never ventured to let them out of his
keeping; emphatically declared that he himself also
could not do so without permission, not only from
the king, who likewise knew that he now had them,
but from the noblemen who took part in the rebellion
against Mary after her nuptials with Bothwell; and
ended at last with saying that when he had again
returned home to his possession he would take forth
the letters and more precisely consider whether he

---

[1] The letters, which are dated
Edinburgh the 8th, 12th, and 24th
November, and the 2d December
1582, are to be found summarily
printed in Robertson's *History of
Scotland* during the reign of Queen
Mary and of King James VI. till
his accession to the crown of England, (the sixth edition, Dublin,
1772, ii. 431-434,) and now more
completely in *The Correspondence
of Robert Bowes of Aske, Esquire*
(a volume of the publications of
the Surtees Society edited by the

Rev. J. Stevenson), London, 1842,
pp. 236-266.
[2] That these writings may be
with secrecy and good order com-
mit to the keeping of her Majesty,
that will have them ready whenso-
ever any use shall be for them, and
by her Highness' countenance defend them and the parties from
such wrongful objections as shall
be laid against them.—Bowes' letter to Walsingham of 24th November 1582.—*The Correspondence of
Robert Bowes*, p. 254.

CHAP. III.

1582.

dared comply with Elizabeth's wish. Accordingly, at a later period, he declared that, after having now looked over those papers, he must necessarily refuse to part with them.[1] This is the last time those papers are mentioned as still extant. After the Earl of Gowrie had taken part in the plot in which James VI., in the year 1582, was suddenly surprised at Ruthven Castle, and the Earl had in consequence of this deed been executed at Stirling in 1584, those original writings altogether disappear.

Previously to their being finally lost, a short time after they had been produced in England, they had meanwhile been speedily made public through the press in different languages.[2] And that these printed versions or translations agree in their contents with the originals, as the latter had been produced by those whom the Scottish Government authorised, seems sufficiently plain from the still preserved abstracts of them which one of the English commissioners at York, the methodical Sir Ralph Sadler, has, in this instance, made, inasmuch as he had immediately noted down the decisive passages for his own use.[3]

---

[1] And he concluded flatly, that after he had found and seen the writings, that he might not make delivery of them without the privity of the king.—Bowes' letter of 24th November 1582.—*The Correspondence of Robert Bowes*, p. 254.

[2] The first three of the letters were previously published in Latin as a supplement to the Latin pamphlet which, in the year 1571, was hurled by the hand of Buchanan against Mary Stuart, and when this publication was immediately afterwards followed by translations in Scots and French, the documents appealed to were then issued as a supplement to these editions, and in these instances entirely in the Scottish and French languages. Besides the above-named editions of Buchanan's pamphlet, these documents are now found in their different foreign versions, along with many other passages, reprinted in Laing's *History of Scotland*, ii. 146-210, 222-234, and in Teulet, *Lettres de Marie Stuart*, pp. 3-76, 105-110.

[3] *The State Papers of Sir Ralph Sadler*, ii. 337.

While Mary Stuart's guilt in respect of Darnley's CHAP.
murder, according to those printed documents, cer- III.
tainly seems undeniable, yet her antagonists have 1568.
sought still further to confirm their genuineness,
alleging that her guilt does not appear in them so
manifest, but that some of her most zealous sup-
porters have, even from the point of view furnished
by them, believed that they could find it to be
capable of dispute ; for, her opponents have asked,
would any one really, after forging the whole of the
documents, or falsifying portions of the genuine ones,
have allowed the least doubt to remain on the
subject of her guilt ? Another and more weighty
argument than this criticism, which really strikes
against the unlucky defenders more than against
the thing itself, is, however, the remarkable agreement, which has been pointed out, between two
letters Mary Stuart, when on a visit to Darnley as
he lay sick in Glasgow, had sent to Bothwell, and a
seemingly independent testimony, which was furnished during the conference in England by a
retainer of the Earl of Lennox, one Thomas Crawford of Jordanhill, who subsequently, in the civil
war in the year 1569, won a name as captor of
Dumbarton, and who, agreeably to his sworn declaration during Darnley's alleged sickness, not only
" was secretly informed by the King of all things
which had passed betwixt the said Queene and the
King," but also, in obedience to the request of the
Earl of Lennox, " did immediately at the same tyme
write the same word by word, as near as he possibly
could carry the same away." [1] As it may also be

[1] Goodall, *Journal of Meetings of the English Commissioners,*
ii. 246.

regarded as unquestionable that the partisans of Mary Stuart would latterly wish to have in their possession all those original letters and remaining documents ascribed to her, so they not unwillingly have found it necessary to assume that these may, on the execution of the Earl of Gowrie, have fallen into the hands of James VI., and that the latter had felt himself inclined to destroy whatever might really show his mother to be guilty of murder; the disappearance of the documents themselves, it is now accordingly said, " demonstrates that they were genuine."[1] In short, the fact that both letters and sonnets are without signature, without statement of time and place, and have not any direct indication whatever of the person to whom they are addressed, has simply been regarded by those who maintain the genuineness of the writings in question as a consequence of that prudent mysteriousness in which it would readily be sought to envelop the crime.

On the part of Mary Stuart and her partisans the genuineness of those documents has at no time been acknowledged. While the conference at York was going on in the autumn of 1568, she herself was not without a knowledge of the dangerous weapons which were being brought from Scotland to her detriment. William Maitland, who, since his separation from Bothwell, and the latter's fall, had now again appeared among her enemies, seems by this time to have begun to repent of his conduct towards her. For whether it was that having accompanied Murray to the conference in England, he felt his national sentiment wounded by a scene which only

[1] Malcolm Laing, *History of Scotland*, i. 230.

too much reminded him of the independent part CHAP.
enacted by his fatherland in the time of Edward I., III.
or that more probably he had been influenced by 1568.
his wife, who did not forget the feelings under whose
sway she had grown up as one of the Queen's
" Maries"; at all events it is certain that he then
communicated to Mary Stuart secret information
that her half-brother had at length resolved to get
her irrevocably condemned.[1] Accordingly when the
Queen, imprisoned in England, drew up full instructions for the Bishop of Ross and her other representatives at the expected conference, she did not now
rest satisfied with stating in general terms that she,
more than all her subjects, had lamented over the
tragic death of her husband,[2] but also expressly declared with respect to her alleged preparation for
Darnley's murder : " In cais thay alledge thay have
ony writingis of mine, quhilk may infer presumptioun
aganis me in that cause, ze sall desyre the principallis
to be producit, and that I myself may have inspectioun
thairof, and mak answer thairto. For ze sall affirm
in my name, I niver writ onything concerning that
matter to ony creature. *And gif ony sic writings
be, they are false and feinzeit, forgit and inventit be
thamselfis, onlie to my dishonour and sclander : and*

[1] That the Erle of Murray was
wholy bent to utter all that he
could aganes the Quene, and to
that effect had carid with hym all
the lettres which he had to produce
aganes the Quene for prove of the
murther.—Declaration of Bishop
Lesley, made in the Tower the 6th
November 1571, and printed in *A
Collection of State Papers relating
to affairs in the reign of Queen
Elizabeth from the year* 1571 *to*
1596, transcribed from original

papers and other authentic memorials never before published,
left by William Cecil, Lord Burgh-
ley, and deposited in the library at
Hatfield House, by William Murdin (London, 1759), fol. p. 52.
[2] Ze sall answer that I lament
mair heichlie the tragedie of my
husband's deith nor any uther of
my subjectis can do.—Mary Stuart's
Instruction from Bolton Castle,
dated the 29th September 1568 :
Labanoff, ii. 201.

*thair ar divers in Scotland, bath men and women,
that can counterfeit my handwriting, and write the*
*like maner of writing quhilk I use as weill as myself,
and principallie sic as ar in cumpanie with thamselfis.* And I doubt not gif I had remanit in my
awin realme, bot I wald have gottin knowledge of
the inventaris and writeris of sic writingis or now, to
the declaratioun of my innocencie and confusioun of
thair falset."[1] That there really was at that time,
especially in Scotland, a very general and strong
inclination to counterfeit and falsify the writings of
others is also evinced with sufficient clearness by
the legal provisions which it was found necessary to
issue against this crime, and which followed each
other in rapid succession, there having appeared in
the year 1540 a law for the punishment of false
notaries, then an ordinance in the year 1551 ex-
tending the punishment against the makers and
users of false legal documents to the falsifiers of any
writings whatsoever, while the preamble to a subsequent Act, passed in the year 1555, speaks of
" the great and mony falsettis daylie done within
this Realme be Notaris."[2] That there was at that
time no less tendency shown to such forgeries when
the object was a political one is an historical fact,[3] and
therefore there cannot but arise suspicion of forgery

[1] Mary Stuart's Instruction from Bolton Castle.—Labanoff, ii. 203.

[2] *The Acts of the Parliaments of Scotland,* ii. 360, 487, 496.

[3] Whitaker, *Mary Queen of Scots vindicated* (London, 1790), iii. 1-54 and 516-543. To the series of examples adduced by Whitaker we may now, agree-ably to Labanoff (vi. 396-398) and Tytler (*History of Scotland,* viii. 439-451), also add one furnished by Walsingham's forgery of Mary Stuart's ciphers in the document which was employed as the prin-cipal motive for her execution. Compare likewise Mignet, *Histoire de Marie Stuart* (Paris, 1851), ii. 347-349.

in connection with the documents produced by the CHAP. III.
representatives of the Scottish government before
the English commissioners at the conference in the 1568.
neighbouring kingdom, more especially seeing that
the oft-repeated desire of the Scottish Queen to be
allowed to inspect them was invariably unheeded.
Her request for a sight of the letters produced as
hers being neglected, Mary Stuart next charged her
representatives at the conference simply to procure
her copies of those letters from "our said guid
sister;"[1] but copies it was just as impossible for her
to obtain, so that, according to her wish, and according to what even English jurists[2] of high standing
were then obliged, in opposition to the government,
to acknowledge to be her right, she might be able
in presence of the Queen of England, the whole of
England's nobles and all the foreign ambassadors,
to reply to all that was urged against her by her
calumniators.[3] As an excuse for Elizabeth, it has
been assumed by the enemies of the Scottish Queen
that the latter in reality did not wish to get the
documents adduced against her, however often she
proposed to become acquainted with them. But
one circumstance which has been too long overlooked decidedly testifies to the contrary, namely
this: that she also asked the French ambassador in

---

[1] Ze sall require our said guid sister that copies be gevin zou thairof to the effect that thay may be answerit particularlie.—Letter of Mary Stuart from Bolton Castle, the 19th December 1568: La-banoff, ii. 263.

[2] Opinion of the English jurists in the supplement to La Motte Fénélon's account of 15th Decem-ber 1568 to Charles IX. and Ca-

therine de Medici.—*Correspond-ance diplomatique de Bertrand de Salignac de la Motte Fénélon, ambassadeur de France en Angle-terre de* 1568 à 1575. Publié pour la première fois sur les manu-scrits conservés aux archives du Royaume (Paris et Londres, 1838-1840), i. 51-54.

[3] Goodall, ii. 185.

England, La Motte Fénélon, to interest himself in her request. During a long audience which Fénélon had in consequence with Elizabeth, he expressed his hope that the letters produced on Murray's side would be communicated to the representatives of the Scottish Queen; but although Elizabeth was at that time induced to promise this[1]—still only, with pretended fear of thereby causing injury to the Queen,—and although the French ambassador, after the lapse of some days, again personally reminded her of her promise,[2] yet the English government again drew back, this time because Mary had hinted that it had not shown impartiality towards her during the conference. This was the last and weakest of all the pretexts of Elizabeth and Cecil under which her desire was rejected ; and if it has certainly been unfortunate for the memory of Mary that afterwards, when she was able to see at least the printed translations of the letters ascribed to her, she did not leave any more precise information as to her judgment of them, still the keeping back of the real documents becomes on this account not less strange, by means of which at a decisive moment there was denied to the Scottish Queen a right conceded even to the worst criminal, the cutting injustice of which rendering the act not the less suspicious, seeing that the honour of the Queen was assailed in writings which would not be shown her. Rather than let her become acquainted with the originals, the Eng-

---

[1] Je vous diray en substance, Sire, qu'elle me promit, que le lendemain elle accorderoit aulx depputez de la dicte Dame la dicte communiquation.—The account of La Motte Fénélon to Charles IX., dated London, 20th January 1569 ; *Correspondance de la Motte Fénélon, i. 133.*

[2] The account of La Motte Fénélon to Charles IX., dated London, 30th January 1569.— *Correspondance de la Motte Fénélon, i. 162.*

lish government preferred, on the 10th January
1569, to close the conference with a general declaration to the effect that there neither had been anything well founded brought forward by Murray and
his friends, nor had a sufficient proof of guilt been
hitherto procured against the Scottish Queen.[1]
Murray was meanwhile for the service rendered by
him rewarded with a loan of 5000 pounds sterling,[2]
and a short time afterwards the English Government made every effort to get the writings which
he had communicated, and which had now been
printed, spread on all sides.

How far Bothwell, during the last years of his
life, may have been able to make himself acquainted
with any edition of the publication connecting the
writings ascribed to the Queen with the representation of his own misdoings, we do not know.   But
yet at this time a testimony by him with respect
to these would have hardly received great consideration.   The defenders of Mary have not
willingly overlooked this fact; that from a much
earlier point of time, and through the statements
of others, there seems to be an apparent confession
by Bothwell, after which he could not be taken as
an authority in reference to the writings about which
they disputed.   In regard to the confession the
matter stands thus : At the close of the year 1580
the Earl of Morton, after having been the fourth
Regent of Scotland since the Queen's deposition, was
at last brought to ruin.   James VI., who had now

[1] On the uther part thair had
bene nathing *sufficientlie* producit
nor schawin be thaime aganis the
Quene thair Soverane, quhairby
the Quene of Ingland sould con-
ceave or tak ony evil opinioun of
the Quene, hir guid sister, for onything zit sene.—Goodall, ii. 305.

[2] Murray's receipt of 10th January 1569.—Goodall, ii. 313.

assumed the government, caused him to be prosecuted as an accomplice in his father's death,
and being declared guilty by a jury, Morton was
executed on the 2d of June 1581.[1] While he went
to death with a Presbyterian's stern firmness and a
Douglas's indomitable pride, he denied to the last
that he had taken any active part in the murder of
Darnley, but confessed having known about the
conspiracy against him, and that he also had,
according to his statement, thought of speaking to
Darnley about it, but believing that behind the
conspiracy he saw the Queen's own person, he had
not ventured to do so for the sake of his own safety,
or according to his words : " For I knew him to be
a bairne of such nature that there was nothing told
him but he would reveill it to hir againe."[2] After
the issuing of the amnesty by the Queen on Christmas Eve 1566, he had returned from England in
the beginning of the following year, and had meanwhile, in Whittingham Castle in East Lothian, where
he was on a visit to his cousin Archibald Douglas,
had an interview with Bothwell and Lethington,
which must have taken place about the 20th
January 1567.[3] At this interview Bothwell had

[1] By " the maiden," or that same
instrument of death which, later,
in France, where this memento of
the Scottish Reformation time was
unknown, got the name of the
guillotine, and whose introduction
into Scotland is generally ascribed
to the Earl of Morton, although it
was still older than his regency,
under which only a more extended
use of it was made. One of the
characters in Scott's novel of *The
Abbot* thus describes this instrument, which is now preserved
in Edinburgh in the Museum of
the Antiquarian Society : " Herod's
daughter, who did such execution
with her foot and ankle, danced
not men's heads off more cleanly
than this maiden of Morton. 'Tis
an axe, man, an axe, which falls of
itself like a sash-window, and never
gives the headsman the trouble to
wield it."

[2] The Earl of Morton's Confession.—Laing, *History of Scotland*,
ii. 326.

[3] Morton was still in England
the 10th of January 1567 when he
wrote a letter of thanks to Cecil

called upon him to take part in getting the King CHAP.
put out of the way according to the Queen's wish, III.
" because," as he said, " she blamed the king mair 1581.
of David's (Riccio's) slaughter than me," and " because so was the Queine's mynd, and shoe wald
have it to be done."[1] " Unto this," Morton asserted,
" my answer was, I desyred the eirle Bothwell to
bring me the queine's handwryt of this matter for
a warrand ; utherwayes I wald not mell (meddle)
therewith ; *quhilk warrand he never purchaissed
unto me.*"[2] From Whittingham Morton had after
this repaired to St. Andrews on a visit to the Earl
of Angus ; here two days before Darnley's murder
Archibald Douglas was sent to him with a letter and
message from Bothwell, who gave him to understand
that the plot was now near its conclusion, and
begged his assistance for its execution ; Morton had
then again answered that he must first see black
upon white from the Queen about the matter ; but,
as he once more repeated, *this Bothwell never let him
see.*[3] This confession of the Earl is in agreement
with a letter from his cousin Archibald Douglas,
written in London after Morton's death. Douglas,
who, when Morton was imprisoned, had fled to England, in this letter begs Mary's intercession with her
son, so that he might be permitted to return to

for his protection of him, and in a
letter to Cecil from Drury, dated
Berwick 23d January 1567, it is
said that Bothwell and Lethington
then had recently visited Morton
in Whittingham Castle.—Chalmers, *Life of Mary Queen of Scots,*
ii. 227.

[1] The Earl of Morton's Confession.—Laing, *History of Scotland,*
ii. 324.

[2] Laing, *History of Scotland,*
ii. 324.

[3] " My answer was to him that
I wald give no answer to that purpose, seeing I had not gotten the
queine's warrand in wryt, quhilk
was promised ; and thairfore, seeing the eirle Bothwell never reported any warrand of the queine
to me, I never melled farther with
it."—Morton's Confession ; Laing,
History of Scotland, ii. 325.

CHAP.
III.

1567.

Scotland,[1] reminds her how formerly, after the death
of Riccio, he too had in company with Morton left
Scotland, but had before this been amnestied by the
Queen, and goes on also to speak of the meeting of
Bothwell and Lethington with Morton at Whittingham, where he, the young cousin of the latter, then
was: " What speech passed there amongst them, as
God shall be my Judge, I knew nothing at that
time, but at their departure I was requested by the
said Earl Morton to accompany the Earl Bodvell
and Secretary to Edinburgh, and to return with
such an answer as they should obtain of your
Majesty, which being given to me by the said persons, as God shall be my Judge, was no other than
these words: ' Schaw to the Earl Morton that the
Queen will hear no speech of that matter appointed
unto him;' when I cravit that the answer might be
made more sensible, Secretary Ledington said that
the Earl would sufficiently understand it."[2]   It
must have been (as the opponents of Mary themselves latterly explained the contested letters) during
her immediately subsequent stay in Glasgow from
the 23d to the 27th January that she wrote Bothwell the first of the letters which they afterwards
laid to her charge; wherefore then could Bothwell
not—the question has been asked—after the interview at Whittingham, show these to the Earl, wherefore not show him the same letters which Morton
some months later found so decisive against Mary?
Must they not always have spoken equally plainly?

[1] He was afterwards ambassador
of James VI. to Elizabeth. His
biography is given in Brunton
and Haig's *Historical Account of
the Senators of the College of*
Justice (Edinburgh, 1832), pp.
125-128.

[2] Letter of Archibald Douglas to
Mary Stuart.—Laing, *History of*
Scotland, ii. 249-251.

There are many other and stronger doubts which CHAP.
might be urged against the genuineness of those III.
letters. We have still the deposition of George 1567-8.
Dalgleish, which was made on 26th June 1567 in
the presence of the Earls of Morton and Atholl,
along with that of Kirkaldy of Grange; but just as
little as Sir James Balfour, in whose custody the
documents had been, was ever required to tell
anything concerning them when confronted with
Dalgleish, so little does there appear in the deposition of the latter any question whatever, even a
single word, with respect to them.[1] Mary's enemies
indeed explain this circumstance by alleging that
it was only wished at that time to have proofs
against Bothwell, while nothing further was aimed
at in regard to the Queen than simply to see her
deposed and try to save her honour, limits over
which, by and by, it was necessary, however re-
luctantly, through the pressure of political circumstances to pass, first in Scotland, and afterwards also
during the conference in England; but neither the
manner in which the Lords of the conspiracy directly
spoke to Sir Nicholas Throckmorton about their
pretended discovery, nor any part of their conduct
in other respects towards the Queen at the time and
subsequently, makes any such alleged intention probable. Another ground for doubt in this matter is
furnished by the language. It is well known that
Mary Stuart until her flight to England was accustomed to make use only of the French language in
her letters,[2] and it is in conformity with this that

---

[1] The Deposition of George Dalgleish, reprinted in Laing, *History
of Scotland*, ii. 249-251.

[2] She writes from Bolton Castle,
in England, the 1st September
1568 to Sir Francis Knollys thus :

all the letters from her, which were produced in the
conference at Westminster and compared with earlier
letters from her to Elizabeth, are also expressly
testified on the part of the English as having been
composed in the French tongue. The fact was
established in the last century by Walter Goodall,
and later, by the elder Tytler, through a critical
investigation of the letters themselves, that the
language of two of the most criminatory letters, or
of the so-called letters from Glasgow, as these are
now styled, was not originally French, but in many
places is evidently only a translation from a Scottish
original, and that therefore the French of nearly two
hundred letters has been unjustly passed off as Mary
Stuart's.[1] The evidence brought forward on this
point was so overwhelming that neither Robertson
nor Hume, who were on the opposite side, attempted
to rebut it, the enemies of the Queen only replying that Goodall could not prove that the French
form in which the letters now appeared is the
same as that in which they were previously produced at Westminster. Against this objection,
which has latterly been especially urged by Malcolm
Laing, it may meanwhile be pleaded that it still

"Mester Knollis, y heuu har (I
have heard) sum neus from Scotland ; y send zou the double off
them y vreit to the Quin, my gud
sister, and pres zou to du the lyk,
conforme to that y spak zester-
nicht vnto zou, and sut hesti
ansur y refer all to zour discretion,
and wil lipne beter in zour gud
delin for mi, nor y kan persuad
zou, nemli in this langasg ; excus
my iuel vreitin for y neuuer vsed
it afor, and am hestet. . . . Excus
my iuel vreitin thes furst tym."—
Henry Ellis, *Original Letters, il-*

lustrative of English History (London, 1824-46), First Series, ii.
252-254. The earlier letters from
Mary Stuart composed in her native language were only dictated,
yet have some few of them, occasionally in their conclusion, one
or two Scottish sentences added
by the Queen's own hand.

[1] Goodall, i. 81-98 ; William
Tytler, *Inquiry, Historical and
Critical, into the evidence against
Mary Queen of Scots* (fourth edit.)
London, 1790, i. 178-233.

seems very strange that the ruling party in England and Scotland, while they afterwards showed themselves so zealous in getting those letters printed and disseminated, should have been so indifferent about insuring for them their correct French linguistic form, and instead of this have only let the Scottish version of the original letters go forth in another and new French translation. Along with this, the disposition which the Scottish government long showed, both before and during the conference, to keep back the French text, cannot but seem strange. The representatives of the government of Scotland at Westminster were at length half forced to come forward with their French originals, but at the beginning of the conference in York they had, on the contrary, as the accounts of the English commissioners indicate, and as the abstracts in the Scottish language transmitted by the English put beyond a doubt, only produced the letters in the latter (Scottish) language. If nevertheless it be not admitted that in this there was any wilful design on the part of the Scots to mislead, but that an attempt was made to explain the matter rather from a perhaps mistaken regard to the possible unacquaintedness of the commissioners with the French language, yet no such regard could in the least be the reason why Elizabeth also, when she had, prior to the commencement of the conference, prompted Murray to come forward with the discovery reputed ruinous for Mary, got the Scottish translation sent to her merely with a view to a preliminary acquaintance with its contents,[1] although but a short time before, on a well-known occasion during his exile in

<hr>

[1] Goodall, ii. 75.

CHAP.   England, she had publicly expressed her desire that
III.   he should speak to her rather in the French tongue
1567.   than in the, to her, more foreign Scottish language.[1]
Again, it is not the less singular that the Scots had
also at York brought forward many more com-
promising proofs against Mary than they themselves
at a later period found it advisable to produce for
the more exact legal examination at Westminster.
At York they had, in the first instance, shown many
other writings also ascribed to Mary, which afterwards disappeared, and one of these may especially
awaken suspicion.   During the conference at York
the Scots admitted that the greater part of their
nobility had, after Darnley's death, at a meeting on
the 19th April 1567, subscribed a declaration, of
which they produced a copy, whose purport was to
recommend Bothwell to the Queen as the most
fitting husband for her, and to assure Bothwell of
their united support in this matter, but they also
protested that the condition upon which they alone
had been willing to accede to it was this : that the
Queen herself should first authorise them to make
such a declaration, and that this was also given in
a written assurance, subscribed by the Queen's own
hand, dated the 19th April 1567, and which they
likewise produced.[2]   Such a writing, it is not at all
impossible, Mary *may* have at that time subscribed.

[1] *Memoirs of Sir James Melvil,*
p. 57.
[2] The words in which the English commissioners at York mention this writing, and the Scots'
contemporary explanation of their
compact are as follows : "And
yet, in prouve that they did it not
willinglie, they procured a warrant, which was now shewed unto

us, bearing date the 19th of Aprill,
signed with the Quene's hand,
whereby she gave them licence to
agree to the same, affirming that,
before they had such a warrant,
there was none of them that did,
or wolde set to their hands, saving
onlie the Earl of Huntly."—Goodall, ii. 140.

But against any such warrant from her both these CHAP.
same Scottish nobles' own statements militate in so   III.
far as they subsequently, after her marriage with   1567.
Bothwell, actually began their revolt against the
latter with the averment that the Queen could not
be assumed to have voluntarily entered into it.
In particular, the certain fact that, before they even
thus resolved to rise against Bothwell, but at a
point of time when his marriage with the Queen had
also been decided on, even then for the first time
they sought, and on the 14th May, also actually
obtained, a letter of assurance from the Queen (still
preserved), which should henceforward protect them
from being held accountable for the assistance which,
by their compact of the 19th April, they had
voluntarily promised Bothwell towards the object
at which he aimed.[1]   At the meeting in Scotland of
19th April so many noblemen were present that no
one would be able to gain credence there for any
such assertion as that which the English commissioners subsequently heard at York ; and however
little acquainted the latter could be with the circumstances of Scotland, however boldly it was
possible for any one to make vague assertions to
them, yet there were still to be found among Mary's
representatives who accompanied the conference to
Westminster at least two, the Lords Boyd and
Herries, that took part in the above-mentioned
meeting of the Scottish nobles, and we may thus
readily assume that regard to the explanation which
these would be capable of communicating was the
reason why Murray's party found it advisable, before

[1] Mary's Declaration of 14th   other authorities now also re-
May 1567 is to be found among   printed in Labanoff, ii. 22.

any examination took place at Westminster, altogether to withdraw the document produced at York.
If therefore we are not also in this case to try to
get out of the difficulty by supposing that the
English commissioners at York had misunderstood
the Scots, it is certainly best to see in the document
in question neither more nor less than a distorted
copy of the declaration of pardon for the confederates
which Bothwell obtained from Mary on the 14th
May; and as the matter stands thus with the missing writing at Westminster, it certainly tends to
increase mistrust in reference to the others produced there, which are well known to us.   Another
thing which brings the genuineness of these writings
into doubt is their style.   Even should some of the
letters printed in French be assumed to be now in
a new form, yet the same thing can hardly at all
events be maintained in respect to the sonnets, also
printed in French.   Regarding the latter, Brantôme,
a contemporary, speaking both in the name of the
well-known French poet Ronsard, who had previously in France addressed some of his poems to
Mary,[1] and also in his own name wrote thus : " She
aspired to be a poet, and composed verses, some of
which I have seen, that were beautiful and very
well written, and by no means like those which it
has been sought to ascribe to her in connection with
her amour with Earl Bothwell, these being too
inelegant and too little polished to be hers.   M.
Ronsard was in this matter entirely of my opinion,
when we one day talked about it, and read them
together."[2]   Mary may nevertheless have been no

---

[1] Ronsard, *Œuvres complètes* (Paris, 1587), viii. 19.
[2] Note E, Appendix.

great poetess, but about her style of letter-writing CHAP.
there can be only one opinion.   In the large collec- III.
tion of her writings, which Count Labanoff has 1567.
edited, in seven volumes, there are hundreds of .
unquestioned letters from the Queen's hand. In
these good taste is discernible throughout; in none
of them is there any approach to rudeness of thought
and inelegance of expression such as very offensively
make their appearance in the disputed writings, and
this feature of them has accordingly been readily
regarded as an obvious sign that in reality they
originated rather with a man than a woman.
These writings in many respects likewise awaken
doubt by their contents, when the events and circumstances to which they point are subjected to a
closer comparison with what is known from other
historical authorities in reference to the same facts.
This holds good particularly in respect to their
chronological arrangement.   One of the so-called
marriage contracts, or more correctly, one of the
promises on the Queen's part of marriage with
Bothwell, the originals of which, along with the
remaining writings, had been produced at the conference in England, thus states, in opposition to the
letters and sonnets, on what day and at what place
this document was drawn up; it is dated from Seton
the 5th April 1567.[1]   The Queen must, therefore,
according to it, have consented to marry Bothwell
before the latter carried her off on the 24th April.
In the same document of the 5th April, mention is
also made in more than one place that a process of
divorce between the Earl of Bothwell and his wife

---

[1] The promise is contained in   234-37, and in Teulet, *Lettres*, pp.
Laing, *History of Scotland*, ii.   107-110.

I

was already being instituted, and yet we know with certainty that this process first began on the 27th April.

On the whole, comparing the reasons which have been adduced for the genuineness of the writings in question with the opposing facts which bespeak their untrustworthiness, the latter seem to us to have the greater weight. The best reason apparently which has been urged for the genuineness of the letters is what has been called the " overpowering" agreement between one of the letters, which the Queen is said to have written from Glasgow, and the declaration made by Thomas Crawford. But, in truth, this agreement must be said to be *far too* overpowering. The two documents are in fact almost identical. What Mary Stuart is said to have written from memory to Bothwell about her conversation with Darnley, and what Darnley is said likewise from memory to have related to Crawford about the same protracted conversation, agree almost word for word with such perfect exactness, that it may amaze every one who has but noticed the divergences met with every day in a court of justice even between such depositions of witnesses as concern only the simplest facts. It seems at first sight impossible, in consideration of this circumstance, that both the aforementioned testimonies can be genuine ; and, when more closely inspected, Crawford's testimony just goes to furnish one of the strongest grounds that bespeak the falsification of the writings in question. Time has more recently brought to light a remarkable letter, written to Crawford by the Earl of Lennox, who also appeared at the conference in Westminster as one of Mary

Stuart's accusers. This letter was certainly called CHAP. forth by the influence of John Wood of Tilliedavy, who was then secretary to Murray, and, as one of 1568. the representatives of the latter at the conference, brought with him those disputed writings.[1] Contemporary letters, which Wood had sent to Murray and Maitland from Chiswick, make it unquestionable that he must have been present with the Earl of Lennox when the latter, on the 11th June 1568, likewise wrote Crawford from Chiswick; and it is no less certain that, under the influence of Wood, Lennox now addressed a request to his "trusty servant, Thomas Crawford," "by all means" to consider how there could be procured further matter of accusation against the Queen, his attention being directed by the letter to the same series of points as those on which his declaration now in question turns. And it seems in that case far more probable that, after being thus reminded by Lennox, Crawford penned his declaration from the recollection of his conversation with Darnley, at the critical period when Mary Stuart had a few weeks before fled from Scotland, and when the conference in England was being arranged for the first time, than that he should, during the last days of its continuance, have found himself called on to do it. Not only so, but it is likewise most probable that some one may then have discovered in Crawford's account the materials for manufacturing false letters from the Queen. If this supposition prove correct, then the

[1] Catalogue of State Papers and Historical Documents preserved at Hamilton Palace, by George Chalmers, author of *Caledonia*, printed in *Miscellany of the Maitland Club*, consisting of *original Papers and other Documents illustrative of the History and Literature of Scotland*, vol. iv. (Glasgow, 1847, 4to), part i. pp. 118-121.

most important support for the trustworthiness of these writings must also be regarded as seriously weakened. For with respect to the reason drawn from the disappearance of the original documents since the reign of James VI., this is so far from being any real proof, that it only assumes the appearance of a proof by the assumption of a genuineness which should first be proved. It is certainly a strange mode of argumentation to appeal to the disappearance of the original documents as making good their genuineness; from the opposite standpoint we may just as well recognise in this disappearance the work of those who were afraid of one day or other seeing another forgery revealed. And lastly, as regards the circumstance that all the writings produced at Westminster were without signature or any other precise indication of their origin, we are not by any means obliged to see in this the mysteriousness arising from the conscious guilt which the opponents of Mary have wished to attach to it. On the other hand, it is in this respect strange, as the advocates of the Queen have long pointed out, that while these writings, in conformity with the record of the meeting of the Scottish Privy Council of the 4th December 1567, are said to be " written and subscribed with her own hand," they are, on the contrary, immediately thereafter, on the 15th December 1567, described by the Scottish Parliament in the same way as they were afterwards presented at Westminster, and as we now alone know them, namely as "wholly written with her own hand." Between these different modes of expression there is a most palpable variance, for, as has been remarked, while it may be imagined that if the first

expression is the more limited and the second the
more comprehensive, the first might, in the natural
course of things, have therefore been quite free from
falsehood, it now seems, as the reverse is the case,
that the second corrects the first by limiting the
same, and another forgery thus unmistakably discloses itself. It was customary at that period for
the name of the writer, along with the date and
address, to be put on the last leaf of the letter, and
hence it may be readily assumed that in this way
possibly the first thought of another forgery was
matured. The Scottish Privy Council may have
found an opportunity of removing this leaf from
some of the letters afterwards produced against her.
Mary's friends have in fact been disposed to assume
that her persecutors, when by her fall they were put
in possession of Holyrood, or by other means, had
really become acquainted with love-letters and sonnets in her handwriting, but of an earlier date,
addressed to Darnley, or perhaps even to Francis II.,
and as a starting-point to such a supposition, they
specially refer to one of the letters ascribed to the
Queen, in which she speaks both of a previous secret
marriage that had to her great joy united her to the
person to whom she writes, and of an approaching
public marriage with the same person.[1]   Now, unless
the nuptial union into which the Queen had already
entered be assumed to have reference to the Scottish
" Handfasting," we cannot help regarding the word
" Marriage " in this letter as unaccountable, since no
one ever heard of any secret marriage between the
Queen and Bothwell.   On the other hand, the fact

[1] The letter is given by Laing,   by Teulet, *Lettres de Marie Stuart*,
History of Scotland, ii. 208, and   p. 65.

is beyond dispute that contemporaries have actually mentioned a previous secret marriage between Mary and Darnley, and in this way we have special reason for assuming that her enemies, after the remark already cited from the Scottish Privy Council Records, may have allowed the signature to drop by the removal of the last leaf from the genuine letters, in order the better to be able to mix them together with those that were manifestly forged. In regard to the latter, in which even the contents are plainly forged, it is not necessary for us in every instance to suppose a complete fabrication, but only to such an extent as that in which certain passages may have been falsified or interpolated. In this light they were looked upon, especially by that section of the Scottish peers and prelates who still took part with Mary after she was at length obliged to seek refuge in England. Thirty-five earls, bishops, and abbots, among whom are found the Earls of Huntly and Argyll, and the most of whom we may assume to have seen the writings when before Parliament, selected, during the sitting of the conference in the neighbouring country, certain plenipotentiaries, who, in their name, were authorised to render assistance to their exiled sovereign in meeting the charges of Murray and his party; and in the instruction, which on this occasion they drew up at Dumbarton, 12th September 1568, they assert, with regard to the writings which threatened such danger to the Queen, that these, "in sum principal and substantious clausis," were only an invention of the Queen's accusers.[1]

On the supposition that these documents have

---

[1] Instruction of 12th September 1568.—Goodall, ii. 361.

been falsified, to a greater or less extent, the question may be asked, Who in such a case was really to
blame for it ? In this matter some have sought to
fix the guilt on Sir James Balfour, who, as a celebrated Scottish historian believed, ought to be
branded as the most corrupt man of that age.[1] Others
have assigned it to the same Scotsman, who was
subsequently the first to circulate these writings in
print, that is to say, George Buchanan; but even if he
could be regarded as morally capable of such a deed,
still these productions hardly agree with his style.
Some have also wished to blame the laird of Lethington as having been the author of the forgeries in
question. Of him the famous Englishman, William
Camden, expressly states in his *Annals of the Times
of Queen Elizabeth*, that Lethington, during the
conference at York, secretly confessed that he had
oftener than once counterfeited the Queen's writing.[2] At the time when the conference took place
Camden was only sixteen years of age, a poor student
at Magdalen College, Oxford, and Sir John Maitland,
a son of Lethington, undertook to reply to him.
When Maitland, some years after the first edition
of the *Annals* had appeared, read Camden's work
during his stay in Belgium, and met with the above-
mentioned statement, among many other passages
in which he thought his father's memory was injured, he wrote to Camden for the purpose of
demanding an explanation from him.[3] Still, notwithstanding this, the later edition of Camden's

[1] Sir James Balfour, the most corrupt man of that age.—Robertson, *History of Scotland*, ii. 51.
[2] Et Lidingtonius clam innuisset, se sæpius reginæ characteres emen- titum esse.—*Annales rerum Angli-*carum et *Hibernicarum regnante Elizabetha*, p. 143.
[3] This letter, which is dated " Bruxellis, 8 Junii 1620," and which has the superscription " D. J. Metellanus G. Camdeno," begins

work, which the latter had even before his death prepared for the press, contains in this respect no omission, change, or correction.[1] There is yet one Scottish grandee whom we may name in connection with this matter. The Earl of Morton was the person into whose hands the casket with those disputed documents is said first to have fallen, through the capture of Dalgleish, and on him who, also, at a later period, was himself condemned for the crime with which he charged the Queen, we are disposed rather to fix as the originator of the forgery in question. He at least has manifestly deserved such a suspicion; for if it is only a guess that Camden's historical writings were inspired by the government of James VI., it is no guess, as will be subsequently shown, that Morton's treatment of the letters of others could be accommodated to a political purpose. Thus when the Earl of Lennox was made Regent in Scotland, and had sent Thomas Buchanan to Denmark for the purpose of there prosecuting, in his own name and in that of Queen Elizabeth, their action against Bothwell after his flight from Scotland, the Earl of Morton was at the same time in England in order that, in conjunction with two other Scottish officials, he might look after another political affair. Thomas Buchanan corresponded from Denmark with both the English and Scottish Go-

thus: "Hisce diebus dum Elizabethæ Annales perlegerem in loca quædam incidi, in quibus parentis mei mentio non satis honesta facta est, jure facta nullo modo mihi possum persuadere." Then follow various citations from the *Annals*, among them being the passage quoted above, after which Maitland concludes as follows: "Hæc præ-cipue sunt loca de quibus plenius cuperem edoceri, qua demum ratione quave auctoritate impulsi libro vestro ea inserenda censueritis."— *Gulielmi Camdeni et illustrium virorum ad G. Camdenum epistolæ.* Londini, 1691, 4to, pp. 305-306.

[1] Gulielmi Camdeni, *Annales rerum Anglicarum et Hibernicarum regnante Elizabetha*, i. 169.

vernments, and accordingly sent off from Copenhagen two letters, dated respectively the 19th and the 20th January 1571, of which the one was addressed to Elizabeth's minister, William Cecil, the other to the Regent, the Earl of Lennox. Morton during his stay in London received the last-mentioned letter, which he, along with his colleagues, took the liberty of opening and reading before it was sent to Scotland, and thereupon the English Government requested to be made acquainted with its contents. How he complied with this request he himself relates in a letter to Lennox, which he did not venture to send him directly by post, but subsequently caused to be conveyed to him by a separate trusty messenger. "We haid no will," writes the Chancellor of Scotland, "the contents of the same suld be knawin, fearing that sum wordis and matteris mentioned in the same, being dispersit heir as novellis, suld rather have hinderit nor furtherit our cause. And thairfor, being desirit at court to shaw the lettre, we gave to understand that we had sent the principal away ; and deliverit a copie, *omittand sic thingis as we thocht not meit to be shawin*, as zour Grace may perceave be the like copie, quhilk also we have sent zou herewith ; quhilk ze may communicat to sic as zour Grace thinkis not expedient to communicat the hail contentis of the principal lettre unto."[1] We wonder any one who has paid attention

[1] The letter from London, 24th March 1571, subscribed by Morton, Robert of Dunfermline, and James Macgill, is found in Goodall, ii. 382-383. The prior, Robert of Dunfermline, and the then clerk-register, James Macgill of Nether Rankeillour, had, like Morton, already during the conferences at York and Westminster, been among the Scotsmen who had followed Murray as the latter's representatives or assistants, and Macgill had, at an earlier period, also been one of the participators in the murder of Riccio.

to these words of Morton is able again to put confidence in him, because the Earl at the time when he
received from Murray a receipt for the due delivery
of the memorable casket, was also certified by this
associate of his that he had honestly kept the written
contents of the casket " without ony alteratioun,
augmentatioun, or diminutioun thairof in ony part
or portion ;"[1] or because Morton himself, when he
was also present at the conference in Westminster,
as is stated in the English official account, here
again protested upon oath that he had at the time
taken the box produced with the writings contained
in it from George Dalgleish, and that the writings were
still the very same, without any manner of change.[2]

The second principal grounds on which the persuasion of Mary's complicity in the murder of
Darnley is chiefly based are the depositions by
Nicolas Hubert, or, as he is also called after his
native place, Paris, who, after being in Bothwell's
service, and subsequently in Lord Seton's, had
lately entered the Queen's household. The first
of the two depositions points to Bothwell as the
ringleader in the murder; the other also impeaches
Mary as an accomplice.[3] Some have sought to find
in the dramatic character of these documents a
security for their trustworthiness, and for their
having originated only from a person who had been
in such a station as Paris. It has been said that

[1] Testifeing and declaring, that he
has trewlie and honestlie observit
and kepit the said box, and haill
writtis and pecis forsaids within
the same, without ony alteratioun,
augmentatioun, or diminutioun
thairof, in ony part or portioun.—
The receipt of Murray to Morton

of 16th September 1568, as found
in Goodall, ii. 90.
[2] Goodall, ii. 256.
[3] They are found, among many
other authorities, reprinted in
Laing, *History of Scotland*, ii.
270-290, and in Teulet, pp. 79-
105.

they are distinguished by a tone so simple that no
question of forgery could easily arise in reference to
them, by details so minute in the subordinate circumstances related, that the cleverest forger would
not be able to invent them. But even if this in
some respects could be said with regard to the first
declaration, it by no means holds good with respect
to the second which concerns the Queen. In the
case of the latter the critic must find the servant's
familiarity with the Queen very improbable,[1] for we
cannot easily understand why the Queen and Bothwell, where they are spoken of as writing letters to
each other, should make the messenger by whom
these letters were sent the oral bearer of expressions, by means of which they must subject themselves to public exposure. Then the second declaration is not only at variance with the first, in as far
as the latter manifestly reveals Bothwell's dread lest
the Queen should learn anything about what he was
arranging, but its statements by no means agree
with the dates which the opponents of the Queen
themselves have fixed on as a sure guidance in judging of the conduct ascribed to her.[2] Especially there

[1] The servant is thus brought forward in one place as he who "took the liberty" to address the Queen in these words: " Madame, Monsieur de Boiduel, ma commande lui porter les clefs de vostre chambre, et qu'il a envie d'y faire quelque chose, c'est de faire saulter le Roy en l'air par pouldre, qu'il y fera mettre."—Examination of Paris in Laing, *History of Scotland,* ii. 285, and Teulet, *Lettres,* p. 98.

[2] This holds good particularly of a Journal or Diary preserved in the Cottonian Library, in which

an endeavour is made day by day to throw light upon the Queen's acting in Scotland after the birth of James VI. It had been communicated on the part of the Scottish to the English Government as a means of guidance, and is therefore commonly, although less properly, designated at one time as Murray's, and at another as Cecil's "Diary." According to this document, which is to be found printed in the Appendices to Malcolm Laing, *History of Scotland,* ii. 81-85, Bothwell was from the 24th to the 28th January absent from

also comes into prominent view the form in which
those declarations present themselves. It was in
the year 1569, when Paris was kept a prisoner in
Murray's Castle at St. Andrews, that he is said to
have made his two declarations, of which that concerning Bothwell is dated 9th August; the other,
called forth by an examination regarding the Queen's
conduct, was emitted on the 10th August. When
Robert Pitcairn, many months after the conclusion
of the conference at Westminster, was for the first
time sent as Scottish ambassador to the court of
Elizabeth, and received his instructions from Murray
on the 15th October 1569, the latter also secretly
furnished him with a new testimony, namely, the
confession of Paris regarding the Queen's guilt, " in
case that otherwise later proofs should be demanded,"[1] and the testimony thus sent is still preserved in the English State Paper Office. While
however it is expressly stated in the confessions of
Dalgleish, Hay, and Hepburn, before what judicial
authority they were made,[2] this is not the case with
that of Paris, the original of which in the English
State Paper Office only mentions that it was

Edinburgh on a visit to Liddesdale;
on the contrary, according to the
second declaration of Paris, we
must assume that the latter had,
on the 25th and 26th January,
met him in Edinburgh, and there
brought him a message from the
Queen in Glasgow. Laing, who
belongs to those authors that believe in the genuineness both of
the writings ascribed to Mary
Stuart, and of the declarations
ascribed to Paris, has here, in
order not to give up the latter,
seen no other way of escape from
the difficulty than to assume the

dates given in the Diary, which
just originated, according to him,
from the opponents of the Queen
by way of excuse for their conduct,
to be—false.

[1] And gif furder pruif be re-
quirit, we have sent with zow the
depositiounis of Nikolas Hubert,
alias Paris, a Frenchman, one that
was present at the committing of
the said murder, and of late execute to the deith for the samin.
—Goodall, ii. 84-88.

[2] Compare these confessions as
given by Laing, *History of Scotland*, ii. 243-259.

latterly read over before Paris, and acknowledged CHAP. III.
by him to be undoubtedly true in presence of George
Buchanan, John Wood of Tilliedàvy, and Robert   1569.
Ramsay.[1] As Buchanan and Wood were notorious
agents of Murray, and Ramsay was his servant,[2] it
seems even on the Regent's side latterly to have
been strongly felt that these names, so far as they
had not from want of others been evidently fabricated, were not greatly fitted to gain credence for
the particulars of the confession. We have in the
Cottonian Library an attested copy of the second
confession of Paris, which was subsequently sent to
England, but attested not like the copies of the
earlier confessions of those under sentence of death
by the Justice-Clerk, Sir John Bellenden, but by
Alexander Hay, who was only secretary of the
council,[3] and in this copy he has entirely omitted

[1] The concluding words of the original, cited by Chalmers in his *Life of Mary Queen of Scots*, ii. 51, are these : "The copie of this Declaration and Deposition, markit every leaf with the said Nicolas Howbert's own hand, being read again in his presence, he avowed the same, and in all parts and clauses thereof, to be undoubtedly true ; *in presence of Mr. George Buchanan, maister of St. Leonard's College in St. Andrews, Mr. John Wood, Senator of the College of Justice, and Robert Ramsay, writer of this declaration, servant to my Lord Regent's Grace.*" By "mark-it" is not meant signed, but having a mark affixed—Paris having been unable to write.

[2] Wood had, as Murray's partisan, taken part in the latter's insurrection after Mary's marriage with Darnley, and, like Buchanan, he was also one of Murray's agents at the conferences in England. He

was murdered on the 15th April 1570 by the avenging hand of Arthur Forbes, the laird of Reres, a short time after the murder of his patron the Regent had taken place. See the unfavourable characteristics given of him by contemporaries in Brunton and Haig's *Historical Account of the Senators of the College of Justice*, pp. 114-115. Melvil says that he privately sold the letters of the Duke of Norfolk to Elizabeth.—*The Memoirs of Sir James Melvil*, p. 99.

[3] " Ita est : Alexander Hay, scriba secreti consilii S. D. N. Regis ac notarius Publicus."—Anderson, *Collections to the History of Mary Queen of Scots*, ii. 205. Alexander Hay became, in March 1564, by the assistance of Lethington, clerk of the Privy Council, and got, in October 1579, the post of Clerk-Register. Sir John Bellenden, Lord of Auchi-

the words about Buchanan, Wood, and Ramsay
having been present at the reading over of the confession before Paris, and his acknowledgment of the
same. Add to this that Buchanan himself seems
finally to condemn the principal testimony here
treated of against the Queen. It was only two
years after the execution of Paris that Buchanan
put forth his severe attack on Mary, accusing her of
complicity in the murder of Darnley; but in this
famous polemical pamphlet, in which he usually
does not disdain to use any argument which could
disgrace the Queen, he has not made any use whatever of, or so much as named, an authority which
must, from his point of view, have been so important. In the *History of Scotland*, which Buchanan
afterwards published, although he frequently mentions Paris, he is equally silent respecting the
declarations ascribed to the latter, and therefore we
may thus justly conclude that in reality he never
either knew or valued any confession such as that at
which he with his two companions is said to have been
present.[1] The alleged confession of Paris was also
concealed from Mary, even more than the writings
ascribed to herself; during the whole lifetime of the
Queen it was manifestly kept a profound secret from
both her and her friends, and it was not until nearly
a century and a half after her death that for the first
time it was made public.[2] On the side of herself

noul, was Justice-Clerk from the
year 1547 until his death in the
year 1577.—Consult Brunton and
Haig, *Historical Account of the
Senators of the College of Justice,*
pp. 91-95 and 171-177.

[1] Buckingham, *Memoirs of Mary
Stuart, Queen of Scotland.* London, 1844, i. 365. A copy of the
sentence pronounced on Paris we
altogether want.

[2] In Anderson, *Collections to the
History of Mary Stuart, Queen of
Scotland,* ii. 192-205, where nevertheless the remarkable concluding
sentence about the witnesses, subsequently added for the first time
by Chalmers, was still omitted.

and her friends at the time there was, therefore, CHAP.
never any difficulty in directly replying to the de- III.
claration which, for the first time, has latterly been 1571.
set up as the second chief evidence of her acquaintance with the design of the murder; but it is so far
from being the case that her adherents have avoided
mentioning Paris, that some of his last words to the
advantage of the Queen are appealed to in a publication which is nearly contemporaneous with the declaration ascribed to him. In the year 1571 Lesley,
Bishop of Ross, published at Liège his well-known
Defence of Mary Stuart,[1] and in it he ventured
not only to state a direct charge against her political
opponents as those who themselves had perpetrated
the murder on Darnley, but also added a positive
assertion to the effect that some of the subordinates
and condemned assistants in this deed, and especially Paris, had before their execution, by their confessions, quite exempted the Queen from all blame.
"We can tel you," says Lesley, "that John Hay
of Galoway, that Powry, that Dowglish, and last
of al that Paris, al being put to death for this
crime, toke God to recorde, at the time of their
death, that this murther was by your Counsayle, In-
uention and Drift committed; who also declared,
that they neuer knew the Queene to be participant
or ware thereof. Wel we can farther tel you of the
greate goodnes of God and of the mightie Force of
the Truth; whereby, though ye have wonderfully
turmoiled and tossed, though ye have racked and
put to death aswel Innocents as Gultie, your owne

---

[1] A Treatise concerning the defence of the honour of the right
high, mightie, and noble princesse,
Marie, Queene of Scotlande and
Dowager of France. Liège, 1571.

CHAP.
III.
1571.

confederats, God hath so wrought, that as for no torments nor fayer Promises they could be brought falsly to defame their Mastresse, so without torments at al they haue voluntarily purged her, and so layed the burden upon your necks and shoulders, that ye shall never be able to shake it of."[1] In opposition to the declarations, which we now know that the Queen's enemies privately ascribed to Paris, Lesley repeats distinctly, with respect to his general assertion, that Paris, just before his execution, is also said to have called heaven to witness that he never, at any time, had been the bearer of such letters as those whose falsehood Lesley maintained.[2]

[1] Lesley, *Defence of the Honour of Marie, Queene of Scotlande*, reprinted in Anderson's *Collections*, i. 77. The judicial proceedings were secret, and that they did not scruple to employ torture against the subordinate persons who were imprisoned on the occasion of the murder of the king, the records of the council themselves furnish evidence. These contain, under the 27th June 1567, an order that William Blacater, James Edmonston, John Blacater, and Mynart Fraser, who had been made prisoners, should be "put in the irins and tormentis for furthering of the tryall of the veritie."—Keith, *History of the Affairs of State and Church in Scotland*, p. 407. On the one side there is in the official account of the confessions which, immediately before their execution on the 3d January 1568, were made by John Hay of Talla, William Powrie, and George Dalgleish (Laing, *History of Scotland*, ii. 263-65), no declaration concerning the Queen such as that mentioned by Lesley, and what concerns Paris, as we know at least now no more with respect to him beyond the declarations ascribed to

him, so as for the others, have we not any confession made before execution to the priests in addition to those emitted under judicial examinations. Only in the confession which Laird James of Ormiston, some years later in Edinburgh Castle, made immediately before his execution on the 13th December 1573, to priest John Brand (Laing, *History of Scotland*, ii. 291-296), do we meet with a passage which could answer to the assertion previously put forth by Lesley : "Being inquyred gif ever the quein spake unto him at any tyme or gif he knew what wes the quenis mynd unto it, ansrit, as I shall ansuer to God, shoe spake never to me nor I to hir of it, nor I knaw nathing of hir part but as my Lord Bothwell shaw me ; for I will not speike bot the trewth for all the gold of the earth."

[2] " For as for him that ye surmise was the bearer of them, and whome you haue executed of late for the said murther, he, at the time of his said execution, tooke it upon his death, as he should answere before God, that he neuer caried any such letters, nor that the Queene was

Considering how the enemies of Mary Stuart, when CHAP.
they began to use the press to spread their charges III.
against her, did not usually disdain any weapon, 1568.
it becomes, after a challenge like Bishop Lesley's,
doubly strange that they continued to find it advisable to keep secret the mysterious declaration
ascribed to Paris.[1]

While there cannot rationally be entertained any
question as to Bothwell's criminality,[2] the writings
ascribed to Mary Stuart whose originals are lost, and
the so-called confessions of Paris, remain always the
sources which must essentially determine whether
the Queen is to be held as having had a share in his
murderous deed, or is to be acquitted of any complicity in it. In connection with the whole questions
in dispute, there are indeed various other considera-
tions on which stress has been laid, but no advance
towards a solution is made by such general consider-
ations as, for instance, that the sixteenth century
under the universal deep passionateness which was
nourished by the world-wide contest between Catholicism and Protestantism had in general another
standard for political murder than after ages, or by
maintaining that Mary Stuart was in this respect

participant, nor of counsayle in the
cause."— Lesley's *Defence of the
Honour of Marie*, in Anderson,
Collections, i. 19.

[1] Dr. Thomas Wilson, one of
Cecil's most zealous assistants also
wished to be able to publish the
declarations ascribed to Paris. In
a letter to Cecil of the 8th November 1571 (printed in Murdin, *State
Papers relating to Affairs in the
Reign of Queen Elizabeth*, p. 57),
Wilson begged that he might get
those declarations "closely sealed,"
and added that "it shall not be

knoun from whense it cumeth ;"
but his request was fruitless.

[2] Only with Goodall the historical scepticism is carried so far
that he devotes a whole chapter
(*Examination*, i. 332-404) to estu-
blish his doubt as to "whether the
Earl of Bothwell had a hand in the
murder of King Henry," and still
in a later publication he has, according to Laing (*History of Scotland*, i. 36), reiterated the assertion
"that there are people who do
not believe that he, Bothwell, was
guilty of that murder."

K

CHAP.
III.

1570.

only a daughter of her age, as evinced especially by the way in which she afterwards, during her imprisonment in England, received the news of the murder of her half-brother, Murray by James Hamilton of Bothwellhaugh, and settled on this Bothwellhaugh, a relative of the archbishop, a pension out of her estate as dowager queen of France.[1] Mary's conduct on this occasion we shall not here justify; but, on the one hand, it may be pointed out how she, at that time, steadily maintained that what had happened had happened without her command or knowledge,[2] and on the other hand it may be pleaded as an extenuating circumstance, that this same Hamilton of Bothwellhaugh had seen himself ruined for his fidelity towards her, since, after having fought at Langside, he had, along with the other Hamiltons, been outlawed, and by Murray's party been stripped of all he possessed.[3] In particular it is of importance to re-

[1] About this Mary wrote her ambassador in France, the Archbishop of Glasgow, in these terms: —"Ce que Bothwelhach a faict, a ésté sans mon commandement de quoy je luy sçay aussi bon gré et meilleur, que si j'eusse ésté du conseil. J'attend les memoires qui me doivent estre envoyez de la recepte de mon douaire, pour faire mon estat, où je n'oublieray la pension du dit Bothwelhach."— Labanoff, iii. 354.

[2] When, at Murray's death, it came to light that among other crown diamonds, which he had presented to his wife, he had also made over to the latter the famous "Great Henry," which was a gift to Mary Stuart from her father-in-law, Henry II. of France, and which the Queen had bequeathed to the Scottish crown, as a remem-

brance of herself and of the prince who had given it her, Mary wrote on this occasion to Murray's widow, and in the letter, which is dated 28th March 1570 (to be found in Strickland, vii. 62, 63) it is said:—"Albeit your late husband had so unnaturally and unthankfully offended us, . . . we desired not his blood shed . . . but maun be sorry for his death."

[3] [The story of Crawfurd about Murray's treatment of Hamilton's wife, although given in the original Danish edition of this work, has been omitted here with the author's consent. He is not, indeed, quite satisfied that Burton (*History of Scotland*, v. 13) has completely made out its want of authenticity. He remarks that in the *Acts of the Parliament of Scotland*, iii. 133 *nothing* is said of Hamilton's *wife*

member here that Mary had for a long time accus- CHAP.
tomed herself to look upon Murray in the same ___III.___
light in which he was also afterwards regarded by 1567.
her son, King James, namely, as the chief cause of all
her misfortunes.[1] In order to form a just opinion of
Scotland's Queen in the year 1567, we ought not to
take into account what she may have become during
years of imprisonment and sufferings, nor to judge of
her character from a few outbursts of an exasperation
which is more recent than the catastrophe by means
of which it was called forth, but rather to consider
what impression her previous character had left behind her. And the friends of her youth tell us that
they had never found in her the harsh or cruel disposition which opponents all at once ascribe to her ;
in the eyes of her French friends she appeared only
as " gentleness itself ; "[2] they fondly remembered
how that, during her stay in France, she never had
had pleasure or the heart to see others suffer, and
how she had, upon her journey back to Scotland,
expressly forbidden her uncle, the grand-prior, to
let any of the crew be punished on the galley which
carried her, as she could not bear to see it.[3] If,

and that the question is not, what
length of time she survived, but
whether she was not for some time
really mad.—*Translator.*]
  [1] Of James VI. Camden writes
in a letter of 22d November 1607
(*Sylloge Scriptorum de Vita Thuani*, Londini, 1733, fol. p. 9) to
De Thou : " Rex tamen noster,
Buchanano infensissimus, Moravi-
um noxæ maximæ damnat, ut
maternæ calamitatis fontem et
fundum, idque a secretorum eo
ævo participibus edoctus, ut
fertur."
  [2] Encore qu'elle fust la douceur

mesme. — Brantôme, *Vies   des
Dames Illustres*, in *Œuvres   du
Seigneur de Brantôme*, i. 495.

  [3] Jamais en France elle ne fit
cruauté, mesme n'a pris plaisir, ny
eu le cœur de voir défaire les
pauvres criminels par justice,
comme beaucoup de Grandes que
j'ai connues, et alors qu'elle estoit
dans sa galère ne voulut jamais
permettre, que l'on battit le moins
de monde un seul forçat, et en pria
le Grand-Prieur son oncle et le
commanda tres-expressément au
comité, ayant une compassion ex-

after all, we are to look away from the proper means
of proof under dispute, or from what is stated respecting these, we think, on the other hand, that a
general regard to the other contemporary averments,
by which the accusers have long ago exposed themselves, must of necessity, on the whole, very soon
weaken confidence in *their* charges; just as the
altered behaviour which latterly many of those
were led to adopt, who, after Darnley's removal,
had begun to take part against the Queen, or at
least had entertained the suspicion of her complicity
in his murder, cannot easily be understood otherwise than as their acknowledged reversal of the
testimony which they had formerly advanced, or,
at any rate, had not openly rejected. The political
party that accused Mary Stuart of complicity in the
catastrophe which ended Darnley's days, is the same
which has also accused her of having formerly wished
to poison him. Accordingly when Darnley, after
the baptism of his son at Stirling, had repaired to
his father in Glasgow, and had become violently
sick, partisans sought afterwards to explain the
bluish pustules which everywhere broke out on his
body as the consequence of poison which was said
to have been handed to him by Mary.[1] Yet un-
suspicious contemporaries, who wrote while Darnley
was still alive, have left express testimony to the
effect that it was the smallpox, which then raged in
Glasgow, by which Darnley became so seriously

trême le leur misère, et le cœur luy
en faisoit mal.—Brantôme, *Vies de
Dames Illustres*, in *Œuvres du
Seigneur de Brantôme*, i. 146.

[1] Cujus fraudis indices liuentes
pustulæ, quum Glascuam venisset,
toto corpore eruperunt, tanto cum

dolore, et omnium partium vexa-
tione, ut exigua vitæ spe duceret
spiritum, quum interim Regina ne
medicum quidem eum adire sit
passa.—Buchanan, *De Maria Scotorum Regina*, p. 13.

affected.[1]   By contemporary incontestable historical CHAP.
testimony it has been transmitted to posterity how III.
the young Mary Stuart took to heart the death of 1567.
her first consort, Francis II.; from it we know how
she day and night watched by his sick-bed, how her
own health after his death was weakened by the exer-
tion; but yet opponents were by no means ashamed
to spread the absurd report that she had already
poisoned her first husband in France, that she next
in Scotland took part in the murder of her second
husband, and here finally she had also destined for
the third, meaning Bothwell, the same fate.[2]   With
however much solicitude both Scottish and English
contemporary rulers, who specially wished to put a
gulf between Mary and her son, willingly sought to
cut off every connection between them, they have
yet not been able to deprive after ages of all
evidence of the cordial sympathy with which the
imprisoned mother in England clung to her " poor

[1] The King is now at Glasgow
with his father, and there lieth full
of *the smallpokes; to whom the Queen
hath sent her physician.*—The Earl
of Bedford's words in a letter to
Cecil, dated Berwick, 9th January
1567, and cited in Chalmers, *Life
of Mary Queen of Scots,* ii. 178.
My Lord Darnley lieth sick at
Glasgow of the small pocks, which
disease beginneth to spread thene.
—Sir William Drury's letter to
Cecil, dated Berwick, 23d January
1567, cited in Chalmers, ii. 548,
and more completely communicated in Tytler, *Hist. of Scot.,*
vii. 364-365.   The Diary of a
contemporary likewise mentions,
on the 14th January 1567, Mary's
consort as "the kingis grace,
hir husband, quha then was
lying seik in the Castell of Glasgow in the polkis" (*Diurnal of

Remarkable Occurrents, p. 105);
and in another Diary it is said as
to this about the same time: "King
Henrey wes layand seike in Glasgow of the small poks, bot some
sayed he had gottene poysone."—
The Diarey of Robert Birrell, in
Fragments of Scottish History, p.
6.   The above-cited account of
Bedford, that Mary had sent one
of her physicians to Darnley, stands
also in direct opposition to the
accusation which makes any such
care to be denied him.

[2] Dr. Thomas Wilson's Account
of the year 1571 in Murdin, *State
Papers relating to affairs in the
reign of Queen Elizabeth,* p. 57.
Although Wilson as his authority
here even refers to the Bishop of
Ross then imprisoned in the Tower,
yet such an appeal to one of Mary
Stuart's faithful friends and de-

CHAP. child" left behind in Scotland.[1]   Yet not the less
III. there came to be added to the other charges by
1568. which she was formerly persecuted by her antagonists this also, that she was said likewise to have
attempted the life of her child, an accusation which
Mary herself has already met with these words
which remind us of the reply of Marie Antoinette
to the tribunal of the Revolution : " A mother's
love to her child confutes them."[2]   Soon after
there appears a change in the conduct of most of
her antagonists.   The year after the conferences

fenders makes the charge certainly
not the less absurd.
    [1] Among the gifts which Mary
during her imprisonment in England frequently sent to her little
son, left behind in his fatherland,
but which, both on the Scottish
and English side, found hinder-
ances in the way of reaching their
destination, are mentioned small
articles of dress, a pair of ponies,
eight small cannons cased in velvet, and similar presents.   One
of her letters to him, which was
stopped and taken from him, speaks
thus : " Deir sone, I send ze this
bearer to see zow and bring me
word how ze do, and to remember
zow that ze have in me a loving
moder that wishes zow to learne in
tyme to love, knaw, and feir God,
and nixt that, conform to Goddis
command and gud nature to remember ye dowtie anent hir yat
hes borne zow in her sydes.   I
send zow a buik to learne the
samyn, and I pray God zow may
learne yat beginning, and that He
vill give zow His blessing, as I do
hartlie give zow myne, in hoip zow
sall deserve it quhan zow come to
discretion, quhilk I pray God to
send zow with ane long and gud
lyf, and to me a blyth sicht of zow
as of my deir belovit sone.—Your

loving and gud moder, Marie R."
The letter, which is written from
Tutbury, 22d January 1569, and
addressed " To my deir sone, James
Charles, Prince of Scotland," has,
with several more after a copy in
the British Museum, been communicated by L. Wiesener in his
Marie Stuart et Jacques VI., cinc
lettres inédites de Marie Stuart, in
Revue des Questions Historiques
(deuxième année, tome troisième,
Paris, 1867), pp. 459-97.
    [2] And as to that quhair thay
alledge " that we sould have bene
the occasioun to cause our sone follow his father haistelie," thay cover
thameselfis thairanent with a weit
sack ;   and that calumnie sould
suffice for pruif and inquisitioun
of all the rest ; for the natural love
of a mother towardis hir bairn con-
foundis thame.—Letter of Mary
Stuart from Bolton Castle, 19th
December 1568 ; Labanoff, ii. 258.
At the accusation for also having
wished to destroy her own son,
Marie Antoinette at a later period
burst forth (Poujoulat, Histoire de
la Révolution Française.   Tours,
1848, ii. 81) : " Si je n'ai pas ré-
pondu c'est que la nature se refuse
à une pareille accusation faite à
une mère ; j'en appelle à toutes les
mères."

in England saw William Maitland, laird of Lething- CHAP.
ton, William Kirkaldy, laird of Grange, and others of III.
the Queen's former accusers take her side ; for after 1573.
Kirkaldy had liberated Maitland from the prison in
which he had been lodged by Murray, both the
deliverer and the delivered set themselves for an
obstinate defence of Edinburgh Castle ; with the
brave garrison of which, or the so-called " Castilians,"
they held the fortress in Mary's name, until at length,
on the 29th May 1573, they were compelled to yield
to the Earl of Morton's besieging army, now rein-
forced by English auxiliaries and English artillery.
Vacillation was indeed generally characteristic of
party men during Scotland's agitated Reformation
time,[1] and though in their heart these thought very
little of the crime of regicide, yet that a wife should
have brought about the death of her consort in the
way in which the Queen had been charged could only
awaken abhorrence in every age. The charge seems
therefore to have been also rejected even by those
who, like Kirkaldy and Maitland, ended their political life as open partisans of the Queen, and as
victims to her cause.[2] The subsequent conduct of
the English commissioners still more strongly tells

[1] This fickleness of political character has, in Maitland's case, been
portrayed in the at that time
well-known personal satire " Cham-
æleon, written by Mr. George
Buchanan against the laird of
Lethington."—Georgii Buchanani
Opera omnia, curante Thoma Rud-
dimanno (Edinburgi, 1715), fol.
ii. 13-18.

[2] The lairds of Grange and Lethington preferred, when Edinburgh
Castle could no longer be kept
possession of, to surrender them-

selves to the English commander,
Sir William Drury, and sent Queen
Elizabeth a written petition to
rescue them. She chose however
to hand them over to the Earl of
Morton, but before the latter caused
the chivalrous Kirkaldy, "the
second Wallace," to be hanged,
Maitland had ended his days, according to the supposition made by
some, by taking poison, or as Sir
James Melvil (Memoirs of Sir
James Melvil, p. 122) expresses it,
" after the old Roman fashion, as
was said."

against the trustworthiness of the proofs of the Queen's alleged guilt with which they had been made acquainted. It has been remarked that the English commissioners, whose number was increased on the removal of the conferences to Westminster, could not, during the very cursory collation made of the letters which the Scots passed off as written by Mary with those which Elizabeth furnished for comparison with them, find any difference in the handwriting, and it was in consideration of this that they so far met the secret wish of Elizabeth, as, without in other respects then pronouncing for or against the guilt of the Scottish Queen, to find it not quite becoming for Mary to be granted admission to Elizabeth's presence so long as the dismal affair stood as it now did.[1] But just as the Earl of Sussex, both a prudent and zealous partisan of Elizabeth, and also one of her commissioners at York, after there seeing the privately produced proofs which the Scots brought along with them, was not then so fully convinced as to be able to withhold the opinion that should the matter be taken up in a purely legal way, the Scottish Queen would, by such an examination of the evidences, have the advantage on her side,[2] and as at least the Spanish ambassador in England was able afterwards during the conference in Westminster to state that some of the English statesmen who took part

---

[1] Goodall, ii. 260.

[2] If her adverse party accuse her of the murder by producing of her letters, she will deny them, and accuse the most of them of manifest consent to the murder, hardly to be denied, so as upon the trial on both sides her proofs will judicially fall best out, as it is thought.— Letter from the Earl of Sussex to Cecil, dated York, 22d October 1568 ; Lodge, *Illustrations of British History in the reigns of Henry VIII., Edward VI., Mary, Elizabeth, and James I.* (London, 1791), 4to, i. 458.

in this had complained of, and partly resisted, the CHAP.
pressure which the English government sought to
exercise to the ruin of the Scottish Queen,[1] so only   1569-72.
a short time elapsed ere Thomas Howard, Duke of
Norfolk, the foremost and most powerful of the
English commissioners at York and Westminster,
appeared as suitor for the hand of the imprisoned
Mary Stuart, and this suitor is supported by several
of the other English grandees, who along with him
had had at Westminster the best opportunity for
enabling them to form a judgment about the forthcoming proofs against the Scottish Queen.   Certainly
it may be said that the Duke of Norfolk by his proposed marriage, for which Elizabeth first sent him
to the Tower and afterwards to the scaffold, allowed
himself to be led away by ambition; certainly the
Catholic sympathies, animating the Earls of Northumberland and Westmoreland, contributed to the
warmth with which these especially also embraced,
to their own ruin, the design of the Protestant Norfolk; but none of them could yet have forgotten how
they had recently seen Mary represented by the
renegade Scots at the conference as a murderess of
the worst description, and human nature must
certainly have, during the last three hundred years,
undergone an incredible change if the Duke of Norfolk still continued to retain any confidence in that
representation when he was seized with the desire
of laying this woman's hand in his, or of placing her
in the highest circles of the English aristocracy,

[1] Dichos señores havian mostrado
algun valor y contrastado un poco
la furia terribile con que el secre-
tario Cecil queria perder aquella
señora.—Account from Don Guer-
aldo de Espes to Philip II. of 1st
January 1569 ; Lingard, *History
of England* (fifth edition, Paris,
1840), v. 162.

and these at the same time approving of the idea,
accepted from the beginning, that she should
also become the recognised successor of Elizabeth.
The most remarkable evidence of a change in the
judgment regarding Mary is however one which
more recent times have enabled us to procure; it
concerns Darnley's own mother. Lady Margaret
Lennox had at last been able to see her son approach
the splendour to which he seemed to her by his relationship to be called both in England and Scotland;
she had lived to enjoy the happiness of being able to
greet her son with the regal title. When this glory
had come so abruptly to an end on Darnley's murder,
Lady Lennox is found at first also among those
who forthwith unhesitatingly condemned Mary as a
murderess; but a mother's strong feeling now drove
her forward in an opposite direction. After Mary
had fled to England she wrote in her despair to
Elizabeth, asking her to take judicial proceedings
against the fugitive,[1] and in this she was backed up
by those English statesmen who at once had wished
to have Mary considered as a prisoner of war, in
remembrance of the use which she had formerly
allowed herself to make of the English coat of
arms, and with reference to Darnley's having been
born an English subject. The mother-in-law's disposition could not long remain unknown, and some
years passed ere Mary from her prison at Chats-

---

[1] Darnlii enim mater, Comitissa
Lenoxiæ, jam pridem lachrymis
oppleta, suo maritique nomine apud
Elisabetham gravem instituerat
querimoniam, utque in judicium
de filii cæde vocaretur, obsecrarat.
—Camdeni *Annales rerum Anglicarum et Hibernicarum regnante*
Elizabetha, p. 138. In a painting
of Lady Lennox of the year 1565
her hair is still fair; in the painting in Hampton Court, in which
she is represented in widow's dress,
she appears as an old lady with
snow-white hair.

worth thus wrote on the 16th July 1570 to her :— CHAP.
III.
" Madam, if the wronge and false reportes of
ennemies, well knowen for traytors to you, and alas   1570.
too muche trusted of me by your advise, had not so
far sturred you against my innocency, (and I must
saie against all kindnes,) that you have not onelie,
as it were, condemned me wrongfullie, but so hated,
as your woordes and deedes hath testefied to all the
worlde a manifest misliking in you against your
owne blood, I would not have obmitted thus long
my duelie in writing to you, excusing me of those
untrew reportes made of me ; but hoping, with
Goddes grace and tyme, to have my innocencie
knowen to you, as I trust it is alreadie to the most
part of all indifferent persons, I thought best not to
trouble you for a tyme."[1]   When Lady Lennox
received the letter from which these words are
taken she sent it to her husband, who had by this
time, in consequence of the death of Murray, become
Regent of Scotland, and in a confidential reply which
the Earl of Lennox on this occasion wrote his wife,
he declared that he was assured of Mary's guilt not
only by his " own knowledge, but by her handwrit,
the confessions of men gone to the death, and other
infallible experience."[2]   The Earl, who assuredly knew
Mary's handwriting, refers here also to the disputed
documents contained in the silver casket.   He continues thus : " It will be a long time, which will be
necessary to bring so notorious an affair into forget-
fulness, to make black white, or to show innocency
where the opposite is so well known.   The most

[1] The letter, which is addressed
"To my Ladie Lennox, my mother-
in-lawe," is found in Labanoff, iii.
77-78.

[2] Letter of the Earl of Lennox.
—Robertson, *History of Scotland*,
ii. 348.

impartial persons upon whom I rely doubt not about the justice of your and my cause and about the righteous occasion of your displeasure. Her right obligation towards you and me, as the parties interested therein, would be a true confession and her sincere repentance for that dolorous deed, as offensive for her to speak of as it is sorrowful for us to think upon. God is just, and will not in length of time let himself be deceived ; but as he has revealed the truth, so will he punish the wrong." After the Earl of Lennox meanwhile had during the continued party strife been slain like Murray, and was succeeded by the Earl of Morton as Regent in Scotland, we find Mary, in one of her letters from Sheffield to her ambassador in Paris, the Archbishop of Glasgow, expressing her joy at the good understanding which had now arisen between her and the widow of Lennox : " I praise God," writes the Queen, " that she now day by day comprehends still more the falseness and the evil designs of those who formerly made use of her name against myself."[1] We meet still more decidedly with the same assurance of her mother-in-law's acknowledgment of her " innocence," in a later letter from the imprisoned Queen, when Lady Lennox was dead, dated Sheffield, 2d May 1578, and likewise addressed to James Beaton in Paris : " Lady Countess Lennox, my mother-in-law," so it is said in this letter, " is dead a month ago. This good lady had, God be praised ! given me good amends, since we have for five out of six years been in correspondence, and has by letters

[1] Je loue Dieu qu'elle congnosse de jour en jour l'infidellité et perverse intention de ceulx qui se sont aultres-foys aydés de son nom contre moy mesmes.—Letter of Mary Stuart of 5th November 1577 ; Labanoff, iv. 398.

written with her own hand, which I preserve,
avowed to me the wrong which she had done me by
her unrighteous prosecutions, set on foot as she has
let me understand with her consent, because she had
been badly informed."[1] With this letter entirely
agree some words in a report furnished to Elizabeth
the 16th April 1583 by the Earl of Shrewsbury and
Robert Beal, the clerk of the Privy Council, who
had, in the name of the English Queen, been sent
to Mary in her prison. Among other expressions of
hers they mention also this : " Not the less doubt I
not that my innocence is already well known to all
the princes of Christendom. Also I am confident
that many others, who at first thought hardly of
me, have now been satisfied, as, for example, my
mother-in-law before her death, whereof I have
letters and tokens." At these words she pointed
to a little diamond ring on her finger as showing[2]
that Lady Lennox had acknowledged that she had
been deceived, and that Mary was guiltless of her
husband's death. Mary's letter to the Archbishop
of Glasgow, which has already been long known,
and her expressions to Shrewsbury and Beal, which
later times first brought to light, have been as a
mere self-written testimony pronounced unworthy of
credit by those authors who are in general most
disposed to see in her only the lying deceiver.[3]
But in the most recent times a proof has come to
light which, at least in this respect, justifies the

[1] Et m'a avoué par lettres écrites
de sa main, que je garde, le tort
qu'elle m'avoit fait en ses injustes
poursuites, dressées, comme elle me
l'a fait entendre, par son consente-
ment, pour avoir été mal informée.
—Labanoff, v. 31.

[2] " As one declaring."—The Account of Shrewsbury and Beal to
Elizabeth.—Raumer, *Die Königinnen Elisabeth und Maria*, p.
332.
[3] By Laing, *History of Scotland*,
ii. 176, and by Raumer, 335.

Queen.   It is a letter from the Countess of Lennox
to Mary, found among the English State papers.
It is written from Hackney, 6th November 1575.
The letter dwells upon their common solicitude for
" our sweet and peerless jewel in Scotland," Darnley's and Mary's son, the little King James VI., and
on their common care lest " the wicked governor
(the Earl of Morton) should have power to do ill to
his person ;" it expresses the warmest sympathy for
the Queen, and is subscribed, " Your Majesty's most
humble and loving mother and aunt, Margaret
Lennox."   " I beseech your Majesty," thus writes
Darnley's mother, " fear not, but trust in God that
all shall be well; the treachery of your traitors is
known better than before."[1]   It is the mother of
the murdered one who thus writes.

[1] Letter of Margaret Lennox to
Mary Stuart in Agnes Strickland's
Lives of the Queens of Scotland
(London, 1852-59), v. 374.   Miss
Strickland has for the first time
communicated this remarkable
letter and accompanied it with a
facsimile ; later it has again been
reprinted by Teulet, pp. 246-48.
Miss Strickland found it among
Cecil's papers ; forgotten or overlooked among these, this justifica-
tion now comes forward from the
same side from which the cruelest
persecution of Mary Stuart formerly proceeded.

CHAPTER IV.

DIFFERENT from the question about Mary's share in the murder of Darnley, although often mixed up with it, is the question whether she had before the death of Darnley thrown herself into the arms of Bothwell. As positive testimonies on this point, there meet us again in the first rank those much controverted documents formerly mentioned. The declaration of Paris has been readily referred to as an evidence of an unusual intimacy which had even before the death of Darnley sprung up between the Queen and Bothwell,[1] and in one of the sonnets ascribed to Mary she herself bluntly says :

" Pour lui aussi ie jetté mainte larme,
Premier qu'il se fust de ce corps possesseur,

[1] Item interrogé des premiér es pryveauté qu'il a connu estre entre la Royne et Monsieur de Boduel ? Respond que c'estoit alors que ledit Sieur de Boduel conduysoit la Royne vers Glasgow, quand elle alloit quérir le Roy. A Calandar après souper assez tard, Lady Reyres vint à la chambre de Monsieur de Boduel, et voyt ledict Paris là et demande : " Que faict ce Paris ici ?" " C'est tout un, ce dit-il ; Paris ne dyra chose que je luy deffende de dire." Et là-dessus elle l'amène à la chambre de la Royne.—Interrogé, s'il scavait aucune privauté entre la Royne et Monsieur de Boduel durant le temps que le Roy gysoit à Kirk-of-Field ? Respond, que Monsieur de Boduel lui avoit dict que, toutes les nuyts, Jehan Hepburn feroit le guet soubs les galleries à Saincte-Croix, ce pendant que Lady Reires yroyt bien tard le quérir pour l'amener à la chambre de la Royne ; lui déffendant, assavoir à Paris, sur la vie, de dire que sa femme estoyt avecques luy.—The Examination of Paris, the 10th August 1569 ; Laing, *History of Scotland*, ii. 284-288, and in Teulet, *Lettres*, pp. 97-103.

Duquel alors il n'avait pas le cœur ;
Puis me donna un autre dur alarme,
Quand il versa de son sang mainte dragme,
Dont de grief me vint lesser douleur
Qui m'en pensa oster la vie, et frayeur
De perdre, las ! le seul rempar qui m'arme.
Pour luy depuis j'ay mesprisé l'honneur,
Ce qui nous peult seul pourvoir de bonheur ;
Pour luy j'ay hazardé grandeur et conscience ;
Pour luy tous mes parentz j'ay quité et amis ;
Et tous autres respetz sont apart mis ;
Brief de vous seul je cherche l'alliance."[1]

While on the side of the defenders of Mary
the first three of these famous lines have been
thus explained, that the forgers have here from
want of attention been led themselves to disclose
an historical fact, namely, that the Queen's affection
for Bothwell first was shown after he had carried her
off by force to Dunbar Castle,[2] and that the two
following lines must be understood of some hidden
fact or other which has not become known to us ;
on the side of her assailants it is stated, on the
contrary, as an unquestionable assertion that by
the lines in question there can only be intended the
manner in which Bothwell had, on the 8th October
1566, been wounded by John Elliot in front of
Hermitage Castle, and the violent fever of the
Queen consequent on her visit to him, and her
return on horseback to Jedburgh, and that we thus
have the sonnets attributed to her, a confession from
herself that she had even before that event, long
ere Darnley's death, entirely given herself up to
Bothwell.

When and how this had really come to pass, that

---

[1] The Sonnets ; Laing, *History of Scotland*, ii. 230, and Teulet, p. 73.

[2] *Mary Queen of Scots vindicated*, by John Whitaker (London, 1790), iii. 78, 83-105.

author undertook to tell the world whom Mary's CHAP.
contemporaries, both countrymen and foreigners, IV.
willingly recognised as the most gifted in Scotland. 1506-20.
George Buchanan wrote his interpretation of the
letters and sonnets ascribed to Mary Stuart, and his
description received such an impress of his energetic
and bright genius that, after the lapse of three
centuries, it still retains its influence. Buchanan's
famous pamphlet is still the foundation for the
common representation of the relations of Mary
to Bothwell, whether it be made use of at first
hand or not.

In order to form a general estimate of the value
of this work, the standpoint must not be left out of
consideration on which its author was then placed.
Born in the year 1506 at a farm-house, in the parish
of Killearn, in the county of Stirling, where the
vernacular language at that time may be assumed
to have been Gaelic, of an ancient race, but of poor
parents, he was sent, when still a youth, by a
maternal uncle, who had early noticed his great
talents, to the University of Paris in the year 1520.
His uncle's death and his own poverty compelled him
after two years to give up his studies there, and he
then enlisted among French auxiliaries who, at that
period, were sent over for service in Scotland against
the English; but a night march through deep snow
speedily threw him upon a bed of protracted sickness,
and sent him back again to his books. He then
became at the University of St. Andrews one of the
students of John Major, the same who, in applying
the doctrine maintained by the councils of the
fifteenth century that the Pope indeed received his
power from God, but in case of need could be

L

deprived of it by the Church, in the sixteenth taught
that kings likewise certainly possessed a power transmitted from father to son, but that equally in the
secular sphere the fundamental authority lay with
the community, so that a ruler injurious to the
people, who showed himself incorrigible, could be
deposed by them. Following Major to Paris, Buchanan became for some time professor in the
College of Saint-Barbe, until the affection shown
him by a young Scottish nobleman, the Earl of
Cassilis, Gilbert Kennedy, induced him to accompany the Earl for five years as tutor; and this
position, when the Earl had come of age, after
their return to Scotland in the year 1534, again
procured him a similar appointment—James v.
having chosen him as tutor for one of his sons.[1] By
this time Buchanan's inclination toward Protestant
ideas manifested itself in the poem which he published against the Franciscans, entitled *Somnium*,
in which he represents St. Francis as appearing to
him in a dream, and requiring him to enter his
Order, against which step Buchanan then adduces his
reasons. James v., who was at that time displeased
with the Franciscans, encouraged him to proceed
further against them, and accordingly Buchanan
next wrote the poem *Franciscanus*, one of the
most biting satires which any language contains,
and consequently found himself assailed, not merely

[1] For James Stuart, whose
mother was Elizabeth Shaw of the
Sauchie family. This son, who
died in the year 1548, has often
been confounded with the most
celebrated of the natural sons of
James v., the afterwards so famous
Earl of Murray, who was also
named James Stuart, but whose
mother was Margaret Erskine,
latterly married to Sir Robert
Douglas of Lochleven.—David
Irving, *Memoirs of the Life and
Writings of George Buchanan*
(Edinburgh, 1817), p. 17.

by the monks, but by the whole Church. The charge of heresy, specially pressed by Cardinal David Beaton, and his abandonment by James V., caused him in the year 1539 to be cast into prison. Many of the Scots, who were at the same period like him committed to prison for Lutheranism, were burnt at the stake, and others were obliged publicly to recant their heresies, but Buchanan succeeded in escaping, and by way of England again reached Paris.[1] But as he here once more met his deadly foe Cardinal Beaton, who was Scottish Ambassador in France, he found it advisable to pass right on to Bordeaux. There for three years he acted as teacher in the College of Guyenne, which was under the charge of the learned Portuguese Andreas Govea. In accordance with its rules, which required that there should be every year new dramatic performances, he penned two specimens of his poetic genius (Latin tragedies), and translated two of the Greek plays of Euripides. Here also he took occasion, in the name of his college, to celebrate the passage through the city of the Emperor Charles V., in a poem which the latter graciously accepted at Bordeaux on the 1st December 1539. To this city also he was, however, pursued by the malignity of Cardinal Beaton, the Cardinal having written to the Archbishop of Bordeaux that Buchanan was a heretic who had fled from a just punishment in his native country ; but the intervention of French friends was able to stop the persecution here. It was the plague which in the year 1543 first drove him from Bordeaux,

---

[1] In his fuit Georgius Buchananus, qui sopitis custodibus per cubiculi fenestram evaserat. — Buchanani, *Rer. Scot. Hist.* p. 167.

and thus it came about that the celebrated Montaigne is able to tell in his Essays how in his youth, on his family estate, he had had Buchanan for one of his instructors. Buchanan's friend and well-wisher, Andreas Govea, was some years afterwards recalled to his native land for the purpose of undertaking the direction of the newly-instituted University in Coimbra. Hither, in the year 1547, Buchanan followed, at the summons of Govea that he should not only come himself, but also bring with him from France a colony of teachers to Portugal, which, at a time when almost the whole of Europe besides was, or was about to be, involved in external or internal war, Buchanan considered (as he has himself said) the corner of the world where it was most likely that he would be able to find rest. But after a brief season of good fortune, persecution by the Church woke up anew on the death of his protector in the year 1548, there being now added to the old complaints about his poem *Franciscanus* new ones for his violation of Lent, and his utterances in favour of the doctrines of the Reformers. When Buchanan for two years and a half had had the Portuguese inquisitors for his tormentors, he was shut up in a monastery in order the better to be taught the principles of the Romish Church ; and it was here that he began his famous Latin translation of the Psalms. On being set at liberty John III. sought still to retain him in his service ; but, without waiting for permission, Buchanan seized the opportunity of getting away offered him by the arrival at Lisbon of a Candiote ship bound for England. From England he again went immediately to France, where some time afterwards

Marshal Brissac, commanding a French army in CHAP.
Piedmont, engaged him as tutor for his son. After IV.
having passed a series of years in this situation, now 1560-71.
in Italy and now in France, and having among other
things written a poem on the occasion of Mary
Stuart's nuptials with the Dauphin, Buchanan at
length returned to his native country in the year 1560
just as Catholicism there was virtually overthrown.
As Murray had become the head of the Government,
he made Buchanan, who henceforward appeared as
his most devoted adherent, Rector of St. Leonard's
College in the University of St. Andrews. Later he
was, though a layman, appointed Moderator of the
General Assembly in the year 1567, and in the following year Murray, after Mary's flight to Elizabeth,
sent him to England as one of the Scots designated ·
to attend the Conferences at York and Westminster,
an opportunity of which he then availed himself to
dedicate some verses to Elizabeth.

This was George Buchanan's position, and thus
had he been prepared for the anonymous publication
against Scotland's Queen which, after Murray's
death, issued from his pen at the close of the year
1571, and was printed in London and addressed to
Elizabeth—the first and most dangerous of all the
writings that have attacked the name of Mary
Stuart.[1]

In this work Buchanan relates how the Queen,
being delivered of a son in the castle of Edinburgh,
in June 1566, afterwards made her escape by the
river Forth from Edinburgh to Alloa, the residence

[1] De Maria Scotorum Regina,   et rabie, horrendo insuper et de-
totaque ejus contra Regem conjura- terrimo ejusdem parricidio : plena
tione, fœdo cum Bothuellio adul-   et tragica plano historia, Londini,
terio, nefaria in maritum crudelitate 1571, 8vo.

of the Earl of Mar, and on her return in September
did not for some days take up her abode in Holyrood Palace, but instead, according to the frequent
custom of the Scottish monarchs,[1] first stayed in a
private dwelling, and afterwards in the so-called
" Exchequer House" in Edinburgh, while Bothwell
resided in the vicinity with his adherent David
Chalmers of Ormond, also well known as an author.
Not without a certain amount of ready sarcasm,
which does not exactly suit well with the " tragic"
character of his history, but in an eloquent style,
and in the flowing Latin in which that period
sought to vie with antiquity, Buchanan sets forth
circumstantially enough how Bothwell is said to
have surprised the Queen by night, but how the
violence of which Buchanan says she afterwards
complained must in reality only pass as feigned,
because she herself, without necessity, some nights
afterwards suddenly caused Bothwell to be summoned to her, employing as her messenger Lady
Reres, one of her Court ladies, who is here designated as a former mistress of Bothwell.[2] On the
ground of this representation, Buchanan then finds
only too explicable the interest which in the following month took the Queen from Jedburgh to
visit the wounded Earl, and thus, according to him,
the relations between the Queen and Bothwell
were before that time plainly enough settled.

[1] Thus when Mary Stuart, after
having fled from Holyrood on the
occasion of the murder of Riccio,
had returned victorious to Edinburgh, she would not immediately
take up her abode in the Palace,
but resided at first in "my Lord
Home's lodging, callit the auld
bishope of Dunkell, his lodging."

(*Diurnal of Occurrents*, p. 94.)
Some days afterwards she removed
to a house on the eminence towards the castle, where her mother
the Queen Regent had formerly
dwelt [on the site now occupied
by the Free Church College].

[2] Note F, Appendix.

With a liberty which only the Latin muse permits, CHAP.
he represents her as one who, long before the death
of ·Darnley, was wont openly to rest in Bothwell's   1566.
arms, and who also, after her husband's death,
had, without shame, already clung to Bothwell ere
he carried her away to Dunbar. In its form the
work reminds us of the most celebrated Philippics
of classic antiquity, in which one single light colour,
one single softening in the picture would have
been contrary to the rules of rhetoric, and the
accusation rises gradually to a climax.

The attack of Buchanan on Mary Stuart called
forth on her part the deepest indignation. Nor
even yet can one easily free himself from an unfavourable impression when he turns over the leaves
of one of the volumes in which Buchanan's collected
writings were published after his death, when in
one part of this volume he finds Buchanan's hateful
attack on the Queen, and in another his beautiful
verses in celebration of " Caledonia's Nymph,"[1] or
turns over the leaves in the other poems in which
his muse at an earlier period, on more than one
occasion, had presented incense to her. Mary
who, since her sojourn in France, was wont
to spend a fixed part of the day in reading,[2] had
been, after her return to Scotland, instructed by
Buchanan in Latin, in which she had already as a
child made great progress. In Scotland, when in
her twentieth year, she read every afternoon a

[1] In the dedication to Mary of
his translation of the Psalms :—
" Nympha, Caledoniæ quæ nunc feliciter
    oræ
Missa per innumeros sceptra tueris avos ;
Quæ sortem antevenis meritis, virtutibus
    annos,
Sexum animis, morum nobilitate genus."

[2] Tant qu'elle a esté en France,
elle se reservoit tousjours deux
heures du jour pour estudier et
lire.—Brantôme, *Vies des Dames
Illustres*, in *Œuvres du Seigneur
de Brantôme*, i. 125.

CHAP.
IV.

1564.
portion of Livy with him.[1] Nor had she withheld her assistance from him ; for though it is not indeed certain that Buchanan is, in so many words, said to have been indebted to Mary for protection from the dangers which had threatened him while in France, yet it is undoubted that in the year 1564 she rewarded his literary and poetical services by granting him the revenues of the Abbey of Cross-raguel on the death of Quintin Kennedy.[2] No wonder then that Mary Stuart, at a later period, described Buchanan's attack as an abominable pro-ceeding. After the publication of his shameless production, she saw in him only a "lewd and atheistical man,"[3] and during her imprisonment in England regarded it as the bitterest injury that the Scottish government resolved to select this man for instructor to her son.[4] When James VI. reached his majority, he also owned himself to be actually of his mother's opinion against Buch-anan ; for though he had the latter not the least to thank, as his teacher, for his learning and the inclination to study, which even in his eighteenth year made him an author, and afterwards led him to publish so great a series of writings, yet the young King caused the Scottish Parlia-

[1] The Queen readeth daily after her dinner, instructed by a learned man, Mr. George Buchanan, some-what of Livy.—Randolph's Letter to Cecil, dated 7th April 1562 ; Calendar of State Papers, Foreign Series, 1561-1562, p. 584.

[2] David Irving's Lives of Scot-tish Writers, Edinburgh, 1851, i. 80.

[3] She said that the worst that was possible had already been done against her, namely, that one had in London and France printed the book of Buchanan, "that lewd and atheistical man."—Account of Shrewsbury and Beal to Elizabeth, of 16th April 1583, Raumer's Die Königinnen Elisabeth und Maria Stuart, p. 332.

[4] In a letter from Sheffield of 4th March 1571, she beseeches the French Ambassador in London, la Motte Fénélon, to get Elizabeth to exert her influence that her son might obtain another teacher in the room of Buchanan.—Labanoff, iii. 201.

ment, in the year 1584, in an Act against de- CHAP.
faming the King or his ancestors, also to issue a IV.
condemnation of the most important of Buchanan's 1584.
works, dedicated to the young King himself, namely,
his famous, almost republican, dialogue *De jure
Regni apud Scotos*, first printed in Edinburgh in the
year 1579, and his great History of Scotland, first
printed in Edinburgh in the year 1582, shortly before
the author's death. Before Buchanan, in the eighty-
seventh year of his age, ended his days (on the 28th
September 1582), his royal scholar repeatedly required him to recall what he had, in the seventeenth
and eighteenth books of his History, again so posi-
tively reiterated about the King's mother, and to
leave to posterity an evidence of his regret ; but Buchanan declined to obey this order, and on the contrary left it to the King so to deal with his writings
after his death as the King might think proper.

The mother's resentment and the son's displeasure have been alike unable to paralyse the
effect of Buchanan's attack. Even more recent
authors, as the elder Robertson, Malcolm Laing,
and Mignet, have not feared to appeal to Buchanan
as a valid witness where there was a question
about Mary's relations to Bothwell. But we may
well ask—Has he a real title to be so regarded ?
Can a really unbiassed critic find in his attack a
reliable historical representation ? A contemporary
of Buchanan has already remarked that, especially
in his older days, he had become too prone to
allow himself to be led by his associates, so that,
without taking heed, he wrote according to what
these said to him ; that he willingly followed the
current of public opinion, and was by no means

free from an inclination to persecute those against
whom he had become prejudiced.[1]   Because he thus
made himself an echo of what his associates accepted
or mentioned as notorious, we need not perhaps
pronounce him destitute of good faith ; the change
in the mood in which Buchanan at the beginning
had bowed himself before the splendour that surrounded Mary's first appearance, may possibly in
part have resulted from the feudal feeling which
bound him to the family of Lennox, just as it had
attracted Knox with a special interest to Bothwell,
partly from the affection which led Buchanan, in one
of his poems, to address a Prince like Darnley as
" *optime rex*,"[2] and which certainly also caused him,
more than many others, to be shocked, and to feel
resentment at the tidings of Darnley's murder ;
but the exaggerations and distortions which filled
the whole atmosphere which Buchanan breathed
cannot by that means be made sure historical evidence.   His attack on Mary Stuart can only be
considered, and must necessarily be judged, as a
party production.   At the time Buchanan accompanied Murray to the Conference in England, the
Scots, having brought from Scotland the letters
ascribed to Mary, drew up a general view of her
previous conduct in Scotland as a means of guidance to the English Commissioners for their
understanding of the letters.   This partial charge
Buchanan made the foundation of his rhetorical

[1] He was also religious, but was
easily abused, and so facile, that he
was led by every company that he
haunted, which made him factious
in his old days, for he spoke and
wrote as those who were about him
informed him ; for he was become
careless, following in many things
the vulgar opinion ; for he was
naturally popular, and extremely
revengeful against any man who
had offended him, which was his
greatest fault.—*The Memoirs of
Sir James Melvil*, p. 125.

[2] Georgii Buchanani *Poemata
quæ extant*, p. 392.

declamation; and as he followed it so far as it CHAP.
ascribed to Mary a guilty hand in Darnley's murder, IV.
so did he also in his representation of the love-rela- 1571.
tions to Bothwell ascribed to her. In some places
he has rendered the language in that accusation
almost verbatim, in others he has either abridged or
expanded it. The last remark holds good of the
manner in which Buchanan's pamphlet represents
the origin of the Queen's dealing with Bothwell
through Lady Reres, Mary's messenger to him.
Admitting that suspicion might thus have been easily
awakened, as there at least occurs in the declaration
which was made by Darnley's valet, Thomas Nelson,
when examined after his master's death—an expression to the effect that the Queen, when at Darnley's
last place of residence, was usually pleased of an
evening with Lady Reres to go down into the
garden to sing and make sport;[1] might it not be
some natural frolicsomeness of the youthful Queen
similar to that which she had shown on an earlier
occasion, which was also misconstrued by her associates as a criminal errand? The authorities to
which Buchanan here refers cannot, at all events,
awaken confidence. He has, indeed, added that the
Queen herself is said to have spoken before different
persons of her misconduct as having occurred in the
manner stated by him; but of these persons he has,
however, expressly adduced only two, and these
two in any accusation against Mary are not
entitled to confidence, since they are no other
than Murray himself and his mother, Margaret
Erskine, sister of the Earl of Mar, one of the mis-

[1] For upon the nyt sche usit with
the lady Rereis to ga furth to the
garding and ther to sing and use
pastyme. — The Declaration of
Thomas Nelson.—Laing, *History
of Scotland*, ii. 267.

CHAP.
IV.
1566-7.

tresses of James v. before he married Mary of Guise. She had never forgiven Mary for being the legitimate child of James v., and even after her marriage to Sir Robert Douglas of Lochleven had been, when Buchanan wrote, the Queen's jailor on her son Murray's behalf.[1] It might seem to have greater weight that Buchanan appeals in support of his narrative to a corresponding declaration made by George Dalgleish, Bothwell's valet, as " confession which is preserved in the Acts ;" but here also, the suspicious circumstance meets us, that neither in the examination of Dalgleish, which was held on the 26th June 1567, nor in the confession which he made immediately before his execution on the 3d January 1568, as we have them now before us,[2] is there the least ground for such a charge against the Queen as that so trenchantly set forth by Buchanan. The untrustworthiness, however, of the accusations, which Buchanan has taken upon him to pen, shows itself most conspicuously in that part of his pamphlet where he relates how the Queen in the autumn of 1566 visited the sorely wounded Bothwell. After telling how Bothwell had been wounded by Elliot, and how his life was in imminent danger in Hermitage Castle, the description of the visit is thus introduced :—" When

[1] [There seems a slight inaccuracy here. It was Sir William, the eldest son of Sir Robert Douglas, to whose custody Mary was committed on Lochleven in 1567. He was served heir to his father in 1555. He married Agnes Lesley, daughter of the Earl of Rothes, and in 1588 became sixth Earl of Morton. — Robert Douglas, *The Peerage of Scotland.* Margaret Erskine could not therefore have been the " Queen's jailor," although there is reason to believe that she was still alive and residing in the neighbourhood of Lochleven while Mary was a prisoner in its castle. See *Nat. MSS.* Pref.—*Translator.*]

[2] Examination of Dalgleish, and Dalgleish's Confession. — Laing, *History of Scotland,* ii. 249-251, and 264, 265.

this was announced to the Queen at Borthwick she CHAP.
flew like one mad, in spite of the severe winter, in $\underbrace{}_{}$
long daily journeys first to Melrose and then to Jed- 1566.
burgh ; and, although certain tidings were got here
that Bothwell's life was not in danger, yet she could
by no means persuade herself to stop."[1]　Now every
one who reads this description must have the idea,
if he knew no better, that the Queen had hurried
at full gallop from Borthwick to Hermitage Castle.
Yet it is demonstrable that Bothwell's fight with
Elliot took place on the 7th October 1566, the
Queen's arrival at Jedburgh on the 8th, and that it
was only after being detained here a week by judicial business that on the 16th she rode over to the
neighbouring Hermitage.　So the Queen's journey
did not take place in midwinter, as Buchanan's
readers must believe, but in the middle of October,
which in the south of Scotland it is as unreasonable
to regard as real winter, as it was for Buchanan to
take great offence at the Queen's retinue,[2] in which
were to be then seen " the Earl of Murray and other
Lords."[3]　The very grave and most disingenuous
neglect of the chronological order to which the
sojourn at Jedburgh has led Buchanan, however, still
remains to be noticed.　After telling how the Earl
of Bothwell, when he began to recover, was brought
over to Jedburgh, Buchanan makes the Queen give

[1] Id ubi Borthuicum ad Reginam delatum est magnis itineribus,
aspera jam tunc hyeme primum
Melrosiam, inde Jedburgum, velut
insana, pervolat.　Eo etsi certi
de ejus rumores perferebantur,
tamen impatiens moræ animus,
sibi temperare non poterat.—De
Maria Scotorum Regina, p. 8.
[2] Cum eo comitatu, cui nemo,

paulo honestior, suam vitam aut
fortunam committere auderet.—
Ibid. p. 9.

[3] Pour ceste occasion elle y alla
en diligence, accompagne du Conte
de Murray et autres seigneurs.
—Compend of a contemporary
French historical sketch in Tytler's
History of Scotland, vii. 48.

CHAP.
IV.
1566.

such loose reins to her passion for Bothwell that he leaves us to judge whether this licentiousness may not, with great probability, be considered as the real cause of the long hopeless illness which at that time brought her near death.[1] For not to dwell on the little likelihood that a man dangerously wounded, and but newly risen from a bed of severe sickness, should immediately be made the object of such a passion, it cannot be assumed that Bothwell arrived at Jedburgh before the 21st October,[2] while, on the other hand, it is absolutely certain that the Queen's violent illness began immediately after her hurried ride on the 16th had brought her back from Hermitage Castle. A letter to the Scottish ambassador in Paris, the Archbishop of Glasgow, written on Wednesday morning the 23d, by the members of the Scottish Privy Council at Jedburgh, communicates the critical news, that her Majesty had been sick for the last six days;[3] and another letter to the same ambassador, written at Jedburgh by John Lesley, Bishop of Ross, and dated Saturday and Sunday morning the 26th and 27th, fully agrees with the foregoing, in so far as it states that, with a

[1] Eoque, illuc transducto, eorum conuictus et consuetudo, parum ex utriusque, dignitate fuit. Ibi, siue ob nocturnos diurnosque labores, ipsis parum decoros, vulgo infames, sive occulta aliqua Numinis prouidentia, Regina in morbum adeo sæuum et exitiabilem incidit, vt nulla prope spes de ejus vita cuiquam superesset.— *De Maria Scotorum Regina*, p. 9.

[2] The Earl of Bothwell came to Jedburgh the 21st instant in a horse litter.—Letter of Sir John Forster to Cecil, dated Berwick, October 1566.—*Calendar of State Papers*, For. Series, 1566-8, p. 141.

[3] "That ze be not ignorant of the trewth, quhilk is, that hir Majestie hes been sick thir sex dayis bypast." Among the signatures to this letter from Jedburgh of 23d October 1566 (Keith, *History of Church and State in Scotland*, p. 352), Bothwell's is still not found. On the other hand, he took part with the rest of the Council in the issue of a proclamation, which is dated Jedburgh, 25th October 1566 (Keith, p. 352), and this accords with the fact that in Lesley's letter of 27th October he is spoken of as newly arrived at Jedburgh.

heavy perspiration, an improvement in the Queen's CHAP.
condition took place on Friday the 25th, which IV.
was considered a favourable turn of the sickness 1566.
because it was on the ninth day.[1] Thus both
these letters in the most decisive manner trace back
the beginning of Mary's sickness directly to the first
day of her home-coming from Hermitage. On one
point of time Buchanan, in his bitter charges, even
comes into collision with himself. According to his
pamphlet it was when the baptism of James VI.
took place at Stirling that the illicit behaviour of
the Queen and Bothwell became so shameless, that
it seemed as if they aimed at revealing it to all.[2]
But we may now ask, where then was Buchanan
himself at this period ? The answer must be that
he himself was present at the baptismal ceremony
in Stirling, and that he also there contributed
to the festivities of the joyous occasion. On this
occasion there was seen in the Castle Hall, ere the
day ended with a display of fireworks from an
artificial fort, one of those grand masked pageants,
which the festivals of that period seldom wanted,
this time consisting of a procession,—satyrs, naiads,
mountain nymphs, and the like ; each group having
some stanzas to recite at the throne, and these
Latin stanzas, of which again some, celebrating the
Queen as a paragon of virtue, were composed by no
other than—Buchanan,[3] by the same Buchanan, whose

[1] Quhilk was halden the releif
of the seykness, because it was on
the nynth day, quhilk commonlie
is callet the creisis of the seykness.
—Lesley's letter to the Archbishop
of Glasgow, dated Jedburgh, "this
Sunday the 26 day of October,
luit at even," and " at morning, the
27 October 1568."—Keith, *His-*

*tory of Church and State in
Scotland*, Appendix, p. 134.
[2] Ad consuetam redierunt pal-
æstram : idque adeo aperte, ut
nihil magis timere viderentur,
quam ne ignota esset sua nequitia.
—*De Maria Scot. Reg.*, p. 10.
[3] Pompæ Deorum Rusticorum
dona ferentium Jacobo VI. et Mariæ

pamphlet, speaking of the same period, only seeks
to excite belief in the flagrant unchastity of the
Queen at the period mentioned.[1] Still more manifest, according to what the pamphlet adds, should
that amour have also become, after one saw on the
occasion of the festival at Stirling the care the
Queen took for Bothwell's splendid appearance, as
if she had been—these are Buchanan's words—" I
will not even say his wife, but his handmaid." [2]
Buchanan's representation has here a certain amount
of truth, but, as usual in his pamphlet, it does not
set this in the correct light. For it is certainly the
case, as Buchanan's pamphlet represents, that the
splendid dress in which Bothwell appeared on the
holiday in question was the gift of the Queen;
but Buchanan either conceals, or has been ignorant
of the fact that the Queen had presented exactly
similar gifts to her other nobles. It is a fortunate
circumstance that among Mary Stuart's Inventories
which recent times have brought to light, are two
giving information of the large collection of silk-
stuffs and other materials for wearing apparel which
she had brought with her from France, or had
acquired in Scotland, and the remarks subjoined by
Servais de Condé, one of her French servants, whom

---

matri ejus, Scotorum Regibus, in
coena quæ Regis baptisma est
consecuta ; Georgii Buchanani
Poemata quæ extant, p. 402. The
Queen is here greeted thus :—
" *Virtute*, ingenio, Regina, et munere
  formæ
Felicibus felicior maioribus ;
Conjugii fructu sed felicissima, cujus
Legati honorant exteri cunabula."
    [1] One of the Queen's earliest
defenders, and not the least, has
already called attention to this
contradiction on the part of Bu-

chanan. — Thomas Innes, in his
*Critical Essay on the Ancient In-
habitants of Scotland*, London,
1729, i. 348-352.

    [2] Hic vt Bothuelius inter Pro-
ceres conspicuus esset, partim ei
ad vestimenta coemenda pecuniam
erogabat, partim mercatoribus
emebat: omnibusque conficiundis
tanta diligentia præerat, quasi non
dico vxor, sed ne ancilla quidem
foret.—*De Mar. Scot. Reg.*, p. 12.

she made "keeper" in Holyrood, and on whom CHAP.
devolved the superintendence of its inventory, not IV.
only show in general how willingly she would have 1566.
distributed from her stores right and left, but expressly state how Servais de Condé, while giving the
silver-edged stuff to Bothwell, was required to give
similar silver or gold-edged stuff to the Earl of
Huntly, to the Earls Murray and Argyll, and to
Maitland of Lethington.[1] Even in September the
Queen, as also Sir John Forster was then able to
report to Cecil, had, with womanly interest, selected
the colours in which her trusted friends should
appear at the coming festival before the expected
foreigners, and had arrayed them in the dresses, as
she herself intended to bear the cost.[2] It may
further be regarded as a pendant to the feature just
exposed of Buchanan's mode of representation, when
in his pamphlet, referring to Mary's flight, after
Darnley's death, to Seton Castle, to Lord William
Seton and his wife Isabella, a daughter of Sir William Hamilton of Sanquhar, he foolishly lays stress
on the circumstance that one so high in position as
the Earl of Bothwell could appear satisfied with a
small and unsightly apartment, merely because it
was not far from the Queen's bed-room.[3] In order

[1] *Inuentaires de la Royne Descosse, Douairiere de France,* pp. 69, 166.

[2] Letter of Sir John Forster to Cecil, from Berwick, 19th Sep-tember 1566. Agnes Strickland, *Lives of the Queens of Scotland,* v. 222, 223.

[3] Ad Setonum *cum paucis,* nec iis adeo mæstis, aduolat, Ibi Bothuelius, quamquam summa, qua tum erat in aula gratia, et majorum nobilitas, et honores postulare viderentur, vt splendid-issime, secundum Reginam, acci-peretur, tamen proximum Culinæ cubiculum ei datur, neque tamen omnino incommodum ad luctus minuendos ; erat enim Reginæ cubiculum subjectum, et si quid repentini doloris accidisset, scalæ erant angustæ quidem illæ, sed quæ aditum tamen Bothuelio ad eam consolandam præberent.—*De Maria Scotorum Regina,* p. 24.

M

that the impression intended may be produced, the
reader must here behold the Queen and Bothwell pro-
ceeding on their flight " with only some few attendants ;" we know, however, from other sources, that
the Queen, when she made her visit to Seton, was
accompanied by a court of not less than a hundred
persons, a larger retinue than any Scottish mansion-
house could at that period accommodate with due
regard to the rank of each person.[1]

By nothing else than its daring charges the attack
of Buchanan on Mary had meanwhile succeeded
in becoming one of the pamphlets which won
the widest circulation and immense influence, both
in the original edition, showing his mastery of the
Latin tongue, and in the subsequent enlarged translations published during the conflict between Catholicism and Protestantism in the second half of the
sixteenth century. It was by no means only the
new Scottish Government which, during the minority
of James VI., made this circulation of the utmost
importance ; the same thing holds good also, and
perhaps in a still higher degree, of the English
Government, since Queen Elizabeth gave Buchanan a
pension of one hundred pounds, congratulated Cecil,
her most trusted minister, and had, with uncommon
eagerness, both the original printed in London,[2] and

[1] It was on the 16th February
1567, that the Queen, under the
advice of her physicians, set out
from Edinburgh to Seton, and in
one of the letters from Sir William
Drury to Cecil, dated Berwick,
17th February, the former reports
thus :—" She this last night, the
16th of February, lay at the Lord
Seyton's, accompanied by Argyle,
Huntly, Bothwell (he was high

sheriff of this shire), Arbroath, the
Archbishop of St. Andrews, the
Lords Fleming and Livingston,
with the Secretary, who followed,
amounting to a hundred people."
—Chalmers, *Life of Mary Queen
of Scots*, i. 208.

[2] In a letter to Sir Francis
Walsingham and Sir Henry Killi-
grew in Paris, Cecil mentions
Buchanan's pamphlet as "newly

copies sent over to the English ambassador in Paris, ordering him "to present it, if need be, to the king (Charles IX.), as from yourself, and likewise some of the other noblemen of his council; for they will serve, to good effect, to disgrace her; which must be done before other purposes can be obtained."[1] The year after a French translation also appeared, which seems to have been superintended by a Huguenot and a decided enemy of the Scottish Queen.[2] But Buchanan's publication did not accomplish the effect intended; if the support which Charles IX. and Henry III. afterwards rendered to Mary[3] certainly did not realise the expectations she cherished, and though we can trace in the historical representation of Mary by De Thou the influence of Buchanan, yet in Catholic France, there was always preserved, from the time of Mary's youthful sojourn, a sympathy for her fate, which followed her even to her affecting death.[4] In Pro-

printed in Latin, and I hear it is to be translated into English with many supplements of the like condition." The letter, dated Richmond, 1st November 1571, is given in Digges, *Complete Ambassador, or two Treaties of the Intended Marriage of Queen Elizabeth.* London, 1655, fol., p. 151.

[1] Chalmers, *Life of Mary Queen of Scots,* ii. 52.

[2] *Histoire de Marie Royne d'Escosse touchant la conjuration faicte contre le Roy et l'adultère commis avec le Comte de Bothwell.* Traduicte en François par Thomas Waltem. Edinbourg, par moy Thomas Waltem, 1572.

[3] Cheruel, *De Maria Stuarta, utrum Henricus III. eam in suis periculis tutatus fuerit, an omni ope destitutam Anglis prodiderit.* Rotomagi, 1849. The cause why

France did not do more for the Scottish Queen is ascribed partly to the unfavourable influence of Catherine de Medici. The latter is said to have formerly felt herself put in the background by Mary Stuart, and could we believe a letter from the Papal Nuncio in Paris, "la Regina di Scotia un giorno gli disse, che non sarebbe mai altro che figlia di un mercante" (Cheruel, *Marie Stuart et Catherine de Médicis.* Paris, 1858, p. 17).

[4] See the "Oraison funèbre" of the Archbishop of Bruges over Mary Stuart in the Church of Notre-Dame in Paris—the same in which she had been married to Francis II.—in Jebb, *De vita et rebus gestis serenissimæ principis Mariæ, Scotorum Reginæ, Franciæ Dotairæ,* ii. 671.

testant England, on the contrary, the soil was far
better prepared for the venomous plant; the English
Queen's envoys in Scotland, and her commanders on
the borders, and still more, the unreliable Scots
news-mongers, who depended on the authority of
these, had ever since Mary's union with Darnley,
been able only too frequently to pander to Elizabeth's well-known humour, by reporting much
idle talk about her rival, and after Mary's imprisonment in England, they went still further in
the same direction. To what a height the calumnies
previously set on foot against Mary, after the
publication of Buchanan's book, at last rose in
England, is evinced in a striking manner by the
correspondence which Mary, during her imprisonment
in England, carried on with Castelnau de Mauvissière, the French ambassador in London. In the
year 1584 the report was spread in England, that
she stood in an illicit relation to her own jailer, the
Earl of Shrewsbury—the same who afterwards, with
the Earl of Kent as Elizabeth's plenipotentiary,
stood by the scaffold on which Mary's head fell,—
and Mauvissière believed that he ought not to conceal this report from her. "I dare neither," he
writes, "conceal from you, that your enemies have
spread a report that you have had a child, and that
now, through connection with your keeper, you
have become *enceinte* a second time."[1] With justifi-
able warmth Mary answered :—" There is nothing I
would not venture for my honour, which, even
though I had not been placed so high on earth, is
yet dearer to me than life. Therefore I most

[1] Mauvissière's Letter.—Raumer, *Die Königinnen Elisabeth und Maria
Stuart*, p. 378.

earnestly beseech you that you will untiringly per-
severe in the course taken for the annihilation of
this abominable slander, until I get sufficient
satisfaction for it, either by a public notification
through the whole kingdom, on which you shall
particularly insist, or by the exemplary punishment
of the authors."[1] In this instance also, her name
obtained a decisive vindication,[2] although the whole
picture Buchanan had presented of the Catholic
Queen was not thereby effaced. One of the chief
steps towards the scaffold, which so many in England
constantly wished to see her ascend, may indeed be
said to have been formed by Buchanan's works. In
Scotland Buchanan had himself taken care that the
attack on Mary, which had at first been published in
the universal language of the learned, should likewise
become accessible to and effective with the common
people of the country; his Scottish translation of his
Latin original became a striking example of the
power of the old Scots tongue, and showed its
ability even to compete in force with the language
of the Romans.[3]

Before Buchanan, in his Latin *History of Scotland*, which he published twenty years later, put
forth anew the accusations made in his pamphlet,
the hideous picture of Mary which he first presented to the eyes of the world had been still more
coloured by his friend and contemporary John Knox,

[1] Letter of Mary Stuart to Mauvissière of 26th February 1584. Labanoff, v. 426.
[2] In a letter of December 1584 Mary Stuart relates that the Countess of Shrewsbury, from whom those calumnies had origi-nated, had been compelled upon her knees to recall them. Labanoff,

vi. 69.—Raumer, *Die Königinnen Elisabeth und Maria Stuart*, p. 392.
[3] *Ane Detectioun of the Doingis of Marie, Quene of Scotland, twich-ing the murther of hir Husband.* Translated out of the Latine, quhilk was written be M. G. B. Sanctandrois be Robert Leck-previk, 1572.

the second of the authors whose representation has
latterly been so much the ground of the opinion commonly held of the Scottish Queen.   Knox's delinea-
tion of the history of the Reformation in Scotland has been definitely placed above all that
Great Britain can show of an earlier date in prose
literature.   It has been thought that we must come
down to the middle of the eighteenth century ere it
is possible to meet with any work, at least in Scotland, which can compete with it; but along with
this it must be said that the hero of the Reformation, in his historic work, also exhibits the same
recklessness and violence which characterise all
his discourses and writings, and by which he occasioned a sensation even among his own harsh contemporaries.[1]   No Dominican monk, as has with
reason been remarked,[2] could, in intolerance, surpass
Knox, who, in the most peremptory manner, maintained that it was a duty to punish "idolaters"
with death, and who in his *History of the Reformation*
bluntly describes the murder of Riccio as "that just
act, and most worthy of all praise."[3]   By Scotland's
Reformer, Scotland's Catholic Queen, ever since her
return home, had been already condemned on the
ground of her creed, and the verdict was certainly
not softened after the meeting which she had with
him, and in which, according to his own account of
it, the superiority, both in argument and modera-

---

[1] It was earlier assumed that
the most offensive passages in this
work which circulated in manuscript before it was spread in
print, were only later interpolations, but this supposition is no
longer tenable after the last and
careful edition of the *History of*
the Reformation by David Laing,
which has been followed in this
examination.

[2] Hallam, *Constitutional History*
of England, London, 1842, i. 138.

[3] Knox, *History of the Reforma-*
tion in Scotland, i. 235.

tion, seems on the side of the young princess.[1] CHAP.
Equally, according to Knox's statements, the disputed letters contained in the silver casket are 1572.
to be regarded as undoubted evidence of Mary's early
passion for Bothwell.[2] Although the picture of the
Queen grows by no means brighter in the *History of
the Reformation* than it is in Buchanan's pamphlet,
yet in other respects it is not, as in the former, her
conduct towards Bothwell which must lend the
darkest colouring, Bothwell being never mentioned
in Knox's work without a certain unmistakable
sympathy. So far Knox added new weight to
all the charges in Buchanan's pamphlet, inasmuch
as he has represented life at Mary Stuart's court
generally as if it were fit only for a " bordell."[3]
In his eyes nothing at this court could find favour.
Even from the Queen's return from France, it had
only been a mark for his unwearied attacks. For
she was not then the heroine whom the more
sentimental delicacy of a succeeding age, and the
romance of younger poets, afterwards created; she
was gay and full of life ere more bitter experiences
and sufferings moulded the character whose serious-
ness of mind knew even how to raise her above the
terrors of death. As one of her earliest defenders
emphatically pointed out in opposition to Buchanan's
pamphlet,[4] she had brought with her, from her sojourn
in France, its freer manners, in contrast to Scotland's

[1] Knox, *History of the Reformation in Scotland*, ii. 277-286. See
also the same, ii. 331-335, 371-377,
387-389, 403-411.
[2] He kept her letters, to be an
awe-bond upon her, in case her
affection should change.—Knox,
*History of the Reformation in
Scotland*, ii. 562.

[3] Knox, *History of the Reformation in Scotland*, ii. 368.
[4] Il ne voit et considère point,
que ceste Royne ayant esté nourrie
en France se ressentoit des libertés
honnestes de ceste royaume, ou
les soupçons sont éloignez des
privautés. Contre les peruerses
calomnies des trahistres accusans

semi-barbarous, and almost savage enthusiasm for "The Reformation." That an old head upon young shoulders is contrary to nature was something not taken into consideration by Presbyterian strictness; her youthful inclination for music, dancing, and masked balls was ever stamped as an abomination in this ultra-Calvinistic country, where the tendency had already appeared, which subsequently caused all places of public entertainment to be closed on Sundays, and even means of escape into the country to be interdicted, and where it is still reckoned almost a sin to visit a theatre.

To the picture of life at the Scottish court which Knox's *History* would leave on the mind, the fate of an unhappy foreigner must especially furnish the background. Among the large retinue of French lords that accompanied Mary when, in the year 1561, she turned homewards to Scotland, was Châtellard, a nobleman from Dauphiné. The celebrated Bayard had been his granduncle on the mother's side,[1] and he further distinguished himself both by genius and bravery, but still more by highly refined manners. With the sentimentalism of a troubadour he hovered about the beautiful young Queen as the moth flutters round the light. On the journey to Scotland he sailed in the same ship with Mary, and when, owing to the darkness, it was necessary to light the lanterns and torches, he seized an oppor-

---

la très-illustre, très-chaste et débonnaire Princesse, Madame Marie, Royne naturelle, legitime, et souveraine de Escosse, 1572. Again printed by Jebb, i. 457.

[1] Brantôme, *Vies des Dames Illustres*, in *Œuvres du Seigneur du Brantôme*, i. 183. According to a reference by Joseph Robertson (*Inuentaires de la Royne Descosse*, Preface, p. lxxv.) to a Journal *La France Protestante*, which we have not in this instance been able to consult, this relative of Bayard is properly called Pierre de Bocsozel, Lord of Chastelard.

tunity of remarking that "this lantern and this torch
are not in the least required to make our way over
the sea clear, for the beautiful eyes of our Queen
are so sparkling that with their fire they are able to
illuminate the whole ocean, yea to kindle it if need-
ful." Before returning to the Continent with the
Duke de Danville, afterwards Constable of France,
who had brought him along with the other French
lords to Scotland, he, according to the fashion of
the times, presented French sonnets to the Queen,
which she at times answered with similar ones, and
when in France he saw the first religious war break
out between the Catholics and the Huguenots,
though he himself belonged to the latter, yet he
would neither fight against his co-religionists, nor
bear arms against his patron above-mentioned, but
after a short absence, passed over again to Scotland
with a letter of recommendation from the duke.
The troubadour brought with him a small volume of
new poems which he presented to Mary. He became
once more a welcome guest in Holyrood, where he
often had the honour to have her as his partner in
the dance, and again overwhelmed the Queen with
flatteries which indeed won for him only her smiles,
but smiles which became to him most fatal, for
they tempted him, as Brantôme expresses it, "like
Phaethon" to strive after a sun so high that he
perished. In February 1563 he presumed to steal,
armed with sword and dagger, into the Queen's
bedroom, where he sought to hide himself under her
bed until she went to rest. But ere she retired he
was discovered, and when the Queen, whom it was
felt undesirable to disturb at the time, learned next
morning the news of his audacious conduct, she for-

CHAP.
IV.
~~~~
1563.

gave him indeed, but dismissed him hereafter from her near presence.[1] Two days after, on the 14th February, when the Queen was on a journey from Edinburgh to St. Andrews, and was passing the night at Burntisland, Châtellard, notwithstanding, again followed her to her bedroom, under pretence of wishing to clear himself from her censure. Mary ordered him instantly to withdraw, and as he delayed doing so, she called with loud screams for help. Châtellard was committed to prison, an action was raised against him for high treason, he was condemned to death, and on the 22d February was executed in the market-place of St. Andrews. Before his departure from the prison he again read the Hymn to Death, one of the odes of his friend the poet Ronsard. On the scaffold he turned towards the place where he supposed the Queen to be, and is said to have sent her his last greeting in these words :—" Adieu, the most beautiful and the most cruel princess of the world." [2]

[1] Mais la Reyne, sans faire aucun scandale luy pardonna.— Brantôme, *Vies des Dames Illustres*, in *Œuvres du Seigneur de Brantôme*, i. 188. Châtellard had, before his second journey to Scotland, given Brantôme, at parting, the adieu : " Car nous estions bons amis."
[2] Adieu, la plus belle et la plus cruelle princesse du monde.—Brantôme, *Vies des Dames Illustres*, in *Œuvres du Seigneur de Brantôme,* i. 188. Brantôme adds :—" Aucuns ont voulu discourir à quoy il l'appelloit tant cruelle, ou si c'estoit, qu'elle n'eut pitié de son amour ou de sa vie. La-dessus qu'eust-elle sçen faire ? Si, apres le premier pardon, elle eut donne le second, elle estoit scandalizée partout."

The judgment would besides present itself in a new light, if Châtellard really had, before his death, acknowledged having only acted as the tool of the Protestants and the enemies of the Guises, who, by the Queen's disgrace, wished to see her debarred from a then dreaded new princely marriage. But it is only in a statement of 3d May 1563 from Perrenot de Chantonnay, the Spanish ambassador in Paris (given in Teulet, *Papiers d'État*, iii. 5), that this account of Châtellard can now be met with, in which it is stated, " enemigos de la casa de Guisa le avian persuadido de passar en Escocia y procurar por todos las vias possibles de hazer alcuna cosa con la qual la honra de la dicha Reyna viniesse a' disputa."

That an occurrence like this was fitted to set malicious reports in circulation, the young Queen, who took occasion from it to let one of her four Maries share her bed-chamber,[1] might well imagine, and indeed it was forthwith notified by Thomas Randolph, who was still Elizabeth's ambassador at that time in Scotland. Randolph, whose accounts then and to a much later period — until Mary's union with Darnley crossed the English plans— otherwise always speak of the Scottish Queen as being " so worthy, so wise, so honourable in all her conduct,"[2] nevertheless only charges the Queen in his report of that " deplorable occurrence, with having shown too much unguardedness unto so unworthy a creature and abject a varlet,"[3] and one who at last wished by force to obtain a favour he could not get in any other way.[4] In Knox's *History* there is also an episode about Châtellard, or, as he is incorrectly called by the writer, " the poor Chattelett," in which, without distinguishing between the two culpable attempts, the idea on the contrary is sought to be conveyed to the reader that the incensed Queen really wished to have him secretly put to death, in order that he should not

[1] She chose for this purpose Mary Fleming, afterwards the wife of Maitland. Randolph's letter to Cecil, dated St. Andrews, 10th March 1563.—*Calendar of State Papers, Foreign Series*, 1563, p. 193.

[2] Randolph's statement to Cecil of 21st May 1565.—Raumer, *Die Königinnen Elisabeth und Maria Stuart*, i. 64.

[3] Randolph's account to Cecil of 14th February 1563.—Raumer, *Die Königinnen Elisabeth und Maria Stuart*, i. 26.

[4] He died with repentance, and confessed privately more than he spoke openly. His purpose was, that night he was found under her bed, to have tried her constancy, and by force to have attempted what by no persuasions he could attain to. Thus your Honour understandeth the effect of the whole matter as truly, I believe, as any man can report it.—Randolph to Cecil, 28th February 1563.— *Calendar of State Papers, Foreign Series*, 1563, p. 167.

utter anything to her dishonour, and that when the
story could not be suppressed the French Protestant
was arraigned and condemned, the conclusion of the
whole being :—"And so receaved Chattelet the
reward of his dansing ; for he lacked his head that
his tonng should not utter the secreattis of our
Quene." But if, as has long ago been shown,[1] we
often cannot rely on Knox's reports where these
relate to things of which he was personally cognisant,
his *History* is in general specially suspicious in those
passages in which it gives descriptions of the court.
And here in the case just hinted at, the connection
between Buchanan and Knox seems also to acquire
a peculiar importance. As there is in Knox's
History of the Reformation a reference to Buchanan's pamphlet,[2] so Buchanan, although the tendency of Knox to exaggeration was not unknown to
him,[3] has yet in his *History* so often satisfied himself with copying Knox that his complete omission
of the story about Châtellard may well be deemed
suspicious.[4] The reason why he has not in this
instance followed Knox is also sufficiently obvious.
According to Knox, that wish to see Châtellard
secretly put to death, which he sought to ascribe to
the Queen, must have been frustrated by the opposition of Murray ; but the reports of Randolph make

[1] By Lord Hailes. *Annals of
Scotland*, Edinburgh, 1819, iii.
260-262.

[2] Knox, *History of the Reformation in Scotland*, ii. 562.

[3] In the year in which the Reformer died, Buchanan writes to
Randolph :—"As to Maister Knox,
his hystorie is in hys freindes
handes, and thai ar in consultation
to mitigat sum part the acerbite of
certain wordis."—Buchanan's letter

in Wright's *Queen Elizabeth and
her Times*, i. 429.

[4] Joseph Robertson has already
called attention to this circumstance of Buchanan's "omission of
the story of Châtellard, which," he
adds, "the Reformer tells with
scandals, so far as I have observed,
told by no one else."—*Inuentaires
de la Royne Descosse*, Preface, p.
lxxvi.

it manifest that it was Mary herself who desired to   CHAP.
save Châtellard from death, and that on the con-   IV.
trary it was the still all-powerful Murray who, with   1565.
the other members of the Privy Council, urged the
carrying out of the sentence.[1] The judicial records
in which a more precise explanation of the offence
for which Châtellard suffered might surely be met
with, are now lost for the whole period from May
1562 to May 1563, but even Châtellard's own verses
simply complain that his burning love for the Queen
had met with invincible coldness.[2]   The confidence
with which Knox has in this instance sought to
ascribe to the Queen an illicit connection weighs no
more than the confidence with which for example
one of his other attacks on Mary's court thus
states :—" It was well known that shame hastened
the marriage betwixt John Sempill, called the
dancer, and Mary Livingstone, surnamed the
lustie."[3] What is intended by this is the marriage
between Mary Livingston, one of the Queen's four
Maries, a daughter of Lord Alexander Livingston,
and the young John Sempill of Belltreis, a son of
Lord Robert Sempill, Mary Stuart having shown
her approbation of the union by a deed of gift of
9th March 1565, conveying to the young couple a
portion of landed property " because it had now

[1] Randolph's Report ; Raumer's
*Die Königinnen Elisabeth und
Maria Stuart*, p. 29.
[2] They are to be found printed
in the Supplements to *Mémoires
de Messire Michel Castelnau Seigneur de Mauvissière. Illustrez par
T. le Laboureur.* Bruxelles, 1731,
vol. i. 549-550, and contain such
lines as these :—
    " Et neantmoins la flâme,
    Qui me brule et enflâme,

De passion,
N'émeut jamais ton âme
D'aucune affection."
    [3] Bot yit wes not the courte
purged of hureis and huredome
quhilk was the fontane of sik
enormities, for it wes weill knawn
that schame haistit mariage betwix Johne Sempill, callit the
Danser, and Marie Livingstoune,
surnameit the Lustie. — Knox,
History of the Reformation, ii. 415.

pleased God to move their hearts to enter into the estate of matrimony."[1] But so far was there from being any haste with the marriage, that even months beforehand we find it announced in the reports of the foreign ministers, of whom Randolph then informs the Earl of Bedford of an expected invitation to the approaching nuptials.[2] Knox also stands alone when he does not even exempt Mary Stuart's mother, the Queen-Dowager of Guise, from his accusations, but unhesitatingly speaks in the most offensive manner of the Catholic Regent, as if she had been the mistress of Cardinal David Beaton, and almost seems to insinuate that she had stood in a like connection to d'Oysel, commander of the French mercenary troops in Scotland.[3]

Thus the matter stands with the authorities whence so many later writers have derived their facts, when they represent Mary as having before Darnley's death abandoned herself to Bothwell in frenzied love. Taken in connection with ecclesiastical and political passions, which willingly credit all that is bad of a dangerous enemy, they may explain why with contemporaries and their immediate successors the prevalent opinion both in Scotland and England so quickly came to an agreement about a point which has so long been matter

[1] *The Acts of the Parliaments of Scotland*, ii. 559.
[2] Randolph's letters to Cecil and the Earl of Bedford, both of 9th January 1565, *Calendar of the State Papers relating to Scotland*, i. 204. Paul de Foix's letter to Catherine de Medici, of January 1565. Teulet's *Papiers d'État*, ii. 32.
[3] Knox, *History of the Reformation in Scotland*, i. 92, 203, ii. 70.

It is a Nemesis that Knox from the Catholic side has himself become down to the latest times an object of like accusations as he was ready so lightly to spread about others. See for example *The Life and Times of John Knox*. Two lectures delivered to the members of the Edinburgh St. Patrick's Catholic Young Men's Society, Edinburgh, 1868, pp. 69-71, 92-93.

of dispute in after times. By themselves they are
positive evidence of Mary's earlier union with
Bothwell, yet they are of such a nature that one
may most readily be induced to see in Mary in this
respect simply a victim of such vague reports as so
commonly plague those in high places. Therefore
it is now also the case that in direct opposition to
the many descriptions which both make Mary
take part in the murder of Darnley, and represent her as having become before this the abandoned mistress of Bothwell, there stands a series of
writings by which the Queen is not only acquitted
of any suspicion of participation in the murder of
her husband, but also with the same positiveness
of assertion is acquitted of any connection with
Bothwell before he carried her off to Dunbar. But
this assurance may nevertheless be too strong. A
middle way seems still capable of being found, which
may come nearer the truth. While it is certainly
not necessary to see the hand of Mary Stuart in the
catastrophe which ended Darnley's days, and while
we may with reason admit the untrustworthiness
of the positive evidence against the Queen of a
previous connection with Bothwell, yet it becomes
always difficult, without the supposition of such an
earlier connection, to comprehend her whole subsequent behaviour in respect to Bothwell's proceedings. Without this supposition it is difficult to
understand how she could so shortly after Darnley's
death agree to marry the Earl, to marry one who
had recently been accused of being—the murderer
of Darnley.[1]

[1] Note G, Appendix.

CHAPTER V.

THE murder of Darnley took place on the night between Sunday the 9th and Monday the 10th of February 1567. After he had for a lengthened period lived virtually in a state of divorce from the Queen, and in Glasgow, on the return of the pardoned rebels, was actually revolving in his mind to leave Scotland and repair to France or Spain, as if from a presentiment of impending danger, a reconciliation took place about the time of the new year. For when Darnley was seized with smallpox during his stay in Glasgow, the Queen sent him her physician, wrote him many friendly letters,[1] and at last went herself to him with the view, when his strength permitted, of having him conveyed in a sedan chair[2] back to Edinburgh. Here she arrived with the King in the evening of the 30th January 1567. In order, as was said, not to expose others, and especially the young prince, to infection, and at the same time to procure for Darnley himself freer air during his convalescence, he was not immediately brought to the low-lying Holyrood, but since he himself objected to reside in Craigmillar Castle, south of Edinburgh,

[1] Buchanan, *Rerum Scot. Hist.* p. 213.
[2] [Birrel calls it " ane chariott." —*Diarey*, p. 6: *Fragments of Scottish History.* Probably it was the Queen's coach mentioned else- where as having conveyed the Earl of Arran to Edinburgh.—*Diurnal of Occurrents*, p. 72. Robertson's Preface to *Inuentaires*, p. xxi.— *Translator.*]

was taken, as had from the first been intended,[1] to
a dwelling which the Earl of Bothwell had previously
undertaken to prepare for the reception of the in-
valid, and which yet lay close enough to Holyrood
to enable the Queen easily to visit him.

Bothwell, who met the King and Queen on the
way with the intelligence of the accomplishment of
his errand,[2] had chosen a lonely and retired house
surrounded by gardens in the vicinity of the so-
called " St. Mary's, or our Lady Kirk-in-the-Fields."
Long before the Scottish capital had extended itself on both sides of the steep and narrow ridge
which stretches from Holyrood up to Edinburgh
Castle, this church stood on the same spot where
the University, instituted in the year 1582 by
Darnley's and Mary's son, has now its site. The
church received its name from the circumstance
that it was originally situated outside the city wall,
but afterward, as the city increased in size, this wall
was extended so as to surround the church with its
adjacent buildings, an hospital or almshouse, and a
parsonage. The wall however had not saved these
buildings from being devastated by the English
invasion in 1544, during which for three days and
three nights Edinburgh was in flames, and ten
years later the ruined hospital had come into the
possession of the ·Duke of Châtelherault, who caused

---

[1] It is one of the many arbitrary
distortions of facts of which Froude
is guilty, that he represents Darnley as being eager to go to Craigmillar, and as only prevented by
the Queen.—*History of England*,
viii. 363. Darnley's servant,
Thomas Nelson, who accompanied
them from Glasgow, has very expressly remarked that it was ·Darn-

ley himself who would not go to
Craigmillar, and that the arrangement was therefore altered.

[2] " And Bothuell, *keipping tryist,*
i.e. trust, met hir upon the way,"
it is said about this, with an allusion to Bothwell's motto, in the
Journal of William Cecil, given
in Laing, *History of Scotland,*
ii. 87.

CHAP.
V.
1567.

a dwelling to be reared for himself on the spot where it stood. The parsonage or deanery had also recently been restored, and as a prebend had been made over to Robert Balfour, a brother of the then adherent of Bothwell, Sir James Balfour. This dwelling its possessor[1] had now left to make way for Darnley. The house, which certainly bore marks of ancient Scottish plainness, judging even from the striking description of it by contemporaries,[2] contained six or seven rooms, divided into two stories, connected by means of a winding stair. It had one principal door to the north, another to the east leading out to a garden, and through the city wall, against which the south gable of the house stood, a back-door led down to a cellar or vault.[3]

Buchanan, who has not been able to conceal that the reason for the choice of the house in the Kirk-of-Field had reference partly to the necessary prevention of infection in Holyrood,[4] partly to the

[1] With respect to him it is later said in the declaration of the laird of Ormiston regarding the proceedings of Bothwell and his followers: " For they had 13 fals keys of the lodging maide and givin, as they said to me, be him that aught the house."—Laing, History of Scotland, ii. 292.

[2] The English ambassador, Sir Nicholas Throckmorton, who, later in the year, stayed for some time with Lord Hume in Fast Castle, describes it in a letter to Cecil of the 12th July 1567 (Tytler, History of Scotland, vii. 128), as "very little, a place fitter to lodge prisoners than folks at liberty ; " and when Brantôme speaks of Holyrood as a very beautiful building, he does not forget immediately to add, that it " ne tient rien du pays."—Vies des Dames Illustres, in Œuvres du Seigneur de Brantôme, i. 143.

[3] In Registrum Domus de Soltre, Charters of the Hospital of Soltre, Edinburgh, 1861, edited for the Bannatyne Club by David Laing, there is a drawing of the ground at the Kirk-of-Field at the time Darnley was murdered. The original was sent by the English ambassador in Scotland to the palace in Whitehall, and is now preserved in the English Royal Archives.

[4] Ducitur Edinburgum non in Palatium. Cur ita? Ne videlicet contagio pestilentis morbi filio adhuc tenello noceret.—Buchanan, De Maria Scotorum Regina, p. 67. Some years before this there occurs in a letter from Randolph himself to Cecil, dated Edinburgh, November 3d, 1564, this remark : " Three of his men are sick of the smallpox, so thinks that he for a time must absent himself from the court."— State Papers (F. S., 1564-5), p. 236.

healthy situation of the place,[1]—which, in later CHAP.
times, has also caused a neighbouring spot to be V.
selected as a site for an infirmary,—is nevertheless 1567.
unable to understand how there should be fresh
air "among dead men's" graves, and seeks after all
to represent the choice of this place of residence as
a setting aside of all decent respect. Perhaps it
deserves not to be passed over in silence that, in
consequence of a discovery made in more recent
times, we are still able to see the list of the
tapestries for the walls, the velvet cushions, and all
the other sorts of furniture, which, on the occasion
of Darnley's residence in the house of the Kirk-of-
Field, had been brought thither from Holyrood,
and which subsequently went amissing. Darnley,
whose sick and bath-room was in one of the
uppermost suites, had also in it "a bed of violet
velvet, trimmed with lace of gold and silver,"[2] and
in the "Hall" or "Saloon" there had, amongst
other furniture, been also erected "a dais of black
velvet."

Although Mary, during the ten days Darnley
spent in the house of the Kirk-of-Field, had
her own residence at Holyrood, yet she was
frequently to be seen on a visit to him during this
time. She very often sat with Darnley in his sick-
room, and as she found pleasure in walking in the
neighbouring garden of what was formerly a monastery of the Dominicans, or brought her choir of
musicians along with her from the palace to the
house in the Kirk-of-Field, so she also chose at least

---

[1] Cur hic potissimum delectus
est locus?   Aeris salubritas præ-
tenditur.—Buchanan, De Maria
Scotorum Regina, p. 68. By Sir

James Melvil (Memoirs, p. 77) we
find the Kirk-of-Field also mentioned "as a place of good air."
[2] Note H, Appendix.

two days a week, on Wednesdays and Fridays, rather to remain there all night than return late to Holyrood. In view of such occasional stays one of the lower rooms right under that of the king had been arranged as a sleeping apartment for her. At this time Darnley also wrote to his father, the Earl of Lennox, who, being sick, had remained behind in Glasgow, of the greater friendliness the Queen now showed him, and how, as she one day found him about to write this letter, she lovingly kissed him. Her older as well as her more recent enemies have laid stress on the contrast between Mary's former ill-will towards Darnley,[1] which she continued to express a few days before her departure for Glasgow,[2] and the whole of this behaviour on her part, in which accordingly they choose to see the most abominable hypocrisy, fitted only to lull her destined victim to sleep. Her contemporary friends and later defenders have, on the contrary, seen in the Queen's sympathy with Darnley's illness the germ of a returning affection for him,[3] and have assumed that

[1] Buchanan, *Rerum Scoticarum Historia*, p. 213.

[2] In her letter to her ambassador in Paris, dated from Edinburgh, 20th January 1567. But in the same letter she nevertheless writes: "And for the king, our husband, God knawis alwayis our part towartis him." And likewise: "Alwayis we persave him occupeit and bissy aneuct to haif inquisitioun of our doyings, quhilkis, God willing, sall ay be sic as nane sall haif occasioun to be offendit with thame, or to report of us any wayis but honorably."—Labanoff, i. 329.

[3] Telle malaventure est advenue au temps, que sa Majesté et le roy estoient au meilleur mesnaige, que l'on pouvait desirer.—Note of the French envoy, De Clernault, at Berwick, the 12th February 1567, contained in Chalmers, *Life of Mary Stuart*, i. 133. The French nobleman just named resided in Scotland, while the French minister, du Croc, had got leave to pay a visit to his home (Sandret, *Ambassade de Philibert du Croc en Écosse, Étude Historique*, Paris, 1870, p. 12), and had departed from Edinburgh two days previously, in order to give, without delay, to Catherine de Medici and Charles IX. more precise intelligence about Darnley's death. He carried with him also a letter to these about the catastrophe, which had been immediately drawn up on the Monday in the Scottish Privy Council, but

it was the fear of this which hastened the work of CHAP. V. the murderers.

1567.

As there cannot be a doubt that the Earl of Bothwell had from the beginning been the only one who conceived the design of removing Darnley in one way or another, so also the belief was long prevalent in Scotland that, not only the different persons of lower rank, who were afterwards seized and executed for complicity in the murder, had given their assistance to it, but that · likewise many of higher rank and authority had taken an active hand in the murderous transaction itself. One of the first of the subordinate agents to suffer for complicity in the murder declared that in the evening of the 9th February he had met on the way to the King's dwelling other conspirators whom he did not know, as they had their faces muffled up[1] just as the conspirators against King Eric Glipping came to Finderup " cloaked and masked "—and among the earliest reports of the perpetration of the murder that reached England from Scotland we meet with the statement, that some one had seen, on the night of the murder, Andrew Ker of Faldonside, the still unpardoned, banished rebel, and other accomplices with him " on horseback in the vicinity of the spot in order to assist in the cruel project, if it had been necessary." During the stormy years which

had likewise by his journey through to Berwick enjoyed an opportunity here to give an account of the tragedy that had happened, which was sent from Berwick to the English court. Chalmers (*Life of Mary Queen of Scots*, ii. 113-115), who has also printed the note of Clernault among his " Proofs of Mary's Reconcilement to Darnley before she set out to bring him from Glas-

gow," gives these the superscription : " Amantium iræ amoris redintegratio est."
[1] Quhilks had cloakes about yare faces.—William Powrie's confession ; Laing, *History of Scotland*, ii. 243.
[2] Letter from Sir William Drury to Cecil of 13th May 1567.—*Calendar of State Papers, Foreign Series*, 1566-1568, p. 229.

CHAP.   followed the murder, not only was a disclosure
  V.   gradually made, as the changed position of parties
1571.   permitted, of several who had been more or less
engaged in the conspiracy, but new accusations of
complicity in the perpetration of the murder itself
were also brought forward. Thus in the year 1571,
during the regency of Darnley's father, when Captain Thomas Crawford of Jordanhill had taken
Dumbarton Castle, where the Queen's party had
constantly maintained themselves since the beginning of the civil war, among others John Hamilton,
the Catholic Archbishop of St. Andrews, fell as a
prisoner into his hands. He was forthwith conveyed
to Stirling, and, without any proper trial, there
hanged ; and to the fact of his having been the first
bishop in Scotland who perished by the hangman's
hand were owing, in no small degree, the numerous
suspicions about his conduct in connection with
Darnley's murder. The proofs of this on which
Buchanan, with the recklessness not unusual with
him, has relied, in the first instance, in his pamphlet,
and afterwards in his *History*, are however, on the
whole, but weak. Thus Buchanan urges that the
archbishop, who had accompanied the Queen in her
journey to Glasgow, did not, while in Edinburgh in
the winter of 1567, reside, as formerly, in the more
populated part of the city, but in the building belonging to his brother, the Duke of Châtelherault,
nearest to Darnley's residence during his illness, and
that from the highest part of Edinburgh there had
been here seen, during the night, a light which was
only extinguished when the catastrophe took place.[1]

[1] Auxit hominum suspicionem, quod tum in ædes fratris Comitis Araniæ divertisset, ei domui pro- pinquas, in qua Rex occisus erat cum semper antea in celebri urbis loco habitaret, ubi commode, et

Buchanan, who always shows himself blinded by the
hereditary hatred of the Lennoxes against the Hamiltons, may himself have found sufficient evidence
when, after the archbishop had been made prisoner,
he along with Lord William Ruthven and Justice-
Clerk, Sir John Bellenden of Auchinoul, brought
forward the accusation against him at Stirling. He
also subsequently represented it in his Scottish History as a thing incontrovertible, that many different
divisions of conspirators from different quarters met
for the accomplishment of the murderous deed, and
that one of them consisted of six or seven of the
Hamilton vassals who had been sent by the archbishop. But, while the latter a few moments before
his execution confessed with regret that he had
subsequently promoted the murder of Buchanan's
favourite, Regent Murray, he continued on the contrary to the last to repel every accusation of having
had any share whatever in Darnley's murder.[1]   In
the year 1581, when the Earl of Morton, after James
VI. had assumed the reins of government, was
executed on the ground of having been privy to the
conspiracy, his cousin, Archibald Douglas, was also
accused of complicity in the murder, and only saved
himself by escaping into England, but a man named
John Binning, who had been in his service at the
time the murder took place, and who was himself

salutationibus celebrari, et epulis
popularem gratiam colligere posset: item, quod, e superioribus
urbis locis, lumen et pervigiliæ
in ejus ædibus tota nocte con-
spiciebantur, ac tum demun, ubi
ruinæ, propinquæ fragor inso-
nuit, lumina sunt exstincta ; et
clientes, qui frequentes, armati
vigilaverant, vetiti egredi.—Buchanan, *Rerum Scot. Hist.*, p. 214.

[1] His answer to the first heid
wes, that he knew nathing of tho
Kingis murther, and that he wes
sa innocent thairaf that he wald
not ask God mercie thairfoir. . . .
And sua he continowit to the
death in his denyall that he haid
na knowlege of the Kingis mur-
thour.—*Diurnal of Occurrents*, p.
204.

CHAP.
V.
1567.

executed in June 1581 for his connection with it, declared that his master also had actually gone out in the evening to the accomplishment of the deed along with him and his fellow-servant Gaimer.[1] But in the year 1586 Douglas, after being acquitted in a manner which somewhat recalls Bothwell's own acquittal, was even taken into favour by James VI. Binning, before his death, also denounced John Maitland of Coldingham, and Robert Balfour, the proprietor of the house in the Kirk-of-Field, as accomplices, and against the brothers of these two, namely, the Secretary of State, William Maitland of Lethington, and Sir James Balfour, the same accusation had been previously directed, but it seems that contemporaries nevertheless, with respect to them, confounded the preceding general confederacy against Darnley, and the knowledge of its intended object, with the execution of the deed itself.

The ringleader in this was, at all events, undoubtedly the Earl of Bothwell. As his immediate assistants he had selected four of the smaller Scottish lairds, vassals of his own, namely, James, laird of Ormiston, in Teviotdale, the latter's uncle (or as he is called in Scots, his father's brother), Hob Ormiston, John Hay of Talla, and John Hepburn of Bolton, a cousin of the Earl. Along with these, whom he had won over for the work by confiding to them the agreement of the nobles at Craigmillar,[2] the Earl employed or took with him on the

---

[1] That his master passed to the deid doing, the said Binning and Gaimer, his servants, being with him in company. — Declaration; Laing, *History of Scotland*, ii. 337.

[2] The earle requyred me to take pairt with him therein, because, as he alledged, I was ane man of activeness (alace theirfor!), quhair I utterly refuisit, and said, God forbid, bot, gif it were upon the field, to fight with your Lordschip unto the death, I sould not feir my skinn cutting. Then the said Earle

night of the murder, of his own servants, William CHAP.
Powrie, Patrick Wilson, and George Dalgleish, the   V.
last of whom solemnly declared, before his execution, 1567.
that he then followed Bothwell not knowing that it
concerned the king's death, until this had taken
place.[1] Among the servants of the Queen he had
moreover made sure of the positive assistance of
the Frenchman, Nicolas Hubert or Paris, who had
formerly been in his own service; to him he applied
for, and through him he at length obtained, the key
of the Queen's room in Balfour's house; this he
wished also to get possession of, although he had
beforehand been able to procure the keys which
could open every apartment in it. Besides the
more subordinate agents in this transaction already
named, the Act of Parliament, which was issued
against Bothwell on the 30th December 1567,
finally mentions also Symon Armstrong and William
Murray as accomplices in the murder.[2]

Lord Robert Stuart, Prior of Holyroodhouse,
Mary's half-brother, had, under promise of silence,
confided to Darnley that imminent danger threatened his life if he did not quickly leave the place
where he was staying.[3] Darnley repeated this to
the Queen, who, on this occasion, as she was passing
the Friday night in Balfour's house, wrote to her

said to me, Tuishe, Ormistoune, ye
need not to take feir of this, for
the haill lords hes concluded the
samen langsyne in Craigmiller.—
Confession of the Laird of Ormiston ; Laing, *History of Scotland*,
ii. 291.
[1] Daglishe suyd, as God shall be
my judge, I knew nothing of the
kingis daith befoir it was done.—
Confession of Dalgleish ; Laing,
History of Scotland, ii. 264.

[2] Anderson, *Collections*, iv. 152.
Six years later the declaration of
the Laird of Ormiston named also
of the Queen's people Archibald
Beaton along with Paris:—"Pareis
and Archie Betoun com and met
us, and said all wes ready preparit
for the setting of the lunt."—Laing,
History of Scotland, ii. 292.

[3] *Memoirs of Sir James Melvil*,
p. 78.

half-brother about it; but Robert Stuart denied
that he had said any such thing, and, if we are
to believe the Queen's enemies, this denial led to
an altercation between him and Darnley so sharp
that each laid his hand upon his sword.[1] The
fatal hour had, however, really drawn near. At
first it had been intended to kill the king while
walking in the neighbouring gardens during his
convalescence, but this plan was abandoned, as the
murder would thus be more easily found out. By
means of barrels of gunpowder, which Bothwell had
caused to be brought from Dunbar Castle to his
rooms in Holyrood, it was deemed that the object
in view could be attained with greater security, and
its execution had accordingly been fixed for the
same Saturday night on which Darnley had the
altercation with Robert Stuart. All the preparations were not indeed, at this time, in readiness,
but that scene, which could not be hidden from
Bothwell, showed that no longer delay was advisable. On the afternoon of Sunday the 9th February
1567, the final consultation was held for two hours
in Bothwell's rooms at Holyrood, between the Earl,
both the Ormistons, John Hepburn, and John Hay.
The Queen had promised that she would be present
at a dance and merry-making in the evening, at the
palace, on the occasion of the wedding, that day, of
one of her servants, Sebastian Pagez, a Frenchman
from Clermont, to a Scots girl.[2] The time could not
be more opportune.

[1] Buchanan, who always knows
how to explain Mary Stuart's
thoughts, makes her not only re-
joice at the huff of the young men,
but says:—" Regina hoc spectaculo
lœta, . . . alterum fratrem Jacob-

um advocat, velut ad litem diri-
mendam : re vera, ut ipse quoque
per occasionem tolli posset."—*Rerum Scoticarum Historia*, p. 213.
[2] He was married to Christily
Hogg. Two days later the wedding

When the consultation was concluded, Bothwell repaired to a banquet, given the same day, on account of the approaching departure of the Savoyard ambassador Moretta, by the Bishop of Argyll, who resided in John Balfour's house in Edinburgh, and which the Queen, who had attended the marriage in the forenoon, had also promised to honour with her presence.[1] But on rising from table, and when all was enveloped in the darkness of a winter night,[2] Bothwell betook himself alone to meet with his assistants in the vicinity of the parsonage. The powder had been put on a couple of horses by William Powrie and Patrick Wilson, at the order of John Hepburn, and, at ten o'clock, was conveyed, not through the city, but outside the city wall up towards the house, the quantity being so great that it required to be brought in two succes-

of Margaret Carwod, one of the Queen's ladies, also took place; she was married on the 11th February 1567, to John Stuart of Tullypowreis (Joseph Robertson's Preface to *Les Inuentaires de la Royne Descosse*, p. lvii). These closely occurring marriages have given occasion to considerable confusion with more recent authors. Thus Malcolm Laing (*History of Scotland*, i. 35), Mignet (*Histoire de Marie Stuart*, i. 302), Wiesener (*Marie Stuart et le Comte de Bothwell*, p. 253; *Revue des Questions Historiques*, iii. 5, 103), Froude (*History of England*, viii. 367), and Gauthier (*Histoire Marie Stuart*, i. 333), all incorrectly make Sebastian Pagez to be married, on the 9th February, to Margaret Curwod, the Queen's confidential lady. Buchanan's pamphlet (*De Maria Scotorum Regina*, p. 18) mentions him as "Sebastianus, Arvernus genere ob psalendi peritiam

et sales Reginæ admodum gratus," and at the baptism of James VI. in Stirling he had the management of the masked ball then given. On the 16th June 1567, when Mary Stuart was dethroned, he also was imprisoned on suspicion of complicity in the murder of the king (*Diurnal of Occurrents*, p. 115), but he must have afterward been set at liberty again, as, in the year 1586, he is still named (Labanoff, vii. 250) among Mary Stuart's servants during her imprisonment in England.
[1] John Hepburn's Declaration; Laing, *History of Scotland*, ii. 257. The so-called Diary of Cecil, *Ibid.*, p. 87. Burton (*History of Scotland*, Second Edition, iv. 188) incorrectly names the Countess of Argyll as the person who gave this entertainment.
[2] Sua sone as it was mirk.—Declaration of John Hay; Laing, *History of Scotland*, ii. 253.

sive loads. The back-door was opened by Paris, and the opportunity was favourable ; for the Queen shortly beforehand, in high spirits, had left the banquet in the city to return to the marriage festivities, but on the way had come, accompanied by the Earls of Argyll, Huntly, and Cassilis, to pay a visit to the king, with whom she remained a couple of hours before the dancing should begin at the palace, and the Queen, after the old custom, should "conduct the bride to bed." As a large barrel, into which the murderers had at first intended to put the bags of powder, could not be got through the back-door, the bags had to be carried in separately by the laird of Ormiston, Hepburn, and Hay, and so Bothwell, who was impatiently looking on, asked whether all were not ready, and "bade them make haste before the Queen came back from the King, for if she returned ere they were ready, they would not find another opportunity so good."[1] When the powder was conveyed in, and a large portion of it heaped up in the very room used by the Queen on the preceding nights, Hay and Hepburn were shut in underneath, in order to prepare everything for the explosion,[2] while the Earl of Bothwell went up-stairs to Darnley's guests. The Queen was still engaged in conversation with Darnley ; at the same time the Earls who accompanied her were busy with a game of dice.

---

[1] My Lord come and speirid gyf all was redy, and bad yame haist before the Queene cum furth of the Kingis house, for gyf she come furth before yay wer reddy, yay wald not find sic commodity. —Deposition of John Hepburn ; Laing, *History of Scotland*, ii. 257.

[2] Be force of gun poulder, qlke a lytle afore was plasit and imput be him and his foresaids under the grund and angular stains, and within the voltis, in laich and darnit (low and hidden) pairts and places. —Sentence on the Earl of Morton ; Laing, *History of Scotland*, ii. 320.

This final interview between Darnley and Mary CHAP.
Stuart bore the impression of a cordiality long V.
wanting; the Queen, full of thoughts of the mar- 1567.
riage, oftener than once kissed the king, and gave
him a ring,[1] and the king, after her departure, continued, until he went to sleep, to speak to his
servants of the joy which her affection now promised
him, only that he had become again disconcerted
when she once happened to mention Riccio's name.[2]
Of his servants, William Taylor remained during
the night in the king's room; besides him there
were also in the house Thomas Nelson, Edward
Symonds, Andrew Mackay, and the boy Glen.

The Earl of Bothwell accompanied the Queen,
when, at eleven o'clock, she came down from the
king—and past her room, which, if she had been
able to enter, she would now have found filled with
gunpowder—and, with torches carried before her,
she wended her way with her retinue back to the
entertainment in Holyrood.[3] Bothwell left the
feast at midnight, and, in his own rooms in the
palace, doffing his silver-embroidered court dress of
black silk and velvet, putting on a simple dress, and

---

[1] "None but those wives," says
Chalmers, "who stand recorded, for
their barbarity and wickedness,
could have given her husband such
a pledge of her fidelity and affection; knowing that he was to be
put to death soon after her departure." — *History of Mary, Queen
of Scots*, ii. 181.

[2] Ibi, cum hilarius solito per
aliquot horas collocuta esset, sæpe
eum deosculata, annulum etiam
tradidit. Post dicessum Reginæ,
quum Rex, inter paucos qui ad-
erant ministros, illius diei dicta
factaque retractaret, inter alios ser-

mones, ad bene sperandum ejus
animum erigentes, paucorum verb-
orum recordatio lætitiam non nihil
turbavit;—injecta est ab ea mentio
Dauidem Rizium, superiore anno,
circa id ipsum tempus interfectum
fuisse.—Buchanan, *Rerum Scoticarum Historia*, p. 214.

[3] "Yay carryit the saids maill
and tronk again to the Abbay,
and as yay came up the Blaik
Frier Wind, the Queenes grace
was gangand before yame with
licht torches," it is said in William
Powrie's Declaration; Laing, *History of Scotland*, ii. 244.

enveloping himself in a trooper's cloak, he forthwith
hurried back to the parsonage, taking with him
Paris and Dalgleish, and followed by Powrie and
Wilson, who like him had returned to Holyrood.
This time the way taken was not round outside the
city wall, but through the suburb of the Canongate,
which then occupied the space between Holyrood
and the Canongate Port, and thence through the
city itself. They left the Palace through its garden,
but did not succeed in eluding, at the outlet of the
latter, the sentinels, who, standing at their posts,
challenged them with the question, "Who is there?"
but they replied, that they were "Friends,"—
"Friends of Lord Bothwell," and this potent name
put an end to further question.[1] When they reached
the Canongate Port, and found it now shut, as it
was past midnight, they were obliged to call out
here again to the porter, John Galloway, to open
for "Friends of Lord Bothwell," and were once more
obeyed. Arriving at the garden-wall of Balfour's
house, Bothwell ordered three of his attendants to
wait quietly, whatever they might see or hear, while
he himself, although his progress was impeded by
his hand not yet being wholly healed since the fight
with Elliot, sprang along with Paris over the wall.
Half-an-hour after, they returned, having with them
Hay and John Hepburn, who had now set fire to the
one end of a thick match leading to the gunpowder,

[1] Thus it is said in the Declaration of William Powrie (Laing, *History of Scotland*, ii. 245):— "And deponis, yat as yai came by the gait of the Quenes south garden, the two sentinellis yat stude at the zet yat gangis to the uther cloiss, speirit at yame, quha is yat? and answerit—Friends. The sentinel speirit, quhat friends? and yai answerit, my Lord Bothwell's friends." A corresponding statement is likewise found in the Declaration of George Dalgleish, *Ibid.* ii. 249.

and forthwith retired, locking the door behind them. It was two o'clock. As it was some time ere the match had burnt out, Bothwell, who would not leave until he saw the end of the matter,[1] became impatient, and asked whether there was any window in the house through which one could see if the match was yet burning. While they were still speaking, the explosion took place, and they hurried away, the report sounding frightfully in the still night.[2] Buchanan even writes, that some buildings in the neighbourhood were shaken by the explosion, and that people in the most distant parts of the city, who were reposing securely in the arms of sleep, awoke in terror.[3] Darnley, along with his servants, Taylor and Mackay, lay like corpses on the ground; Mackay and Glen were crushed; Nelson and Symonds were so far unhurt, as to be able to rise from among the ruins. As Darnley, who at some distance outside the garden wall, lay under a tree, in his linen only, but with his remaining clothing and his boots by his side, and was neither

---

[1] And quhen my Lord saw yat ye matter came not hastily to pass, he was angre, and wald have gen in himself in the house, and the said John Hepburn stoppit him, saying this wordis, ze neid not.— Hay's Declaration; Laing, *History of Scotland*, ii. 255. And speirit gyf yair was ony part of the house yat they mycht se the lunt, gyff it was burnand anouch.—The Declaration of Hepburn, *Ibid.* ii. 258.

[2] In the Declaration which is ascribed to Nicolas Hubert or Paris, it is said about himself and Bothwell:—" Voylà comme ung tempeste on ung tonnoyre qui va eslever. De la peur que j'eu je

cheus en terre, les cheveux dressés comme allaines, dysant : Hélas, Monsieur, qu'est-ce cecy ? Il me dict. Je me suis trouvé à des entreprises grandes, mais jamais ne me feit ay grand peur que cest-ycy."—Laing, *History of Scotland*, ii. 279.

[3] Tanto cum fragore, ut ædes aliquot vicinæ quaterentur, et in longinquioribus urbis partibus, qui somno gravissimo erant oppressi, velut attoniti expergiscerentur. —Buchanan, *Rerum Scoticarum Historia*, p. 214. Swa that thair remainit nocht ane stane upoun uther undistroyit. — *Diurnal of Occurrents*, p. 106.

bruised by any fall, nor had his body scorched,[1] this circumstance occasioned afterwards, when the explosive action of gunpowder was less known than it is now, the suspicion that before being blown up, he had been suffocated with a pocket-handkerchief stuffed into his mouth,—a suspicion which the rumours current about the period coloured with increased exaggeration.[2] But as the body of Darnley, had he been really murdered beforehand, would certainly not have been laid so far away from the house, so it is expressly said in the declaration about the explosion, which we still have from Darnley's servant, Thomas Nelson, who slept in the room just by the side of the king's, that he and his comrades had not been sensible of the least thing before the house in which they lay fell about them.[3] In later times, when by and by John Hepburn, John Hay, and James Ormiston were apprehended, they too unanimously protested before their execution, that the king died by the blowing up of the house, without having been suffocated by any one's hand.[4] The

[1] Sir James Melvil tells in his Memoirs, that Bothwell himself, the morning after the murder, called his attention to this circumstance :—" He desired me to go up and see him, how that there was not a hurt nor a mark on all his body."—*Memoirs*, p. 78.

[2] *Memoirs of Sir James Melvil*, p. 78. One of the earliest rumours has recently been again brought to light by a despatch from the Papal Nuncio in Paris to Cosmo I. de Medici, which Prince Labanoff has printed in his well-known collection. In this we meet not only with the report to the effect that the fugitive Darnley had been suffocated, but even with a kindred story, according to which "alcune donne, che allogiavano vicino al giardino, affermano d'haver udito gridar il Re. 'Eh fratelli miei, habbiate pietà di me per amor di Colui che hebbe misericordia di tutto il mondo.'"—Labanoff, vii. 108, 109.

[3] Quhilks newir knew of ony thing, quhill the hous quherin thay lay wes fallin about thame.—Declaration of Thomas Nelson ; Laing, *History of Scotland*, ii. 268.

[4] In the confession of John Hepburn of 3d January 1568, it is said :—" He knowis nat other, but that he was blowin in the ayre, for he was handilit with na men's handes as he saw, and if he was, it

belief that by such an explosion one could quite certainly be got rid of by his enemies, seems also at a later period, during the Reformation contest, to have gained general acceptance. Already, under the government of Elizabeth, the Catholics of England had proposed to blow up the Queen, together with her parliament.[1] And when the rule of James VI. failed to realise sufficiently all the expectations which the Catholics had formed, they actually attempted in London, in the year 1605, by the so-called Gunpowder Plot, to repeat on a larger scale the Scottish tragedy. On this occasion, when Thomas Percy had written one of his friends, Lord Mounteagle, the note intended to warn him against being present at the opening of Parliament, and the latter felt that he ought to show it to the Secretary of State, Lord Salisbury, and when Salisbury showed the king himself the note in the Privy Council, it was he who first guessed the meaning of the mysterious warning. The words with which it concluded, " The danger is past as soon as you burn this letter," reminded him of his father's sudden death, and accordingly having, on the evening before the opening of Parliament,

was with others, and not with tham." In the confession of John Hay of the same day, we likewise read :—" He affirmit, that in Setoun my Lord Bothwell callit on him and sayd, quhat thought you quhen thou saw him blowin in the ayre." In the confession of the Laird of Ormiston of 13th December 1573, are found furthermore these words :—" Being requyrit be the said minister, gif he knew not that the king was utherways handilit be menes handes, for it is commonlie spokin he was brought furth and wirryit, quha anserit, as I sall answer to my God, I knew nothing but he was blawin up ; and did enquyre the samyn maist dilligentlie at John Hepburne and John Hay, and all that tarreit behind me, quha swore unto me they never knew nae uther thing bot he was blawin up." —Laing, *History of Scotland*, ii. 263, 264, 293.

[1] Ranke, *Englische Geschichte vornehmlich im sechszehnten und siebzehnten Jahrhundert*, i. 587.

O

CHAP. caused a search to be made of the cellars under the
V.   house in which it was to meet, Guy Fawkes was
1567. there seized while he was, with a light in his hand,
in the act of making the same preparations with
gunpowder which John Hepburn and John Hay
completed for the Earl of Bothwell.

When at daybreak the people of Edinburgh
assembled about the ruins of the parsonage, the
Earl of Bothwell was also among the first to step
towards the corpse of the king. As soon as he had
seen his work accomplished, and the echoes from
Arthur's Seat and Salisbury Crags caused the crash
to reverberate over Holyrood, he had as quickly
as possible hurried with his confederates back to
the palace. They would now have willingly avoided
passing again through the Canongate Port, and
have rather climbed over the city wall at a part
where it was partially broken down, but Bothwell,
notwithstanding, found the place too high for his
weak hand, and they were obliged once more to
wake the gate-keeper, John Galloway, in order to
get through, and had after that to submit a second
time to describe themselves as "Friends of Lord
Bothwell" to the guard at the palace, who in vain
inquired what the great crash meant.[1] They had
nevertheless reached the palace so speedily, that
Bothwell himself, after demanding something to
drink, could lay himself in bed, and half-an-hour
later, pretend to be terrified when some one knocked

---

[1] Twa of the watchis speirit
quhat yai were, and ye deponar
answerit :—We are servants of
the Erle Bothwell, gangand to
him with news out of the town.
—Declaration of John Hepburn ;
Laing, *History of Scotland*, ii. 258.
Als speirit quhat crak yat was,
and yai answerit, yai knew not.—
Declaration of William Powrie ;
Ibid. ii. 246.

at his door, and, almost speechless with fright, succeeded at length in telling what had happened.[1] He immediately rose, put on again the magnificent dress of the previous day, and repaired along with his brother-in-law, the Earl of Huntly, and several others, to the Queen's apartments, where she also was now informed of the death of the King. The Earl, to whom, as Sheriff of Edinburghshire, it immediately belonged to institute judicial investigation in the matter, next appeared, followed by a company of soldiers, before the spectators at the Kirk-of-Field, and caused Darnley's corpse to be carried to a private house in the neighbourhood, where, by command of the Queen, it was examined by surgeons, who pronounced death to have resulted from the explosion, and where, at the same time, it was also viewed by the other members of Council. From this place it was borne to Holyrood, where it was embalmed, and lay in state. Amongst those who, during this latter proceeding, scanned the body, and could notice that it had no trace of external violence, was also Mary herself, who for a long time in silence fixed her eyes upon Darnley's corpse.[2] On the evening of Saturday the 15th of February, the body was quietly deposited by torch light in the Royal Chapel of Holyrood,[3]

CHAP. V.

1567.

---

[1] Mr. George Hacket come to the zet (palace gate) and knocks, and desired to be in ; and quhan he came in, he appeared to be in ane greit effray, and was black as any pik (pitch), and not ane word to speik. My Lord enquirit, quhat is the matter, man ? And he answerit, the kingis hous is blawn up, and I trow (believe) the king be slayn. And my Lord cryet, Fy, treasoun ! And yan he

raise and pat on his claiths.— Declaration of William Powrie ; Laing, *History of Scotland,* ii. 246.

[2] Ipsa corpus, omnium illius ætatis formosissimum, avide spectavit, nullo in alterutram partem indicio, animi secreta prodente. —Buchanan, *Rerum Scoticarum Historia,* p. 214. A subject for a painter.

[3] The ceremonies indeede were the fewer, bycause that the greatest

and Darnley's coffin obtained a place in the same vault which had already received the earthly remains of Mary's father, James V., and of the latter's first consort, Magdalene, daughter of Francis I.—the body of Mary of Guise had been conveyed over to Rheims in France—as well as the two little coffins containing the dust of Mary's brothers that died immediately after their birth. On Sunday the 23d of March, by command of the Queen, a solemn requiem was there sung over the remains of the King thus cut down in his prime, and five days afterwards, on Good Friday the 28th of March, the Queen, accompanied by only two of her ladies, came over to Holyrood Chapel and remained in prayer from eleven o'clock in the evening till three next morning.[1]

From the very first, after Darnley's death, Mary had kept away from the Palace of Holyrood. As for greater security, before the birth of her son James VI., she had repaired to Edinburgh Castle, so now also, after the murder of the King, by which all were surprised, she got like occasion for again taking refuge in the rocky fortress. Henry Killigrew, the English ambassador, who had been immediately sent by Elizabeth to Edinburgh to assure her of the sympathy of the Queen of England, on the 8th March, still found " Her Majesty here in a dark room, so that he could not see her countenance, but by her words she seemed to be very sorrowful."[2] Three weeks later it is stated in

part of the Counsaile were Protestantes, and had before enterred their owne parentes, without accustomed solemnities of ceremonies.—Lesley's Defence of the Honour of Marie Queene of Scotlande ; Anderson, *Collections*, i. 23.
[1] Letter of Sir William Drury to Cecil from Berwick, 29th March 1567.—*The Calendar of State Papers, Foreign Series*, 1566-8, p. 198.
[2] Killigrew's letter to Cecil, dated Edinburgh, 8th March 1567. —*The Calendar of State Papers, Foreign Series*, 1566-8, p. 185.

another English correspondence about the state of matters in Scotland :—" The Queen has been for the most part either melancholy or sickly ever since, especially this week—upon Tuesday and Wednesday often swooned." "The Queen," continues Drury, "breaketh very much. Upon last Sunday divers were witness, for there was mass of requiem and dirige for the King's soul."[1] That Mary nevertheless, during the forty days required by the strictness of the Scottish custom of mourning, did not submit to pass the time amid the light of candles burning in the day-time, but permitted the windows to be opened for the admission of the sunshine, and latterly, in order to enjoy the fresh air, undertook journeys from Edinburgh on two occasions to Seton, was soon eagerly laid to her charge, and was, by those of the party recently meditating the ruin of Darnley, interpreted in the bitterest manner as a sign of her satisfaction at the murder.[2] In this instance her friends not only pleaded that Darnley could not be placed on a level with the crowned kings of former times, but her most zealous defender, the Bishop of Ross, who himself was then a member of the Privy Council, also goes on to say, after describing her mode of life in the apartments from which the daylight was excluded :—" who had a longer time in this lamenting wise continued,

[1] Letter of Sir William Drury of 29th March 1567, given by Strickland, v. 229.

[2] Buchanan writes: "Nam, quum in more esset, a priscis usque temporibus, ut Reginæ, post maritorum obitum, complures dies, non modo coetu hominum, sed lucis etiam obstinerent aspectu, simulatum quidem luctum agressa est, sed, animi superante lætitia, foribus occlusis, fenestras aperit, et —coelum solemque adspicere sustinuit : Et ante diem duodecimum, confirmato adversus vulgi rumores animo, in agrum Setonium, ad septem ab oppido millia passuum, excurrit." — *Rerum Scoticarum Historia*, p. 215.

had she not ben moste ernestly dehorted by the
vehement exhortations and perswasions of her counsaile, who were moued therto by her physitian's
informations, declaring to them the great and imminent dangers to her health and life, if she did not
with al spede breake vp and leaue that kind of
close and solitarie life." [1]

The same day on which Darnley was found dead
judicial examinations began to be instituted.[2] The
day after, Tuesday the 11th of February, Mary
wrote to the Earl of Lennox in reference to his
son's death, and in a letter, giving the intelligence about it, on the same day sent to her ambassador in Paris, the Archbishop of Glasgow, she
expresses the confidence that God in His grace
had preserved her in order that she might bring
weightier punishment on the crime. " Allvayes
quha ever," she adds, " have taken this wicked
interprys in hand, we assure ourself it wes dressit
als weill for us as for the king ; for we lay the maist
part of the last oulk (week) in that same loging,
and wes thair accompayit with the maist part of the
lordis that are in the town that same night at
midnight, and of very chance tarryit not all night,
be reason of sum mask in the abbaye ; bot we
beleive it wes not chance, bot God that put it in
our hede." [3] In conformity with such utterances
an announcement was made on the 11th February

[1] Lesley's Defence of the Honour
of Marie, Queen of Scotlande.—
Anderson, *Collections*, i. 24. The
bishop adds : " Al which yet, notwithstanding, this her fact is with
these most seuere and graue
censors taken for and reputed as
the very next sin of al to the most

greuous sinne against the Holy
Ghoste."
[2] In the Declaration of Thomas
Nelson it is said that " on the
Monounday at efter none he was
callit and examinat."—Laing, *History of Scotland*, ii. 268.
[3] Mary's letter of 11th Feb-

promising, in the Queen's name, a reward of CHAP. two thousand pounds Scots, and an annuity to the first person who would give information of the murderers; and he, if he had himself been their accomplice, was also assured of forgiveness. Bothwell, who, the same morning on which the crime was committed, sought at first to explain it as caused by lightning,[1] was himself obliged later in the day to subscribe his name to a letter to the Queen-dowager Catherine de Medici and Charles IX. of France, in which the Scottish Council state their assurance that God would never allow such an atrocity to remain concealed or unpunished,[2] and some days afterwards Parliament was summoned in consequence of the king's death. Bothwell still assumed that the death of Darnley would not call forth any great sympathy, at least in Scotland, where the king had wellnigh been mortally hated alike by the powerful family of the Hamiltons, who, through his marriage, had seen their hereditary pretensions to the throne set aside by Murray, who, with arms, had resisted his preferment, and by Morton and his confederates, whom he had betrayed;

ruary 1567 to the Archbishop of Glasgow.—Labanoff, ii. 4.

[1] I came to the door the next morning after the murther, and the Earl of Bothwel said that her Majesty was sorrowful and quiet, which occasioned him to come forth. He said the strangest accident had fallen out which ever was heard of, for thunder had come out of the sky, and had burnt the King's house.—*The Memoirs of Sir James Melvil*, p. 78.

[2] Vostre Majesté et tout le monde cognoistra, que le pays d'Ecosse ne vouldra longuement endurer, qu'une si grande honte luy debastante pour la rendre odieuse par toute la Christianneté, si semblables malheuretez demeurassent cachées ou impunyes. The letter, dated Edinburgh (Lislebourg) the 10th February 1567, is printed in Laing, *History of Scotland*, ii. 97. It is subscribed by the Archbishop of St. Andrews, the Bishops of Ross and Galloway, the Earls of Atholl, Argyll, Cassilis, Huntly, Bothwell, Caithness, and Sutherland, the Lords Fleming and Livingston, the Justice-Clerk, Bellenden, and the Secretary of State, Maitland.

where the king had been despised by the people for his whole behaviour after the murder of Riccio ; and where, in the sixteenth century, all classes were so far removed from the more recent humaneness of feeling which, among the people as a whole, has but a short history, that even men like Buchanan and Knox depict to us such events as the death of Riccio not only with a characteristic coolness, but sometimes almost with manifest pleasure. Should nevertheless any lively sympathy make its appearance, Bothwell might moreover suppose, not without reason, that suspicion would more readily turn against the older enemies of Darnley than against him who thought that he had acted prudently, and believed that he could safely rely on the fidelity of his more immediate accomplices. He had the morning after the murder given Hay of Talla a brown steed and Hepburn of Bolton a white one, caused the last-named to throw the keys used into the crevice of a stone-quarry between Holyrood and Leith,[1] promised Powrie and Wilson that he would send them to the Castle of Hermitage where they should enjoy an honourable maintenance, and in the evening charged all his followers of the previous night " to hold their tongues, for they should never want so long as he had anything."

Bothwell was however disappointed in both his suppositions. Had Darnley died a natural death he would have been quickly forgotten, but the tragical circumstances in which the young sick king was called from sleep into the arms of death now

---

[1] Quhilk the deponar keist in the quarie hole betwixt ye Abbay and Leith.—Declaration of John Hepburn ; Laing, *History of Scotland*, ii. 259.

awakened in a portion of the people a sympathy CHAP.
V. which was purposely fostered by the older enemies of Bothwell. For while, both in foreign countries 1567. and in Scotland, it was at first certainly thought that Murray and Morton were originators of the murder,[1] yet the most common suspicion speedily turned against him who had actually accomplished it. Nor indeed had the caution used in its perpetration been very great, since the Earl's accomplices had, during the fatal night, been repeatedly challenged, and had as repeatedly replied that they were the Earl of Bothwell's friends. Very soon it was commonly said that Bothwell was the perpetrator; voices were heard at night crying out that Bothwell was the murderer: "Some drawing his pourtraict to the life, set above it this superscription: 'Here is the murtherer of the king,' and threw the same into the street;"[2] placards were secretly posted up which also named him at the head of those charged with the crime. But although Bothwell's expectations were thus far disappointed, and notwithstanding that even now, under the suspicion threatening him, he was usually seen, when he spoke with strangers, to lay his hand on

---

[1] Morton had however remained at Whittingham, and Murray had been so prudent, or, according to Buchanan, on account of a premature delivery by the Earl's wife, so fortunate, as to leave Edinburgh on the same Sunday, which was the last day of the king's life. If we may believe a report communicated by the Bishop of Ross, Murray is nevertheless alleged, after having crossed the Forth, and was riding on his way through Fife, to have said in the evening to a confidential servant: "This night ere morning the Lord Darnley shall lose his life."— Lesley's Defence of the Honour of Marie, Queene of Scotlande ; Anderson, *Collections,* i. 75.

[2] Spottiswood, *History of the Church of Scotland, beginning the year of our Lord 203, and continued to the end of the Reign of King James the VI.* (the third edition, London, 1668), fol. p. 200. There is not now to be found in the whole of Scotland any portrait of Bothwell.

CHAP.
V.

1567.

his dagger,[1] yet he could still rely on the influence which he, the highly exalted Earl, and his powerful friends in the council, were able to bring to bear on the mode in which the investigation into the murder was conducted.[2] Some few persons, and especially some poor people who dwelt in the neighbourhood of the parsonage, were examined, but good care was taken to prevent any greater light on the subject from appearing. The Queen, whose earlier breach with her husband was generally known, and in reference to whom therefore the first guesses concerning Darnley's death were far from favourable, had been reminded by her exalted relatives in France and from other quarters of the necessity of a grave judicial prosecution in connection with it; but in a matter like this a queen must still lean upon her council, and feeling herself to be really innocent, and being then, as Mary protested she was, ignorant of who had been the actual perpetrator,[3] she must also have been so much the less inclined to permit another, a member of her Privy Council, to be imprisoned in consequence of those denunciations by anonymous writers, who themselves refused to come forward. As the Queen's own name was by no means always spared,[4] it was so much easier for

[1] And his hand, as he talks with any that is not assured unto him, upon his dagger.—Report of Sir William Drury to Cecil from Berwick, dated 28th February 1567; Tytler, *History of Scotland*, vii. 371.

[2] Sed quis auderet Bothuelium attingere, quum idem reus, judex, quæsitor, pænæ exactor, esset futurus?—Buchanan, *Rerum Scoticarum Historia*, p. 215.

[3] The Bishop of Ross, who at that time constantly took part in the meetings of the Privy Council,

writes: "For she, good innocent Ladie, hath, upon her honour, protested and plainly declared, that afore her taking and imprisonment she neuer knew, who were either principal or accessarie, or by any meanes culpable and blame-worthy concerning the said murther."— Lesley's Defence of the Honour of Marie Quene of Scotlande; Anderson, *Collections*, i. 42.

[4] According to the reports of Sir William Drury to Cecil in England the market women could even one

Bothwell, on the other hand, to give the investiga- CHAP.
tion begun such a direction that the prosecution for V.
the murder was almost swallowed up by the prose- 1567.
cution of the lampooners.[1]

The matter first became really dangerous for
Bothwell when at length a man ventured openly to
put his name to the charge. Darnley's father, the
Earl of Lennox, whom the Queen had immediately
apprised of his son's death, had in consequence
been in correspondence with her about the institu-
tion of a judicial process in reference to it. As
Lennox, who, in a letter from his castle at Hous-
ton, of the 20th February, had been still unable
to bring forward any definite accusation, subsequently stated in a letter of the 26th of the same
month, that he had heard of certain placards posted
up in Edinburgh, denouncing certain persons as
guilty of the murder, and that therefore he must
desire these persons to be taken into custody, Mary,
on the 1st of March replied to him, that there
were so many placards, with so many different names,
but that if the Earl himself would fix upon some of
these names, the parties concerned should be pro-

day be heard, when Mary was
passing the market of Edinburgh,
crying out : "God preserve your
grace, if you are saikless (guiltless)
of the king's death."—Tytler, *History of Scotland*, vii. 83.

[1] Ita omissa de Regis morte
quæstione, subit altera, multo
acrior, adversus libellorum auctores,
et (ut ipsi loquebantur), Bothuelli
calumniatores.—Buchanan, *Rerum
Scoticarum Historia*, p. 215. There
was then no opposition against
Bothwell in the Council. On the
8th March Murray had, beside the
Earls Huntly and Argyll and

State-Secretary, the laird of Lethington, also Bothwell at dinner
with him three weeks after that the
latter had been publicly accused of
the murder. This is proved by
Killigrew's letter, written on the
above-mentioned day, to Cecil.—
Chalmers, *Life of Mary Queen of
Scots*, ii. 231. Under a proclamation from the Privy Council of
14th March 1567 (printed in Anderson, *Collections*, i. 38) against
some of the offensive caricatures of
the Queen which had been posted
up in Edinburgh, we meet with
Murray's name also along with
Bothwell's and those of his friends.

V.

1567.

secuted, and, if guilty, should be punished according to their deserts. Darnley's father then at last took courage, and in a letter of the 17th March, in which he expresses his surprise that these names seemed to have been concealed from Her Majesty, he alleged as persons whom, for his part, he also highly suspected,[1] according to one placard, the Earl of Bothwell, James Balfour, David Chalmers, and a certain John Spens; according to another, among the servants of the Queen, the foreigners Francisco de Bisso, Sebastian Pagez, Jean de Bordeaux, and Joseph Riccio, the brother of David. The Queen laid this letter before her council, at the meetings in which Bothwell also was constantly present, and the answers, consisting of two documents. One of these is a letter to Lennox from Mary, dated Edinburgh, 24th March, in which the Queen apprises him that the persons named by him shall be subjected to such a judicial examination as the laws of the kingdom authorise, and desires him quickly to make his appearance in Edinburgh in order to see that the cause was conducted in a right manner.[2] The other is

[1] Quhilk personis, I assuyre zour majestie, I, for my part, greitlie suspect. — Letter of the Earl of Lennox to Mary Stuart, of 17th March 1567 ; Anderson, *Collections*, i. 48.   David Chalmers of Ormond, originally trained for the Church, had afterwards become a spiritual member of the Supreme Court, as well as a member of the Privy Council. He supported the side of Mary Stuart on her escape from Lochleven, and after her flight to England he retired to Spain and France. Here he dedicated in the year 1572 to Charles IX., his " Abridgment of the History of Scotland, France,

and England ;" in the year 1573 to Catherine de Medici " A Discourse on the Legitimate succession of Women ;" and in 1579 to Mary Stuart, " La Recherche des Singularitez plus remarquables concernment le État d'Escosse." Subsequently, on being pardoned, he got back his place in the Supreme Court, and died in Scotland in the year 1592.—Brunton and Haig, *Historical Account of the Senators of the College of Justice*, pp. 123, 125.

[2] And thairfore we pray zou, gif zour lassour and commoditie may sut, addres zou to be at ws heir in

an Act issued on the 28th March by the members of CHAP.
the council, Bothwell being also among them, which, V.
after stating how the Earl of Lennox had wished 1567.
the Earl of Bothwell, and the other persons named
in certain anonymous placards, to be put in custody
and prosecuted, without agreeing to their imprisonment, appoints a court of assize to be held the 12th
of April next, and this to be publicly proclaimed at
the market-places of Edinburgh, Glasgow, Dumbarton, and other places where it was judged
necessary, in order that all and every one who wished
to accuse the Earl, or the other persons suspected
by Lennox, might be able to meet before the court
in Edinburgh at the appointed time. On the side
of Lennox, who assuredly saw that it was easier to
accuse than to convict a man so powerful as Bothwell,
it was matter of complaint that the respite was too
short, while Bothwell, on his part, pretended that
he found the time too little for the preparation of
his defence; but in fact it was simply the law of
Scotland that fifteen days should elapse betwixt the
summoning and the holding of the court of assize.[1]
As the court day drew near, a scene was repeated
similar to that which had been witnessed in 1565,
when Bothwell himself wanted courage to make his
appearance. But this time it was Bothwell who
assembled the immense following, the Hepburns,
his vassals and other adherents thronging into

Edinburgh this oulk approcheand, quhair ze may see the said triall, and declair thay things quhilk ze knaw may further the same ; and thair ze sall haue experience of our ernest will and effectuus mynd to haue an end in this mater, and the auctours of sa unworthie a deid realie punist, als far furth, in effect, as befoir this, and now presentlie we haue writtin and promist.— Letter of 24th March 1567 to the Earl of Lennox, signed " Zour gud Dohter, Marie R. ;" Anderson, *Collections*, i. 49.

[1] Hume, *Law of Scotland respecting Trial for Crimes.* Edinburgh, 1800, 4to, ii. 257.

CHAP.
V.
1567.

Edinburgh in so great a multitude, that when the Earl, on the morning of the 12th April, rode from Holyrood to the Assize court, he was accompanied by a whole host of friends. The Earl of Lennox could not present a similar array of attendants; his vassals had, during his long exile in England, become accustomed to a certain measure of independence, and he had not been able as yet to regain the strong authority over them which a Scottish chief was wont in other circumstances to exercise. Immediately before the holding of the assize, he wrote on the 11th April to the Queen from Stirling, stating that he had become sick, and craving the postponement of the case, just as he had also begged Elizabeth to write Mary to the same effect. The bearer of Elizabeth's letter, which was written on the 8th April, did not reach Edinburgh till six o'clock in the morning of the 12th April; he was not in time with his message, to be able to press through the crowds of Bothwell's followers, who were swaying backwards and forwards while waiting in front of Holyrood for the Earl, and who met him with threatening speeches about "such Englishe vilaynes as sought and procured the stay of the Assiss,"[1] and refusals to see to the delivery of his letter. Only when all the noblemen and vassals had mounted their horses, and Bothwell, along with Lethington, came out from the palace, could these even receive Elizabeth's letter, with which they turned back to the palace; and when, on the lapse

[1] Letter of Sir William Drury to Cecil, dated Berwick, 15th April 1567.—Chalmers, *Life of Mary Queen of Scots*, ii. 245. Sir William Drury on the 11th April, at ten o'clock in the evening, received Elizabeth's letter at Berwick, and thence without delay transmitted it by "the Provost Marschall" to Edinburgh.

of a short time, they rejoined the waiting crowds of CHAP.
V. horsemen, Lethington told Elizabeth's messenger, in answer to his question whether it had really been 1567. given to the Queen, that she was still asleep, that therefore he had not given it, and that on this busy day there would hardly be time for doing so until after the assize was held.

Attended by a large number of noblemen and vassals, which the envoy of Elizabeth estimated at four thousand,[1] Bothwell rode to the assize. This was held at that time in a building reared in 1561, and finally demolished in 1817, which was called the Tolbooth, but which has become better known through Sir Walter Scott's novel, under the name of "The Heart of Mid-Lothian." As assessors in the court we find named James Macgill, Henry Balnaves, of Hallhill, Robert Pitcairn, Prior of Dumfermline, and Lord Lindsay;[2] it was presided over by the Earl of Argyll as chief justice, the latter, although two years before the enemy of Bothwell, during his contest with Murray, having now for a length of time been his political confederate.

When Bothwell, however, advanced to the bar, he was pale and downcast. The laird of Ormiston, one of his associates, who had followed him to the process, which in reality also concerned himself, approached him, and in a low voice said to him :— "Fye, my lord, what devill is this ye are doand? Your face shawes what ye are, hald up your face, for

[1] So giving place to the thronge of people that passed, wch was greate, and by the estimaçon of men of good judgments above IIII· gentelmen besids other.— Letter of Sir William Drury quoted by Chalmers, ii. 246.

[2] Keith, *History of the Affairs of the Church and State in Scotland,* i. 375. Laing (*History of Scotland,* i. 69), however, holds that this statement must only be considered as a mere guess by Keith.

Godis sake, and luik blythlie; ye might luike swa and ye were gangand to the deid. Allace, and wo worth them that ever devysit it, I trow it sall garr us all murne." Bothwell, however, only answered him :—" Had your tongue ; I wald not yet it wer to doe ; I have ane outgait fra it, cum as it may, and that ye will knaw belyve." [1] The Earl of Lennox had really not ventured to appear in court ; on his behalf stepped forward only Robert Cunningham, a member of the Lennox clan, who had taken part in the plot against Riccio, and who now moved the postponement of the process. On Bothwell's side, on the contrary, it was maintained that the case should be proceeded with, and this course was at last adopted. The jury, numbering fifteen members, consisted of the Earls Andrew of Rothes, George of Caithness, and Gilbert of Cassilis, Lord John Hamilton, a son of the Duke of Châtelherault, Lords James Ross, Robert Sempill, John Herries, Laurence Oliphant, and Robert Boyd, John " Master " of Forbes, and Lairds John Gordon of Lochinvar, James Cockburn of Langton, James Somerville of Cambusnethan, John Mowbray of Barnbowgall, and Alexander Ogilby of Boyne. Some negotiations in the matter seem to have taken place before the court, for the meeting, which began in the morning, only ended at seven o'clock in the evening. After a little hesitation the jury, through the Earl of Caithness, a nobleman related to Bothwell by marriage, whom they had chosen as their foreman, gave in the

[1] The declaration of James Ormiston.—Laing, *History of Scotland*, ii. 294. This account must have been overlooked by Mignet (*Histoire de Marie Stuart*, i. 323), who, in his narrative, makes Both- well appear on this occasion altogether otherwise :—" L'accusé, le Comte de Bothwell, se présenta d'un air assuré et confiant devant la cour de justice."

unanimous verdict of "Not Guilty." The general
accusations of Cunningham against those impeached
by Lennox, who were said to be "notoriously
known" as the perpetrators of the murder, were
certainly valued as by no means any proof. On
the other hand, some of the jurymen were even
quite ignorant up to that moment, how far the
guilt of Bothwell extended, and the members of
the jury who were not previously favourably
decided towards him, had by this got a special
ground for quieting their conscience, since the
literal interpretation was as characteristic of the
Scottish as of the English legal proceedings, and
the question, perhaps not inadvertently, had been
so put to the jury that they were asked about
the murder as having taken place on the 9th
of February, whereas it had not actually occurred
until two hours after midnight, or on the next
day.[1] Immediately after his acquittal Bothwell,
in conformity with a custom which had not then
quite gone out of use in Scotland, finally issued
a public declaration of his willingness to fight a
duel with any one who should hereafter ascribe
to him the guilt of the king's murder, on which
account the Earl of Lennox, as soon as he received
intelligence of the issue of the trial, sought and
obtained permission to leave Scotland. After visiting his grandson in Stirling Castle, he embarked on
the 17th April, in the "Thirteenth," a ship on the
west coast of Scotland, and sailed through the Irish
Sea to England,[2] in order to seek out Lady Lennox

[1] Sir James Melvil writes about the jurymen that they "cleansed and acquitted him, some for fear, some for favour, and the greatest part in expectation of advantage.— Memoirs, p. 78.
[2] Diurnal of Remarkable Occurrents, p. 119.

P

whom Elizabeth, at the news of Darnley's union
with Mary Stuart, had formerly deprived of liberty,
but whom, on now receiving tidings of Darnley's
death, she had set free again, after having, at her
despotic caprice, for about two years, kept her
shut up in the Tower.

CHAPTER V.I.

THE Parliament summoned in consequence of the death of Darnley was opened almost immediately after the court of assize was held, an interval merely of two days elapsing between them. It sat only from the 14th to the 19th of April, but during this short period made various important enactments. Among these was a parliamentary recognition of the recovered rights of the Earl of Huntly, which some in more recent times have sought to ascribe to the presumed influence of Bothwell, who, in view of his approaching divorce, is said to have wished by this means to secure his brother-in-law's consent. The possessions of the Gordons had, after the battle of Corrichie, been confiscated, but when Murray manifestly proved himself a rebel, Mary restored to George Gordon the earldom of Huntly, and made him chancellor. In consequence of a parliamentary enactment dating from the preceding century, none of the possessions which had devolved to the crown could be finally alienated without the assent of Parliament;[1] the confiscation of the estates of the Gordons having been meanwhile ratified by Parlia-

[1] But avyz deliverance and decret of the haill parliament. —The Act of 4th August 1455;   *The Acts of the Parliaments of Scotland,* ii. 42.

CHAP.
VI.
1567.

ment, it was thus necessary that their restoration should be similarly confirmed, and this Parliament of April 1567 was the first that Mary Stuart had seen assembled since the one which at the murder of Riccio had been immediately dissolved. It was thus no new favour to the Earl of Huntly which in this instance was in question. The promise of the Queen to Huntly was already twenty months old, six months older than Bothwell's marriage to his sister. Besides, it was not Huntly alone who now obtained the final confirmation of his possessions and dignities, but the same favour was shown at this time to many others of the nobility whose earlier conspiracies were in no small degree occasioned by the fear lest Mary should resume, in name of the crown, the numerous ecclesiastical estates which the nobles, under her minority, had either appropriated, or at least got transferred to themselves, but whose tenure they had nevertheless seen threatened by that other enactment according to which the sovereign, during the first four years after his majority, could, in cases where full payment had not been given, still forbear to confirm such transfers, and instead thereof revoke them. Amid the turbulence which ensued on the murder of Darnley, many from the most opposite factions now endeavoured to get their titles confirmed. Accordingly in this Parliament there were so confirmed about thirty such deeds from the crown, some of which were really in favour of those who had been the worst enemies of the Queen. In respect to what concerned himself Bothwell also obtained the ratification of his possession of Dunbar Castle, but so far as any special influence exerted

by Bothwell during this brief meeting of Parliament is in question, we may more readily find this
in certain legal provisions enacted to the advantage
of Protestants, just as certainly as that the Earl of
Huntly from this period, and soon undoubtedly in
combination with his sister, must be assumed to
have come to an agreement with his brother-in-law
Bothwell about the latter's rapidly following divorce.
Parliament also expressly ratified the acquittal of
the Earl of Bothwell by the Court of Assize, at the
same time issuing a threatening Act against those
who presumed after the king's death to circulate
infamous placards against diverse persons.

At the close of Parliament, ere its members had
returned to their homes, Bothwell did not neglect,
on the 19th of April, to meet with almost the whole
of the principal nobility at the evening entertainment, which, from the inn where it was held, is
known in Scottish history under the name of
" Ainslie's Supper."[1] When the entertainment was
at its height there was laid before those present a
document for signature, with which Bothwell gave
them to understand that the Queen would be well
pleased, and in which they not only anew declared
themselves convinced of Bothwell's innocence, and
engaged to defend the Earl against every calumnia-
tor, but besides, in consideration of his birth and

---

[1] Bothwell mentioned later in
Denmark the place and those
present thus : " Après que j'eus
gaigné ma cause, vindrent deuers
moy en mon logis du dict parla-
ment de leur franche et propre
volonté, sans estre pryez, qui es-
toyent douze contes, huict évesques
et huict seigneurs." In the apology
of the so-called *Book of Articles*,
with which the enemies of Mary
Stuart afterwards came forward
during the conferences in England,
it is said on the contrary that the
members of Parliament had been
" callit to suppar be Boithuille at
his hous than kepit within the
Palace of Halyroudehouse." —
Hosack, *Mary Queen of Scots and
her Accusers*, p. 542.

services,[1] recommended this noble lord, being a native, in preference to any foreign prince, so truly " as we are nobillmen, and will answer to God," as a befitting husband for the Queen, whose continued widowhood was hurtful to the country. Bothwell's most intimate followers, and those who were afraid that if he were disappointed of the Queen's hand he would expose them as leaders in what had been done,[2] first set the example of subscribing; after this the others promised likewise to forward his claim to the Queen's hand, with their honour, life, and estate, and to consider all who should hinder it as " their common enemies and foes." Among those present on this occasion are also mentioned the Bishop of Ross, Lord Herries, and other individuals,[3]

[1] Considdering the anciencie and nobillenes off his Houis, the honorable and guid service done be his predecessoris, and speciallie himselffe, to oure soverane, and for the defence of this her Hienes Realme againis the enemyeis thairof, and the amitie and friendshipe quhilk sa lang hes perseverit betwix his Houis and everie ane of us, and utheris our Predecessoris in particular.—Document in Anderson, Collections, i. 108.

[2] Ne Bothuelius, promissis nuptiis exclusus, eos ut totius sceleris architectas insimularet.—Camdeni, Annales, p. 138.

[3] During the conference at Westminster Cecil received a copy of the Bond which had been entered into by the Scottish gentlemen on the 19th of April 1567 in favour of Bothwell. The copy was however without the undersigned names, and the person who brought it to Cecil, John Read, a writer with Buchanan, was obliged then from memory to state the names to Cecil, who, with his own hand, noted them down on that copy which is still preserved in the Cottonian Library with these words appended : " The names of such of the nobility as subscribed the band, so far as John Read might remember, of whom I have this copy, being in his own hand, being commonly called in Scotland Aynslie's Supper." The first of the alleged names (in Anderson, Collections, i. 112) can however by no means awaken implicit confidence in the correctness of the list, for this name is—Murray's, who, at the period treated of, was not in Scotland, but, foreseeing the coming storm, had sought and obtained the Queen's permission to repair to France. He was still present in Scotland the 2d April 1567, when, in striking contrast with his later accusations against Mary Stuart as a murderess, by a testament he installed the Queen as guardian of his only child, or, according to the language then used, as " oueriswoman to se all thingis be handillit and reulit for the weil of my said

who were the Queen's faithful and devoted adherents, and however low the moral sense had then
sunk in so many of the gentry of Scotland, yet the
conduct which they are said now to have shown can
only be understood of a part of them on the supposition that they really did not know at the time Bothwell's share in Darnley's murder.   Afterwards, for
the first time, when it was wished to give the affair
the appearance of having been submitted to only as
a matter of necessity, the assertion was put forth on
the other side that the place where the banquet was
held was surrounded by two hundred arquebusiers,
and that therefore only Earl Hew Eglinton was
able to escape without subscribing.   The whole
occurrence, almost as strange, reminds us of the
bond which, at the well-known similar banquet at
Pilsen, was afterwards subscribed by the adherents
of Wallenstein, and in which the guests likewise
promised not by any means to separate their cause
from his, to give him the last drops of their blood,
and to prosecute every one acting otherwise as a
perfidious and infamous person.[1]   Of Wallenstein's
forty-two colonels, who, on the 12th January 1634,
subscribed the bond at Pilsen, there were, as is well
known, not a few natives of Scotland.

What took place at "Ainslie's Supper" could
certainly not long remain a secret.   And when Mary

dochter (*Registrum Honoris de
Morton:* A Series of ancient Charters of the Earldom of Morton, with
other original Papers, Edin. 1853,
4to, i. 17), but on the 19th April it is
expressly said in one of the Acts
of Parliament of this day, that he
was then out of the kingdom of
Scotland.   If notwithstanding, in
this instance, the list of Cecil is
still held to be valid, it must be
by assuming that Murray may
either have signed the document in
question before his departure, or
have empowered some other to
sign it in his behalf.

[1] Hurtur, *Wallensteins vier letzte
Lebensjahre.*   Wien, 1862, pp. 364-
366.

CHAP.
VI.

1567.

Stuart also during the action brought against Bothwell continued to keep him in her favour; when, according to a report made by Sir William Drury to Cecil in England, it was even said, that from a window in Holyrood, while standing by the side of Lady Mary Lethington, she had nodded a greeting to Bothwell when he rode up to the Court of Assize, or still later, during the sitting of the court, had sent a message to learn how it was going with him,[1] it began henceforward, especially in England, to be foreseen what was at hand, and the rumour got quickly into general circulation that Bothwell was about to marry the Queen. Sir James Melvil tells in his *Memoirs* that good subjects who loved the Queen were pained by this rumour, and adds, that there were several who, at their own risk, ventured to remonstrate with the Queen. Thus he relates that Lord John Herries came well attended to Edinburgh, confided to the Queen all that was said about Bothwell and his designs, and kneeling, begged her not to marry the Earl. The Queen seemed to wonder how such rumours could have got abroad, and assured him that she had no thought of anything of the kind. Lord Herries besought the Queen to put a good construction on his remonstrance, and from fear of Bothwell, immediately rode home from Edinburgh after causing every one of the fifty horsemen with whom he had come to purchase a new spear. But this tale does not seem to agree well with the fact that Herries was in Edinburgh during the session of Parliament, or

[1] According to Drury's account to Cecil (Tytler, *History of Scotland,* vii. 375, 376). It is founded on a misunderstanding when Tytler, however, also brings forward as a specially noticeable sign of favour for Bothwell after the death of Darnley, the fact that the Earl,

with the statement that he also subscribed the document at " Ainslie's supper," just as he generally about this period showed himself as a facile ad- herent of Bothwell, having accordingly been one of the witnesses to the subsequent marriage-contract between Bothwell and the Queen, and three days afterwards, on the 17th May, having attended a meeting of the Privy Council over which Bothwell presided.[1] More remarkable is another tale of a like nature told by Melvil, inasmuch as this is communicated by him from personal knowledge. He likewise tells that another Scotsman, Thomas Bishop, who had resided long in England, and had laboured there with zeal for the rights of Mary, wrote him a letter which he adjured him to show the Queen, and in which this devoted adherent of hers expressed himself to the same effect as Lord Herries, but with the greater freedom which absence in a foreign country permitted; if the Queen married the Earl, so it was said in this letter, she would lose God's favour, and all hearts in England, Ireland, and Scotland. Sir James Melvil actually showed the letter to the Queen, who, after reading it, silently returned it to him, but called the Secretary of State, William Maitland, and asked him also to read this remarkable paper. The laird of Lethington then

when the Queen rode to the Parliament both at its opening and at its close, bore the royal sceptre before her, while the Earl of Argyll bore the crown and the Earl of Crawford the sword (see *Diurnal of Remarkable Occurrents*, pp. 108, 109). This was a manifest consequence of his position, and had already been the case long before the year 1567. When Mary Stuart, on the 7th of March 1565, proceeded

to the Parliament then opened in Edinburgh, it is said : "In hir Majesties cuming thairto, George Lord Gordoun, eldest sone to vmquhile George, Erle of Huntlie, bure the croune, James, Erle of Bothwill, the ceptour, and Dauid, Erle of Crawfurd, the sword of honour."—*Diurnal of Remarkable Occurrents*, p. 89.

[1] Goodall, ii. 61.

CHAP. said to Melvil that he had acted more honourably
VI.   than wisely, and advised him to withdraw ere Both-
1567. well came forth to the Queen, an advice which
Melvil found it well to follow, for the Earl immediately burst out in a rage at what the Queen now
communicated to him, until Mary Stuart—so much
sway had she still over his savage temper—quieted
him by beseeching him not to deprive her of her
best servants.[1] Melvil relates this as something
which occurred before the Queen's abduction to
Dunbar, but his *Memoirs*, which he first penned
when advanced in life, prove, on the whole, not very
reliable wherever dates are in question,[2] and as the
rumour of the purpose of marriage between Mary
and Bothwell can hardly have gained entrance into
England before the news of the subscription of the
Bond on the 19th April, so neither can the above-
mentioned warning be easily assumed to have
reached Scotland until after the Queen's abduction,
when it would arrive too late. But, even if any
such warning had come forward earlier, it was at all
events not the same thing as a direct accusation
against Bothwell, so unanimously acquitted, and
recommended by the nobles, that he had really had
a share in the murder of Darnley, and that at least
no such accusation whatever was brought before
her by any of her subjects previously to their rising
against Bothwell, Mary Stuart at a later period

---

[1] *Memoirs of Sir James Melvil,* pp. 78-79.

[2] Thus Melvil represents the visit of Mary Stuart to Jedburgh, as if it had taken place after the baptism of James VI. ; he refers to the signing by the nobles of the document, in which the Queen was called on to marry Bothwell, to the period after her abduction, although it had previously occurred on the 19th April ; he makes also Dalgleish be first taken prisoner in Orkney in the autumn of 1567, while he had already been im-prisoned in Edinburgh in June (*Memoirs,* pp. 77, 80, 85).

solemnly protested, with the additional assurance
that if she had had any idea of it, she would certainly never have allowed things to go so far as they
did.[1]
It was only a few days after the close of Parliament and the subscription of the Bond that Bothwell undertook the famous surprise by which he
carried off Mary as a prisoner. On Monday the
21st of April Mary left Edinburgh with a small
retinue, to pay a visit to her little son in Stirling
Castle, where, in view of the threatening period
which the murder of Darnley seemed to herald, he
had, on the 2d of March, been intrusted to the care
of John Erskine, who formerly, while he was known
only as Prior of Inchmahome, was one of Mary's
earliest instructors, but now, since the death of his
father and of his elder brother, had become Earl of
Mar.[2] When returning homewards after a short
stay in the beautiful castle of Stirling, where Mary
now saw for the last time her little son, and where
this child of hers had afterwards to remain during
the whole of his minority, on the 23d of April she
was suddenly seized by the way with such violent

---

[1] With respect to Darnley's murder, she says : – " For nane of my subjectis did declair unto me, befoir my taking and imprison- ment, that thay quha ar now haldin culpabill and principal executouris thairof, wer the prin- cipal auctoris and committaris of the samin ; quhilk gif thay had done, assuritlie I wald not have proceidit as I did sa far."—Instruc- tion of Mary Stuart to her repre- sentatives at the Conference in England, dated, Bolton Castle, the 29th September 1568. Labanoff, ii. 202.

[2] It was on the occasion of this visit to Stirling that the blind hatred against Mary culminated in such a way as to lead to her being even accused of having there attempted to destroy her little son : —" She offered him an apple, but it would not be received of him ; and to a greyhound bitch having whelps was thrown, who eat it, and she and her whelps died presently." —Letter of Sir William Drury to Cecil, dated Berwick the 20th May 1567 ; *Calendar of State Papers, Foreign Series,* 1566-8, p. 235.

pains, that she was obliged for some time to take up her abode in a small cottage. On recovering, she continued her journey, and had passed the night in the palace of her birth at Linlithgow, when on Monday, the 24th April, she was surprised by Bothwell at a bridge over the river Almond.[1] The Earl of Bothwell had made it appear as if he intended to repair again to the unquiet Border districts; he had thus spoken in presence of his associates, and had accordingly been able to assemble so many men, that he was accompanied on this occasion by nearly a thousand mounted spearmen, so that the inconsiderable retinue which attended the Queen had not any hope of being able, even if they had been willing, to make a stand against the superior force with which they were now surrounded. Bothwell spoke only some hurried words about the Queen's being threatened by an impending danger from which he wished to save her,[2] and while some of her attendants got permission to pass on without hindrance, he himself took hold of the bridle of the Queen's horse, his men in like manner secured George Earl of Huntly, William Maitland, laird of Lethington,

[1] *Vide* Note I, Appendix.
[2] Onde lui un giorno che la Regina se ne andava, quasi sola per videre il figlio, la assalto in strada con molti de suoi, et con buone parole et con mostrarle che la Maestà Sua si trovava in grandissimo pericolo, la condusse in uno delli suoi castelli." The Representation sent from Mary Stuart's side to the Christian Princes, written at Carlisle in June 1568. Labanoff, vii. 317. Froude understands much more fully how to represent this occurrence, and it may serve as a small example of his romancing way of writing history,

that, without any warrant whatsoever from authorities, he relates (*History of England*, ix. 64) the surprisal thus:—"As the royal train appeared, he (Bothwell) dashed forward with a dozen of his followers, and seized her bridlerein; her guard flew to her side to defend her, when, with singular composure, she said she would have no bloodshed; her people were outnumbered, and rather than any of them should lose their lives, she would go wherever the Earl of Bothwell wished. Uncertain what to do, they dropped their swords."

and Sir James Melvil, and these prisoners were then
hurried off to the well-fortified castle of Dunbar,
lying at the mouth of the Firth of Forth, which had
been given up to Bothwell in reward for his services.
When, at a later date, Mary, during her imprisonment in England, was asked about Bothwell's relations to her, she either answered only with vague
words, or began to weep.[1]   But at a period not
long after her abduction, we have from herself a
more precise account of what had taken place
between her and Bothwell, ere she gave him her
hand.   It is contained in an instruction which,
immediately after her marriage to Bothwell, she
communicated to William Chisholm, Bishop of
Dunblane, who was deputed to explain to the King
of France, the Queen-Dowager Catherine de Medici,
the Cardinal of Lorraine and her other relatives on
the Continent, the step she had then taken, just as
Sir Robert Melvil, brother of Sir James, was deputed to explain it to Elizabeth in England.   After
touching on the never-to-be-forgotten meritorious
services which the Earl of Bothwell had rendered at
the beginning of her reign, she goes on to say that
it was first "sen the deceis of the King oure
husband, yat his pretensis began to be heichar."
"His deportmentis," she remarks, "in this behalf
may serve for ane exempill, how cunninglie men can
cover yair designeis, quhen thai haif ony greit inter-
pryis in heid quhill yai haif brocht yair purpois to
pas.   We thocht his continewance in the awayting
upoun ws, and reddines to fulfill all oure command-
mentis, had procedit onelie upoun the aknawlegeing

---

[1] The account of Sir Francis   *nen Elisabeth und Maria Stuart*,
Knollys.—Raumer, *Die Königin-*   p. 221.

of his dewtie, being oure borne subject, without furder hid respect ; quhilk movit ws to mak him the bettir visage, thinking nathing less yan that the same being bot ane ordinarie countenance to sic nobellmen as we fand affectionate to oure service, sould encourage him, or gif him bauldnes to luke for ony extraordinar favour at oure handis."[1] At the outset Bothwell, when he ventured to reveal his thoughts to the Queen, only sought to gain her assent by humble attention, but he found her answer anything but corresponding to his wishes.[2] It was then in consideration of the Queen's unwillingness, of the hindrances which her friends or his foes might put in his way, and of the possible change of their mind, whose consent he had already obtained, that the Earl determined to try his good fortune, and undertook the surprise at Almond Bridge, and the abduction to Dunbar. " In quhat part we tuke that maner of dealing, bot speciallie how strange we fand it of him, of quhome we doubtit less than of ony other subject we had, is easie to be imagined. Being thair (at Dunbar) we reprochit him, (reminding him of) the honour he had to be sa estimit of ws, the favour we had alwayis schawn him, his ingratitude with all uther remonstrances quhilk mycht serve to red ws out of his handis. Albeit we fand his doings rude, zit wer his answer and wordis bot gentill, that he wald honour and serve us, and nawayis offend us ; askit pardoun of the bauldnes he had tane to convoy ws to ane of oure awin housis, quhairunto he wes drevin be force, als weill as constrainit be lufe, the vehemencie quhairof

[1] Instruction of Mary Stuart to the Bishop of Dunblane. — La-banoff, ii. 32-44, and 45-49.

[2] " But finding oure answere nathing correspondent to his de-syre."—Ibid. ii. 37.

maid him to set apart the reverence quhilk naturallie
as oure subject he bure to ws as alswa for saiftie of
his awin lyff. And thair began to mak ws a discours of his haill lyff, how unfortunate he had bene
to find men his unfreindis quhome he had nevir
offendit; how thair malice had nevir ceasit to assault
him at all occasiounis, albeit onjustlie ; quhat cal-
umpnyis had thai spred upoun him twiching the
odious violence perpetrated on the persoun of the
King oure lait husband ; how unabill he was to safe
himself from conspiraceis of his innemeis, quhome
he mycht not knaw, be ressoun everie man professed
him outwartlie to be his friend ; and zit he had sic
malice, that he could not find himself in suirtie,
without he wer assurit of oure favour to indure
without alteratioun ; and uther assurance thairof
could he not lippin in, without it wald pleis ws to do
him that honour to tak him to husband ; protesting
alwayis that he wald seik na uther soveraintie bot
as of befoir, to serve and obey ws all dayis of oure lyff,
joyning thairunto all the honest language that could
be usit in sic a cais.   And quhen he saw ws lyke to
reject all his sute and offeris, in the end he schowed
ws how far he was procedit with oure haill nobilitie
and principallis of oure estaittis, and quhat thai had
promeist him undir thair handwrittis.   Gif we had
caus yan to be astoneist, we remit ws to the jugement
of the King, the Quene, oure uncle, and utheris
oure friendis.   Seing oure self in his puissance,
sequestrat frome the cumpany of all oure servandis,
and utheris of quhome we mycht ask for counsale ;
zea, seing thame upoun quhais counsale and fidelitie
we had befoir dependit, quhais force aucht and mon
manteine oure authoritie, without quhome in a

maner we ar nathing :—for quhat is a Prince without
a peopill—befoir hand alreddie zealded to his ape-
tyte, and swa we left allane as it wer a pray to him ;
mony thingis we revolved with oure self, but nevir
could find ane outgait. And zit gaif he ws lytill
space to meditate with oure self, evir pressing ws
with continewall and importune sute."[1] Among the
many thoughts which had then forced themselves on
the Queen she mentions expressly that she now felt
herself almost broken down by the frequent rebel-
lions, that the kingdom rent asunder into parties
needed to have a man at its head, and how difficult
it was to get her people to accept of a foreigner, and
then it is finally said in reference to Bothwell :—
" Eftir he had be this meanis, and mony utheris,
brocht ws agaitward to his intent, he partlie extorted, and partlie obtenit oure promeis to tak him
to oure husband.　And zit not content thairwith,
fearing evir sum alterationis, he wald nocht be satis-
feit with all the just ressounis we could allege to
have the consummatioun of the mariage delayit,
as had bene ressounabill, quhill we mycht communicat the same to the King, the Queen, oure
uncle, and utheris oure friendis; bot as be a bravade
in the begynning he had win the fyrst point, sa
ceased he nevir till be persuasionis and importune
sute, accumpaneit notheles with force, he hes finalie
drevin ws to end the work begun at sic tyme
and in sic forme as he thocht mycht best serve his
turne."[2]

At the same time as Mary gave the Bishop
of Dunblane this instruction, she also wrote to her
ambassador asking this very devoted friend of hers

---

[1] Labanoff, ii. 38-39.　　　　　　　[2] *Ibid.* ii. 41.

to afford, in the way he deemed best, assistance to
the Bishop in his difficult commission to her relatives.
And just as on this occasion she repeated that all
she had said in that instruction was truth,[1] so at a
later period, when she empowered another envoy in
Rome to labour for the dissolution of her marriage
with Bothwell, she again repeated that only against
her will, only by force, had she entered into this
marriage.[2]

With the substance of Mary's representation, according to which it was contrary to her
knowledge and will that Bothwell took her prisoner,
the first proclamations and writings which the leaders
of the rebellion against Bothwell afterwards issued
also agree.   For these simply advance as one of
the chief complaints against the Earl that he had
now become guilty of high treason by having used
force against the Queen's most noble person.[3]   It is
of still greater significance that Sir James Melvil,
who along with the Queen was taken a prisoner
to Dunbar, likewise expresses himself to the same
purport.   In his Memoirs we read that after the
arrival at Dunbar in the evening, Bothwell boasted
that he would marry the Queen whether she would
or would not,[4] and in the same place it is subsequently stated that the Queen could not help
marrying him after he had forcibly carried her off

[1] In our instructioun to the
Bischop of Dunblane we have maid
discours of the verie trewth of the
mater ; we have mentionat the
samyn sincerelie from the very
beginning. — Letter of Mary to
the Ambassador in Paris, the
Archbishop of Glasgow, dated
Edinburgh, 27th May 1567 ; Labanoff, ii. 54-56.

[2] Contro nostra voluntá—contro
nostra voglia. — Instruction of
Mary to Robert Ridolfi, of March
1571 ; Labanoff, iii. 232.
[3] Note K, Appendix.
[4] There the Earl of Bothwel
boasted he would marry the Queen,
who would or who would not, yea
whether she would herself or not.
—Memoirs, p. 80.

Q

and dishonoured her.[1] Finally, what a contemporary
also relates is in harmony with the substance of the
Queen's representation :—" The rumour of the re-
vissing of hir Majestie come to the Provest of Edinburgh, incontinent the commoun bell rang, and the
inhabitants thairof ran to armour and wappynnis,
the portes wes steikit, the artailzerie of the castell
schot.—Upon the samin day, it wes alledgit that
it wes devisit, that William Maitland, zounger of
Lethington, secretare to our souerane ladie, being
in hir cumpany the tyme foirsaid, suld have been
slane."[2]

This impression was however soon forced to
give way before the opinion which subsequently
prevailed in Scotland, according to which no doubt
could be entertained, even from the beginning, that
what Bothwell had undertaken was done in consequence of an agreement with Mary.[3] His conduct
was more precisely accounted for at the time in
three ways. It was in Scotland an old practice that
when papers were drawn up, by which any one
obtained pardon for crimes, this was so done that
only the chief crime was expressly mentioned,
while merely a clause was added, describing in
general terms what offences the person concerned
had besides committed. Buchanan accordingly
holds that as the murderers of the King, and
especially Bothwell, were afraid that there might

[1] And then the Queen could not
but marry him, seeing he had
ravished her and lain with her
against her will.—*Memoirs of Sir
James Melvil*, p. 80.
[2] *A Diurnal of Remarkable
Occurrents*, p. 110.
[3] Tytler's *History of Scotland*,
vii. 88. This opinion was even

announced during the abduction
itself to Dunbar by one of Bothwell's own confidants :—" Capitain
Blachater, who has taken me,
alledged, that it was with the
Queen's own consent," it is said in
the Memoirs of Sir James Melvil,
p. 80.

come a time when it would be seriously resolved to
punish them for the deed, they had found out that
by the help of such a clause they would be able to
get the crime pardoned, the express mention of
which in a document might appear as dangerous to
the perpetrators as it would be unseemly for the
pardoner.[1] The murder of the Queen's husband
could not be mentioned, but another crime of high
treason, which was less odious, must be found out,
under screen of which the murder of the King as by
a piece of sophistry could be concealed and forgiven.
An attack upon the Queen's exalted person was such
an aggravated crime, and therefore nothing more
fitting for the purpose could be contrived than that
feigned abduction. Others explained the strange
transaction by alleging that its design was to stop
the mouths of those who had long thought that the
Queen stood in a too intimate relation to the Earl.[2]
More natural than both these far-fetched explanations is that which, while still seeing in the abduction merely a pre-concerted piece of acting, inter
preted it as a direct result of an immoderate love
for Bothwell[3] which made her impatiently long to
be able to call him her own. As they who favour

[1] Nam, quum in Scotia mos esset,
ut diplomata, quibus scelerum
gratia fit, qui veniam petit, gravis-
simum facinus nominatim expri-
mant, ac cetera generalibus verbis
adjiciat, decreverunt paricidii pub-
lici conscii, nominatim de manus
injectione in principem veniam
petere, deinde velut in cumulum
subjicere, cæteris nefariis factis.—
Buchanan, *Rerum Scoticarum Historia*, p. 217.

[3] Bot it was rather done for the
stanche of the mouthes of the
peopill, that allegit that the said

erle wes mair familiar with bir
grace lang of befoir, nor honestie
requyrit.—*A Diurnal of Remarkable Occurrents*, p. 110.

[2] Already on the 20th April
1567, Kirkaldy of Grange wrote
in a letter to the Earl of Bedford
that the Queen of Scotland was
reported to have said that "she
cared not to lose France, England,
and her own country for him, and
shall go with him to the world's
end in a white petticoat before
she leave him."—Tytler's *History
of Scotland*, vii. 88.

this mode of explaining the hurried marriage proceed upon the supposition that the passion had long
before led Mary to give herself up to the Earl, so
one of her later defenders believes that he is able
to expose the foolishness of any such explanation by
asking the questions :—" Where was the necessity
for a precipitate marriage at all ?   Was Mary so
eager to become Bothwell's wife, with whom she
indeed had long been indulging in an illicit intercourse, that she could not wait the time demanded
by common decency to wear her widow's garb for
Darnley ?   Was she really so entirely lost to every
sense of female delicacy and public shame,—so utterly
dead to her own interests and reputation,—or so
very scrupulous about a little longer continuing her
unlicensed amours, that, rather than suffer the delay of a few months, she would thus run the risk
of involving herself in eternal infamy ?"[1]   These
questions are not without force for those against
whom they are directed, but if the relation be apprehended somewhat differently, it would be possible
to meet them.   There is with regard to the abduction and the subsequent sudden marriage a circumstance which is not ordinarily taken into consideration in this connection, but to which we might
refer as an answer.   Immediately after Mary's third
marriage her opponents declared that she had again
become pregnant,[2] and when the Queen was confined a prisoner at Lochleven, Sir Nicholas Throckmorton, who had been sent by Elizabeth to

[1] Bell's *Life of Mary Queen of
Scots*, ii. 86.
[2] The Prince is in greater danger than before, by reason the
Queen is with child.—Letter of
the Earl of Bedford to the Earl
of Leicester, dated Garendon the
15th of June 1567 ; *Calendar of
State Papers (Foreign Series)* 1566-
1568, p. 252.

Scotland to negotiate her release, wrote in a letter
from Edinburgh of 18th July 1567, to his mistress:
—" I have also persuaded her to conform herself to
renounce Bothwell for her husband, and to be contented to suffer a divorce to pass betwixt them; she
hath sent me word that she will in no ways consent
unto that, but rather die, grounding herself upon
this reason, taking herself to be seven weeks gone
with child; by renouncing Bothwell, she should
acknowledge herself to be with child of a bastard,
and to have forfeited her honor, which she will not
do to die for it."[1]   Might not Mary, under the supposition of which she makes mention, have at this
time or earlier believed her pregnancy to be of older
date?   And, if the Queen had such fear after Darnley's death, might not Bothwell then have found
the final encouragement to venture on the abduction,
and the Queen afterwards an incentive for not at
this time rejecting his hand?   Even if the abduction
to Dunbar had not taken place with the Queen's
will, yet the opposition which she there exhibited to
Bothwell was at all events so small in comparison
with her former brave behaviour during the catas-

---

[1] Letter of Throckmorton, Robertson's *History of Scotland*, ii.
311. " Elle eut du Comte de
Bothuel, son troisième Mary, une
fille qui fut Religieuse à Notre
Dame de Soissons," it is said, in
accordance with this, in Laboureur's Supplement to Mémoires
de Messire Michel de Castelnau, i.
648.   But although it has been
stated by one on the other side of
the Channel that Mary Stuart
was delivered of a child at Lochleven (Wright's *Queen Elizabeth
and her Times*, i. 266), yet not
many will, with Prince Labanoff,
ii. 63, find in such legends any
real fact.   Mary herself, in July
1570, names James VI. in her letter to Lady Lennox, " Your little
sonne (*i.e.* grandson) and my *onelie
childe* " (Labanoff, iii. 78), and
seems even to have felt proud of
only having borne one child, in as
far as we may venture to conclude from one of her favourite
devices, which shows a lion and its
young one, with the legend *unum
quidem, sed leonem* (Selectus Di-
plomatum et Numismatum Scotiæ
Thesaurus, Collegit J. Andersonus,
Edinburghi, 1739, fol. tab. clxxvii.
nr. 4).

trophe which put an end to Riccio's life, that this
weakness becomes the weightiest—and properly the
only incontrovertible—reason for assuming an earlier
and more intimate understanding between her and
the Earl than she has plainly admitted. When
some one mentioned to David Hume that a new
treatise had been published, the author of which
was believed to have successfully vindicated Mary,
the historian only asked : " Has he also proved that
the Queen did not marry Bothwell ?" and when no
affirmative answer could be given, he signified that
the attempt had failed.[1]

While the Queen's sojourn at Dunbar continued,
Bothwell hastened a divorce from his former wife,
in the way which, during the disorganisation of
the Reformation period, was so common, that it
caused foreigners to say, that " in England, and
still more in Scotland, they had a strange custom,
being able to divorce each other when they were no
longer pleased with one another,"[2]—an easy mode of
which Mary, even in her own family, had immediate
examples, since her grandmother, Queen Margaret,
after the death of James IV., had married Archibald
Douglas, Earl of Angus—father to the Countess of
Lennox—and Henry Stuart, Lord Methven, and

[1] Taylor's *Pictorial History of
Scotland.*—London, 1859, ii. 57.
[2] " Il ont une coustume estrange
en Angleterre, mais plus prattiquée
en Escosse, de pouvoir se répudier
l'un l'aultre quant ilz ne se trou-
vent bien ensemble. La chose est
remarquable par les exemples qui
s'en sont ensuivis."—Letter of the
French minister Du Croc to the
king, of 27th May 1567 ; Teulet,
Papiers d'Etat, ii. 157. Du Croc
conjectures here that this custom
dates in royal families dates " de Matilde,
fille Henry Ier, troisiesme filz de
Guillaume le Conquérant, laquelle
ayant espousé Henri III., empe-
reur, elle le laissa pour prandre
Galfroy de Plantagenet."   Bothwell expresses himself in a like
manner in Denmark:—"Au mesme
instant ils consultérent comment
je pouvrois légitement répudier
ma première princesse, selon les
lois divines de l'Eglise et la coustume du pays."

afterwards got a divorce from both of them, and CHAP.
her grand-uncle, Henry VIII., the brother of Queen VI.
Margaret, had followed in his sister's footsteps by 1567.
his divorces from Catherine of Arragon and Anne of
Cleves. Bothwell's process for obtaining a divorce
from his wife was however begun before the abduction of the Queen,[1] and was being carried on at
once under the jurisdiction of both the new and
the old churches. The previous authority of the
Catholic clergy to judge in processes of marriage and
divorce had been abolished by the Parliament which
was summoned by the provisional government
set up in 1560, after the death of Mary of Guise,
and which abrogated the Episcopal jurisdiction. In
order to supply the want of a jurisdiction in causes
such as those mentioned, a special court indeed was
afterwards constituted in 1563, in which four commissioners had seats, but the abolition of the
Episcopal jurisdiction in the country nevertheless
was one of the acts of the Reformed party, to which
the Queen had never given the assent of the Crown,
and by an ordinance of the Queen the Consistorial
Court had been at a later date formally re-established
with the Archbishop of St. Andrews at its head.
This had already taken place on the 23d December
1566, a few days after the Archbishop and the other
Catholic Prelates celebrated the baptism of the
young prince at Stirling, and that ordinance which
was then issued plainly therefore cannot by any
means be connected with the divorce which Bothwell now sought to obtain, as some have held.
Before this resuscitated Catholic ecclesiastical court
he raised an action against his wife for the dissolu-

---

[1] Laing, *History of Scotland*, ii. 83.

tion of their marriage, because entered into within too near a degree of relationship. That his wife must now have been gained over to the cause, either by Bothwell, or by her brother, the Earl of Huntly, cannot be doubted, nothing being more improbable than the assertion that there did not exist any collusion between the parties. It may here be remarked that, just as it was not unusual in those days for prudent relatives of the bride to procure even before marriage the dispensation of the Catholic Church as a security against its being made null and void in consequence of near relationship, so Buchanan has alleged that such a dispensation was really obtained at the time of Bothwell's marriage with Jane Gordon, but that it was kept concealed during the process,[1] and in this instance his assertion seems not to be without foundation, since that dispensation was itself discovered a short time ago.[2] At the same time as the Protestant Earl sued the Catholic Lady Jane Bothwell before the Romish Court, she on her side also raised an action of divorce before the Reformed Court against her husband for previous infidelity. With so great speed was the process carried on, that the marriage was declared by the Protestant, or the so-called Commissary Court, on the 3d of May, to be

[1] Cælato interim pontificis Romani diplomate, quo venia ejus culpæ facta erat.—*De Maria Scotorum Regina*, p. 29.

[2] Report of the Records and Manuscripts at Dunrobin, belonging to His Grace the Duke of Sutherland, in *Second Report of the Royal Commission on Historical Manuscripts.* London, 1871, fol. pp. 177-180. The Dispensation is issued by the Papal Legate in Scotland, the Archbishop of St. Andrews, and must be assumed to have been taken by Bothwell's divorced wife along with her to Dunrobin. [A fuller discussion of this subject will be found in the admirable monograph of Dr. John Stuart, entitled, "A Lost Chapter in the History of Mary Queen of Scots Recovered," 4to. Edinburgh, 1874.]

dissolved, and that a corresponding decision was CHAP.
given by the Catholic Consistorial Court, on the 7th VI.
May. The process unquestionably had been insti- 1573.
tuted in both courts, so that Protestants as well
as Papists should have every assurance that the
Queen's subsequent marriage with Bothwell was
lawful.

On the separation Bothwell surrendered to Lady
Jane Gordon for life the estate and village of Nether
Hales in Haddingtonshire, a transfer which after his
marriage with the Queen was confirmed by letters-
patent issued under the Great Seal.[1] Bothwell's
young divorced wife subsequently, in the year 1573,
married at Strathbogie, Alexander, Earl of Sutherland, who likewise had at that time got a divorce
from his former spouse—Barbara Sinclair—under
the charge of infidelity. After the Earl's death in
1594, she entered into a third marriage with Alexander Ogilvy, laird of Boyne, one of the judges
who acquitted Bothwell, and was now a widower in
consequence of the death of his wife Mary Beaton,
one of the Queen's "four Maries." After surviv-
ing both Mary and her three husbands, Both-

[1] Of 10th June 1567.—Chalmers,
Life of Mary Queen of Scots, ii.
234. Perhaps it is only this deed
of gift which forms the ground of
an expression of William Maitland in the letter of the French
ambassador, Du Croc, to Queen
Dowager Catherine de Medici, of
17th June 1567 (Teulet, *Papiers
d'État*, ii. 170), to this effect:—
"Mais nous ne doubtons point en
ce royaulme, qu'il n'aime mieux
sa première femme que la Royne."
If there is reported in the same
letter another of the many unfavourable utterances about Bothwell, according to which the latter
was said to have written letters to
his divorced consort, "par les-
quelles il mande à ladicte contesse
la tenir pour sa première femme et la
Royne pour sa concubine," yet this
utterance stands at least in direct
conflict with Du Croc's own testimony in a second letter (of 27th
May, Teulet, *Papiers d'État*, ii.
157), according to which Bothwell
is on the contrary reported to have
said regarding his first spouse,
"qu'il ne l'avoit jamais espousée,
et l'avoit toujours tenue pour concubine."

well's former wife ended her days at the age of
eighty-four.[1] By prudence she was able to keep
until her death the estate transferred to her by
Bothwell, without seeing it confiscated at the forfeiture of his other possessions, and after her second
marriage, by which she became the mother of five
sons and two daughters, she understood how to
manage with ability the Sutherland estates during
the minority of her eldest son. She was the first
who took care to have the coal mines of Sutherland worked on the banks of the Brora, and to
begin salt-making there. On her death at Dunrobin Castle, the 14th May 1629, her remains were
deposited by her sons in the Cathedral of Dor-
noch, in the family burying-place of the Earls of
Sutherland, and she left behind her the reputation
of having been " a vertuous and comlie lady, judi-
cious, of excellent memorie, and of great vnderstand-
ing above the capacitie of her sex."[2]

After a sojourn under Bothwell's roof, from the
24th of April to the 3d of May, the same day on
which the sentence of divorce between him and
Lady Jane Gordon was pronounced by the Commissary Court, the Queen left Dunbar and rode to
Edinburgh in company with the Earl and his men.[3]

[1] Joseph Robertson : Preface to
Inuentaires de la Royne Descosse,
pp. xliii., cxiv.
[2] *A genealogical History of the
Earldom of Sutherland, from its
origin to the year* 1630. Written
by Sir Robert Gordon of Gordon-
ston. Edinburgh, 1813, fol. pp.
168, 409. The author of this work,
created by James VI. Baron of
Nova Scotia, was the second of her
sons by the Earl of Sutherland.
A fine copy of the Legenda Aurea
—the edition of the year 1470—in
which her name is very often found
written, seems also to show that
Lady Jane Gordon was a woman,
who, according to the circumstances of her times, was not without culture.
[3] Diary of William Cecil ;
Laing, *History of Scotland,* ii. 89.
According to another authority,
which on this occasion also mentions George Earl of Huntly and
the Secretary of State, William
Maitland, as having been among
the attendants of the Queen, the

Before Mary Stuart in this fashion entered her capital, CHAP.
Bothwell's attendants put away their spears as if to VI.
show that the Queen was at liberty, and the Earl 1567.
himself, dismounting from his horse, took the
Queen's ambling steed by the bridle, and led it with
seeming respect.   The Queen entered the city by the
West Port, and rode through the Grassmarket up
to the Castle of Edinburgh, all the way conducted
by Bothwell—a sight to which Mary's friends were
witnesses only with sorrow, while it made the
enemies of her government exult.

A week afterwards, during which Mary remained
in Edinburgh Castle, constantly attended by Bothwell, a message was sent from her to the authorities
of the Reformed Church to publish the banns of
the marriage into which the Queen now wished to
enter.   A verbal request to this effect was brought
by one of Bothwell's kinsmen, Thomas' Hepburn, to
John Craig of St. Giles Kirk, and subsequently a
written one by the Justice-Clerk, Sir John Bellenden,
as the minister had refused to comply with the first
order, unless he saw the Queen's signature.   Nevertheless the bold pastor, whose character seems to
have resembled that of the Danish master, Ole Vind,
did not yet cease from his opposition, but demanded
beforehand to be admitted into the presence of the
parties themselves, otherwise he would either entirely
abstain from publishing the banns of marriage, or at
the same time openly tell what he thought about
the matter in the Church.   Afterwards, on being
called before the Privy Council, at which Bothwell
was present, he remonstrated with the latter in the

return of the latter to Edinburgh   *Diurnal of Remarkable Occurrents,*
first took place on the 6th May.—   p. 110.

CHAP.
VI.

1567.
most serious manner about all that was laid to his
charge—infidelity, abduction of the Queen, and even
participation in the murder of the King; and when
Bothwell did not answer him satisfactorily,[1] he concluded with saying, that he could not but publicly
state his conviction before the congregation. At
divine service in St. Giles Church, on Sunday the
9th May, he did indeed obey the order given so far
as to announce the approaching marriage, but after
that he added:—"I tuck heaven and erth to
witnes that I abhorred and deteastit that mariage,
because it wes odious and sclandrous to the warld;
and seing the best part of the realme did approve it,
ather be flatterie or be thair silence, I desyrit the
faithful to pray earnestlie that God wald turn it to
the comfort of this realme, that thing quhilk they
intend it agains reason and guid conscience."[2]

After the decree of divorce between Bothwell
and Lady Jane Gordon was pronounced by the Protestant and Catholic Courts, and the approaching
marriage of the Queen with Bothwell duly announced
by the publication of banns in the Church of St.
Giles, and by proclamation on the same day at
Holyrood, the Queen passed on the 12th May from
the Castle of Edinburgh down to the Palace.[3]   On

[1] The Declaration of Mr. John
Craig, minister of Edinburgh,
concerning his proclaiming the
banns of marriage betwixt Mary
Queen of Scotland and James,
Earl of Bothwell; Anderson, Collections, ii. 280.
[2] The Declaration of Mr. John
Craig; Anderson, Collections, ii.
280. Craig, on the ground of
having in this instance overstepped
his calling by describing the marriage of the Princess as "odious

and sclandrous to the warld," was
afterwards again summoned to
appear before a meeting of the
Privy Council; but when at last he
wished here, in presence of Bothwell, to show that his impression
agreed with God's Word, with
good law and order, the meeting
ended, as he himself writes, with
this, that "my Lord pat me to
silence, and sent me away."
[3] Diary of Wm. Cecil; Laing,
Hist. of Scotland, ii. 90. The 11th

the way, however, she stopped at the Chief Court of
Justice, or the so-called Court of Session.   Here she
presented herself in person, and made a declaration
before the Chancellor and judges of the court, and
before an assembly of the nobles whom she summoned to meet in this place.   She declared that
she had learned that the judges entertained some
doubt whether they could constitute the court after
their sovereign was detained in imprisonment at
Dunbar by the Earl of Bothwell, but she charged
them now to give up these scruples ; for though she
had at first been offended at the said Earl for his
abduction of her person, yet in consideration of his
previous good services, and of the good services she
further expected of him, she had afterwards forgiven him, as she forgave all the accomplices that
had been in league with him, and intended to exalt
him even to still higher dignity.[1]   In the evening of
the same day, the Earl was with great pomp created
Duke of the Orkneys—and with these the transferred Shetland Isles—and the Queen herself put
the ducal coronet on his head.   To add greater
splendour to the stately occasion, four gentlemen
were at the same time knighted, namely, the lairds
James Cockburn of Langton, Alexander Hepburn of
Benston, Patrick Whitlaw, and James Ormiston,
whom we know as one of the ringleaders in the
catastrophe which ended Darnley's life.   Another of
Bothwell's adherents, Sir James Balfour, who had
drawn up in writing the bond to be entered into by
those who were to put Darnley out of the way, and
whose brother, Canon Robert Balfour, had vacated the

May is stated as the day, in *Diurnal*   [1] Declaration of Mary Stuart ;
of *Remarkable Occurrents*, p. 111.   Anderson, *Collections*, i. 87-89.

house in which Darnley passed his last days, had previously been made Commander of Edinburgh Castle,
in the room of Sir James Cockburn, laird of Skirling.
Although Mary had already publicly forgiven all
the accomplices of Bothwell, yet the nobles still did
not deem themselves secure from the consequences
of having at " Ainslie's supper " subscribed the bond
for Bothwell, but by which perhaps they had hardly
supposed, at the time, that he would consider himself
warranted to employ force for gaining the object to
which it referred. They must have demanded that
Bothwell, whose power over the Queen so unmistakably showed itself in these days, would procure
for them from the Queen a special assurance of
immunity, and this two days later was also granted.
On the 14th May, Mary put her name to a short
declaration which was subjoined to the bond
given by the nobles to Bothwell, and which was
expressed in these words :—" The Queenes Majestie
haveing sene and considerit the band above writtine,
promittis in the word of a princesse, that she, nor
her successoris, sall nevir impute as cryme or offence
to onie of the personis subscryveris thairof, thaire
consent & subscriptioun to the matter above writtin,
thairin contenit ; nor that thai, nor thair heires, sall
nevir be callit nor accusit thairfoir ; nor zit sall the
said consent or subscryving be onie derogatioun or
spott to thair honor, or thai esteemit undewtiful
subjectis for doing thairof, notwithstanding quhatsumevir thing can tend or be allegeit in the contrare.
In witnes quhairof her Majestie hes subscryveit the
samyne with her awin hand."[1]   The same day also

[1] The Declaration of Mary
Stuart of 14th May 1567 ; Labanoff, ii. 22. Bell adds in reference
to this declaration : "Here is

a marriage-contract was at length signed which had CHAP.
been very cleverly drawn up, striving as it does VI.
with adroitness to hide the inequality of the match 1567.
between the royal widow and " the richt noble and
potent Prince James, Duke of Orknay, erle Boith-
vile, lord Halis, Chreichtoun and Liddisdall, greit
admirall of this realme of Scotland." One of the
articles stipulates that all state documents shall
hereafter have the signatures of both parties, both
the Queen's and her intended husband's.[1]

The day after, or the 15th May, the marriage
took place in Holyrood Palace. Of the higher
nobility of Scotland, civil or clerical, there were present only Earls Crawford, Huntly, and Sutherland ;
Lords Aberbrothock, Oliphant, Fleming, Livingston,
Glammis, and Boyd ; the Archbishop of St. Andrews and the Bishops of Dunblane and Ross ; the
rest present — among whom, however, could also
be observed John Craig—were mostly insignificant
petty nobles in Bothwell's train.[2] To those who
knew the Queen's character, the mode in which
the marriage was performed must have been the
most striking sign of the sway which Bothwell now
exercised over her ; for just as when he married the

another argument against the idea
of collusion between Mary and
Bothwell ; for in that case, so far
from having anything to fear,
Bothwell's friends would have
known that nothing could have
recommended them more to Mary,
than the countenance they gave
his marriage."—*Life of Mary
Queen of Scots*, ii. 94.

[1] " Furthermair, it is concluded
and accordit be hir Majestie, that
all signatours, lettres, and writingis to be subscrivit be hir
Majestie in tyme to cum, efter

the completing and solemnizatioun
of the said mariage, othir of giftis,
dispositionis, graces, privilegis, or
utheris sic thingis quhatsumevir
sall be alsua subscrivit be the said
noble Prince and Duke, for his
interesse, in signe and takin of his
consent and assent thairto, as hir
Majestie's husband." — Marriage-
Contract of 14th May 1567 ; in
Labanoff, ii. 4-28.

[2] *Diurnal of Remarkable Occurrents*, p. 111 ; Tytler, *History of
Scotland*, vii. 97.

CHAP.
VI.
1567.

Catholic Jane Gordon, he had secured the celebration
of the ecclesiastical ceremony by one of the Reformed
clergy, so he was now able to enforce the same thing
when the Queen was to give him her hand. The
Queen, who, on this occasion, still made her appearance in her widow's weeds, was early in the morning
married to the new Duke by Adam Bothwell, the
Protestant Bishop of the Orkneys,[1] who prefaced the
ceremony with a sermon on the second chapter of
Genesis, in which he enlarged on the regret of the
bridegroom at the past, and his purpose in future
to conform himself to the discipline and order of the
Reformed Church. The festivities which it was
customary to witness at a princely wedding were
now wanting; Bothwell had in vain sought to persuade the French ambassador, Du Croc, who had
returned to Scotland, to honour it with his presence;
the people looked on with dislike, and Sir James
Melvil, a contemporary very unfavourable to Bothwell, who was present as an eye-witness on the
marriage day, had not, even when in his old age he
wrote down his recollections, forgotten the dismal
impression it made upon him.[2] The day after an

---

[1] Adam Bothwell was no relation
of the Earl of Bothwell, but had
been one of the four Scottish Prelates who joined themselves to the
Reformers. His action at the
marriage was charged against him
by the Reformed Church; it gave
Knox occasion to say: "If there
be a good work to be done, a
bishop must do it."—*History of the
Reformation in Scotland*, ii. 555;
and Adam Bothwell was afterwards suspended by the Church
for his conduct in this instance,
and was obliged to make a public
apology before he was again re-

stored.—Anderson, *Collections*, ii.
283, 284.

[2] I found my Lord Duke of
Orkney sitting at his supper, who
welcomed me, saying, I had been
a great stranger, desiring me to sit
down and sup with him; the Earl
of Huntly, the Justice-Clerk, and
diverse others being sitting at
table with him. I said, I had
already supped; then he called for
a cup of wine and drank to me,
saying, You had need grow fatter,
for, says he, the zeal of the commonwealth hath eaten you up, and
made you lean. I answered, That

unknown hand wrote on the gate of Holyrood the
Ovidian line :—

"Mense Maio malas nubere vulgus ait."[1]

And the wide-spread popular belief made marriages in May be long afterwards regarded among all classes as unlucky. It is said that among the people in Scotland, since this wedding-day, there are still but few marriages contracted during this month.[2]

It has been a subject of dispute how far the solemnisation of the marriage in the first instance after the Protestant mode was subsequently repeated according to the rites of the Romish Church, and this question is not without significance with respect to the attitude which the Queen afterwards assumed towards Bothwell. In the account to Philip II. from the Spanish ambassador, Don Frances de Alava, the latter states, in accordance with what the Bishop of Dunblane, just arrived from Scotland, had communicated to him, that the whole of the religious ceremony was only after the Calvinistic mode; Sir James Melvil also mentions only one marriage ceremony according to the fashion of the Reformed Church, and a corresponding testimony is likewise furnished in the diary of an anonymous Scotsman which records contemporaneously the events of the period.[3] Other contemporaries assert, on the

every little member should serve to some use, but that the care of the commonwealth appertained most to him, and the rest of the nobility, who should be as fathers of the same. I knew well, says he, he would find a pin for every bore. Then he fell in discoursing with the gentlewomen, speaking such filthy language that they and I left him and went up to the Queen, who expressed much satisfaction at my coming.—*Memoirs of Sir James Melvil*, p. 80.

[1] Keith, *History of Church and State in Scotland*, p. 386. The line is from Ovid, *Fast.*, lib. v. l. 490.

[2] Taylor, *Pictorial History of Scotland*, ii. 57.

[3] Toda la cerimonia fue à la Calvinista.—Letter of Don Frances

R

contrary, that the marriage on that morning was solemnised after the rites of both the Catholic and the Reformed Churches.[1] There seems, however, no room for doubt in reference to this when we notice the way in which Mary has herself expressed her dissatisfaction with Bothwell on account of the form in which the marriage was celebrated. " Quhairin," she writes immediately after her marriage to her relatives in France, " we cannot dissembill that he hes usit ws utherwayis than we wald have wyssit, or zit have deservit at his hand, having mair respect to content thame by quhais consent grantit to him befoir hand he thinkis he hes obtenit his purpois, althoch thairin he had bayth frustrate ws and thame, than regarding oure contentatioun, or zit weying quhat wes convenient for ws, that hes bene norissed in our awin religioun, and nevir intendis to leif the samyne for him or ony mon upoun earth."[2]

de Alava to King Philip II., dated Paris, 16th June 1567 ; Teulet, *Papiers d'État*, iii. 31. In the great hall, where the council useth to sit, according to the order of the reformed religion, and not in the chappel at the mass, as was the King's marriage.—*Memoirs of Sir James Melvil*, p. 80. Within the auld chappel, not with the mess, but with preitsching.—*Diurnal of Remarkable Occurrents*, p. 111. There is, however, in the latter account with respect to the place where the marriage was held, an obvious contradiction to Melvil's statement.

[1] Accomplishit on baith the fashionis.—The bond of the Scottish nobles of 16th June 1567 ;

Anderson, *Collections*, i. 136. After bathe the sortis of the kyrk, re-formed and unreformed. — Diary of William Cecil ; Laing, *History of Scotland*, ii. 90. There are other concordant authorities to be found in Laing's *History*, i. 90-91.

[2] Mary Stuart's instructions to the Bishop of Dunblane.—Labanoff, ii. 41. She immediately adds after stating what is given above : —" For now sen it is past, and cannocht be brocht bak agane, we will mak the best of it, and it mon be thocht, as it is in effect, that he is oure husband, quhome we will bayth luff and honour, swa that all that professis thame-sellis to be oure friendis mon profess the lyke friendschip towartis him quha is inseperablie joynit with ws."

CHAPTER VII.

At the same time that Mary, after the wedding, gave her instructions to the Bishop of Dunblane and to Sir Robert Melvil of Murdocairny, whom she sent to Paris and London to explain her sudden marriage with the Earl of Bothwell, the latter also himself wrote to the monarchs of France and England. His words to Charles IX., whose Scottish guard he had formerly commanded, were only a respectful greeting ;[1] his letter to Queen Elizabeth was on the contrary written in a bold, almost kingly tone. He was, so he expressed himself, not unacquainted with the Queen's dislike towards him, but he asserted that this was undeserved, and declared his resolution to maintain friendship between the two kingdoms. Men of higher rank than he, so he concluded, might have been chosen for the exalted position which he now occupied, but none, he dared say, was more willing than he to show the English Queen every attention. The style was different from the servility which ordinarily marked the utterances of contemporaries to England's proud mistress,

---

[1] Letter of Bothwell to King Charles IX., dated Edinburgh the 27th May 1567.—Teulet, *Papiers* *d'État, relatifs à l'histoire de l'Écosse au* xvie *siècle*, ii. 156.

an evidence of the self-importance which, as well as his guilt, distinguished this audacious man.[1]

William Cecil, the trusty minister of Elizabeth, was at the same time also written to by Bothwell, as well as by Mary herself, both of whom expressed their hope that he would do his best to preserve friendly relations between the two Queens;[2] but when these letters were written, Elizabeth had already promised her assistance to the enemies of Bothwell in Scotland.[3] Those who even had joined with him in the plot against Darnley, or who afterwards recommended him as the most fitting husband for their Queen, were, nevertheless, speedily filled with rancour at "his immoderate ambition," at seeing the chief castles of the kingdom in his hands, with the object which they ascribed to him, "that he might be able to invest himself with the crown of the realm." To them it indeed seemed as if they had only been originally attached to him in order to become tools against him who was now away, and they began to fear, not less than formerly, the introduction of French absolutism into Scotland. The nobles were obliged, so they expressed themselves, after overthrowing Bothwell, to see the monarch "environed with a continual guard of two hundred harquebusiers as well day as night wherever she went,

---

[1] Abstract of Bothwell's letter to Queen Elizabeth, dated Edinburgh, 1st June 1567.—Tytler, *History of Scotland*, vii. 103-104.

[2] Letters of Mary Stuart and Bothwell to Cecil, both from Edinburgh, the 1st of June 1567; *State Papers, Foreign Series*, 1566-1568, p. 242.

[3] Already the 8th April 1567, had the Earl of Bedford, Commander on the Borders, been written to, that "he is to give them comfort" (*Calendar of State Papers, Foreign Series*, 1566-1568, p. 202), and on the 23d of May 1567 it was notified to the Earl of Morton that in England they could "by no means allow of Bothwell," and that, therefore, assistance was to be also expected of "such as before and after the murder were deemed to allow of Bothwell."— Caird, *Mary Stuart*, p. 148.

besides a number of his servants." Bothwell had CHAP.
"by these means brought the nobility to that VII.
miserable point, that if any man had to do with the 1567.
prince, it behoved him, before he could come to her
presence, to go through the ranks of harquebusiers
under the mercy of a notorious tyrant, as it were to
pass the pikes : a new example, and wherewith
this nation had never been acquainted, and yet few
or none admitted to her speech ; for that his suspicious heart brought in fear by the testimony of an
evil conscience, might not suffer her subjects to have
access to Her Majesty, as they were wont to do."[1]
Others among the grandees of the realm also found
it intolerable that the young son of the king, the
heir to the throne, should so soon come into the
hands of the man who passed for his father's
murderer, and to whom were already ascribed, either
seriously or feignedly, designs threatening danger to
the child's life.[2]

Finally, as a further reason for rising against
Bothwell, solicitude for Mary Stuart herself was
also alleged. It seems quite certain that, whether
passion or other views induced Mary to com-
mit the irreparable mistake of marrying Bothwell,
it was not long ere she was awakened from every
dream that her new connection could bring happiness. Even before the marriage was consummated,

<hr />

[1] Answer of the Scottish Lords
of 11th July 1567 to Sir Nicholas
Throckmorton, who had then, as
Queen Elizabeth's ambassador,
arrived in Scotland, printed in
Keith, *History of Church and
State in Scotland*, i. 418-20.

[2] Is autem, nemo dubitabat,
quin puerum, primo quoque tem-
pore, per occasionem de medio
tolleret, ne vel cædis Regiæ ultor
superesset, vel ne esset, qui liberos
suos, in hæreditate regni adeunda,
præiret.—Buchanan, *Rerum Scoticarum Historia*, p. 220. Compare
letter of Kirkaldy of Grange
of 8th May 1567 to the Earl of
Bedford ; Tytler, *History of Scotland*, vii. 92-93.

it was said in Scotland that Bothwell, by his extraordinary jealousy, would make it an unhappy one,[1] and the French minister, Du Croc, who had refused to be personally present at the ceremony, but who conversed with the Queen shortly before, heard her state, when he saw her sadness on the wedding day, that it was because she would never more be glad, and only wished herself dead.[2] If we may believe in this instance the enemies of Bothwell, she quickly found in him no longer that tender regard of which she had previously been the object. So far we can neither be surprised that Bothwell's foes, when they rose against him, likewise stated that they were also anxious to deliver the Queen from her new husband,—from the man who, as they asserted, would otherwise, in half a year, hand over the mother to the same death as he had prepared for the father, and destined for the son.[3] But it

[1] There has been a great unkindness between her and Bothwell for half a day. He is held the most jealous man that lived, and it is believed that they will not long agree after the marriage.—Letter from Sir William Drury of 13th May 1567 ; *Calendar of State Papers, Foreign Series,* 1566-1568, p. 229.
[2] Teudi (*i.e.* 15th May) sa majesté m'envoya quérir, où je m'apperceus d'une éstrange façon entre elle et son mary ; ce qu'elle me voullut excuser, disant que, si je la voyoy's triste, c'estoit parce qu'elle ne se voulloit resjouyr, comme elle dit ne faire jamais, ne desirant que la mort.—Letter of Du Croc to Catherine de Medici, 18th May 1567 ; Teulet, *Papiers d'État,* ii. 155. When Du Croc goes on to add :—" Hier, estant renfermez tous deux dedans ung

cabinet avec le comte de Boudoell, elle cria tout hault que on luy baillast ung couteau pour se tuer. Ceux, qui estoient dedans la chambre, l'entendirent," his statement agrees with what Sir James Melvil (*Memoirs,* p. 81) has at a later period related :—" In presence of Arthur Arskine, I heard myself her ask for a knife to stab herself, or else, said she, I shall drown myself."
[3] In the answer of the Scottish Lords of 11th July 1567, among the chief explanations of their insurrection is mentioned also this, that they had had " Bothwell suspected, seeing him keep another wife in store, to make the Queen also to drink of the same cup, to the end he might invest himself with the crown of the realm." Further, in the same document, it is likewise said that they were

may indeed be questioned whether this reason was CHAP.
yet very sincerely entertained by at least the real VII.
leaders of the movement. Nor does it accord 1567.
with this view, that hardly was Mary out of
Bothwell's hands, before they themselves imprisoned
her, and removed her from the throne. Although
the Scots Lords would so far explain this contradiction by alleging that "plat contrary to our expectation," they had now discovered her passion for
Bothwell to be as strong as ever,[1] and that, therefore, they had previously been obliged to hold her
in custody, yet this agrees but ill with the testimonies from their own side which more recent times
have brought to light. These more recent dis-
closures not only sufficiently show that the secret
alliance of the Lords, which older historians have
represented as first formed after Bothwell's marriage
with the Queen, was really entered into a month
previous, but also that her enemies, while seeking
support from England, even before Bothwell carried
her off to Dunbar, had already been anxious to
ascribe to Mary the same unbounded devotion to
Bothwell, the surprising discovery of which, after
they rose in rebellion, they subsequently brought

afraid not only for the life of the
King's young son, but also for that
of the Queen, "who should not
have lived with him half a year to
an end, as may be conjectured by
the short time they lived together,
and the maintaining of his other
wife at home at his house."—
Keith, *History of Church and
State in Scotland*, p. 418. Instead
of with Bell (*Life of Mary Queen
of Scots*, ii. 102) inferring from the
above expressions about Jane
Gordon, that Bothwell's divorce

from her had only been an act *pro
forma*, it may perhaps be more
correctly assumed that they are
founded on the fact that, after the
divorce, he made over Nether
Hales to his former wife.
[1] For plat contrary to our expectations, we found her passion
so prevail in maintenance of him
and his cause, that she would not
with patience hear speak anything
to his reproof, or suffer his doings
to be called in question.—Written
answer of the Scottish Lords to Sir

forward as a reason for the imprisonment of the Queen.[1]

The sojourn of the little prince in Stirling Castle happened at this time to furnish a point of union to the nobles of Scotland for their new conspiracy,—for a conspiracy which, in this instance no less than formerly, found its support from the neighbouring country. The Earl of Mar, whose duty it was to see to the security of the heir to the throne, had formerly, as Prior of Inchmahome, been an adherent of the old faith, but, like so many others who both separated from the Catholic Church and, at the same time, were careful to preserve to themselves the abbeys received from the latter, he had, since the previous year, been also enfeoffed with Stirling Castle by a deed of gift bearing the signatures of Mary Stuart and Darnley. It was his sister Margaret Erskine who had by James V. become mother of James Stuart, afterwards Earl of Murray, and in now taking part with the other Lords that began the insurrection, the Earl of Mar had certainly been specially influenced by his sister's son, who had so long coveted the supreme power in Scotland, and who, although previously absent, was nevertheless, from a distance, also making his influence felt. The safety of the King's son, punishment for the King's murder, and the rescue of the Queen, had already, during the Queen's stay with Bothwell at Dunbar, been chosen as the watchword which even the circumstances seemed to offer; with it the Earl of Argyll rode from Stirling to the west country, the

Nicholas Throckmorton of 11th July 1567; Keith, *History of Church and State in Scotland*, p. 419.

[1] See letter of Kirkaldy of Grange to the Earl of Bedford, of 20th April 1567.—Tytler, *History of Scotland*, vii. 87.

Earl of Atholl to the northern districts, and the CHAP. VII. Earl of Morton to Fife, Angus, and Montrose ; with a watchword like this they gained adherents every-where among the nobility of Scotland, always too easily moved. Even to the most intimate associates of the Queen and the Earl the secret alliance ex-tended ; William Maitland, laird of Lethington, Sir Robert Melvil, and his brother Sir James Melvil had secretly joined it,[1] and the Lords confidently anti-cipated the issue of the movement when, a few weeks after the marriage, there seemed to present itself an easy prospect of taking the Earl by surprise.

The first week after the wedding Bothwell and Mary remained at Holyrood, during which time meetings of the Privy Council were very often held.[2]   Bothwell intended, at this time, to set about in earnest an expedition to the Border districts intrusted to his special care, the same by whose wild inhabitants he had, in the previous year, been so nearly losing his life, and whose untamed population had latterly very seriously disturbed the more peaceable inhabitants.   The Queen on this occasion caused proclamations to be issued in her name and " with advice of hir derrest spouse, James Duke of Orknay, Erle of Bothwell, Lord Hails,

---

[1] *Memoirs of Sir James Melvil,* p. 82.   As Melvil relates that Bothwell, when he began to ob-serve that William Maitland too was joined to his opponents, had wished to put him out of the way, if the Queen had not saved him, -so Buchanan, who seems not to have had correct knowledge of the period, since the Earl of Murray had left Scotland, gives a corre-sponding, but more romantic story

how Bothwell had likewise very nearly effected the destruction of Murray.—Buchanan, *Rerum Sco-ticarum Historia,* p. 215.

[2] Thus we have still Acts of the Privy Council of the 17th, 22d, and 23d of May 1567. On the 22d of May the Secretary of State, William Maitland, was still pre-sent.—Keith, *History of Church and State in Scotland,* p. 386.

CHAP.
VII.

1567.

Chrichtoun, and Liddisdaill, Greit Admirall of this Realme, and Lordis of Secreit Counsall."[1] The proclamations contained a command to her vassals in the southern parts of the country to meet her and the Earl on a certain day at Melrose. As meanwhile the report was spread that the special design of summoning the troops to arms did not concern the Borders, but that in reality it was intended to march with them to Stirling Castle, with· the view of securing the surrender of the King's son by the Earl of Mar, so when these rumours came to the ears of the Queen she forthwith caused them to be met on the 1st June 1567, by a " Declaration upon the Brutis (rumours)."[2] In this declaration the subjects are reminded that since the Queen had returned home to the realm they had not felt the pressure of any foreign host, but had enjoyed peace with other countries ; that neither had any internal disturbances shown themselves without these being immediately suppressed, " so that they might justly compare their state, in this her Majesty's reign, to the most happy time that has occurred in man's memory." " But," so it is subsequently said, " as envy is enemy to virtue, and that seditious and unquiet spirits ever seek to entertain trouble and unquietness, so can Her Majesty never mean so sincerely and uprightly, nor ever direct her doings so perfectly, but instead of thankful hearts and good obedience, Her Highness' clemency is commonly abused and recompensed with untowardness and ingratitude ; when she thinks least of any

[1] The proclamations are printed in Keith's *History*, pp. 395, 396.
[2] The Quenis declaration upoun the Brutis. — Keith, *History of Church and State in Scotland*, pp. 396, 397.

novation, ever some invention or other is brought in, and the people persuaded to believe it." In so far as it was now said that she designed to reject the assistance of the nobles in the government of the country and, in opposition to the custom of past times, to decide all things alone, Her Majesty, in reference to this, declared that it was not her intention to subvert the laws "in any single iota." As it was likewise reported that the troops which the Queen had caused to be summoned against the Borderers, who were harassing her peaceable subjects, were to have another destination, the truth on this point would show itself in a few days, and when finally her maternal heart was adjudged to be destitute of right feeling for her very dear son, she also confidently trusted to time, so evidently would it manifest to all her motherly affection for him.[1]

After the issue of this declaration, the Queen, in company with Bothwell, left Edinburgh on the 7th June attended by two hundred arquebusiers, who now formed her guard. The remainder of the troops summoned for the expedition had as yet only met in so small numbers that Bothwell, as well as the Queen, was obliged to betake himself, for some few days, to Borthwick Castle, which is situated on an acclivity surrounded by the little stream Gore, about fourteen miles from Edinburgh, and which, in the following century, was strong enough to withstand, for some time, the victorious host of Cromwell. On the 10th of June, as they were sitting at table in Borthwick Castle, they received the unexpected news that the Earl of Morton and Lord

CHAP. VII.

1567.

[1] Sa sall hir Majesties moderlie affectioun towartis him appeir evidentlie.—Keith, p. 397.

Alexander Hume, with a troop of twelve hundred
horsemen, were hastening to the castle, in order,
after their hurried night-ride, to take its guests
prisoners. The surprise did not however succeed.
The troop that first arrived called out indeed before
the castle that they came as fugitives pursued by
rebels, but Bothwell did not allow himself to be
caught by this stratagem. As he nevertheless did
not consider the castle strong enough to enable him
to hold out, he made his escape by a secret postern
gate, accompanied only by a son of the Laird of
Crookstone.[1] Some of Lord Hume's men, while
advancing, met the two fugitives and made chase
after them, but when their enemies were only a
bowshot from them they separated in different
directions, and their pursuers taking the wrong
direction, Bothwell escaped to Haddington. As
after Bothwell's escape the hostile troops did not
believe that they could long maintain themselves
before Borthwick Castle, the Queen also subsequently found an opportunity of getting away from
the castle, mounted on horseback and clad in men's
clothes.[2] Bothwell, turning back, waited her arrival
at some distance, and now again repaired with her
to Dunbar, which they reached on the 11th June
at three o'clock in the morning.

[1] Understanding the weakness of the place, he escaped. — Sir William Drury's letter to Cecil, dated Berwick, 12th June 1567; *Calendar of State Papers, Foreign Series*, 1566-68, p. 248.

[2] With respect to this escape of the Queen the Lords stated after-wards in an answer to Sir Nicholas Throckmorton, who, as ambassador from Queen Elizabeth, had been sent to Scotland in consequence of Mary's imprisonment:—"It ap-peared well when at first we came about Borthwick, we meant nothing to the Queen's person in so far that hearing he (Bothwell) was escaped out of the house, we insisted no further to pursue the same, it being most easy to have been taken."—Answer of the Lords to Throckmorton of 11th July 1567; Keith, *History of Church and State in Scotland*, p. 419.

The same day the enemies of Bothwell, on the contrary, being disappointed before Borthwick, marched towards Edinburgh, and on the way were joined by the Earl of Mar, Lord Lindsay, the Lairds of Tullibardine, Lochleven, and Grange, with another band of seven hundred horsemen.[1] The Earl of Mar, when he found the gates of Edinburgh shut, caused these to be broken open, and without any hindrance from the citizens the Lords marched in. The adherents of the Queen who had repaired to Edinburgh, George Gordon, Earl of Huntly, John Lesley, Bishop of Ross, John Hamilton, Archbishop of St. Andrews, Gawin Hamilton, Prior of Kilwinning, and Lord Claude Hamilton, Prior of Paisley, sought to rouse the citizens to oppose the entrance of the Confederate Lords, but only few of these joined their armed men, so that they found themselves forced to retire into the Castle of Edinburgh.[2] Its commander, Sir James Balfour, indeed admitted them, and also gave them, some mornings afterwards, on the 15th June, means of escaping unhurt on the opposite side, but even he did not allow the castle to fire a single shot against the Confederate Lords. Sir James Melvil had, as he relates in his *Memoirs*, already frightened Balfour, by stating that one of Bothwell's confidants, the commander of

[1] The contemporary French account of the events in Scotland from the 11th to the 15th of June 1567.—Teulet, *Papiers d'État*, ii. 159. The anonymous author speaks of himself in this account as commander over "l'Isle aux chevaux," which was the ordinary name among the French for the little island of Inchkeith in the Firth of Forth, and has therefore certainly been one of the French soldiers who remained behind in the service of Mary Stuart.

[2] Hi, quum sensissent hostes suos in urbem acceptos, in forum provolantes, duces multitudini sese offerunt. Sed quum rari admodum ad eos sese aggregarent, retro cedendo ad arcem usque compulsi fuerunt.—Buchanan, *Rerum Scoticarum Historia*, p. 220.

CHAP.
VII.
1567.

Dunbar Castle, Laird Patrick Whitlaw, had assured him that Bothwell intended to take Edinburgh Castle from Balfour, and to give the command of it to the Laird of Benston, a member of the Hepburn family.[1] Without openly breaking with either party the lukewarm Sir James Balfour now wished only to wait till he saw which of them showed itself the stronger. He obeyed the orders which the Queen sent him so far as in compliance with them to call upon the Lords to leave the city, but he was disobedient to them in so far as he forbore to use force in expelling them from the town.

When the Confederate Lords assembled in Edinburgh the French minister, Du Croc, at the Queen's wish, offered them his mediation, and they repaired in consequence to his residence. Here he put them in mind that Bothwell had been acquitted by the assize-court, that the Parliament itself had recently confirmed this acquittal, and that subsequently very many Earls, Bishops, and other leading men of the realm had subscribed the declaration which recommended Bothwell as a husband for the Queen, and which he had laid before her at Dunbar Castle. The Lords demanded three days to give a decided answer, but yet, in the interval, they did not omit to print and circulate proclamations against Bothwell, and promised five pounds a month to all who should join them and serve against the Earl. In Edinburgh, nevertheless, adherents did not flock to them to the number they expected, some of the associates of the Lords of the same rank remaining neutral, and, as they were exposed to the great guns of the castle, they were on the eve of giving up the whole

[1] *Memoirs of Sir James Melvil*, p. 81.

undertaking. Even Buchanan and Knox expressly CHAP. VII. declare that if Bothwell had only for two days remained quiet with the Queen in the fastness of 1567. Dunbar, which the Lords were unable to capture, those in Edinburgh would have disbanded, and every one would have sought to care for himself alone.[1] But flatterers at this juncture represented that all would throw away their weapons if the Queen but showed her face in the field. For Bothwell had by no means been idle; a summons had gone forth from Dunbar calling upon all loyal men between sixteen and sixty capable of bearing arms to fight in the Queen's service, and besides Bothwell's own kinsmen and vassals there are others mentioned who showed themselves willing to obey this call, viz., Lords George Seton, John Borthwick, and William Hay of Yester, along with a considerable number of lesser noblemen.[2] On the morning of Saturday, 14th June, Mary Stuart marched from Dunbar with her guard of two hundred arquebusiers, together with sixty horsemen and several cannon, and passed on towards Edinburgh, on whose castle it was still supposed that she could reckon, and into which she therefore believed herself sure of making her entry on the following day.

The expedition from Dunbar was to some extent delayed in consequence of arms having had to be distributed by the way to the rural population

[1] Buchanan, *Rerum Scoticarum Historia*, p. 221; Knox, *History of the Reformation in Scotland*, ii. 558.

[2] These Lords are mentioned in a letter, addressed by Sir James Beaton to his brother Andrew Beaton, for the information of the Archbishop of Glasgow; it is dated from Edinburgh, 17th June 1567, and is printed among the supplements to Laing's *History of Scotland*, ii. 106-115. Their names likewise occur in the French eye-witness' account.—Teulet, *Papiers d'État*, ii. 158-170.

CHAP.
VII.

1567.

summoned from the surrounding country, by whose influx the force drawn from Dunbar was constantly increased. Bothwell did not, however, stop at Hadington as had been expected, but in order to gain time continued his march right to the castle of Seton, where he arrived with the Queen in the evening, and where they remained over night, while their numerous troops were quartered in the adjacent villages of Preston and Prestonpans. At sunrise on Sunday morning, 15th June, at the news of the approach of the enemy, the expedition advanced, and a new proclamation in the Queen's name was issued to her soldiers, in which all the charges made by the rebels were contradicted as idle inventions. They spoke, she said, of wishing to avenge the former King's death, but no one had a better title to avenge him than the Queen herself, if she only knew the authors of his murder; they came forward with accusations against the Earl of Bothwell, although he had used all possible means to manifest his innocence, although the court of law had acquitted him, the Parliament had to the utmost confirmed this acquittal, and he himself in the fullest manner had announced his willingness to decide the matter by a duel with any accuser of equal birth; they talked of wishing to defend the young prince, and yet this young prince was really in their own hands. "The samyn day the Quenis majestie causit mak proclamatioun in the camp, that quha sould sla ane erle suld have XL pund land, ane lord XX pd. land, ane barroun X pd. land, and ane gemane his escheit."[1] It was still morning when they reached the top of Carberry Hill, and the enemy came in sight. On

[1] *Diurnal of Remarkable Occurrents*, p. 115.

Carberry Hill, which is only about seven miles from
Edinburgh, were still found some old redoubts and
trenches which the English had thrown up when at
Pinkie, in the immediate vicinity of this point, they
gained their victory over the Scots in the year 1547.
The Earl of Bothwell, who rode on a splendid
charger, and with the royal banner which displayed
the lion rampant of Scotland,[1] posted his troops
behind these redoubts.   Near them was a stone
which is still pointed out as that on which the
Queen for a long time was seated, having dismounted from her steed to enjoy some rest.   She
sat here with velvet hat and veil on her head, and
wearing a simple dress with sleeves laced together,
and a red skirt which scarcely reached down to the
calf of the leg.[2]
     It was almost midnight when the Lords in Edin-
burgh became aware that Bothwell and the Queen

[1] La Royne en sa bandière portoyt ung lion, qui sont les armes
de ce royaume.—Letter of Du
Croc to Charles IX. of 17th June
1567 ; Teulet, *Papiers d'État*, ii.
177.   Monsieur le Duc portoyt le
lion rouge.—Account of a contemporary eye-witness ; *Ibid.* ii.
167.   The lion, which occurs in
the Scottish arms as early as the
twelfth century (Taylor, *Pictorial
History of Scotland*, ii. 71, 72), and
which reappears in those of Norway, Denmark, Holland, Hainault,
Flanders, Normandy, and, in
reality, in those also of England
(the leopard), corresponds generally
in the arms of North-westerly
Europe to the eagle in those of
Easterly Europe.   In the chapel
of Henry VII. in Westminster
Abbey, where Mary Stuart—her
son King James VI. in the year
1612 having caused her remains
to be brought hither from Peter-
borough—now rests right over
against those of Queen Elizabeth,
there is seen the Scottish lion
carved above on the lower part of
her splendid sepulchral monument.
[2] The Queen's apparel in the
field was after the fashion of the
women of Edinburgh, in a red
petticoat, sleeves tied with points,
a partlyte, a velvet hat and muffler.
—Letter of Sir William Drury to
Cecil, dated Berwick, 18th June
1567 ; *Calendar of State Papers,
Foreign Series*, 1566-1568, p. 254.
Elle estoyt abillée d'une cotte
rouge qui ne luy venoyt que à
demie de la jambe.—The contemporary account ; Teulet, *Papiers
d'État*, ii. 162.   Tunicula tantum
vestita, eaque vili et detrita, ac
paulum infra genua demissa.—Buchanan, *Rerum Scoticarum Historia*, p. 221.

S

CHAP.
VII.

1567.

had taken the field with a view to compel them to leave the city. The Lords then mounted their horses, and in the middle of the night their troops were heard by the inhabitants marching out with the blare of trumpets and the noise of drums. From Leith they hurriedly passed along the Firth of Forth onwards by the shore road which now nearly unites the hamlets and villas bordering it into one unbroken suburb of Edinburgh. At daybreak they reached the village of Musselburgh, and after passing this, it was seen that Bothwell, by hastening his march, had arrived first on Carberry Hill, which lies more than two miles to the south-east. The Lords never-theless secured the bridge for themselves—Magda-lene Bridge, which led over a brook rushing down in front of the hill—and here they drew up their men in two divisions, the first of which was under the command of the Earl of Morton and Lord Alexander Hume, and the second under that of the Earls of Mar, Glencairn, and Atholl. The strength of the Lords is variously stated, but was about as great as that of their opponents; according to the highest estimate given both armies amounted alto-gether to 8000 men.[1] The Lords, who were entirely wanting in cannon, had, on the other hand, this advantage over Bothwell, that all their men were trained soldiers. Their banner, which was calculated

[1] Son armée estoit de quatre mil hommes. Les enemys ne pouvoient estre plus de trois mil cinq cens hommes au plus. Les deux armées faisoient nombre de huit mil hommes.—Letter of du Croc ; Teu-let, ii. 176. The statement of the force present on this occasion by other authorities is only half as large. According to the letter of 17th June 1567 from James Bea-ton, for the Archbishop of Glas-gow, the army of the Lords was "jugit to be 18 hundereth horse-men, and better and four hundereth futmen or ma," and the Queen's "hail companie on hors and fut wus noucht nommerit to twa thousand men."—Laing, *History of Scotland*, ii. 110, 111.

to make an impression on the multitude, had on it a

picture of Darnley's corpse lying under the tree, where in the morning it was found, with the little prince kneeling at his side, and underneath the words : " Judge and avenge my cause, O Lord."

About the catastrophe, of which Carberry Hill was on this Sunday the scene, there are not few accounts, but they are difficult to harmonise, especially because they ascribe to the events of the day a different order. So much however is clear that there was no real battle, that the final decision did not take place till late in the evening, and that before this, as a contemporary tells, messengers were to be seen the whole day passing to and fro between the armies.[1]

The first of these messengers was the French ambassador, Du Croc. In Edinburgh he had, during the night, been witness to the departure of the Lords, but had remained in the city for three hours later, so that he might not seem to have taken part with them. Subsequently, with a small retinue, he rode after the warlike array that had set out before, and at eight o'clock in the morning overtook it in the neighbourhood of Musselburgh, on the bank of the stream at the foot of Carberry Hill. The Frenchman, who, in a letter to his king, has himself left behind a detailed description of the mediation attempted by him, represented to the Lords, that however otherwise they might judge of the circumstances, they yet stood now in direct opposition to their sovereign ; that perhaps, if they should be

---

[1] The uther armey stoode over against it, messingers going betwixt them all day till neir night. —The Diarey of Robert Birrel, burges of Edinburghe ; *Fragments of Scottish History*, p. 10.

fortunate enough to gain the battle, they might
afterwards find themselves in greater perplexity
than ever ; and moreover, that he had always found
so much goodness in the Queen that possibly he
might still be able along with her to discover a way
out of the present difficulty.[1]   The Lords made
answer to him, that they would rather be buried
alive than that the truth with regard to the King's
death should not be known, believing, as they did,
that if in this they neglected to do their duty God
would make them smart for it.   " They knew only
two possible ways to avoid the shedding of blood :
either the Queen must withdraw from those unhappy ones who now had her in their power,[2] in
which case they, as humble and obedient subjects,
would receive her on their knees ; or Bothwell must
place himself in the midst of the two armies, when,
in such an event, one from their ranks would go
forth to fight with him as being the former King's
real murderer ; yea, should one or even four not be
enough for him, ten or twelve would not be wanting."
The Lords with these words gave the French ambassador a company of horsemen to accompany him
over the bridge to Carberry Hill, where another
band of horsemen from the Queen came to meet
him, and conducted him to Mary.   After greeting
her and kissing her hand, Du Croc again began to
talk about reconciliation with those who were still
equally her subjects, and who even called themselves
her respectful and devoted servants.   The Queen

[1] Que je l'avois toujours cognue
princesse de si grande bonté que,
peult-estre, je trouverois quelque
moyen avec elle.—Letter of Du
Croc to King Charles IX., dated
Edinburgh, 17th June 1567 ; Teulet, *Papiers d'État*, ii. 174.
[2] Si la Royne se voulloyt tirer à
part de ces malheureux qui la
tenoient.—*Ibid*. ii. 173.

answered him : " They now show it very badly
indeed by acting contrary to what they themselves
have subscribed, and by still accusing him whom
they have acquitted, and to whom they have given
me in marriage. Yet I am ready, if they only will
repent and ask forgiveness, to receive them with
open arms." Bothwell, who had been much occupied with the marshalling of his army,[1] came
forward at this moment and inquired in a confident
voice, which he purposely raised so high that it
might be heard by the troops :[2] " Is it I with whom
they want to pick a quarrel ? what have I done to
them ? I never intended to harm a single one of
them, but, on the contrary, only sought to satisfy
them. What they now say, they say simply from
envy at my elevation. But fortune belongs to him
who can seize it, and there is not one among them
that does not wish to be in my place." He added,
however, that he had deep sympathy with the Queen
in the painful position in which he now saw her,[3]
and that therefore, in order to avoid bloodshed, in
God's name he was ready, notwithstanding his royal
marriage, to try single combat with any one that
would meet him between the two armies, provided
he was his equal in rank. Accordingly he besought
the ambassador to report this to the Lords, for his
quarrel with them was so just that he relied upon
having God on his side. As the Queen meanwhile
would not hear of this proposal, and Bothwell at

[1] Qui estoyt fort ententif a la
conduicte de son armée.—Letter of
Du Croc ; Teulet, *Papiers d'État,*
ii. 175.

[2] Il me demanda tout hault,
affin que son armée l'entendist,
d'une parolle fort assurée, si c'es-

toyt a luy qu'ils en voulloient.—
Ibid. ii. 175.

[3] Pour mettre la Royne hors de
la peine ou il la voyoit, de la
quelle il disoit porter une peine
extrême.—*Ibid.* ii. 175.

the same time saw his enemies cross over the stream,
Du Croc was obliged, with deep regret, to say farewell to the Queen, whom he left with tears in her
eyes,[1] and descended the hill only to say to the
Lords that he had found the Queen full of kindness,
and prepared for granting them forgiveness if they
went to her themselves for it.   Alexander Earl of
Glencairn—one of the violent zealots of the period,
who some days after went with his men into the
Queen's chapel at Holyrood and pulled down its
altar and sacred images[2]—answerèd in the name of
the Lords : " We are not come hither to beg forgiveness for ourselves, but to grant it to them who
have themselves offended."   The Lords again put
on their helmets, and the mediation, which had
occupied two 'hours, was broken off.[3]   Du Croc was
obliged to return to Edinburgh without gaining his
object.

It deserves to be particularly noticed that
although this French ambassador was by no means
favourably disposed towards Bothwell, yet he con-
fesses that he witnessed with great interest the
superior ability with which Bothwell managed everything.   If Bothwell could only rely upon his troops,
Du Croc did not doubt that he would be victorious,
for while he was sole commander on Carberry Hill,
there were contrary orders passing from one to the
other in the army of the Lords,[4] and the French

---

[1] La laissant la larme à l'œul.—
Letter of Du Croc ; Teulet, *Papiers
d'État*, ii. 177.

[2] Knox, *History of the Reformation in Scotland*, ii. 561.

[3] Et prirent oppinion que parle-
ment leur porteroit dommage, pour-
quoy misrent tous leur morions en

la main.—Letter of Du Croc ; Teulet, *Papiers d'État*, ii. 177.

[4] Et aussi l'estimois beaucoup
qu'il commandoit tout seul, et je
faisois doubte des autres pour ce
qu'ils estoient plusieur testes, et y
avoit une grande cryerie parmi
eulx.—*Ibid.* ii. 177.

ambassador also reported to his sovereign thus : " I CHAP.
cannot but say that I saw a great captain present ⌣̲ VII.
himself with the utmost confidence, and one who 1567.
led his troops with bravery and prudence."[1]   How
certain Bothwell still was of the issue of the day at
the departure of Du Croc, he also showed, when, on
seeing his foes cross the stream, he advised this
mediator " to imitate him who wished to establish
peace and friendship between the armies of Scipio
and Hannibal when these two armies were about to
come to blows, just as the two before them were
going to do, but who, when he could do nothing and
was unwilling to take part with either side, chose
for himself a place as a spectator, and thus became
witness of the grandest sight which he had ever
seen ; if Du Croc would now do the same he would
never live to witness a greater entertainment, for
he should see them fight bravely."[2]

The battle which Bothwell had imagined at hand
when he saw his enemies pass over the stream did

[1] Il fault que je dise que je veiz
ung grand cappitaine parler de
grande asscurance et qui con-
duisoit son armée gaillardement
et sagement.—Letter of Du Croc ;
Teulet, *Papiers d'État*, ii. 176.

[2] Du Croc, who replied, "que
ce n'estoit pas de la Royne et de
ces deux armées que je vouldrois
veoir ce plaisir, mais que au con-
traire je n'aurois jamais veu chose,
qui m'enyast tant que ce que je
verrois (Teulet, ii. 176), has probably misrepresented Bothwell's
reference to antiquity, or Bothwell
has himself confounded together P.
Cornelius Scipio Africanus major
and Africanus minor. We may conjecture that he had rather in view
the last named, who in vain came
forward as mediator between Mas-

inissa and the Carthaginians, about
whose internal contest Appian
(viii. 71) on this occasion thus
relates : " Scipio looked from an
elevated spot at this battle as at
a spectacle. He often said afterwards that, though he had been
present at many battles, he had
never found any pleasure such as
in this. For only once at this
martial exploit, where an hundred
and ten thousand men stood against
each other, had he been a sorrow-
less spectator." He adds however
with a feeling of self-complacency,
" that only two before him had
seen such a sight, viz., in the
Trojan war, Zeus from Ida and
Poseidon from Samothrace."—*Vide*
Homer, *Iliad*, viii. v. 51-67, and
xiii. v. 10-16.

not however take place. On the one hand, the latter perceived the preponderance which the position chosen by their opponent gave him, the hill being too steep to be seized from the westward without very great danger, while they would have to expose themselves to the cannon which the Earl had brought with him,[1] and to fight with the sun right in their eyes ; on the other hand, Bothwell having so many untrained soldiers, would not abandon his strong position in order to throw himself upon the more experienced troops of his enemies, especially as it was said that the Hamiltons, Lord Herries, and others of the Queen's adherents, had assembled large bands of horsemen, and were already in the neighbourhood, or might be expected the following day. Only now and then Bothwell made his artillery fire some shots on their out-posts, but these were too far distant to allow of them being struck by the cannon. After crossing the stream the Lords contracted their lines, made a movement to the right in the direction of Dalkeith, and occupied a height beyond the range of the cannon where they no longer had the sun in their faces, and whence access to Carberry Hill was less difficult. Dalkeith belonged to the Earl of Morton, and thence, on the clear, hot summer day, when, according to the custom of the country, the horsemen dismounted and fought on foot, and while the two armies only stood watching each other,[2] was brought abundance

[1] Maiores machinæ.—Buchanan, *Rerum Scoticarum Historia*, p. 221. And thair plaissit 7 or 8 pieces of artillerie, the quhilk they had broucht wyth thaim of Dunbar.— Letter of James Beaton ; Laing, *History of Scotland*, ii. 111. Il

avoit trois pièces de campagne.— Letter of Du Croc ; Teulet, ii. 176. Ung double et deux simples fauconneaux. — Contemporary Account, *Ibid.* ii. 162.

[2] Ils furent depuis les onze heures du matin jusqu'à cinq heures du

of meat and drink to the armed companions of CHAP.
Morton. In the Queen's army, on the contrary, VII.
notwithstanding all the attempts of the commanders 1567.
to maintain order, large bands were to be seen completely exhausted leaving the ranks to seek refresh-
ment in the neighbourhood ; only the arquebusiers
of the Queen, under Captains Alexander Stuart and
Hew Lauder, and another troop of Bothwell's firmest ·
adherents, steadily kept the ranks, but these, the
Lords trusted, would also become so tired out that
in the evening they would be obliged, in order to
refresh themselves, to give up the advantage of
their position.

Before that time, however, another way of
escape from the impending fight offered itself.
While the Earl of Bothwell could not rely upon his
own kinsmen and vassals, others were to be found
in the Queen's army who " were of opinion that she
had intelligence with the Lords," while " part of
them believed that her Majesty would fain have
been quit of him, but thought shame to be the doer
thereof directly herself."[1] And thus it happened
that at the out-posts, before the two armies, a
parley was held in which it was concluded that it
would be best to leave the decision of the quarrel to
a duel. The Queen, who had in the morning been
unwilling to hear this expedient spoken of, could
not with the same confidence refuse it, seeing the
proposal for thus preventing further bloodshed was
brought forward by her own people. For such a
mode of deciding the matter still harmonised with

soir à se regarder, ayant tous mis   Croc ; Teulet, *Papiers d'État*, ii.
piedz à terre, comme c'est la façon   178.
du païs, qui vout à cheval jusqu'au   [1] *Memoirs of Sir James Melvil*,
point de combattre.—Letter of Du   p. 82.

CHAP.
VII.

1567.

the spirit of the times ; not many steps from Carberry Hill the former Earl of Huntly, immediately
before the battle of Pinkie in 1547, had, as commander of the Scottish army, offered to meet the
Duke of Somerset, the leader of the English invading army, in knightly fashion, with a company of
twenty against twenty, of ten against ten, or only
man against man,[1] and it was only a few years more
than a generation since, that in the South, during
the second of the wars between Francis I. and
Charles v., the French King was seen to send, and
the Emperor to accept, a challenge to single combat,
and even at a later period in the North, during the
Kalmark war, the King of Sweden is known to have
addressed a like challenge to the King of Denmark
and Norway.[2] Mary sent for Sir William Kirkaldy,
the laird of Grange, the most distinguished warrior
in the hostile army, and to him the task was
intrusted of bringing Bothwell's readiness for the
proposed combat to the knowledge of the Lords.[3]

As, however, the duel of those princes did not
really take place, so neither was the duel on Carberry Hill actually carried out. What happened

[1] Burton, *History of Scotland,*
iii. 211.

[2] At a more distant period, to
mention here only the wars in
the North, Frederick III. is said, on
the second attack of Charles Gustavus upon Denmark, to have
offered the Swedish king to decide
the contest by single combat (*Memoires du Chevalier de Terlon,*
Paris, 1681, i. 254), just as King
Charles XII. still later wished to
have challenged Peter the Czar
to a duel (Norberg, *Anmärk-
ningar wed Konung Carl XII.'s*

Historia, Kjöbenhavn, 1754, pp.
30-32).

[3] *Memoirs of Sir James Melvil,*
p. 82. Melvil, who also makes the
laird of Grange in vain offer himself for the duel, has about this
first conference between the Queen
and Kirkaldy volunteered the
statement that "as he was speaking with Her Majesty, the Earl of
Bothwel had appointed a soldier
to shoot him, until the Queen gave
a cry, and said that he would not do
her that shame, seeing she had promised that he should come and
return safely."

there vividly recalls the circumstances in the North **CHAP.**
in olden times where it was not deemed becoming **VII.**
for kings or earls to appear against men of lower   1567.
origin or of less renown.[1] After Bothwell rode forth
in front of his army, willing now to redeem the
offer he made on his acquittal,[2] the first that wished
to accept his challenge was James Murray, a young
nobleman who had in Edinburgh been engaged in
posting up the secret placards against the Earl.
As he was meanwhile rejected by the other side as
beneath Bothwell in rank, his elder brother, Sir
William Murray, laird of Tullibardine, offered in
his stead to fight out the quarrel, asserting at the
same time that neither with respect to the antiquity
of his family nor in point of fortune would he yield
to the Earl. Yet was he also rejected, as he was
not like Bothwell one of the Peers of the realm ;
the Queen and the kinsmen of Bothwell wishing to
have only an Earl or a Lord as his opponent, and
Bothwell himself accordingly named the Earl of
Morton, who is said to have stated his readiness for
the combat. Lord Patrick Lindsay, who along with
Morton and Lord Ruthven, had played his part at
the murder of Riccio, now begged that it might be
allowed him, as a reward for his services, to undertake it in room of the Earl. It is related that the

---

[1] N. M. Petersen, *Danmarks
Historie i Hedenold*, Kjöbenhavn,
1834-37, iii. 394. About the
challenge of the Polish Crown-
General Zamoiski by Duke Charles
of Sudermania, afterwards Charles
IX., Lelewell remarks (*Histoire de
Pologne*, Paris et Lille, 1844, ii.
86) :—" Le Grand Zamoiski même,
qui refusa en republicain le titre
de Prince, vouloit dans sons âge

avancé obtenir le titre de comte,
afin de se mesurer en duel avec
Charles duc de Sudermanie Prince,
usurpateur de la Suède."

[2] Ibi Bothuelius, equo insigni
ante aciem provectus, per præ-
conem postulat, quo cum ipse singulari certamine decernat.—Buchanan, *Rerum Scoticarum Historia*,
p. 221.

Lords at first would not permit Lindsay to take upon himself alone a business which was as much theirs as his,[1] but that afterwards they expressed their satisfaction at his readiness. Morton, who drew back in his favour, lent him for the approaching duel an old two-handed sword, which one of his ancestors, Archibald Earl of Angus, had formerly made famous, and Lindsay was then seen to fall on his knees in presence of the whole army, and with a loud voice to pray God that His favour would preserve the innocent and make His justice strike the murderer who bore the guilt of the King's innocent blood. The warrant of arrest issued at a later period by the Lords against Bothwell affirms, as both Buchanan and Knox also do, that, as the result of cowardice on the part of the Earl, the Queen also rejected Lord Lindsay as of unequal birth to her husband,[2] but Bothwell protests that he himself induced both the noblemen who came with him, and also the Queen, to accept Lord Lindsay, and as his testimony does not in this instance stand alone, it can hardly be pronounced

---

[1] The Laird of Grange being retornit to the Lords wyth that anser, the Laird of Trebrowne was sent sone after him to knaw, quhair the plaiss sould be appointit, and in quhat appareill thay suld cum to the feild, quha, at his retorning, rapported to the Queinis Majestie and to my Lord Duk, that the Lordis wald noucht suffar my Lord Lindsay to faicht, and to tak all the haill bording upon him that was equallie thairs and his; and swa that proposs stayit.— Letter of James Beaton of 17th June 1567; Laing, *History of Scotland*, ii. 112.

[2] Efter that he had cowardlie refusit singular combat, baith of a Baron and gentleman undefamid, and of a Lord and Baron of Parliament.—The Scots Privy Council's warrant of arrest of 26th June 1567; Anderson, *Collections*, i. 140. Ibi quoque quum Bothuelius tergiversaretur, nec se honeste expedire posset, Regina suam interposuit auctoritatem, atque, eo depugnare vetito, contentionem diremit. — Buchanan, *Rerum Scoticarum Historia*, p. 221. Bothwell seeing that there was no more subterfuge nor excuse, underhand made the Queen to forbid him.— Knox, *History of the Reformation in Scotland*, ii. 561.

destitute of weight.[1]   All that remained now was   CHAP.
VII.
that the seconds, five noblemen from each side who
were to be present at the duel as eye-witnesses,[2]   1567.
should agree about the place and the conditions of
the combat.

Why was the quarrel not then brought to an
issue by the final decision of single combat ?   Why
did not Lindsay and Bothwell meet for its determination in the manner for which the latter has
subsequently said that he in vain waited until far
on in the summer evening?[3]   It seems as if the
Lords at the last moment preferred another mode of
deciding the quarrel after the frequent parleying
had given them better knowledge of their opponents'
want of unity, and possibly they were also influenced by fear lest the affair should be protracted in
order that the Queen's friends might obtain their
reinforcements.   After Sir William Kirkaldy of
Grange, Sir William Douglas of Drumlanrig, Sir
William Kerr of Cessfurd, and Sir John Home,
laird of Coldingknowes, with two hundred horse-

---

[1] The Queinis Majestie was lang
or sche could be persuadit to that,
bot at the last, albeit sche fand it
not noucht gud, sche consentit to it
noucht wythout grat difficultie.—
Letter of James Beaton, of 17th
June 1567 ; Laing, *History of Scotland,* ii. 112. A la fin ung nommé
milord Lindesay s'y presenta :
on faisoit semblant d'accepter
celuy-là.—Letter of Du Croc in
Teulet's *Papiers d'État,* ii. 178.
Et Monsieur le Duc se travaille et
ses barons, de son cousté, envers la
Royne pour luy faire accorder de
permectre. Et, après avoir longtemps persuadé, elle feust contante
plustot que d'avoir entré en effu-
sion de sang, et fut longtemps après

devant qu'elle le vouleust accorder.
—The contemporary account ; *Ibid.*
ii. 164.
[2] Thair was 20 gentlemen in
ether syd to see thair partes.—
Letter of James Beaton of 17th
June 1567 ; Laing, *History of
Scotland,* ii. 112.
[3] "Peu après" Bothwell protested
in Denmark, "je allay au lieu du
combat pour y attendre mon ennemy, où je demeuray jusques au
soir bien tard, sans qu'il se mou-
trast, ne feist semblant de vouloir
comparoir, comme je prouveray
(quand il en sera besoing) par ung
mille de gentilzhommes, sur peyne
de perdre la vye." — Teulet, *Lettres,* p. 175.

men, had gone before eastward round the hill
for the purpose of cutting off Bothwell from Dunbar, the Lords were seen about eight o'clock in the
evening to be on the point of assailing the hill in
front. The Queen, who had again mounted her
steed, found at this crisis, that though the kinsmen
and vassals of Bothwell and her own arquebusiers
were ready to fight for the Earl,[1] yet the army was
in a state of complete disintegration,[2] and she forthwith announced in consequence her determination
to repair to the army of the Lords. She caused
Kirkaldy of Grange to be again summoned, and as
he had lately told her how willingly the Lords
would receive her as their mistress, if she abandoned
Bothwell, she said that if they promised this, she
was now prepared to comply with their wish. In
vain would Bothwell, while Grange rode down the
hill with this message to the Lords, have even then
besought Mary rather to turn back to Dunbar, and
let him fight with her subjects; in vain would he
have warned her against the fair words which only
concealed treachery;[3] he saw—as he has himself
remarked, and which but little accords with the
blind passion for him that Mary's enemies have
ascribed to her—that for him it " was impossible to
move her from her purpose, or to get her to listen

---

[1] Bothuelii propinqui et clientes
confligere cupiebant.—Buchanan,
Rerum Scoticarum Historia, p.
221.
[2] On the oder partie the Queinis
Majestie's folks haid na will of
straiks bot rather was drawand
thamselfs asyd, and sum of thaim
steilland away.—Letter of James
Beaton; Laing, *History of Scotland*, ii. 113.
[3] " Sur quoy," Bothwell after-

wards wrote, " je la pryai d'adviser
à ce qu'elle vouloit faire, et que
par sa bonté elle ne se perdist, car
je congnoissois assez leur cueur
plain de trahison."—Teulet, *Lettrs*,
p. 176. James Beaton also notices
in his letter this separation of the
Queen from Bothwell as that " the
quhilk hir Majestie haid persuadit
to him nocht wythout gryat difficultie."—Laing, *History of Scotland*, ii. 113.

to any objection," and he could simply beg of her, ere she carried it into effect, to obtain all necessary security from the Lords. The shades of evening had already spread themselves over Carberry Hill, when Bothwell held this conversation with Mary, and was seen not without emotion to part from her, in order, with a small company of horsemen, to gallop back to Dunbar.[1]   It was the last time they met in life.

When Kirkaldy of Grange again ascended the hill, and met the Queen alone, she was prepared to follow him, if the Lords promised not to seek to do injury to her men, but to permit every one to return to his own home.   As soon as Kirkaldy gave her an assurance to this effect,[2] and Bothwell was now a good way off, she said aloud :—" Laird of Grange, I render myself unto you, upon the conditions you rehearsed unto me, in the name of the Lords."[3] Upon this the Queen gave him her hand, which he kissed ; he then took her horse by the bridle, and led it down from the hill.   When she reached the first rank of the army of the Lords, where, on bended knee, these received her with wonted respect, she told them that it was not from fear or doubt of victory, but only to spare blood that she now came to those to whose counsel she would rather listen.[4] But when she spoke about wishing to advance to

[1] Et plus souventefois s'entrebessèrent au départit.   Sur la fin, Monsieur le Duc luy demanda si elle ne voulloit de sa part garder la promesse de fidellité que elle luy avoit faicte, de quoy elle luy assura.   Là dessus, luy bailla sa main ainsi que il départoit.—The anonymous contemporary's account ; Teulet, *Papiers d'État*, ii. 165-66.

[2] The qubilk being fund gud be the Lordis, they causit mak ane proclamation incontinent defendant all, that was of thair parte, to persue or invaid any, that was of the Queenis parte.—Letter of James Beaton ; Laing, *History of Scotland*, ii. 113.

[3] *Memoirs of Sir James Melvil*, p. 83.

[4] Knox, *History of the Reformation in Scotland*, ii. 561.

meet the Hamiltons, she encountered a dismal coldness, and on approaching the second division of the
army, she was stunned with a cry which saluted her
as a murderess.[1] Her emotion was violent, resem-
bling what she displayed at the murder of Riccio,
and her despair at being, as she complained, deceived
by her own subjects, knew no bounds.[2] It was not as
a princess, but as one vanquished, over whom they
triumphed, that late in the same evening she was
obliged to make a humiliating entrance into Edinburgh. In agreement with a promise with which
Bothwell says that she separated from him, and
according to which she was to let him hear from her in
Dunbar, she is said during the night secretly to have
written him a letter, but the letter was given up to
the Lords, and they, interpreting it as her own
opinion, that she neither had left, nor would leave
him,[3] declared it to be unavoidably necessary to retain her in custody, and accordingly she was taken
as a prisoner, the night after, from Edinburgh to the
island castle in Lochleven, the same prison as had
been intended for her at the rebellion of Murray two
years previously, long before any one could plead her
connection with Bothwell. This investigation cannot

[1] Quum ad secundam aciem per-
venisset, concors ab omnibus
clamor sublatus est, ut meretricem,
ut parricidam cremarent.—Buchanan, *Rerum Scoticarum Historia*,
p. 222.

[2] Minas, maledicta, lacrymas et
cetera, quæ muliebris amat dolor,
profundebat.—*Ibid.* p. 222.

[3] Sir James Melvil, always so
very mild in his treatment of
Mary Stuart, whose representation
makes it appear that she had now
in fact left him, adds here :—" For
she could not do that so hastily

which process of time might have
accomplished."—*Memoirs of Sir
James Melvil*, p. 84. But against
the whole assertion about the com-
promising letter, speaks strongly the
fact, that no such letter was ever
produced at the conferences in
England, instead of which the
document brought forward there,
the so-called " Book of Articles "
(Hosack, p. 547), only says, that " in
farther pruif of hir inordinat affectioun towardes him she convoyit a
purs with gold to him be David
Kintor the same xvi. day."

follow her in her subsequent escape, effected during
the following year from this Scottish imprisonment,
nor in her fatal flight to the neighbouring country,
after the adverse battle at Langside, nor in the new
and long-continued confinement that there awaited
her, nor in her passage to the tragical death which
was at last prepared for her by the same hand that
had been the primary cause of her misfortunes, by
the kinswoman who had never been able to forgive
her for being beautiful, Catholic, and successor of the
Tudors, by that

> "false woman,
> Her sister and her fae."

CHAPTER VIII.

THE history of Bothwell and Mary Stuart, till the events on Carberry Hill divided them from each other, is so entwined together, that a sketch of the fortunes of the one can rarely be separated from an account of those of the other. After that fateful day—the 15th of June 1567—drove them away in opposite directions, the condition of the one, in spite of the increasing distance between them, did indeed still continue to exercise an influence upon that of the other, yet they never more met, and from this period the remainder of Bothwell's life demands its own history. But a difficulty now meets us in respect to this, that while the Scottish sources of information, although almost incessantly conflicting with each other on every single point, have been hitherto sufficiently numerous, they now suddenly and all but entirely cease, the stormy and eventful times continuing henceforward uninterruptedly to occupy the attention of Scotland, so that the conclusion of Bothwell's life became only a misty recollection to the next generation. It is only in more recent times, and especially from the North, that some greater light has been shed over his latter

days. After Suhm, at the close of the last century, CHAP.
had directed attention to the manuscripts in the VIII.
North which could throw light on Bothwell's later for- 1779-1829.
tunes,[1] one of the literati in Denmark, while engaged
not many years afterwards in issuing a translation of a
sketch by Gentz of the History of Mary Stuart, was
enabled from a communication by Thorkelin from
the Danish Privy Archives, to bring to light other
contributions relating to the subject.[2] On the
other hand, it was longer ere a leading document
giving information from Bothwell himself, to the
presence of which, in a Swedish manuscript Suhm
had previously called attention,[3] became more widely
known on the other side of the North Sea,[4] but after
this happened, a copy of it was obtained from the
library of Drottningholm, where it was then preserved, and was combined with the contributions
drawn from the State Archives in Denmark, in a
special publication which was printed for the Bannatyne Club.[5] As, however, only very few copies
of the Bannatyne Club Publications are printed,
this little volume became very soon a bibliographic
rarity even in Scotland, and as good as unobtain-
able on the Continent, so that even Prince Alexander Labanoff-Rostoffski, in whom Mary Stuart
has almost found a new lover in the nineteenth
century, was ignorant of its existence when he pub-

[1] *Samlinger til den danske Historie.* Kjöbenhavn, 1779-1784, 4to,
ii. 2, 99, 101-102. *Nye Samlinger
til den danske Historie.* Kjöbenhavn, 1792-1795, 4to, iv. 108.
[2] *Den Skotske Dronning Maria
Stuarts Historie med et Anhang
af forhen utrukte Papirer af M. C.
Bergenhammer, og en Fortale af
K. L. Rahbek.* Kjöbenhavn, 1803.

[3] Note L, Appendix.
[4] An English translation of it
was given in the New Monthly Magazine (June 1825), xiii. 521-37.
[5] *Les Affaires du Conte de Boduel,*
l'an 1568. Presented to the members of the Bannatyne Club by
Henry Cockburn and Thomas
Maitland. Edinburgh, 1829, 4to.

CHAP.
VIII.
1837-62. lished the extensive collection of his unhappy
heroine's letters, with illustrative notes. The contributions to Bothwell's history drawn from Denmark and Sweden were therefore printed, first in a
separate small volume by Prince Labanoff,[1] and
later, as this did not come into the hands of the book-
sellers, in a supplement to the letters which Alexander Teulet has added to his great edition of political
documents connected with the History of Scotland
in the sixteenth century.[2] The papers thus hitherto
obtained from the Danish royal archives constituted
meanwhile but a part of what they contained, which
was fitted to throw light on Bothwell's later fortunes,
and accordingly the learned Icelander, Thorleifr
Gudmundson Repp, who, while in Edinburgh holding an appointment in the Advocates' Library, had
rendered his assistance to the editing of the Bannatyne Club's costly publications, undertook, on his
return to Denmark in 1837, to procure a fuller
collection from the Danish State Archives. He did
not, however, succeed in getting his work, which
was written in English,[3] published, and from the

---

[1] *Pièces et Documents relatifs au Comte de Bothwell.* St. Péters-bourg, 1856.

[2] *Lettres de Marie Stuart.*—Par A. Teulet, Membre de la Société Impériale des Antiquaires de France. Paris, 1859.

[3] The manuscript a few years after his death was, through the intercession of Counsellor of State Worsaae, made over by the family to the English tourist, Captain Horace Marryat, who has given notices of Bothwell in his sketches of travels in Denmark (*A Residence in Jutland, the Danish Isles, and Copenhagen,* London, 1860, i. 410-419), and in Sweden (*One Year in Sweden, including a visit to the Isle of Götland,* London, 1862, i. 13-20), but fails to distinguish be-tween Earl James Bothwell, the husband of Mary, and the for-mer's nephew, Earl Francis Both-well. Captain Marryat wished also himself to have instituted re-searches with respect to Bothwell in the State Archives, but in reference to this it is said in the survey of visits to the archives' office during the year 1860 :— " Captain Marryat wished in April to be obliged with the communi-cation of notices of Earl Bothwell's sojourn in Denmark ; but after having previously learned the

extracts made from it, given in other works, it is CHAP. VIII. manifest that he too has not had his eye upon all the documents which the archives can furnish. 1567. From this the conclusion seems obvious that although the Danish State Archives furnish most of the contributions to the later history of Bothwell, yet these necessarily require, in order as far as possible to clear up the subject, to be combined with the information which to the careful investigator is supplied by other sources.

In some of the Scottish records of the history of Mary, which have been brought to light in more recent times, it is related that when Kirkaldy of Grange was sent to the Queen to negotiate with her while still on Carberry Hill, he carried with him a secret message and token from the Earl of Morton to Bothwell, by which the latter was advised on the ground of the rage of the multitude to betake himself out of the country for some time till the Earl could bring matters into another course, and it was also intimated by the same means that no one would be allowed to pursue Bothwell.[1] This testimony about such an express understanding between Bothwell and his opponents is indeed too unsupported for confidence to be placed in it,[2] yet the way in which Bothwell was suffered in the evening

nature of the documents preserved here (they are almost all in Danish) he withdrew his request."—Wegener, *Aarsberetninger fra det Kongelige Geheimearkiv*, Tredie Bind, p. xi.

[1] Historical Memoirs of the reign of Mary Queen of Scots, and a portion of the reign of King James the Sixth, by Lord Herries. Edited and presented to the Ab-

botsford Club by Robert Pitcairn. Edinburgh, 1836, 4to, pp. 94.

[2] Yet Camden seeks to maintain : —" Re vera submonuerunt, ut sibi fuga consuleret, non alio consilio, quam ne apprehensus totam machinationem renudaret, et ipsius fugam in argumentum ad Reginam regicidii accusandam arriperent."—*Annales Rerum Anglicarum et Hibernicarum regnante Elizabetha*, p. 117.

to withdraw seems capable of being understood only
when it is remembered that both the Earl of Morton and the other chief leaders in the army of the
Lords had taken part with Bothwell in the transac-
tions connected with the league which was entered
into against Darnley in the previous year, and thus
were they even in a position to convict Bothwell of
his crime, yet on the other hand he might become a
dangerous witness against themselves, so that they
must have felt at the outset that their own interests would be best served if he would privately
steal away. But when this had happened, and they
had returned with Mary to Edinburgh, a bond was
subscribed on the following day in which they not
only banded themselves together upon honour, word,
and promise, to get the Queen's marriage with Bothwell dissolved, but as solemnly, as they had formerly
assured the Earl of assistance, they now pledged
themselves not to rest till they got him duly
punished, " as truly as we are noblemen, and love the
honour of our native country."[1] A week afterwards a
herald was heard in the Market Place of Edinburgh,
and in similar places throughout the towns of the
realm, making a proclamation from the Privy
Council, which forbade all and every one from
affording the Earl of Bothwell shelter or support by
land or sea, and offering a reward of a thousand
crowns to whoever should seize and deliver him into
the hands of justice.[2]

---

[1] Bond of the nobles of Scotland
against Bothwell, subscribed in
Edinburgh the 16th June 1567.—
Anderson, Collections, i. 138.
[2] Proclamation of the Privy
Council of 26th June 1567, Ibid.

i. 139-141. Anderson does not
mention here that this proclamation had also been circulated in a
printed form.—Imprentit at Edinburgh be Robert Lekpreujk. Anno
Do. 1567.

After learning at Dunbar that Mary had met
from the Lords the fate which he had foreseen,
Bothwell left the castle on the 27th June,[1] and,
with a couple of vessels fitted out by him, sailed
past the Firth of Forth northward. The reason
why Bothwell did not remain in Dunbar Castle can
hardly have been any fear as to his safety, as some
allege,[2] for he had a trusty commander at that time in
charge in Patrick Whitlaw, who had been made knight
when he himself was created Duke ; many faithful
members of the Hepburn family voluntarily repaired
to Dunbar[3] to take part in its defence, and in spite
of repeated summonses to surrender, the castle continued to be held for Bothwell, and that even after
Sir James Balfour had betrayed Edinburgh Castle
to his enemies ; nor was it till after having made

[1] " Le Duc, mary de la Royne,"
Du Croc communicated on the 30th
June 1567 from Edinburgh to
Charles IX., " est sorti, il y a trois
jours, et s'est mis sur un navire,
l'on ne sçait pas où il a fait voille.
Si croy-je qu'il ne c'esloignera point
de la coste de ce royaulme."
—Teulet's *Papiers d'État*, ii. 186.
This letter of Du Croc is referred
by other authorities, probably incorrectly, to the 21st of June
(*State Papers relating to Scotland*,
i. 248. *State Papers, Foreign Series*,
1566-68, p. 258), but that Bothwell
before finally leaving Dunbar
Castle had made thence a short
visit to Fife is hinted at in the
accounts of Sir William Drury
from Berwick of the 16th and
27th of June 1567 (*Calendar of
State Papers, Foreign Series*, 1566-
1568, pp. 255, 263).
[2] For that he feared to be en-
closed.—Spottiswood, *History of
the Church of Scotland*, p. 213.
[3] Among the members of the
Hepburn family, who along with

Patrick Whitlaw took part in de-
fending Dunbar for Bothwell until
the fortress, on the 1st October
1567, came into the hands of
Murray, are mentioned William
Hepburn of Gilmerstoun, Patrick
Hepburn of Wauchton, the latter's
brother, Adam Hepburn of Smea-
ton, and Thomas Hepburn of
Auldhamstocks (see *Diurnal of
Remarkable Occurrents*, p. 122).
Besides those who had taken refuge in Dunbar, and for whose
surrender the new government of
Scotland laid claim by a specially
threatening summons of the 26th
August 1567 (printed in Anderson's *Collections*, 148-150), was also
Patrick Wilson, who in company
with William Powrie, had brought
the gunpowder with which Bothwell caused Darnley's dwelling to
be blown up. Wilson is still mentioned in a document of the 30th
July 1572 as not apprehended
(*Diurnal of Remarkable Occurrents*, p. 309), and had therefore
probably saved himself.

a serious resistance, and the heavy guns from the
Castle of Edinburgh had been brought against it,
that by a capitulation it came in the autumn following into the power of the new Government.[1]
The real cause why Bothwell fled from the fastness
of Dunbar to the north-west of Scotland may with
more correctness be affirmed, as he himself states,
that he had wished there to effect a meeting with
the Hamiltons and the many other friends whom
the Queen still had in these districts, and who
during the following year, when she succeeded in
escaping from Lochleven, actually rose to fight
against her enemies.[2] When, on the other hand,
Bothwell also asserts that it was in consequence of
a consultation held between him and the adherents
of the Queen that he was obliged to repair to the
Continent to procure assistance in opposition to the
new order of things caused by the catastrophe on
Carberry Hill, there is certainly ground to call in
question his veracity. For supposing an advice had
really been given him to withdraw from the country, yet as this could hardly be accompanied with
any warrant or authority to speak in the name of
others on the Continent about the affairs of Scotland, it must have had its origin merely in the fact
that it had become evident to the adherents of the
Queen that his presence in Scotland just then furnished a main hindrance to the cause of Mary.
Where any such consultation was held, whether in
the north or west of Scotland, he has not by any
means exactly indicated. That Bothwell on the

[1] *Diurnal of Remarkable Occur-*
rents, p. 125.
[2] Bothwell's account of events in
Scotland from 1559 to 1568.—
Teulet, *Lettres*, pp. 178-180.

contrary had not at this time omitted to visit his CHAP.
former brother-in-law may be assumed from one of VIII.
the accounts sent to Queen Elizabeth by Sir 1567.
Nicholas Throckmorton, in which the latter, on the
16th July 1567, announces from Edinburgh that
Bothwell had recently been staying in the north
with the Earl of Huntly at Strathbogie, and had
sought to enlist troops and raise a rebellion, but
that the Earl, although the new rulers were not on
good terms with him, had yet seen that Bothwell in
all quarters had only small support, and therefore
would not venture anything for him.[1]

"I also hear," the English ambassador adds,
"that Bothwell during the night has suddenly departed from the Earl's residence ; that he has gone
to Spynie, and will probably proceed to the Orkneys,
but will hardly find there a good reception." The
letter shows, as will be seen, how well informed
they were then in Edinburgh about the position of
matters in the North, although they did not put
any serious hindrance in the way of Bothwell's
withdrawal. It is evident from an Act which was
drawn up a day or two after by the Scottish Government, that Bothwell must have for some time found
refuge with his granduncle, Patrick Hepburn, Bishop
of Moray, in Spynie Castle, near Elgin, where he
had been brought up as a child, since the Act on
this ground forbids under threat of punishment all
lessees in the bishopric of Moray to give any payment or service either to the bishop or to any of his
agents.[2]   An offer was also sent at this time from

---

[1] Throckmorton's account of 16th
July 1567.—Raumer, *Die Königinnen Elisabeth und Maria Stuart,*
pp. 153-54, and *Calendar of State*

Papers, Foreign Series, 1566-68,
p. 286.
[2] This Act, issued by the government on the 21st of July 1567 is to

Spynie to Edinburgh to seize Bothwell, or to put him to death. The offer came from an adventurer, an English Catholic, who had fled from London to escape arrest for debt, and had afterwards under-taken to serve Cecil as a spy in Scotland. Having by his conduct incurred suspicion, the Scottish Government had caused him the year previously to be apprehended and examined, and as the letters which were found upon him, and which exposed Cecil, substantiated his guilt, he was compelled to remain a prisoner for a length of time in the strong castle of Spynie. By connections which he had here established, he believed he was now in a posi-tion to lay hold of Bothwell or to put him out of the way, and a brother of his, Anthony Rokesby, presented a proposal to this effect to the ambassador of Queen Elizabeth, Sir Nicholas Throckmorton, who was still in Edinburgh. The wary diplomatist, thinking that it would not be very easy to seize Bothwell alive, and not wishing to authorise murder, let the matter rest after referring Rokesby with his proposal to the Laird of Lethington at Stirling, and this Scottish statesman probably preferred to see Bothwell withdraw from the country than to see him again a prisoner.[1] Bothwell at all events had

be found printed in Anderson's *Col-lections*, i. 142-45. The Bishop was afterwards, on the ground of that reception of Bothwell, prose-cuted as accessory to the murder of Darnley, but was acquitted on the 28th November 1567 (*Calendar of State Papers, Foreign Series*, 1566-68, p. 367).

[1] Letter of Throckmorton to Queen Elizabeth, dated Edin-burgh, 31st July 1567.—*Calendar of State Papers, Foreign Series,*

1566-68, p. 305. The same letter also states that it was said that Bothwell, during his stay at Spynie Castle, had killed one of the Bishop of Moray's illegitimate sons, but this statement is not more credible than the story told in one of the accounts from Sir William Drury at Berwick of 27th June 1567, in reference to Bothwell, that " it is said, that since his retreat, by his consent a French page, whom he had, who knew of his proceedings,

met with no hindrance as yet when he parted with CHAP.
VIII.
his aged relative at Spynie Castle to pass from
Morayshire to the Orkneys. 1567.
When Bothwell first determined on leaving
Scotland the idea of previously visiting the Orkneys
must have been uppermost in his mind. It was
only two months since he had received his ducal
title, and the islands of Orkney and Shetland were
by their situation in a greater or less degree withdrawn from the party-movements prevailing in the
rest of Scotland. They had also a population that
had not yet lost its Norse nationality, and whose
disposition and interests had always shown themselves very widely different from those of the Scots.
When Bothwell embarked in the north of Scotland
and for ever retired from its coasts, he caused the
two small vessels conveying himself and his followers to steer their course towards "the dukedom"
which had as yet not seen its master. He landed
on the Mainland of Orkney. But here disappoint-
ment speedily met him. The bailiff of Orkney was
Gilbert Balfour of Westray, who also held the office
in Bothwell's name of "Keeper" of the castle in
Kirkwall. Gilbert, like Sir James Balfour, belonged
to those whom contemporaries in some cases accused
of having a share in Bothwell's crime,[1] but Gilbert

is drowned."—*Calendar of State
Papers, Foreign Series*, 1566-68, p.
262. The last mentioned report,
which manifestly points to Paris,
is undoubtedly false, and the Scottish communications to English-
men became in general at this
time so unreliable, that even Sir
William Drury found himself obliged to complain to Cecil that
"they so often fail in their re-

ports."—*Calendar of State Papers,
Foreign Series*, 1566-68, p. 254.
    [1] Among "those that laid hands
on the King to kill him, by Bothwell's direction," Knox could thus
along with Sir James also name
Gilbert Balfour.—*History of the
Reformation in Scotland*, ii. 551.
Gilbert Balfour afterwards became
with Archibald Ruthven chief
commander of the three thousand

CHAP.
VIII.
1567.

Balfour, if the suspicion really had any ground, hastened, like Sir James, to turn round just as those in power turned. Even before the latter contrived to sell the castle of Edinburgh to Scotland's new government, Gilbert Balfour refused, in the castle of Kirkwall, to come to any terms with Bothwell—nay, showed him such opposition that, as Bothwell subsequently states, his stay there lasted only two days.[1] Like a strange passing meteor the Orkney Isles saw their duke vanish towards the north.

On the Shetland Isles, whose bailiff, Olaf Sinclair, belonged to the same family as Bothwell's mother, Jane Sinclair, circumstances proved more favourable. For the maintenance of the men whom Bothwell brought with him, every benefice in Shetland submitted to give the duke an ox and two sheep,—a voluntary gift, which in consequence of the system of oppression and extortion so long enforced by the Scottish Lords upon the old Norse population of the islands of Orkney and Shetland, still continues to be exacted as one among the more

Scots that entered into military service with John III. of Sweden. Here he was accused in the year 1573 of taking part in the conspiracy by means of which Charles Mornay is said to have wished to put John III. out of the way, and to again elevate the imprisoned Eric XIV. to the throne. King John was to have been cut down while they represented for his diversion in the palace of Stockholm the Scottish sword-dance, which was performed by a band of warriors armed with helmet, coat of mail, and drawn sword. The project was not, however, carried into execution, but the conspiracy afterwards became divulged, and among those committed to prison in consequence was also Gilbert Balfour, who was condemned to death and beheaded in the year 1576.—Celsius, *Konung Erik den* XIV*des Historia*, Stockholm, 1774, p. 288-90. Girs, *Konung Johan den* III*des Chrönika*, Stockholm, 1745, 4to, pp. 41-42. Tryxell, *Berättelser ur Svenska Historien*, Stockholm, 1828-73, iii. 333-35.

[1] Barry, *History of the Orkney Islands*, Edinburgh, 1808, 4to, p. 248. David Balfour, *Odal Rights and Feudal Wrongs. A memorial for Orkney*, Edinburgh, 1860, p. 56.

recent taxes imposed on them.[1] Bothwell since
leaving Dunbar had only had two small vessels
with him, but now he met off the Mainland of
Shetland with some that were larger and armed
as the times required, and of these he also got
command. At this time commerce had begun in
these islands. Ships in multitudes from the Hanse
Towns as well as from Denmark brought to them
corn, beer, Danish whisky, and linen cloth, and received in payment fish, wadmal (a coarse cloth), and
horses. Thus at Bothwell's arrival a Hanseatic
merchant, Geert Hemelingk, from Bremen, was
staying in Dunrossness, the southernmost parish
on the Mainland, where a ship of his named " The
Pelican " was lading at Sumburgh Head, the most
southerly point of the island, on which a lighthouse
now stands. Hemelingk consented that Bothwell
should have command of the ship and its crew ; he
concluded a contract with the Earl by which the
latter was to give him a certain sum as long as he
retained " The Pelican " in his service, and compensation if the ship was lost or not returned.[2] In like
manner Bothwell succeeded in securing another
Hanseatic ship belonging to a Hamburg merchant,
then also residing on the Mainland. Both ships
were taken by his own men up Bressay Sound or

CHAP.
VIII.

1567.

---

[1] The exaction is recorded in the Exchequer under the name of " Ox and Sheep Silver," and is paid at the present day.—Hibbert, p. 288. [Not correct. For a more accurate and fuller account of this exaction, see note M, Appendix.—*Translator.*]

[2] The contract between Both-well and Geert Hemelingk, of which a copy exists in the Danish Privy Archives, is dated " jnn

Schvineborchouett den vofftein-denn Augusti nha der gebort Christi 1567." That the name Sumburgh must previously have had the form of Svinborg was con-jectured by Munch in his " Geo-graphiske Oplysninger om de i Sagaerne forekommende skotske og irske Stednavne."—*Annaler for Nordisk Oldkyndighed*, 1857, Kjö-benhavn, p. 376.

CHAP.
VIII.

1567.

the Sound which, close beside the town of Lerwick, separates the Mainland from the lesser island of Bressay, lying to the east.[1] His prospect of being able either to remain in safety in Shetland, or to betake himself whither he would, seemed now so much greater as the autumnal storms of the North Sea were at hand.

To the charges of which Bothwell had already been the object a new one was now added. The same maligners who, while he was still in the heyday of his power, readily spoke of Bothwell as surrounded with a band of " pirates,"[2] now asserted that with his visit to the Orkney and Shetland Isles he had begun in due form the life of a pirate.[3] This representation was, however, contradicted by a con-

[1] Bressay Sound is the old "Brideyarsund" where King Hakon IV., Hakonssön, arrived after two days' sailing, when on his expedition against Scotland in the summer of 1263, and where he lay almost half a month before he sailed to the Orkneys.—Annaler for Nordisk Oldkyndighed, 1857, Kjöbenhavn, p. 349.

[2] After Mary was delivered of a son, in Edinburgh Castle, on the 19th of June 1566, she paid a visit on the 20th July to the Earl of Mar at Alloa House. As she could not bear to ride, she embarked at Newhaven on board a small ship, and sailed up the Forth to Alloa, accompanied by Murray, Mar, and Bothwell, the High Admiral of Scotland. Those who eagerly wished to spread the belief that Mary was at this period the mistress of Bothwell, represent these few hours' sail in such a way that in the Diary dictated by the Scottish enemies of the Queen but ascribed to Cecil, we read regarding it thus :—" She fled the King's company and past be boytt with

the pyrattis to Alloway."—Laing, History of Scotland, ii. 85.   In the same manner Buchanan likewise states, as well in his pamphlet (De Maria Scot. Reg., p. 5), as afterwards in his History (Rerum Scot. Hist., p. 212):—" Apparaverunt autem eam naviculam Gulielmus et Edmundus Blacateri, Eduardus Robertsonus et Thomas Dicsonus, Bothuelii clientes et notæ rapacitatis piratæ."

[3] Forsamekill as James Erle of Bothuile—accumpaneit with certane notorious pyrattis, ar past to the sey, mynding to continew in thair reif and piracie, bayth aganis the subjectis of this realme, and all nationis ; and first ar begun at his Majesties propir landis of Orknay.—Letter of the Scottish Privy Council to the Municipal Government of Dundee of 10th August 1567. Anderson, Collections, i. 145. Bothuelius rerum omnium inopia circumventus piraticam facere coepit.—Buchanan, Rerum Scot. Hist., p. 222. [See also The Register of the Privy Council of Scotland, 1545-69, i. 544-5.]

temporary only a few years after Bothwell's death,[1] and unless we explain the accusation as based on some pressure exerted on those Hanseatic merchants,[2] it ought certainly to be regarded as having had its origin in a misconception or in a too one-sided view of the matter. For it is well known that, during the Scandinavian seven years' war then being waged, the North Sea not less than the Baltic swarmed with privateers, and those who suffered from them were at all times ready to stamp them as pirates. It will, for example, be remembered how Christopher Walkendorff, a generation later, in the same century, caused, at the demand of Queen Elizabeth, the famous Magnus Heinesen to be condemned and executed as a pirate for having taken a London ship, although it was afterwards proved to his satisfaction that he had done so by authority from the Duke of Parma, Alexander Farnese, then Spanish Governor of the Netherlands,

CHAP.
VIII.

1567.

[1] Mais les conjurez, voyans qu'il ne se retiroit, mais qu'il se pourmenoit de lieu à autre sans faire démonstration de vouloir abandonner le royaume, semèrent un bruit qu'il faisait le corsaire et escumeur de mer. Adam Blackwood, *Martyre de la Royne d'Escosse*, Edinburgh 1587, according to the copy in Jebb, *De Vita et Rebus Gestis Mariæ Scotorum Reginæ*, ii. 227. The author, Adam Blackwood, whose name occurs in the letters of Mary, had received, through her recommendation, an appointment in France, and was at this time member of the Superior Court of Justice in Poitiers.

[2] One of them, Geert Hemelingk of Bremen, subsequently explained, when he knew that "The Pelican"

had been captured, his assent to the contract which he entered into regarding it, by a representation of, "wie das mir inn Hittlandt ein Herr ausz Schottlandt mitt etzlich hundertt Mannen unvohrsehnlich angeszenn, der alszbald mein Schiff eingenommen denn fisch vnnd andere wahre, zu meinem mercklich vnnd vnnüherwindtlich schadenn vnnd nachteil, an den strandt auszgeworfen vnnd mich dahin gedrungen Ime mein vnnd meiner Schiffsfreunden Schiff entweder zu verkauffen oder aber an die zwey Monatt lang zu verhurenn zu willigen." Representation of Geert Hemelingk to the Burgo-master and Counsellors of Bremen, dated the 3d of March, preserved in the Privy Archives of Denmark.

CHAP.
VIII.
1598.

who, during the naval war between England and
Spain, issued letters of marque with a liberal hand.[1]
Nothing is more likely than that among the Scottish
seamen, with whom Bothwell, as High Admiral, was
previously in contact, were some who had either by
Dano-Norwegian or Swedish authorisation taken
part in privateering, and it can likewise hardly be
matter of doubt, after what was subsequently explained, that at least a portion of the crews on
board the Hanseatic ships which Bothwell found
lying in the Shetland Isles, and chartered for his
greater journey, were privateers. But this being
the case, how easily might the Earl of Bothwell be
represented as a pirate, how nearly identical with it
was this made by the very term used. The Latin
language, still so common at that period, did not
furnish any expression for the more recent notion of
privateers, but designated both these and the real
sea-rovers, as " piratæ." In 1598, when the Historiographer, Niels Krag, Doctor-of-Law and Professor
in the University of Copenhagen, was sent, in the
reign of Christian IV., to Queen Elizabeth on a
diplomatic errand, having, as its object, to demand
back the ships of Danish subjects, which the English,
during their war with Spain, had plundered or condemned as prizes, he kept a diary of his sojourn in
England, and specially of his negotiations with the
English Commissioners; and here we read, that
while the English " Senators asserted that he could
not call those pirates, who, by public authority, at
their own cost, carried on privateering," yet in reply
it was maintained that " in the Latin language this

[1] C. P. Rothe, *Christoffer Walkendorffs Liv. og Levnet.* Kjöbenhavn,
1754, pp. 54-57.

distinction did not admit of being made."[1] And just as the old term from the South then caused confusion, the same thing has happened from the use of the newer one from the North. A privateer during the seven years' war was called a freebooter (in the Dano-Norwegian privateering regulations of Frederick II., or, as its provisions were named, "Freebooters' Articles"),[2] but when privateers did not at once learn to respect the conclusion of the war, this word soon became synonymous with pirate. When the West Indian waters presented in the seventeenth century the same spectacle which in the olden times the Cilician pirates, rooted out by Pompey, had so long caused the Mediterranean to show, the more recent piratical Republic was inscribed on the page of history with the name of "Flibustier," which is but the French form of free-booter.[3]

It was, however, not any intention of suppressing piracy which at length brought Bothwell's foes to Shetland. When the Scottish Lords had deposed the imprisoned Mary Stuart, and put the crown upon the head of her child at Stirling, on the 29th of July 1567, Murray, as First Regent during the minority of James VI., was recalled from France, where he had been waiting the foreseen outbreak of the storm. He arrived in England on the 23d of July, and having paid a visit to Elizabeth, by whom

[1] Niel Krag's Relation of his Embassy to England, 1598-99. *Nye danske Magazin*, udgivet af det kongelige danske Selskab til den nordiske Histories og Sprogs Forbedring, iv. 191.

[2] The privateer regulations are

communicated by Werlauff in *Nye danske Magazin*, vi. 215, 216.

[3] Formed exactly after the English Freebooter.—Archenholz, *Histoire des Flibustiers*. Paris, 1804, p. 42 ; Jal, *Glossaire Nautique ; Répertoire polyglotte des termes de Marine Anciens et Modernes*. Paris, 1848, 4to, p. 701.

U

CHAP.
VIII.

1567.

he also saw with gladness some English war-ships despatched in pursuit of Bothwell,[1] he passed on the 8th of August, after an absence of four months, over the Scottish Borders, and on the 11th he entered Edinburgh. At once the previous want of vigorous proceedings against Bothwell ceased. After the municipal authorities of Dundee had, on the 10th of August, been communicated with about procuring the requisite crews and fitting out the ships necessary for the King's service,[2] Murray, the same day on which he arrived in Edinburgh, issued commissions for these ships,[3] and under the influence of his old grudge against Bothwell, he so hastened their equipment, that a Scottish squadron was able to start on the 19th of August in pursuit of his mortal enemy.[4] It consisted of the ships "Unicorn," "Primrose," "James," and "Robert," was well provided with cannon, and had, besides the seamen, a company on board of four hundred arquebusiers.[5] Two of Bothwell's chief antagonists on Carberry Hill, Sir William Kirkaldy of Grange, and Sir William Murray of Tullibardine, acted as leaders of the expedition. They were accompanied by the brother-in-law of Gilbert Balfour, Adam Bothwell, Bishop of Orkney, the same who had lately married Mary to Bothwell, but who sought to blot out the recollection of this deed by a zeal which,

[1] According to the letter of Throckmorton to Elizabeth, dated from Edinburgh, 22d August 1567. —Keith, *History of Church and State in Scotland,* p. 448.

[2] The letter is in Anderson's *Collections,* i. 145-147.

[3] The Authorisation.—*Ibid.* i. 147-148.

[4] The Diarey of Robert Birrel.—

Fragments of Scottish History, p. 26. According to Buchanan the equipment of the ships was also assisted by the Earl of Morton "qui tum impendio privato publicæ necessitatis onus sustinuit."—*Historia,* p. 224.

[5] *Diurnal of Remarkable Occurrents,* p. 119.

before this, had led him to perform at Stirling the CHAP.
ceremony of anointing the little King James VI., and VIII.
which afterwards caused him, as one of the agents 1567.
of Murray, to appear against the Queen at the Conferences in York and Westminster. Authority was
given to him and the two other commanders to hold
a court-martial on Bothwell should they be able to
capture him.

After touching at the Orkneys, in order to procure more exact tidings of the Earl, the four
Scottish ships sailed, on the 25th of August, into
Bressay Sound. Here the four ships of which
Bothwell had command lay at anchor, but part of
their crews had gone ashore, as well as Bothwell
himself, who happened to be just then the guest of
the Bailiff, Olaf Sinclair.[1] When those on board
Bothwell's ships caught sight of the enemy, the
cables were at once cut, and all sail was set, with
the view of running through the northern channel
of Bressay Sound. Kirkaldy of Grange confessed
his want of seamanship, but had promised before
his departure from the South, that if he only met
Bothwell, the Earl would not escape from him this
time, but that either Bothwell would take him
prisoner, or he would bring the Earl, alive or dead,
to Edinburgh.[2] Kirkaldy, along with Bishop Adam

[1] Being in the tyme foirsaid
vpoun the Ile of Zetland, at his
dinner with Olave Sinclare, foude
of Zetland.—*Diurnal of Remarkable Occurrents*, p. 123. This
authority is corroborated by Bothwell's own representation (Teulet,
Lettres, p. 181):—" Mais quelques
ungs de mes ennemys survindrent
cependant que j'estois en terre au
logiz du receveur."

[2] And for my owne part, albeit I
be no gud seeman, I promess unto
your Lordship, gyff I may anes
enconter with hym, eyther be see
or land, he sall eyther carie me
with him, or ellis I sall bryng him
dead or quik to Edinburgh.—
Letter of William Kirkaldy to the
Earl of Bedford, dated Edinburgh,
10th August 1567, preserved in
"The State Paper Office," and

Bothwell, was on board "The Unicorn" as commander, and he now ordered all sail to be set. The
helmsman not being acquainted with the channel,
was somewhat afraid, but was forced to obey.
Forward it rushed at flying speed, and Kirkaldy
gained more and more on the hindmost of Bothwell's
ships. This was a bad sailer, but its helmsman
being better acquainted with the channel, held
away from the deep water, and close in upon a
sunken rock, over which it slipped, although not
without damage. The unwary Kirkaldy, still pur-
suing, ran his ship, one of the strongest in Scotland,
with so great force upon the rock, that it broke in
pieces and went down. While he and Bishop Adam
Bothwell, with very great difficulty, saved themselves and their crew by getting on board the ships
that followed, those of the Earl escaped to Unst
or Ornist, the most northerly of the islands. The
rock in Bressay Sound on which "The Unicorn"
foundered still bears the name of the ship.[1]

When Bothwell heard of the arrival of his
enemies in Shetland, he succeeded, ere the latter
had landed, in escaping unobserved across Yell
Sound and the island of Yell, to his ships at Unst.
Thence he sent back one of them to the west coast
of Shetland, where it had orders to run into the

---

printed in Ellis, *Latter Years of
James Hepburn Earl of Bothwell.*
London, 1861, 4to, p. 9.

[1] From the accident that befell
Kirkaldy's ship, the bank has ever
since, from the name borne by the
vessel, acquired the title of "The
Unicorn Rock."—Hibbert, *Description of the Shetland Islands,* p. 289.
With the exception of this fact,

the rest of Hibbert's traditional
account, which has been disseminated through more recent representations, is only confusion. "The
circumstance that James Bothwell
was Duke, and Adam Bothwell
Bishop of Orkney, has," as one
remarks, "involved local history
in a strange comedy of errors."—
Balfour, *Odal Rights and Feudal
Wrongs,* p. 57.

Bay of Scalloway to get those of his men on board that had been left on the island, and then to follow him farther, as the Earl had now determined to withdraw altogether from Shetland. Before, however, he was able to retire from it, he was overtaken by his pursuers.[1] For many hours the three Scottish ships, which carried the enemy, fought with Bothwell's ships, the best of which had its main-mast snapped by a cannon-shot, and Bothwell himself simply owed his deliverance to the south-west wind, which, rising to a gale, drove the Earl with two of his ships far out on the North Sea. Only one of his vessels had fallen into the hands of his enemies, probably the same bad sailer that struck in Bressay Sound, and which he may possibly have himself in consequence determined at Unst to give up;[2] but when the three Scottish ships returned on the 13th and 14th of September to Dundee and Leith, Kirkaldy of Grange, Murray of Tullibardine, and Adam Bothwell were obliged to report that Bothwell himself had escaped.[3]

---

[1] "Les dicts séditieux," writes Bothwell (Teulet, *Lettres*, p. 182), "me poursuyvirent et pressèrent de telle façon que fusmes au combat l'espace de trois heures, et enfin d'un coup de canon coupèrent le grand matz du meilleur de mes navires." One of Mary's superficial biographers (Dargaud, *Histoire de Marie Stuart*, Paris, 1850, i. 384) has confounded this attack on Bothwell in the vicinity of the Shetland Isles with his subsequent seizure in Norway, and this confusion has in turn given rise to an unhistorical sea-piece, since some years ago the usual Danish " Catalogue of the Works of Art publicly exhibited at the Royal Academy of the Fine Arts" (Copenhagen, 1858, p. 12) described a painting by Anton Melby, thus : —"A Danish man-of-war attacks and overcomes Bothwell in the neighbourhood of Shetland. After Dargaud, *Histoire de Marie Stuart*."

[2] Note N, Appendix.

[3] The Diarey of Robert Birrel. —*Fragments of Scottish History*, p. 12 ; *Diurnal of Remarkable Occurrents*, p. 122.

CHAPTER IX.

BOTHWELL has more than once taken occasion to assert that it was his original intention when on the other side of the North Sea to visit Frederick II. of Denmark, and then to go to Charles IX. of France. And certainly such a plan in the second half of the sixteenth century might have special attraction for the Scottish peer. Ever since Christian I., king of Denmark, Sweden, and Norway, had given, in the year 1469, his daughter Margaret in marriage to James III. of Scotland, the most intimate relations had existed between the lines of kings of the same descent ruling on both sides of the North Sea.[1] The Scottish troops that followed Christian I., King John, and Christian II. in their expeditions against Sweden had been led to the North by the same warlike spirit which long previously made so many Scotsmen enter the service of France;[2] they had only been forerunners of the increasing emigration that through two centuries was to continue to lead Scotland's sons to take part in so many wars in foreign lands,[3] and to give the Scottish race a place

[1] Note O, Appendix.
[2] *Les Écossais en France et les Français en Écosse.* Par Francisque Michel. Londres, 1862, vol. i.-ii.
[3] *The Scot Abroad.* By John Hill Burton. Edinburgh and London, 1864, ii. 131-223. Lists of some of the Scotsmen who at a later period entered into the Danish military service are given in Robert Monro's work: *Expedition with the worthy Scots Regiment,*

of honour among the *élite* of so many foreign nations. Even in the year 1567, when Bothwell finally left Scotland, a large number of his countrymen were in the army of Frederick II. during the Northern seven years' war. Besides the political or military ties between the two peoples were others of a more peaceful kind. The capital of Denmark had, as we learn from a " grace for the Scottish nation" issued in the year 1539 by Christian III., an entire guild of Scotsmen, which, during the sway of Catholicism in the sixteenth century, established ecclesiastical institutions at Copenhagen, and after the Reformation founded special " Scottish beds" for their sick countrymen requiring hospital treatment.[1]   As we meet with a series of Scotsmen as Professors in the University of Copenhagen during the first half of the century, including, for instance, Peter David and Johannes Macchabæus (John Mac-Alpyne) in the Theological Faculty, Alexander Kynghorn in the Medical, Thomas Alame in the Philosophical,[2]

CHAP.
IX.

1539-67.

---

levied in August 1626, by Sir Donald Mackey, Lord Rhees, Colonell for his Majesty's service of Denmark, and reduced after the battle of Nerling to one company in September 1634 (London, 1637, fol.). From this work Sir Walter Scott has mainly drawn the materials for his characteristic description of a Scotsman that had returned from these military emigrations, Captain Dugald Dalgetty in *The Legend of Montrose.*

[1] Hofmann, *Samling af Fundationer og Gavebreve, som forefindes udi Danmark og Norge.* Kjöbenhavn, 1755-65, 4to, x. 155. The *St. Nynan's* Altar in Lady Kirk mentioned in this work is only a mistake for *St. Ninian's;* this was Ninian, who as Beda (iii. 4) reports,

had, in the year 394, converted the Picts in South Scotland to Christianity.—Bedæ, *Historia ecclesiastica gentis Anglorum. Cura Roberti Hussey.*   Oxonii, 1846, p. 122. When, as is very often the case in Danish works of the sixteenth century, " skotter" are found mentioned, it must not be assumed without further investigation that men from Scotland are meant, for " skotter " has sometimes only the same import as sutlers or merchants who carried on a retail business in petty wares.— Cronholm, *Skånes Politiska Historie.* Lund and Stockholm, 1847-1851, i. 536 ; ii. 623.

[2] Werlauff, *Kjöbenhavns Universitet fra dets Stiftelse indtil Reformationen.* Kjöbenhavn, 1850, 4to, pp. 60, 61, 65, 66, 72.   A more

so we also find until the close of the century not only many Danish students at the University of Aberdeen,[1] but likewise Scots at that of Copenhagen.[2] Thus the Scottish peer might, as a rule, be sure of obtaining, on his arrival as guest with Frederick II., a favourable reception both from the king and the people of the country. Only Bothwell himself seems not to have been able to reckon upon any specially kind reception. With regard to this, however, too much importance need not be attached to the fact that Frederick II., like his opponent, Eric XIV., had himself been a suitor for Mary's hand when she became a widow on the death of Francis II. of France,[3] although certainly this circumstance would not be in the Earl's favour if he meant to present himself before the still unmarried king as the husband of Mary. It is of more importance, on the other hand, that in a letter addressed to Frederick II. in the name of James VI., still a minor, written and sent off on the same day

detailed biography of Johannes Macchabæus is given by Holger Rördam in *Kjöbenhavns Universitets Historie fra 1537 til 1621*. Förste Deel (Kjöbenhavn, 1868-69), p. 587-597.

[1] In *The Autobiography and Diary of Mr. James Melvil*, edited by Robert Pitcairn, Edinburgh, 1842, p. 418, we find it said in the year 1597 of the author's uncle, the famous Andrew Melvil, thus: " Ther was a number of strangers, Polonians, *Dences* (Danes), Belgians, and Frenchmen, schollars, wha, at the fame of Mr. Androes lerning, came to the Vniuersitie of St. Andros that yeir, and war resident within the sam."

[2] For instance, Andrew Robertson from Aberdeen, who, while he was studying at the University of Copenhagen, translated into Latin the poems of his renowned countryman, Sir David Lindsay, and subsequently, in the year 1591, published them in a Danish translation made by Jacob Madsen. Sir David Lindsay had himself visited Copenhagen in the year 1544 on a mission to Christian III., and at Copenhagen, the place where it was printed, there was issued some years afterward : "Ane Dialog betuix Experience and ane Courteour, compylit be Schir David Lindesay of the Mont, and imprentit at the command and expensis off Doctor Machabeus, in Copmanhouin," 1552, 4to.

[3] Note P, Appendix.

as Bothwell's ships began to be chased among the CHAP. IX.
Shetland Isles, Murray has asserted that the reason
why a Scottish warrior, whom Frederick had sent   1567.
home to enrol more of his countrymen for service,
was not able for a long time to accomplish this
object, was simply that Bothwell, in the hey-day of
his power, had put obstacles in the way.[1] The day
after, the 26th of August, when all in Scotland must
have been quite ignorant whither Bothwell would
direct his course, his enemies, according to their
subsequent communication to Frederick II. when
seeking to prejudice him against Bothwell, sent
abroad an open letter in the king's name, which was
ordered to be published in the market-places of all
mercantile cities.   In this letter Scotland's new
government solemnly revoked a privilege issued
under the former government through the influence
of Bothwell, granting to two of his adherents,
William Blacater and James Edmonston, liberty
everywhere to pursue and capture the enemies of
the King of Sweden.[2]   Of these Scotsmen William

[1] Sed ei in hoc negocio Comes Boithuallus, qui tum forte malis artibus summam in rebus administrandis auctoritatem obtinuit, impedimento fuit quo minus, quod a Regina, matre nostra, petierat, impetraret.—Recommendatory letter of Murray issued in name of James VI. in behalf of John Clark, written at Stirling (Ex regia nostra Striuiligensi), 25th of August 1567, in Danish Privy Archives. The letter arrived previously in Copenhagen the 9th September.

[2] This open letter of 26th August 1567 began thus: "Ad aures Maiestatis Regiæ carissimique avunculi sui Jacobi comitis Moraviæ domini Abirnethiæ prorege ac summi regni sui administratoris amplissimo-

rumque virorum, qui illi in consilio adsunt, pervenit, carissimam suæ maiestatis matrem circumuentam atque deceptam a comite Boithuallo, magno omnium qui regno ac ditione sua vivunt incommodo, Jacobo Edmonston atque Gulielmo Blacader priuilegio sub secreto suo sigillo concessisse, ut omnes omnium regionum homines, qui buscum regi Suetiæ bellum esset, vi et armis terra marique impune persequerentur." The words are taken from a copy of the letter verified by Alexander Hay, then Clerk of the Privy Council. In other respects it is remarkable that while the letter, according to this very plain copy, bears as having been issued in the first year (anno primo)

CHAP.
IX.
1567.

Blacater is well known as one of Bothwell's companions at the abduction of Mary at the bridge over the Almond. He was captured at sea two days after the catastrophe on Carberry Hill, and was hanged on midsummer day, 24th June 1567, but continued till the last moment to protest his innocence of Darnley's murder.[1] According to what was afterwards asserted he had formerly been able, along with his fellow-prisoner, Edmonston, to secure through Bothwell's influence an authorisation from the Scottish Government to sail in the character of a Swedish privateer, and this justified his enemies in alleging that by it there was given the King of Denmark every occasion to break off his earlier friendship.[2] In so far as the Earl of Bothwell really had the intention of visiting one of the kings in the North before proceeding to France, we should rather suppose that this visit was designed for Eric XIV. of Sweden. When, however, a higher Power had brought the Earl to the kingdom of Frederick II. of Denmark, it may be easily imagined that he found

of the reign of James VI., the latter is marked side by side as "Anno Dominicæ incarnationis millesimo quingentesimo sexagesimo sexto," instead of septimo.

[1] A contemporary discloses his cautious criticism of the sentence of death in this case by these words about the court : " The assyise wer of the gentilmen of Lennox, for the maist pairt vassallis and servandis to the erle thairof."—Diurnal of Remarkable Occurrents, p. 116.

[2] Quo quidem privilegio non modo ipsius regis maiestas violata civibusque suis iniuria allata, sed etiam regi Daniæ, aliisque suæ maiestatis sociis ac confœderatis, ansa a pristina amicitia ac societate

descedendi si quidem illi aliive illorum permissione potestate concessa usi fuissent supeditata videtur. In opposition to the letter mentioned above, from which these words are also taken, nevertheless speaks a letter written to Frederick II. by Mary on the 3d of June 1566, and likewise preserved in the Royal Archives. The King, on 25th April 1566, had informed the Queen about a rumour of some one in Leith who was fitting out a ship for the service of the King of Sweden (nomine regis Sueciæ), but the Queen answers, that after having instituted exact inquiries, no ground whatever had been found for any such suspicion.

it most prudent to give his coming the appearance
of a definite errand, but here so little confidence
was placed in Bothwell's veracity that no words of
his as to his intentions were sufficient to dispel
suspicion.

When the storm of the wild North Sea, on whose
billows were formerly borne to Scotland swarms of
Vikings, had driven the Earl towards the rocky land
whence these issued on their marauding expeditions,
he found himself on the south-west coast of Norway,
without any knowledge of its navigable waters, and,
owing to his hurried departure from Shetland, without provisions.   Outside the populous island of
Karm, where he first caught sight of land, he was
however so fortunate as to meet in the evening with
a Hanseatic vessel from Rostock, the master of
which undertook next morning to pilot Bothwell's
two ships into Karm Sound, the arm of the sea
which, north of Bukkefjord, separates the island of
Karm from the mainland.[1] But scarcely had they
gone so far, and had cast one of their anchors, before
there appeared a new sail carrying the Danish flag.
This was the Dano-Norwegian war-ship " Björnen,"
which is more than once mentioned in the history of
the Northern Seven Years' War before its capture
by the Swedes, and the expulsion of the Danish

[1] " En un lieu appelé carmesund,"
writes Bothwell (Teulet, *Lettres*,
p. 282). Perhaps the reported
meeting by the Earl with " ung
navire de Rostock" has had its
share in originating the subsequent
rumour in Scotland to the effect
that Bothwell, on the coast of Norway, had taken " ane ship of Lubky
(Lubeck)," which at last became
" a ship of Turkey."—*Diurnal of
Remarkable Occurrents*, p. 123.

The Abstract of Crawford's manuscript, *Histoire and Life of King
James the Sext;* Keith, *History of
Church and State in Scotland*, p.
459. On the contrary, Cecil still
wrote in a letter of 2d October
1567: " Bothwell is not yet taken,
to our knowledge, though it be said
he should been taken on the seas
by a ship of Bremen."—Keith, p.
458.

fleet from the Baltic into the Sound by Admiral
Claes Fleming in the last year of the war. It was
commanded by Captain Christiern Aalborg, one
of Frederick Second's highly distinguished seamen, whom the king selected next year to conduct an expedition to Greenland, the explora-
tion of which he had again resolved on during
the war.[1] Bothwell's two ships, or, as they were
called in Norway, the two Scottish "Pinker,"[2]
saluted the foreign war-ships, casting anchor beside
them,[3] whose captain demanded to see their ships'
papers, which they were obliged to have "in His
Royal Majesty's seas and rivers." Bothwell made
answer that "they were Scottish gentlemen who
wished to proceed to Denmark to serve His Majesty,"
and ordered one of his companions, or, as he himself
calls him, "one of my gentlemen,"[4] to repair to
Captain Aalborg to explain to him that he whose
duty it was to issue such papers in Scotland was
now in close confinement. As, therefore, Christiern
Aalborg found these Scottish "Pinker," as he himself

---

[1] *Grönlands Historiske Mindes-
mærker.* Udgivne af det kongelige
nordiske Oldskriftsselskab. Kjöbenhavn, 1838-1845, iii. 200, 203,
634. By letter from Fredericksburg of 15th April 1568, the King
also permitted that " Os Elskelige
Christiernn Olborg maa bekomme
nogenn Anndworskouff closters
Boder vdj vor kjöpsted Kjöpnne-
haffnn vdi Kattesund liggendes."
—O. Nielsen, *Kjöbenhavns Diplo-
matarium.* Andet Bind. Kjöbenhavn, 1874, p. 332.

[2] Two-masted lesser war-ships
are called " Pinker."—Garde, *Den
danske-norske Sömagts Historie,*
1535-1700. Kjöbenhavn, 1861,
p. 95.

[3] " Je commanday," writes Bothwell, " qu'on feist l'honneur accous-
tumé ès mer et juridiction des
princes estrangers." — Bothwell's
Representation ; Teulet, *Lettres,* p.
183.

[4] Ung de mes gentilzhommes.—
Ibid. p. 183. In a letter from
Frederick II. (in the Royal Archives)
in which, on the 14th November
1567, he communicated from
Aalborg the news of the detention
of the Scots to his father-in-law,
Duke Ulrich of Mecklenburg, it is
said that there were among them
forty "gentlemen." The same
letter makes Bothwell, when met
by Christiern Aalborg at Karm
Sound, to have in all with him two
hundred men.

afterwards reported, "without any passport, sea-brief, safe-conduct, or commissions which honest seafaring people commonly use and are in duty bound to have," he determined to bring them to Bergen. The task, however, was not so easy. The men on board Bothwell's two ships, amounting, according to his own statement, to an hundred and forty, were more numerous than the crew of the "Björnen," and Bothwell, had he suspected the captain's intentions, might, in his own words, "have been able to show him and his company what seemed to me best." But the Danish Admiral knew how to help himself. During the night he summoned the Norse peasants around Karm Sound to arms, telling them they must assist the King's naval force to take some privateers (freebooters) prisoners.[1] He also got eighty of Bothwell's men on board his own ship under pretence of wishing to furnish them with provisions. Next, he put on shore another part of Bothwell's men, and distributed them among the peasants. Having thus separated the Scots, and also manned the vessels in which they had come with a part of his own crew, he then declared before the strangers, whom he had detained on board, that he would take them and their ships along with him.[2] In vain did

---

[1] "Pour venir secourir les navires de Roy de Dannemarch," it is said in Bothwell's account (Teulet, *Lettres,* p. 184). One could be tempted to see more in these expressions than an incorrect phraseology, more especially as the rumour went in Scotland that "The capitane of Birrame (Bergen) in Norroway addressit tua greit schippis to tak the said erle."—*Diurnal of Remarkable Occurrents,* p. 123. But Bothwell expressly mentions only

the war-ship "Björnen" (l'Ours) in Karm Sound, and the case is the same with the examination afterwards made at Bergen. Absalon Pederssön (*Dagbog over Begivenheder, især i Bergen,* p. 148) confounds the war-ship "David" with the war-ship "Björnen," but nevertheless instances only one ship.

[2] Darauf unser Hauptmann die Capitenen und die von Adel zu sich genommen und das ander Volk zu

318   JAMES HEPBURN EARL OF BOTHWELL.

CHAP.
IX.
1567.

Bothwell, who had hitherto kept in the background, make himself known to the Danish commander. In vain did the Earl offer objections to a course of procedure which to him was unaccountable, since he had never either injured His Majesty, or wronged the least of his subjects, or acted against the laws of the sea, or even taken the worth of a farthing without payment. Bothwell, as he subsequently explained, had his clothes in the ship which he sent back from Unst to the Mainland of Shetland, and Christiern Aalborg could, with difficulty, see in the man who now appeared before him " attired in old torn coarse boatswain's clothes, the highest of the rulers in all Scotland." Accordingly Bothwell was obliged to accompany Captain Aalborg when the latter, with the war-ship under his command, and the two Scottish " Pinker," sailed out of Karm Sound.

On the 2d of September 1567, a week after Bothwell's companions had escaped out of Bressay Sound, the three ships anchored outside of Bergen, and Christiern Aalborg gave to the commandant of Bergen Castle, Eric Ottessön Rosenkrands of Valsö, an account of the remarkable foreigner whom he had brought with him. This functionary then ordered an examination to be made by a commission, consisting of George Daa of Udsteen-monastery, Axel Gynstersberg of Torgen, Eric Hansen, Judge of Nordmör, the Bishop of Bergen, Dr. Jens Skjelderup, along with a number of Norse freemen, councillors in Bergen and representatives[1] of the

Lande gesetzt und bis an weitern Bescheid unter die Bauern vertheilt und ihre Schiffe mit unsern Volk besetzt.—Letter of Frederick II., of 14th November 1567, to Duke

Ulrich of Mecklenburg, in Danish Privy Archives.
[1] Of " Garperne," that is to say, " the counting-house clerks" or " the eighteen at the pier."

Association of German merchants in Bergen. This CHAP.
Commission, which numbered together four-and- IX.
twenty members, proceeded on board the war-ship 1567.
"Björnen,"and to them the Earl of Bothwell explained
that he was " the husband of the Queen of Scotland,"
that he came from that country, and that he was
going to His Royal Majesty of Denmark, and after
that to France. On being asked if he had any
passport or sea-brief with him, he only answered
" disdainfully, and inquired of us from whom he
should get passport or letter, being himself the
supreme ruler in the country." Bothwell desired
permission to be given him to take up his residence
at an inn in the town, and there to stay at his own
expense, and this permission was willingly granted
by Eric Rosenkrands.

In Bergen, where so many Scottish merchants
usually resided at this period, that the Earl's recognition was in the highest degree probable,[1] he
remained during the month of September. He
could walk about in the city wherever he pleased,
and enjoyed much outward attention from the
provincial governor. In a contemporary diary,
which for twenty years gives very full notes about
Bergen and the life of its inhabitants, we thus read
under date of 25th September 1567 :—" The Earl
came to the castle and Eric Rosenkrands showed
him great honour;" and again, under date of 28th
of the same month :—" Eric Rosenkrands made
the Earl and his gentlemen a magnificent banquet."[2]
But this outward respect could not outweigh the

---

[1] Note Q, Appendix.
[2] Absalon Pederssön, *Dagbog
over Begivenheder, iser i Bergen*,
p. 149. By the " gentlemen "
mentioned in this statement we
are led to think of lairds James
and Hob Ormiston, of whom the
last is never known to have been

series of mortifications to which the Earl was subjected from the beginning of his stay in Bergen.
First, he could not but feel himself an object of
suspicion to the German traders in regard to the way
in which he had come into possession of the largest
of his ships " The Pelican," they knowing that it had
formerly belonged to a Bremen merchant, although
to this suspicious circumstance the Earl could now
reply that he had arranged about it with the owner,
and, without being requested, he was prepared to
let both ships lie at Bergen so as to permit of any
one coming who had cause of complaint with respect
to them.[1]

He had next the mortification of seeing one of
his companions sent to prison. For the crew with
whom he had come to Norway were likewise
judicially examined, and as we may assume that
when he came on board at Shetland, he kept his

seized in Scotland, and the first
was not imprisoned before the 10th
of November 1573.—*Diurnal of
Remarkable Occurrents*, p. 338.
Respecting James Ormiston's life,
during the years 1567-1573, we
have only a general remark by
himself in the confession which he
made before his execution to the
priest John Braw, and in which it
is said—" For it is not mervell
that I have bein wickit, for the
wickit companie that ever I have
bein in, bot speciallie within this
seaven yearis bypast, quhilk I
never saw twa guid men or ane
guid deid, bot all kind of wickedness."—Laing, *History of Scotland*,
ii. 295.

[1] Geert Hemelingk, who was
still remaining in Shetland, having
received intelligence of Bothwell's
detention, afterwards applied to
the authorities in Bremen with a
request that they would assist him

to get back " The Pelican," or to
obtain the sum of indemnification
promised him by Bothwell. To
support his representation he had
affixed to it a certificate, dated
" Lassefirde " (Laxfirth), the 15th
September 1567, in which Olaf
Sinclair of Bru, " Kemener vnd
ouerste principall van Hidtland,"
" mit miner handt op de fedder
gevohrdt " attests that Hemelingk,
from his first arrival in the country,
had shown himself a true and
honest merchant. Both Hemelingk's representation and Sinclair's
attestation have, like Hemelingk's
contract with Bothwell, been
added as vouchers to a letter to
King Frederick II., in which the
Burgomaster and counsellors of
Bremen, on the 8th March 1568,
recommended the representation,
and are therefore now found together with the latter in the Danish
Archives.

name concealed from all but his most intimate
friends, so the rest must necessarily have been
ignorant of it. Accordingly the most of them unanimously declared, that, as far as they knew, the
Earl of Bothwell was still in Scotland; and affirmed
that their captain was a certain David Woth.[1]
Since rumour in Bergen indicated that such a man
had shortly before captured "a ship trading to the
country," and had taken from it twenty-two barrels
of beer and four barrels of bread, this captain of
Bothwell's, who had conducted his "Pinker" across
the North Sea, was immediately subjected to a prosecution by the German merchants,[2] and as he could
not deny the charge, he was therefore placed in
close confinement in the Town-house of Bergen.
This action of the merchants was followed by a quite
unexpected complaint from Lady Anne, daughter of
Christopher Throndssön, who had been the Earl's
bride, and who now, under altered circumstances,
met in Bergen with her faithless lover. After her

CHAP.
IX.

1567.

[1] "Tha gaffue the Alle samptli-
gen enn Berettniing och thet met
theris Eeder bekrefftede At de
icke wüste aff thenn herre att siige
anndet ennd hand enndda wor y
skotlanndt." Thus it is said in
the original examination which is
preserved in the Danish Archives.
Bergenhammer first printed it
among the supplements to his
translation of Gentz's *Sketch of the
History of Mary Stuart*, but he
has given in this document, perhaps by a misprint "y skotrnndt,"
in place of "y skotlanndt," and
this has since bred the most per-
plexing confusion. In the reprint
by the Bannatyne Club, the idea
of Repp, who understood the
meaningless word as corresponding
to the Isl. Skógarmaðr, was re-

peated thus:—"That they knew
nothing of this gentleman, but
that he was still a wanderer," and
again in the latest reprint by
Teulet, thus:—"Qu'ils ne con-
naissaient rien de ce gentilhomme,
si ce n'est qu'ils le regardaient
comme un aventurier."

[2] "Och strax bleff aff de kontorske her for rethe thillthallet."
The here necessary "aff," which is
found in the original examination
in the Danish Archives, has been
left out in the reprint of Bergenhammer, and subsequently in the
following copies, of which the
Bannatyne Club's so incorrectly
renders "de kontorske" by "the
Custom-house Officers," and Teulet's
by "les gardes-côtes."

X

brief union with Bothwell, and her eventful flight
abroad, Lady Anne, or "The Scottish Lady," as she
was commonly called by her countrymen, took up
her residence in Norway, whither her mother, on
the death of her father, Christopher Throndssön,
also returned from Denmark. In 1565 Anne
Throndssön is mentioned as being in Bergen,[1] but
her real place of abode was perhaps at some one of
the farms of her sisters or brothers-in-law in the
southern part of the diocese. When the tidings of
Bothwell's unexpected arrival reached her, she at
once seized this opportunity of seeking redress for
the losses she had suffered for his sake; she summoned the Earl before the Court, and read in his
presence the letters in which he had promised to
marry her, "Lady Anne being of opinion that this
promise had been of no weight in his eyes, since he
had three wives alive, first herself, another in Scotland from whom he had procured his freedom, and
the last, Queen Mary."[2] By promising Lady Anne
an annuity to be sent from Scotland, and handing

[1] In one and the same month of
this year, she is named as being
present at two noble entertainments, first at a christening feast
on the 18th August with George
Daa, feudatory of Utsteen-Cloister,
whose son Herluf was then bap-
tized, and next on 27th August at
the wedding of the noble maiden
Brynhild Benkestok with the
young nobleman Eric Hansön, the
entertainment being given at the
expense of Eric Rosenkrands in
his house, which is still preserved
in Bergen (Absalon Pederssön,
Dagbog, p. 104 and p. 107). From
the manner in which Lady Anne
is spoken of in the latter instance,
she seems, since her sojourn in
foreign countries, to have acquired
greater taste for foreign magnificence than was common in her
native land. It is said in the
description of Absalon Pederssön
with respect to the bride :—"And
Lady Anne Trons, the Scottish lady,
was decked out as a Spaniard,
that is, that she had a gold chain
round the forehead, and besides, a
necklace, full of precious stones,
and a wreath of pearls, and feather
of pearls in it, with a red damask
tunic."

[2] Absalon Pederssön, Dagbog, p.
148.

over to her the smallest of his ships, Bothwell got
this prosecution also quashed.[1]

But yet the most humiliating thing for the
Earl was that, in spite of the outward respect shown
towards him, he could not but feel that in Bergen
he was no longer free. When he spoke of wishing
to go to Holland or France, or even of returning to
Scotland, his words were unheeded. In vain did he
write to Eric Rosenkrahds, requesting him to issue
a passport for him, in order that he might as
speedily as possible go " in a yacht or boat along the
coast " to Denmark, and there get access to the
king, his knowledge of the geographical positions
of the two countries seeming not to be very great.
Scotland's High Admiral has explained, that on the
North Sea he had suffered from sea-sickness, and
that therefore he now wished to be rowed along the
coast ; but suspicion in Bergen interpreted his wish
to mean that it " was mainly his desire with a yacht
or boat to reach Varbjerg, or where he could soonest
get to Sweden." In a courteous manner Eric
Rosenkrands refused his request, telling him that it
was to be feared that when he arrived at the
Swedish frontiers, he would perhaps be obliged to
cross the enemy's country, and the wished-for passport would in that case very speedily become a
hindrance to him in his errand. The Governor,

[1] Like Jane Gordon, the Norse
bride, whom Bothwell cast off,
also long survived him. In his
Visitation-book Bishop Jens Nielsen of Oslo, has noted in the year
1594, that " Anne Thronsdatter"
was present on the 21st of April in
Ide Church in Smaaland, and that
on the following day he spoke
with her in Berg's Parsonage
(*Norsk Magazin*, ii. 151-152), and
in the year 1607, Lady Anne made
over her father's principal farm
Seim in Kvind district, of which
she had become proprietress, by
exchange to her sister Else (*Samlinger til det norske Folks Sprog og
Historie*, vi. 242).

CHAP. under the hostile relations then existing between
IX.   Denmark and Sweden, therefore found it unadvis-
1567. able to give him such a passport, but "perpetually
and unceasingly" counselled him to proceed to Denmark on board the royal war-ship.

If Eric Rosenkrands entertained any doubt as to
how far he ought to comply with the Earl's wish,
this certainly was removed by the discovery of the
papers which the latter had brought with him, and
in which, before any accusation by his enemies could
reach him, he carried along with him to Denmark
the most unfavourable proofs against himself. During the judicial examination made on board the
war-ship "Björnen," the Earl was asked whether
there were in his ships gold, silver, jewels, clothes, or
letters, as in that case he required only to make that
fact known in order immediately to receive whatever of these he wished. Bothwell replied, "that
he had really nothing which he either valued or
desired." But towards the close of his stay in
Bergen, when he probably foresaw that he would
very soon be separated from his ships, he sent, as is
stated in the official record of his residence in Bergen,
"three of his servants to the castle to say that their
master had deposited in the ballast of one of the
'Pinker,' a letter-case with some letters, and was
therefore desirous of obtaining it, although he had
before denied that there was such on board.
George Daa and Christen Aalborg immediately
went, and with the three servants of the Scottish
Lord, took up the aforesaid letter-case, and carried
it to the castle. The next day the good man, Eric
Rosenkrands, summoned to the castle certain
freemen, certain counsellors, and certain of the

'eighteen,' with some of the Earl's servants, who
had keys to the same letter-case, and, in the presence of all these good men, it was opened. There were then found in the afore-mentioned letter-case in particular, many and diverse letters, written or printed in the Latin or Scottish tongue, which we immediately glanced over, and caused to be read and explained to us, so that we could understand them. And among the afore-described letters was one on parchment in Latin, in which the Queen appointed the Earl of Bothwell Duke of Orkney and Shetland, vesting in him and the male descendants begotten of him the perpetual possession and inheritance of these islands. Next there were found many diverse letters, both in print and in writing, which the Council of the realm, with the nobility of Scotland, had published, in which they severely impeached the aforesaid Lord with being a tyrannical murderer, robber, and traitor, alleging that with his own hand he put to death his rightful Lord and King; and in the same letters of theirs declared him an outlaw, and offered to all who would lay hands on and apprehend the said Lord of Bothwell, and would send him to Edinburgh, a thousand crowns for their pains. Besides, it was stated, that the Scottish Lords in question had fitted out some war-ships, and sent them to sea, in order to seek for him. We also found among the aforesaid papers a letter written with the Queen's own hand, in which she bewailed herself and all her friends, so that, in the same letter which he had with him, we could clearly remark, that he had for no good reason withdrawn from his native country."
All these documents, along with the declaration

drawn up regarding Bothwell's detention, were
afterwards sent from Bergen to Denmark, and were
at one time in the Archives there, but have now for
the most part disappeared, and among the rest,
which is specially to be lamented, the letter of complaint written by Mary Stuart to Bothwell.[1]

Bothwell subsequently complained in Denmark
that Captain Christiern Aalborg had deceived him
at Karm Sound, since the Earl, in his declaration,
stated that he had given his word of honour that
the Scots should be free to return from his ship
"Björnen," to their own, and to set sail if they
wished.[2] On the other hand, he mentions only with
favour the Governor of Bergen Castle, or, as he calls
him, "ce bon sieur Erik Rosenkrands." But from
the Scottish Earl's point of view, the treatment
which he met with in Bergen must nevertheless
appear in such a light that it may well be believed,
since the men who drew up the account of Bothwell's
residence in Bergen have alleged it, that "he heard
daily there many diverse mocking words, which he
publicly declared he would repay some day in the
future." The prudent citizens and merchants therefore add the remark, that the Scottish Earl ought to
be required "to enter into an agreement never at
any time to inflict injury on the kingdom, or on any
subject of His Majesty, or even on any of those who
trade to His Majesty's country."

But every such assurance was rendered super-

---

[1] The Patent by which Orkney
and Shetland, on the 12th May
1567, three days before Bothwell's
marriage to Mary, were erected
into a dukedom for him, is still
found in the Danish Privy
Archives, but only in a Danish
translation.

[2] He has even added :—"Dont il
nous donna lettres cachettées de son
cachet."—Teulet, *Lettres*, p. 184.

fluous by the fate that awaited Bothwell. After CHAP.
the twenty-four men whom Eric Rosenkrands had $\underbrace{\qquad}_{}$ IX.
appointed for Bothwell's examination subscribed in 1567.
Bergen Castle on the 23d September 1567 the
declaration made by them regarding the detention
of Bothwell, the latter was given to understand, that
he must hold himself in readiness to sail to Denmark
in one of the King's war-ships, and that on this
voyage he could take along with him only four or
five of his servants, the rest of his followers being
left free either to return to Scotland, or to proceed
whither they would. Accordingly, when Christiern
Aalborg set sail from Bergen on the 30th of September, Mary's husband, whom he had brought to
Bergen, again accompanied him to Copenhagen.

As a result of the Earl's detention, the ship
which had followed him across the North Sea, and
had actually arrived on the coast of Norway, suddenly
turned about. "The ship," writes Bothwell, "which
I had sent to Shetland to take on board my men
that I had left there, and in which I had my property, my silver-service, clothes, and jewels, had
already sailed along the coast of Norway, but after
having learned that I was detained, and my followers
had been sent away, it turned back." A number
also of the Earl's men who had followed him to
Bergen went back to Scotland on the 10th October
1567, in a little ship which was given them by Eric
Rosenkrands, and report in Norway subsequently
stated that on their arrival they were put to death.[1]
Perhaps it is to them that Mary's ambassador, James

[1] "Droge een part aff Grevens karle til Skotland paa en liden pinke, Erik Rosenkrantz lente dem. Sigis de were afliuede, da de hiem komme." — Absalon Pedersson, *Dagbog*, p. 149.

Beaton, Archbishop of Glasgow, alludes in a letter
of the 8th February 1568, in which he gives the
Cardinal of Lorraine the latest news from Scotland,
and thus has occasion to mention that about last
Christmas there were twelve or fifteen of the Earl of
Bothwell's chief servants taken prisoners in Orkney
by the Prior of Holyrood, one of the illegitimate
brothers of the Queen, who has now made himself
Lord of the said islands. A storm on the sea had
forced them to land there, and having been conveyed
to Edinburgh and charged as murderers, they were
condemned to death, and executed in prison."[1]

[1] "Pour ce que," it is added,
"quelques ungs d'eux, ayant de-
mandé de grace estre ouy par le
Conte de Mourray, confessérent
bien avoir merité la mort, declar-
ant l'innocence de la Royne et
accusant les plus grands et princi-
paux de son conceil, qui assistoient
lors avec lui, et mesmes le Conte
de Morthon et le secretaire Ledin-
ton et Balfour, qui estoit capitaine
de chatteau de Lislebourgh, et le
dit Conte leur maître en Dane-
mark."—Letter of the Archbishop
of Glasgow; Laing, *History of
Scotland*, ii. 24-25. Laing, who
was not acquainted with the Norwegian Journal, however, assumes
that the sole ground for the whole
of the Archbishop's account is his
mistaking the execution of Hay,
Hepburn, Dalgleish, and Powrie on
the 3d January 1568, for that of
those mentioned above.

CHAPTER X.

AFTER being conveyed in the foreign ship of war past the coasts of Norway and Denmark, the Earl of Bothwell at length saw, on one of the last days of the autumn of 1567, the metropolis of the latter country—" Cawpmanhowin," as the Scots called it[1] —lying before him. He did not, however, meet here with Frederick II., he being then, as was very often the case during the seven years' war, absent from the capital on a journey into the provinces. He was, however, received by the High Steward of the realm, Peter Oxe of Gisselfeld. The latter had been able since the 9th of September to make himself acquainted with the account which Murray had sent to the Dano-Norwegian Government of the events in Scotland in the early part of the year,[2] and therefore found it now advisable to retain in custody in the castle of Copenhagen the unexpected guest who had arrived under so peculiar circumstances. Here the Earl hastened to write two French letters. One of these he addressed to Charles IX. of France. In it he mentions that he had left Scotland to lay before the Danish king the wrongs to which his near

[1] Knox, *History of the Reformation in Scotland*, i. 55.
[2] Ceterum quæ in Scotia superioribus hisce mensibus gesta sint, et quo in statu nunc res nostræ versantur, ut S. T. exponeret, Ioanni Clerk in mandatis dedimus.—Murray's letter written in the name of King James VI., dated the 25th August 1567, but which did not arrive in Copenhagen till the 9th September, and the original of which is in the Danish Privy Archives.

CHAP. relative, the Queen of Scotland, had become a victim,
X.   and after that to repair to France, but that a storm
1567. had driven him upon the coast of Norway before he
reached Denmark. He begs the French king favourably to take into account the good-will with which
through his whole life he had striven, and would
further strive, to be of service to him, and requests
him to grant a gracious answer, as his hope now
rested, next to God, upon his Majesty alone.[1] Bothwell also met in Copenhagen with Charles Dancay
(Carolus Dancæus), the French minister, who, after
visiting Denmark as ambassador in the reign of
Christian III., subsequently resided there, in the
same capacity, from the accession of Frederick II.
till his death in 1589, at the advanced age of about
eighty, having probably held this office at the Danish
court longer than any. As he was one of the medi-
ators in behalf of Denmark at the peace of Stettin,
which at last put an end to the war between the
Scandinavian kingdoms, and as the friend of Tycho
Brahe had laid the foundation-stone of Uranienburg
upon Hveen,[2] so he was also expressly instructed by
the French sovereigns, Henry II., Francis II., and
Charles IX., to use his influence in Denmark in the
interests of the Scottish Government. For this
reason, Mary of Guise and her daughter Mary Stuart,

[1] Comme à celuy qui n'a, après
Dieu, aultre espérance qu'en Voustre
Majesté. The letter, the original
of which is now found in the great
Library in Paris, was dated by
Bothwell, "De Copenhaguen, le
douziesme jour de Novembre," and
is subscribed "Vostre très-humble
et très-obèissant serviteur, James
Duc of Orknay." It has been
printed by Teulet in *Lettres*, p. 150.

[2] Jacobsen, *Bidrag til Danmarks
Personal-og Tids-Historie i det
16de Aarhundre; Historisk Tidsskrift*, v. 481-495.
[Hveen or Huen, a small island
in the Sound, granted by Frederick
II. to Tycho Brahe, with a magnificent castle erected upon it for the
purpose of making astronomical observations.—*Translator.*]

never sent any ambassador to Denmark without en-
joining upon him to regulate his actions by the counsel
of Dancay. The latter could therefore testify that he
had just as much trouble in acting for the Scots as in
behalf of his fellow-subjects of France.[1] Bothwell,
who had given the French minister a circumstantial
explanation of his whole position, begged him, not
by any means in vain, to hasten to transmit his
words to Charles IX. by a special messenger. In
another letter, also composed in French, Bothwell
endeavoured to give Frederick II. a corresponding
explanation of the circumstances under which he had
arrived in Copenhagen. From Peter Oxe, whom he
made acquainted with its contents, he obtained permission to get the letter conveyed to the King by one
of the servants that had accompanied him from Scotland, and had still been allowed to remain with him.

Frederick II. was staying in North Jutland when
he received the tidings of the detention of Bothwell
in Norway and his arrival in Copenhagen. The
earliest documents in which Peter Oxe conveyed
the news to the King have gone amissing, as well as
those which would have shown what was the first
impression this surprising news made on the King.
But after Frederick II. received a later account
which Peter Oxe sent him by the man who could
himself give the fullest information on the subject,
namely, by the captain of the war-ship " Björnen,"
Christiern Aalborg, he wrote, on the 18th November
1567, from Aalborg to the High Steward an answer
which, as it has not been hitherto printed, deserves

---

[1] In one of his letters preserved
in the Danish Privy Archives he
himself writes to King Charles IX.
from Copenhagen, the 10th of
June 1570 :—" Et pour vray, Sire,
ie n'ay moins eu de peine pour les
Ecossais que pour voz propres sub-
iectz."

to be communicated to the reader because of the peculiar way in which Bothwell is still designated in it :—" Our particular Favourite.   We have received, along with our naval commander, Christiern Aalborg, your letter, read it over and understood what you therein mention, and which you make known about *the Scottish King.*   As we have before written you about him, we trust the same, our letter, has come to hand ; and it seems to us to be best that he remain in the castle till our arrival, or until our further written communication thereanent be received by you."

Three days afterwards, and before this reply could have reached its destination, the King received a written advice from Peter Oxe and John Friis of Hesselager, how in their opinion he ought to act towards his foreign guest.   In this advice, which was drawn up in the Castle of Copenhagen on the 13th November, it is said that " according as I Peter Oxe very lately wrote your Royal Majesty about the Scottish Earl who was married to the Queen in Scotland, how he came hither to the city, and I asked him up to the castle, as I have here with a good guard caused him to be kept safely. But since he is very cunning and inventive, according as I John Friis will furthermore inform your Royal Majesty when I return again to your Royal Majesty, we think it not advisable nor convenient for him to be long here in the castle.   But we consider it advisable, with your Majesty's pleasure, that your Royal Majesty should order him to go to one of your Royal Majesty's castles in Jutland, wherever it may be most convenient, and may be done with least danger.   At the same time he has desired of me Peter Oxe that he might write by his own

messenger to your Royal Majesty, which I, in your
Royal Majesty's behalf, have not refused to allow
him to do. And whereas he let me see the letter,
and I knew not whether there were any one with
your Royal Majesty that could understand French,
I have caused the same letter of his to be translated
into Danish, so that your Majesty may learn his
meaning therein. And we consider it to be well, that
when your Royal Majesty has decided in which castle
your Royal Majesty wills that he shall be kept, that
your Royal Majesty then write to him, that since
your Royal Majesty cannot so speedily come hither,
he repair to the same castle there to await information and answer from your Royal Majesty."

In the following not quite tasteful translation of
Bothwell's letter, which accompanied the advice of
Peter Oxe and John Friis, the King could read how,
according to the representation of the former, "after
the last alliance, imprisonment, and invention of
false complaints against the Queen of Scotland, your
Royal Majesty's kinswoman and descendant, and
against me, both her councillors, your Majesty's
obedient servants, as also the greatest part of the
nobility of the Scottish kingdom, have considered it
to be right, that I come before your Majesty to
declare her cause, and to desire your Majesty's good
counsel and assistance for her deliverance, as from
the Lord and Prince on whom, both on account of
kinship and descent, as also on account of the ancient
alliance which has been between both your kingdoms
from time immemorial, she altogether relies. I was
forced by stress of weather into Norway at a place
which is called Arsond (Karmsund), where I intended
to stay and wait for some of my ships which, by the

same stormy weather, after that I had hastily fled from Scotland, were scattered from me at sea. Thereupon came one of your Majesty's ships which detained me for two-and-a-half months until now, as I had not a passport. I have come hither to Copenhagen, that your Royal Majesty should know the whole affair, uproar, and clamour which have happened in Scotland. As I have been so long hindered and detained, and since I am not quite certain what time your Majesty returns, I have requested your Majesty's Stadtholder, Peter Oxe, that, by this bearer, my servant, I might learn your Majesty's good-will and intention." [1]

Frederick II., after being made acquainted with Bothwell's account, did not feel inclined to follow the advice given by Peter Oxe and John Friis as to sending Bothwell to one of his castles in Jutland. The King allowed the Earl, according to his former arrangement, to remain at Copenhagen till he himself, at the end of the year, returned to Zealand. But he could not any longer delay coming to a more precise determination with respect to the fate of Bothwell. For already, towards the close of the month of September, information reached Scotland of Bothwell's detention in Norway through the return home, it is said, of Scottish merchants. Accordingly, on the same day as Christiern Aalborg sailed from Bergen to convey Bothwell to Denmark, Murray wrote in the name of James VI. from Stirling a request to Frederick II. for the surrender of the Earl ;

[1] This Danish translation of Bothwell's letter, which is subscribed " James Duke of Orkney," is, also with the advice of Peter Oxe and John Friis, and a copy of the previously written reply of the King to Peter Oxe, still preserved in the Danish Archives, but there is wanting the French original of Bothwell's letter to the King.

and the Scottish Herald, Sir William Stuart, who CHAP.
departed with it on the 7th October,[1] was at length, X.
after being long detained by stormy weather, able, 1567.
on the 15th December 1567, to deliver this request
into the hands of the Danish king in Zealand.
The King would not now hear of the surrender
of the Earl. On the one hand the Scottish Government accused Bothwell of being the murderer of
Darnley; on the other he maintained to Peter Oxe
that he had already in Scotland been legally
acquitted of this charge, that he was himself the
real Regent of Scotland, that the Queen was his
consort, and that his opponents were only rebels.[2]
One thing was indeed certain, that Mary Stuart was

---

[1] Upoun the sevinth day of October 1567 my lord regent directit Williame Stewart Ross, herauld, away to Denmark to the king thairof, to obtene his favour for delyuering to thame of James Erle of Bothwill, upoun thair expenssis.—*Diurnal of Remarkable Occurrents,* p. 125. The herald is mentioned in this authority (pp. 137, 146) only as William Stuart, but as Sir William Stuart in the Diarey of Robert Birrel, who reports his appointment as herald of the kingdom thus: "The 22 day of Februarii Sir Villiam Steuarte wes inaugurat Lyone king of armes in the kirk, after sermone in ye forenoone, in presence of ye Regent and Nobilitie."—*Fragments of Scottish History,* p. 14.

[2] Intelleximus autem ex relatione nostrorum, se, cum de his argueretur, purgandi sui causa plurima in medium adduxisse; inter cætera, purgationem ejus, cujus insimularetur, criminis, in Scotia a se legitime factam, ideoque in decisorio judicio per sententiam absolutam, se Regem Scotorum, serenissimam Reginam, consan-

guineam nostram, conjugem suam, contrariam factionem subditos rebelles asserens, nec ullam hac in causa Reginæ accusationem intervenire.—Reply of Frederick II. of 30th December 1567, according to a copy in the Danish Privy Archives. This letter was first printed from another copy in the State Paper Office among the many supplements to Laing's *History of Scotland,* ii. 300-302, and therefrom reprinted in the writings about Bothwell by the Bannatyne Club by Prince Labanoff, as also by Teulet. It is thus incorrect, when Ellis (*Latter Years of James Hepburn Earl of Bothwell,* pp. 10-11), who once again has reprinted this letter, thinks that he is giving it as "not hitherto printed." On the other hand the latter gives the subscription of the letter correctly as "*ex Regia nostra Haffnia,*" instead of that by Laing, "*ex Regia nostra Hostenia,*" which Teulet (p. 151) translates by "Palais de Holstein." [Haffnia, the true reading, is the Latin name for Copenhagen.—*Translator.*]

CHAP.
X.
1567.

now kept in confinement and cut off from all communication on the solitary Lochleven, and it was
consequently not from her,—not from Scotland's
imprisoned Queen, that any complaint against
Bothwell was now sent to her Danish relative, who
readily recognised as here applicable the old proverb
to which he himself had recently given utterance
during persecutions in another country, that genuine
friends are only to be known in the hour of need.[1]
It is thus not difficult to understand that Frederick
II. would, in a consultation with Peter Oxe at Kronborg, agree with him, that even without taking into
account the violation of the royal jurisdiction which
would seem to be involved in the surrender of Bothwell, it would not be proper for him in the circumstances to accede to any such measure. The matter
was accordingly allowed to rest with the offer of
permission to the Scottish envoy himself to prosecute Bothwell in Denmark for the crimes alleged
against him, as soon as the council of the kingdom

---

[1] When William of Orange, in
the year 1567, went into exile from
the Netherlands at the approaching
arrival of the Duke of Alva,
Frederick II. wrote him with fine
sympathy a letter from Soroe, 9th
March 1567, in which, in consequence of that event threatening
danger of life (leibsgefahr) to the
Silent, he invites him to come to
him in Denmark. It is said *leaf*
A in this letter : "Weil dann die
rechtenn, wahrenn freundt, dem
alten sprichwort nach, inn der nott
erkandt und wir E. L. dafür gehal-
ten, auch dieselbigen im werck
gegen uns bis daher nit anderst
erspürt, wollten wir dasselbig nit
wenigers auch mit der that erweis-
senn. Da sich demnach E. L.
dergestalt zubefahren und ausser

ihrer landt in sorgen schwebtenn,
wollen die sich, zu verhüttung und
abwehrung desselbigen, unges-
cheucht herein ins Reich begebenn
und die gelegenheit dieser örter zu
freundtlichem gefallen und so gut
als wir habenn."—*Archives ou Cor-*
respondance inédite de la Maison
d'Orange Nassau. Première serie,
iii. 109, 110. William of Orange
thanked the king in a letter from
Dillenburg, 22d July 1567, for the
offer of which he had not taken
advantage (*Ibid.* iii. 111-113), and
subsequently, 12th June 1584,
named his renowned son, Frederick
Henry, after Frederick II. and
Henry III. of Navarre and IV. of
France.—Motley, *Rise of the Dutch*
Republic (London, 1856), iii. 597.

met,—a course however which Sir William Stuart did not presume immediately to undertake.[1] On the contrary, he was satisfied on receiving an assurance that for the present they would take care that Bothwell remained in Denmark, where, for the sake of greater security, the King now resolved to assign him a residence in Malmoe. This assurance was expressly stated in the written reply with which Sir William Stuart returned home, and in which the views already mentioned were set forth in a courteous way, they being supposed to be in accordance with the wishes of the Scottish Government.

Before the departure of Sir William Stuart with that promise it was felt that both the answer and the demand which had called it forth ought to be communicated to the Earl in the Castle of Copenhagen. How Bothwell received the tidings, a letter from Peter Oxe, written in the same place the 30th December 1567, furnishes the following information: " Your Royal Majesty, my most willing, plighted, faithful, obedient service as always heretofore. Most mighty, high-born Prince, most gracious Lord and King, I very lately, in Elsinore, spoke with your Royal Majesty about the Scottish Earl who remains here in the castle, and your Royal Majesty then saw proper that he should be sent to Malmoe Castle, and there be held in safe custody for further information till such time as his case could be better considered, and your Royal Majesty could arrive at additional knowledge of everything about it. As I

CHAP.
X.

1567.

---

[1] "Memorato vero Serenitatis Vestræ feciali, cui prosecutionem hujus causæ, et rei accusationem commissam esse, literæ Serenitatis vestræ testabantur, potestatem fecimus, in proximo procerum nostrorum conventu, legitimo judicio contra eundem experiundi, discep_tandique."—Answer by Frederick II. of 30th December 1567.

Y

CHAP.
X.

1567.

could not myself go out, I sent to him to-day licentiate Casper Vaselich and Niels Kaas, who informed him of your Majesty's intention, and that the Scottish herald had come hither with letters and instructions from the King of Scotland, in which were orders to accuse him as a murderer, and as one who had taken part in the counsel and act of putting to death the King of Scotland, and they read the same Scottish letter to him. But for as much as your Royal Majesty had learned from me the statements which he had alleged in opposition to the same accusation, and that in reference to it your Majesty might be able to obtain further and complete knowledge, and might not act unjustly towards any of the parties, they also informed him that your Royal Majesty at this time wrote to the King of Scotland an answer which was also read to him, and that meanwhile your Royal Majesty would cause him to be kept in custody in another place, and be provided with suitable maintenance till such time as the matter could come to a judicial examination, and all things be treated according to justice, your Royal Majesty as a Christian and wise prince taking care that none of the parties should meet with any wrong. He then complained most vehemently that his enemy and defamer should be free to charge him with unfair accusations, and to spread lying stories about him, while he himself was held in arrest and custody, since it was his meaning and purpose to repair to your Royal Majesty, and from your Majesty, as the next kinsman and blood relation of the Queen, to ask help and comfort. But for what concerned the court of justice, he would in no way be apprehensive, only

he desired that he might have liberty to send one CHAP
of his servants to Scotland and France for his letters, X.
proofs, and witnesses as to how the event had 1567.
happened, so that he might be able to defend himself before the court. And it appears to me, with
your Majesty's pleasure, that your Majesty may most
prudently allow this to be done; your Majesty will
deign to make known to me your Royal Majesty's
command thereanent." In a postscript to the foregoing letter, Peter Oxe added these words :—" Most
gracious Lord and King, since this letter was
penned, the Scottish Earl has sent me a note in
which he desires that he may have possession of a
copy of the letter which the King of Scotland has
written your Royal Majesty as to the complaints
the Scots have against him; your Royal Majesty
will deign to let me know if your Royal Majesty
wishes him to receive a copy of the said letter."[1]

Frederick II. being made acquainted with the
Earl's wishes on New Year's Eve at Fredericksburg,
allowed both to be granted on the first day of 1568,
with the condition, however, "that, should he
write anything, he should as heretofore show the
letters before they were sealed and sent off." On
the same day as Bothwell at Copenhagen was made
aware of this decision, the King, as he had before
determined, wrote from Fredericksburg to Björn
Kaas, the commander of Malmoe Castle, in these
words :—" Know that we ourselves have given

---

[1] The letter of Peter Oxe in the
Danish Archives having the above
postscript, concludes thus about
Bothwell :—" At the same time he
also desires that he may obtain
200 dollars on loan, for he has
nothing with which to buy clothes.
Your Royal Majesty will therefore
deign to write me as to whether I
shall advance him anything on
your Royal Majesty's behalf."

orders to beloved Peter Oxe, our trusty servant, councillor, and High Steward of the Kingdom of Denmark, to send the Scottish Earl, who is detained in the Castle of Copenhagen, to our Castle of Malmoe, there to remain for some time. Therefore we command you, and will that you cause the arched chamber in the same castle, which High Steward Eyler Hardenburg had for his room, to be put in order, and that you also wall up the secret closet in the same chamber, and if the windows with the iron trellis be not strong and quite secure, that you see to that, and when he arrives, that you let him lie in the same chamber, and procure him a bed and good maintenance as Peter Oxe may further instruct, and that ye above all things have strict watch and care of the same Earl, in the way you may think best, so that he do not get away. Such is our will and pleasure."[1]

[1] Copies of both the letter of the King to Peter Oxe, dated Fredericksburg, New Year's Day, 1568, and of that to Björn Kaas, are found in the Danish Privy Archives. The last-mentioned letter has already been printed by Bergenhammer, subsequently by Henry Cockburn and Thomas Maitland in a publication for the Bannatyne Club, likewise by Prince Labanoff, and lastly by Teulet. All these, however, have taken the statement "written in Fredericksburg, 28th December, after the birth of Christ 1568" too literally, which is equally the case in T. Becker, *Skildring af Adelersborg i Folkekalender for Danmark.* Tredie Aargang, p. 53. The old custom, which is followed in this statement, of reckoning the beginning of the year from the birth-day of our Lord, or from Christmas day, 25th of December, and the different countries in which it prevailed, are treated of in detail by Brinckmeier in his *Handbuch der Historischen Chronologie.* Leipzig, 1843, pp. 67-73.

CHAPTER XI.

It was on a day in January 1567, that Bothwell rode out from Edinburgh to receive Mary when she returned with the sick Darnley from Glasgow, and on a day in January 1568, after the lapse of a year, to which he could look back as the stormiest of all in his past life, he was conveyed from the Castle of Copenhagen across the Sound to the Castle of Malmoe. Of the present Malmoe Castle, only the northern wing with the tower over the gate on the north was built in the time of Christian III. ; the great western wing, which some years ago was destroyed by fire, was first built by Christian IV., and the rest probably at a still later time. The portion which formed the state-prison in 1568 must consequently be sought for in the northern wing, and here there is actually shown an old apartment, consisting of a large, oblong, vaulted hall with windows to the south, which, according to the description, apparently must be the room that Eyler Hardenberg occupied as Governor of the Castle, and which, through many years, was now to form a residence for the most distinguished state-prisoner of Frederick II.[1]

[1] Neither the records of the castle, nor those of the command-ant in Malmoe, extend back to the Danish period ; the archives of the Government, which correspond to those of the former commanders

During his stay in the Castle of Copenhagen, Bothwell composed a detailed memoir for the purpose of justifying to the King and the Danish Council his complaint of the restraint by which it was now forbidden him, on the part of the other princes and lords, to operate for the deliverance of the Scottish Queen ; and " in order that the King and his Council might better and more clearly know the malice and treasons of his accusers, he had, as concisely as it was possible for him, comprehensively and truthfully explained the causes of the disturbances and movements that had taken place, of which they themselves were alone the special instruments and sources from the year 1559 until this present day."[1] This account, which is written not without a certain ability, has very often been made use of in the foregoing narrative, though only with great caution, since in it Bothwell not merely clears himself of all share in Darnley's death, but even entirely passes over such plain facts as the surprise of the · Queen at Almond Bridge and her abduction to Dunbar. In concluding this account on the 5th of January 1568, in the Castle of Copenhagen,[2] Bothwell not only affirmed that he came with authority both from the Queen's friends and also from Mary her-

---

of Malmoe, also contain only few documents which go so far back, and although many documents from the Castle archives, during the Danish period, have found their way to those of the Council-house in Malmoe, yet these are equally destitute of any information with respect to Bothwell's sojourn there.

[1] Afin que le Roy de Dannemarck, et le Conseil de son Royaume puissent mieulx et plus clairement congnoistre les meschancetez et trahisons des mes accusateurs, cy-dessous nommez ; J'ay, le plus sommairement qu'il m'a esté possible, comprins et véritablement déclairé les causes des troubles et esmotions aduenues, desquelles eux seulz les principaulz autheurs et commencement, depuis l'an 1559 jusques aujourd'huy.

[2] A Copenhaguen, la veille des Roys, MDLXVIII.

self, who, notwithstanding her close confinement on
Lochleven, was said to have found an opportunity
of confirming in every particular what these had
admitted,[1] but also still assigned as the sole object
of his mission to Frederick II. that he should ask
the latter for assistance by counsel and deed.[2] But
when a few days afterwards he saw himself a
prisoner within the walls of Malmoe Castle he went
a step further. He now appended a smaller document in which he did not rest satisfied with repeat-
ing that he had come to beg help by land and sea,
but specially added that he was empowered to offer
the King as a recompence for this the islands of
Orkney and Shetland,[3] and that if only the King
and his council would themselves state how they
wished bonds to be drawn up with respect to the
surrender of these islands, the Earl became surety
that they would be so drawn up and sealed by the
Queen, by himself, and by the Scottish Privy
Council.[4] This document which Bothwell penned
on the 13th of January,[5] he gave along with the

---

[1] Mais pour plus grande secureté, je feiz tant, que j'en euz son advis, qui estoit, qu'elle trouvoit fort bon, tout ce que les Seigneurs m'avoy-ent conseillé, me pryant d'effec-tuer le tout, le plus diligentment qu'il seroit possible.

[2] Estimans pour vray que cecy pourroit induyre le dict Roy à me donner son bon conseil, secours, ayde et faveur, et pour l'obtenir plus facilement, je luy débuois présenter mon service, et tout ce qui estoit en ma puissance.

[3] Premièrement, que je debuois demander à Sa Majesté de Danne-marck, comme allié et confédéré de la Royne, ayde, faveur et assist-ance, tant de gens de guerre, que

de navires, pour la délivrer de la captivité où elle est. *Item*, Pour les fraiz, qui y pourroyent estre faictz, que je fisse offre à Sa dicte Majesté de rendre les Isles de Orquenaj et de Schetland libres et quittes, sans aulcun empeschement, à la couronne de Dannemarck et de Norvegue, comme ils avoyent cy-devant quelque temps esté.

[4] Et je prometz en bonne foy, que les dictes lettres seront scellées de la Royne, de moy et du Conseil du Royaume d'Escosse, et signées de chascun de nous de noz propres mains.

[5] De Malmoë, le xiii° de Jan-vier 1568.

preceding on the same day in Malmoe to the French
ambassador, Charles Dancay, who must have visited
him, and who has remarked that three days afterwards, on the 16th January 1568, he had the opportunity in Helsingborg of delivering them to Peter
Oxe and John Friis.[1]

Whether the offer of the islands of Orkney and
Shetland which Bothwell now proposed really was
the "intention and final will"[2] of the Scottish
Queen and council, or whether only a reminiscence
of the period when Bothwell attended the meetings
of the Scottish Privy Council caused him in Malmoe to seize this idea as the last means of safety,
he could yet reckon with tolerable certainty upon
such an offer meeting with ready attention.   The
step which Christian I. took when, instead of the
marriage portion with which his daughter should
have been dowered, he pledged Orkney and Shetland to Scotland, has not brought this king greater
praise in the history of Norway than he obtained
in that of Denmark for the way in which, in order
to be chosen Prince of Holstein, he also allowed
Sleswig to be united to a foreign country.   Under
Christian III. the Danish government had begun the
great series of attempts by which it was vainly
sought at a later period to win back the islands.[3]
To no purpose had Christian III. offered the Scots
to pay the sum of money which had been promised
as dowry by his grandfather.   French mediation
also induced him to abandon the idea he had for a
long time afterwards entertained of enforcing his

---

[1] Note R, Appendix.

[2] L'intention et finale volonté de

la dicte Royne, et de Messieurs de
son Conseil.

[3] Note S, Appendix.

claims upon the islands by a great naval armament.[1]   CHAP.
Frederick II. had likewise, from his accession to the   XI.
throne and until the northern seven years' war   1529-68.
wholly occupied his attention, in vain prosecuted
his father's negotiations with Scotland to get the
islands back again.   And what then is more reason-
able than to take for granted that the offer of Bothwell did not a little contribute to the lenity and
care with which the Scottish state prisoner was
through many years protected in Denmark?   How
could it be otherwise than that King Frederick and
his council would indeed listen to such an offer now
made by a man who was himself "Duke of Orkney,"
as the patent brought with him showed,—an offer
which was proposed in the Scottish Queen's name,
and which the constantly continued party-contests
in Scotland might well make more than a dream
before a period should elapse that was only removed
a little more than a generation from the day of the
battle of Summerdale—7th June 1529—when once
more the abandoned Norse population of the Orkneys
were victorious over the invading foreigners from
Scotland?   It is indeed only a mere guess whether
Bothwell from a distance exercised any influence
on the attempts made in favour of Frederick II. by
his successor in the feudal proprietorship of the
islands which at last led the Scottish government

---

[1] The French Minister, Charles
Dancay, writes in a memoir of 12th
April 1575, after having mentioned
his first embassy to Denmark :—
"Apres que j'eus satisfait à cette
charge, je retournai en France, où
je ne fut longtems, que Marie,
Reine Douairière d'Ecosse, mère de
la Reine d'Ecosse qui est à present
envoya devers Monseign. le Roi
Henri pour l'advertir que le Roi
Christiern de Dannemark dressait
une grande armée de mer, pour se
joindre avec celle de la Reine
Marie d'Angleterre, pour l'esper-
ance qu'il avait de recouvrer par
ce moyen les isles Orcades et autres
terres que les Ecossais tiennent."—
*Nya Handlingar rörande Skandi-
naviens Historia*, i. 46.

CHAP.
XI.

1567-71.

for a long time to imprison him during Bothwell's stay in Denmark,[1] but it is not without significance that, when in the year 1570 some war-ships appeared on the northern coasts of Scotland, rumour declared that it was the Earl of Bothwell who had come back from Denmark.[2] It is also of importance to remark that his opponents, even in the following year, continued to entertain the fear lest Mary should find opportunity to despatch from her prison in England the bonds promised by Bothwell,[3] and that Frederick II. wished to fit out ships and crews for Bothwell, so that he might restore to him the islands unjustly separated from the kingdom of Norway.[4]

The Scottish Government had, however, not failed to make repeated attempts to induce Frederick II. to surrender Bothwell. While Sir William Stuart, towards the close of 1567, was in Denmark as bearer of Murray's first request for the surrender of Bothwell, the Parliament met in Scotland which con-

[1] This was the Queen's half-brother, Lord Robert Stuart, whose " dangerous and treasonable practices with Denmark" are vaguely hinted at by David Balfour in his *Odal Rights and Feudal Wrongs*, p. 62.

[2] Les aultres disoient que c'estoit le comte de Boduel qui venoit de Danemarc avec quelques gens qu'il avoit ramassez.—Account of La Motte Fénélon to King Charles IX. and Catherine de Medici of 27th of March 1570; *Correspondance Diplomatique de la Motte Fénélon*, iii. 98.

[3] Lettres of favour from the Kynges moder to this king that the mordorer Bothwell be not delivered to be punished, with sum promes of kyndnes to hym thairfore of the yles of Orknay

and Schetland.—Letter of Thomas Buchanan to Cecil, dated Copenhagen the 19th January 1571, and given from copy in the State Paper Office in Ellis's *Later Years of James Hepburn*, p. 13.

[4] Ceulx cy avoient eu adviz que le roy de Dannemark estoit après à accomoder le comte de Boudouel de quelque nombre d'hommes et de vaysseaulx, pour faire une descente en Escose, et que le dict Boudouel luy promettoit de luy mettre entre les mains les Orcades, mais cella n'a pas continué dont ceulx cy n'ent sont plus en payne. —Account of La Motte Fénélon to King Charles IX. of 6th March 1571 ; *Correspondance de Bertrand de Salignac de la Motte Fénélon*, iv. 8.

firmed in every particular the regulations of the new CHAP.
government and demanded the complete overthrow XI.
of Catholicism. At the same time the fugitive Earl 1568.
and the rest of those supposed to be accomplices in
Darnley's murder that were still at large were
summoned to appear before the Parliament which,
on the 20th December, condemned the absent Bothwell to the forfeiture of nobility, honours, life, and
possessions.[1] When Sir William Stuart, in the beginning of 1568, returned from Denmark without
having effected his object, it was taken up by
Murray with increased zeal. Murray applied both
to Queen Elizabeth, who had always shown herself
an enemy to Bothwell, and also to Charles IX.,
desiring that they would support the demand of the
Scottish Government to the King of Denmark.
Elizabeth willingly complied with this request, and
wrote to Frederick II. from Westminster on the
21st March, and again from Greenwich on the 4th
May 1568. In these letters, while pledging her
royal word that Bothwell, if surrendered, should
have his cause tried anew in Scotland with the utmost
impartiality and equity, she specially insisted that
Darnley was her relative, and that it was a matter
which concerned every monarch, whose majesty
ought, according to a higher law and God's own will,
always to be sacred, and never violated without
punishment.[2] On the other hand, Murray was not
so fortunate in France, for, in spite of the very

[1] *Parliamentary Decisions; Acts
of the Parliaments of Scotland.*
Edinburgh, 1814-1844, fol. iii. 5.
Compare Anderson's *Collections*,
iv. 152.
[2] It is said in the second of
those letters from Elizabeth, both of

which are in the Danish Archives,
and that just named being first
printed by Bergenhammer (p.
324):—" Hoc facinus, privati in
principem, subditi in suum do-
minum, re exsecrabile, exemplo
intolerabile plane existit, cunctis

forcible representations of one of his agents, he did not succeed in leading Charles IX. or Catherine de Medici in the same direction. So far was Dancay from receiving instructions to support the proposal of the Scottish Government as had been desired,[1] that the French King, whom Bothwell had so urgently addressed from the Castle of Copenhagen, on the contrary charged his minister to put forth his efforts in opposing the Earl's surrender. In these circumstances it was deemed in Scotland most suitable to transfer the accomplishment of the matter to a Scotsman for whom there was reason to suppose Frederick II. had a personal regard, and such a person was believed to be found in Captain John Clark, or, as he was called in Denmark, Captain Johannes Clark. At the beginning of the Northern seven years' war this Scottish gentleman had repaired to Denmark with recommendations from both Mary and Elizabeth, and had received a command in the army.[2] In this capacity he had during the war done Frederick II. good service;[3]

quidem hominibus, præcipue vero regibus, quorum majestatem, ratio vult, et Deus ipse sacrosanctam esse jubet." This notion of the sanctity of majesty, however, Elizabeth did not continue to hold at a later period, when, in the year 1587, she addressed the letter concerning Mary Stuart's execution to Frederick II. (given from the original in the Danish Archives in *Nye dansk Magazin*, iv. 268-69), yea, it was really given up a couple of weeks afterwards, when a fishing-boat had conveyed the fugitive Queen across the Solway Firth to the coast of Cumberland. But when Elizabeth wrote her letter at Greenwich on the 4th May 1568, in which the

Scottish Queen still gets the name of her dearest sister (sororis nostræ charissimæ), Mary had just escaped from Lochleven, and was still at the head of an army of devoted adherents who were destined on the 13th May to suffer such a defeat at Langside.

[1] Memorandum of an anonymous agent sent by Murray to the King and Queen-Dowager of France.— Teulet, *Papiers d'Etat relatifs à l'Histoire de l'Écosse*, ii. 943.

[2] His commission as captain over 206 Scottish cavalry soldiers, dated Bordesholm, the 15th June 1564, is to be found in the Danish Privy Archives.

[3] By Resen, who describes him as "the distinguished Captain

and in the year 1567 was sent from the country to France, England, and Scotland to enlist more mercenary troops for the Danish king.[1] On this occasion he went first to France, but, as he afterwards explained, when relating the history of his mission, the impending outbreak of a second religious war having prevented him from obtaining a sufficient number of soldiers to enlist in that country, he had, on the contrary, in Scotland got what he sought, and had recently returned to Denmark with the hired troops. It was during his stay in Scotland that the plot against Bothwell was formed, and Clark did not hesitate on this occasion to join the insurrection ; an eye-witness, who has described the expedition of the Lords from Edinburgh on the night between the 15th and 16th June, expressly mentions Captain Clark and the soldiers, already enlisted by him,[2] as present among the troops that marched out to Carberry Hill to meet in hostile array Bothwell and his men from Dunbar. Subsequently, on the 17th of June, Clark, with equal

CHAP.
XI.

1567.

Johannes Clark, an erudite, well-trained, widely-experienced brave soldier who, at the beginning, was brought here from England," it is laid to his charge that in the year 1565, while he was ordered to lie at Varbjerg with his lieutenant, David Stuart, and the best part of the troops, he, of his own will, betook himself down to Daniel Rantzau at Halmstad, which the Swedes, during the latter's absence, unexpectedly besieged, and, after a bloody engagement, retook the castle. — *Kong Frederichs Den Andens Krönicke*, pp. 131, 261.

[1] He had undertaken to enlist "vier feindlein hackenschützen, jedes drittehalb hundert starck."

—Commission by Frederick II., dated Frederiksburg, 2d March 1567, in the Danish Privy Archives. The King, who here describes Clark as " den erbare vnd manhafften vnsern Obristen," on the day after, in a letter to Mary Stuart (*Calendar of State Papers, Foreign Series*, 1566-68, p. 184), recommended Clark to the favourable support of the Queen's party.

[2] And Captain Clark with sa many as he had luftit on his awin expense in deliberation to pass thairefter in Danmark to the nommer of fourscoir of men or thairby.—Letter of James Beaton, dated Edinburgh, 17th June 1567 ; Laing, *History of Scotland*, ii. 110.

CHAP.
XI.

1567.

zeal, also distinguished himself by capturing at
sea William Blacater, one of Bothwell's confidants, who was the first to be executed as
an accomplice of the Earl.[1] When Captain
Clark passed in autumn to Denmark with his re-
cruits, the new Scottish Government, to which he
had rendered such service, gave him a letter to
Frederick II. In this letter his share in the fight
against Bothwell was carefully concealed, and his long-
continued absence excused as a consequence of his
having had at first obstacles put in the way of his
recruiting. At the same time it was added that they
did not know better hands in which to confide the
task of representing to the Danish King the causes
of the insurrection of the Lords and of the Queen's
imprisonment, and of proposing an alliance between
the kingdoms to meet the imminent peril with which
the evangelical party seemed to be threatened by
the adherents of the Pope.[2] On his return to Denmark this zealous Presbyterian did not however rest
satisfied with merely communicating these represen-

[1] William Blacader capitane,
suspectit in lykwise for the said
slauchter, wes takin be Capitane
Johne Clerk, servand to the King
of Denmark, quha come heir to
raise men of weir, vpoun the sey,
quhen he wes fleand away.—*Diurnal of Remarkable Occurrents*, p.
115. Cappitaine Blarkatonna été
priz sur la mer par le Cappitaine
Clerque.—An account by a contemporary French soldier of the
events from the 7th to the 15th
June, 1567; Teulet, *Papiers d'État*,
ii. 168. Sir Nicholas Throckmorton, who describes Clark as
"Captain Clark, which hath so
long served in Denmark and served
at Newhaven," expressly speaks of
this achievement of his in his

letter to Queen Elizabeth, dated
Edinburgh, 18th July 1567.—
Robertson, *History of Scotland*, ii.
311.

[2] To the recommendatory letter
of Murray to Clark on his return,
written in the name of James VI.,
and dated Stirling Castle, 25th
August 1567, and which is preserved in the Danish Privy
Archives, there is joined a " Brevis
declaratio eorum, quæ Illustrissi-
mus Dominus vicerex et consiliarii
Regni Scotiæ Serenissimo et
potentissimo principi Frederico IIo.
Danorum etc. Regi, et sui Regni
consiliariis per nobilem virum
Joannem Clarck Scotum, ejus Mis
Capitaneum, significari voluerunt."

tations and proposals in the name of the Scottish
Government, but accompanied them with a memoir
from himself.[1] In this is set forth as an indubitable
fact, that, on the arrival of Alva in the Netherlands,
a conspiracy against the common cause of the evangelical party had been entered into by the Pope,
the chief Italian princes, the Emperor, the King of
Spain, and Dukes of Savoy and Bavaria. Clark
also affirmed that, during a late visit paid to the
Netherlands, he had had opportunities of convincing
himself that the first blow would be aimed at
Denmark by the conspirators;[2] that there was therefore a common ruin impending over the evangelical
party if every one sought to fight only by himself,
while the King, by placing himself at their head,
would be able to form an ecclesiastical alliance such
as the world had never seen from the days of our
Saviour.[3] The Danish King, in his reply to these
proposals which he addressed to the Scottish Government from Copenhagen, 1st October 1567, rather
coldly dismisses the idea of any such common league
against the Papists, convinced as he was that God
well knew how to protect His Church from unrighteous violence, and contents himself with
a renewed assurance of his own unalterable attachment to the Protestant cause.[4] On the other hand,

---

[1] Monita quædam privata dicti Capitanei Clarck.—The Danish Archives.

[2] Præterea postrema mea in Belgium profectione ego omnes fere incolas tantopere a Serenissimo Danorum Rege alienatos reperi, et tam aperte de impedimentis et incommodis, quæ in hujusce baltici maris angustiis, hoc bello perpessi sunt, conquerebantur, ut maxime metuam, ne Hispani initium istius

nefariæ conjurationis potius ab ejusdem Majestate quam a quovis alio faciant. Monita quædam privata dicti Capitanei Clarck.—Ibid.

[3] Futurus enim ille est caput et dux talis actionis, quæ omnium, quæ ab adventu Salvatoris Jesu Christi tentatæ sunt, erit maxime memorabilis.—Ibid.

[4] Etenim nos in professione doctrinæ cælestis, quæ nobis a Domino parente nostro tradita est, et quæ

CHAP.
XI.

1568.

he expresses his ready acceptance of the excuse made by the Scottish Government for Clark's prolonged absence, highly eulogises Clark's proved bravery and fidelity, and states that in his opinion his countrymen could not have found any more fitting advocate for the prosecution of Bothwell than the agent whom they had selected. Murray continued to press on the matter with all his accustomed energy. On the 16th July 1568, he wrote Frederick II. an urgent request that he would allow Captain Clark to make a short visit to Scotland in order to have a personal interview with him about a matter of the greatest importance,[1] and before the Danish King had an opportunity of complying with this request, Murray hastened to draw up on the 21st August an authorisation for Bothwell's execution in Denmark. At the same time he again wrote Frederick II., calling attention to the fact that, according to the judicial procedure of Scotland, the Act of Parliament of the 20th December condemning Bothwell had the most complete legal validity, and consequently it was certainly much to be preferred that Bothwell should be sent to suffer his punishment in Scotland. As, however, he could not doubt that so long as the North Sea swarmed with privateers, there was no possibility of his being conveyed across without such an armed naval force

Domini beneficio in ecclesiis et scholis Regnorum nostrorum viget, perpetuo perseveraturi sumus.—Letter of King Frederick II., dated 1st October 1567 ; Danish Privy Archives.

[1] Rem nobis gratissimam Tua Serenitas factura est, si, remisso ad breve tempus militari, quo est ille jamdiu obstrictus, sacramento, veniam largiri velit in Scotiam transmittendi et nobiscum, qui hoc a Serenitate Tua vehementer contendimus, colloquendi.—Letter of Murray in the name of James VI., as yet a minor, preserved in the Danish Privy Archives, dated Stirling Castle, 16th July 1568.

as could not be readily obtained,[1] he would restrict his demand to the surrender of Bothwell into the hands of Clark, so that he might cause the Earl's head to be taken off, and this at least transmitted for exhibition at the place where his crime had been committed.[2] To insure the consent of the Danish King, Murray, although Scotland's own troubles might seem to forbid such a step, with great friendliness gave permission to Axel Wiffert of Naes, another of Frederick's recruiting officers, to enlist two thousand new mercenaries for the military service of Denmark; and this gentleman accordingly believed himself also obliged, on the same day on which Murray wrote Frederick II., to write the King that he found the clamour of the Scots against Bothwell so great that he ventured most humbly to request him to comply with their desire.[3] On the following day another Scottish gentleman, who had also entered the King's military service, Gawin Elphinstone, left Edinburgh, carrying with him the sentence of Parliament against Bothwell, which, in the opinion of the ruling party in Scotland, abundantly supplied the proofs demanded last year by

[1] Verum quum per sævitiam bellorum, quibus vicina regna atque adeo universus fere Christianus orbis conflictatur, mare a piratis obsessum sit, satis tutum non videbatur, illum mari committere, sine valenti navium et strenuorum militum comitatu, ut in Scotiam sine periculo transportari posset.— Letter of Murray, drawn up in the name of James VI., dated Edinburgh, 21st August 1568, and first printed from the original copy in the Danish Archives by Bergenhammer, pp. 328-333.

[2] Quam ob causam igitur Sereni-tatem Tuam maxime rogamus, ut illum eidem Capitaneo ad extremum supplicium dedi curet, utque is abscissum a cervicibus parricidæ caput ad nos in Scotiam transmittat, quod pro more palo præfixum in loco, quo cædes perpetrata est, defigendum curemus. —Ibid.

[3] Do ist mein gants vnderthenigst vnd demuethiges bitt Euer Kon. Mat. wolle Innen solches gnedigst zulassen vnd vergunnen.—Letter of Axel Wiffert to Frederick II., geschreben zu Edinburg jn Schottlandt am 21 tag Augusti 1568.—Ib.

CHAP.
XI.   the Danish Government, and the letters of Murray
        and Wiffert, to Frederick II.[1] Still Murray gave
1568.   himself no rest. For when Axel Wiffert, having
discharged his commission, a few days later followed
Elphinstone to Denmark, Murray furnished him,
on the 26th of August, with a new letter to Frederick
II., in which he again represented that, if Bothwell
could not be safely brought over to Scotland, the
King must at least not suffer "this pirate, condemned alike by divine and human laws," to escape
also in Denmark his deserved punishment.[2]

When Captain John Clark presented himself in
October at Roskilde with the special authorisation
given by the Scottish Government, Frederick had
meanwhile received increased encouragement not to
comply with a desire so singular. On the supposition that the Scottish Government would not allow
the matter to rest, he had before Clark's arrival
applied to other princes, to whom he represented
how difficult and doubtful any complete satisfaction
of the Scottish Government seemed to him, on the
ground alike of his own jurisdiction and supremacy,
his near relationship to the Scottish Queen, care for
his royal reputation, and consideration of the disturbed and altogether insecure condition in which
things still stood in Scotland, and had concluded
with begging that "other Christian authorities"

[1] Vpoun the xxij day of the said moneth of August thair wes ane commissioun send be my lord regent with ane gentilman callit Gawin Elphingstoun to the King of Denmark.—*A Diurnal of Remark-able Occurrents*, p. 137.

[2] Ut divina humanaque sententia damnatus latro, aut tuto in Scotiam transportetur, aut meritas in Dania pœnas luat, suppliciumque de eo sumatur ab iis, quorum fidei, sen-tentiæ a senatu latæ exsecutio, a nobis mandata est. This letter from Murray, dated Edinburgh, 26th August 1568, and issued in name of James VI., was also first printed by Bergenhammer, pp. 325-328.

would assist him with their enlightened counsel.   CHAP.
The princes thus appealed to had, for the most part,   XI.
thrust the matter aside in a polite and almost ironical   1568.
manner, expressing themselves persuaded that the
Danish King and the Danish Council, with their
"highly-gifted understanding," would themselves be
quite able to know how to advise in such an affair.
In as far, however, as the princes consulted inciden-
tally touched upon the question itself, about which
the King of Denmark asked their opinion, only one
of them declared himself at all in favour of complying with the wish of the Scottish Government. This
was his brother-in-law, Elector Augustus of Saxony,
who alleged that such an " extradition" of criminals
had been established between himself and the Emperor and Crown of Bohemia, and he thought in this
case such a course much less doubtful for the King,
if, as was reported, the Earl of Bothwell had during
the Northern war been opposed to him, and had in
Scotland rather favoured the Swedish King.[1]   The
King's uncle, Adolphus Duke of Sleswig and Holstein, Julius Duke of Brunswick-Wolfenbüttel, and
Ulrich Duke of Mecklenburg, were on the contrary
of opinion that regard to his royal jurisdiction
demanded that the case should be tried within the
King's own dominions, before impartial judges, with
the assistance of advocates for both parties,—a view
which the King had last year maintained in his

[1] Vnd weil wir den auch aus
Euer Kon. Wirden hieuorigen an
vns ergangenen schriefften vor-
nehmmen, dass der Graff Euer Kon.
W. in werendem Schwedischen
Kriege fast zu wieder gewesen, vnd
nicht alleine Euer Kon. W. in der
bey Schottlandt gesuchten nach-
barlich hulffe vnd beistand gehin-
dert, dem Könige zu Schweden
aber alle fürderung erzeigt.—Letter
of Elector Augustus of Saxony,
dated Dresden, 1st September 1568,
in the Danish Privy Archives.

reply to the Scottish Government.[1]   The other of
the King's uncles, John the Elder, Duke of Sleswig
and Holstein, did indeed admonish Frederick II. to
avoid offending the Scots and English, who, during
the King's war with Sweden, had shown themselves
well-disposed neighbours, but confined himself only
to exhorting him to wait for time to bring him the
best counsels, and that, to meet the pressure of the
Scottish Government, he should suggest entering into
the negotiations for peace then opened up.   In this
way the King might perhaps in the future be able
to get an opportunity of effecting something for the
unhappy Scottish Queen, if not towards her complete
restoration to her throne, yet at least with the
result of obtaining for her " a respectable State allow-
ance,"[2] since what in this matter they ought above
all things to remember was their near relationship
to the Queen, originating in their common ancestor,
Christian I.[3]   To such opinions was wholly opposed
the demand which, solely on the ground of the sentence pronounced in Scotland, required, without
further delay, the execution of Bothwell in Denmark.   After receiving these the King needed no

[1] Letters of Adolphus Duke of
Sleswig and Holstein, Julius Duke
of Brunswick-Wolfenbüttel, and
Ulrich Duke of Mecklenburg,
dated Gottorp, 27th August 1568,
Wolfenbüttel, 11th September
1568, and Wismar, 19th September
1568, all in the Danish Privy
Archives.

[2] Wo E. Ko. W. vnter solcher
handlung was gutes zu erledigung
der Khonigin, vnd wo nicht zu der
vullenkhomenen Khoniglichen Re-
gierung, jedoch vff ein stadtlich
leibgedings gelegenheit werden vor
sich vnd durch andere befurdern

khonnen, Die wollen an Ihrem
muglichen vleisse, wie wir dann E.
Ko. W. darzu ohne das woll geneigt
wissen, nicht erwinden lassen.—
Letter of Duke John the Elder,
drawn up "in abwesen unserer
rethe," and dated "uff vnserm
hausse Hansburgh, 25th Aug. 1568,"
in Danish Archives.

[3] Fürnemblick aber die nahe
Bluttsverwandtniss der Khoniginn
von vnserm loblichen Grossvattern
Khonig Christian, Christmilter
gedechtniss, dem Ersten, herru-
rendt.—Letter of Duke John the
Elder, in Danish Archives.

longer to fear for his reputation among his princely
friends and relatives, because he quite agreed with
them not to allow Bothwell's head to fall by the
hand of a foreigner.

But though Clark's authorisation, as far as it
concerned the execution of Bothwell in Denmark,
could not be carried into effect, yet in other respects
it was not without fruit. It has already been stated,
that when Bothwell was separated from his followers
in Bergen, he was nevertheless allowed to take with
him a few of his servants; and in order to effect the
prosecution of two of those who were held in Scotland to have been accomplices in the murder of
Darnley, the powers vested in Clark were extended
so as also to embrace them.[1] What the Scottish
warrant aimed at may here be given in his own
words :—" I John Clark," so he wrote in Roskilde
the 30th October 1568, "commander of the Scottish
military detachments, acknowledge, by this my
handwriting, to have received from the noble and
distinguished gentleman, Master Peter Oxe of
Gisselfeld, High Steward of Denmark, two men,
namely, William Murray and the Frenchman, Paris,
who are impeached as traitors and murderers of
Henry King of Scots of blessed memory, which
before-mentioned men I engage to produce before
the judges of the Scottish realm, in order to have
their case examined and themselves punished if
they be guilty, and to have them set at liberty if

---

[1] Dantes, concedentes et commit-
tentes illi nostram plenam potestatem speciale mandatum, expressum
præceptum et onerationem, memo-
ratum Jacobum olim comitem de
Boithuile, Paridem Gallum et alios
de dicto crudeli murthiro delatos
et convictos de manibus talium,
cum quibus presentialiter detenti
sunt, recipiendi. — The Scottish
authorisation for Captain Clark in
the Danish Privy Archives.

they be acquitted, yet so as that they shall have
the space of one month allowed them to summon
witnesses or friends, if they have any, who can or
may purge them of the charge which rests upon
them; and in order that this acknowledgment shall
be firm and certain I have here willingly attested
it with my family seal."[1] As the William Murray
mentioned above was also one of the men that, by
the Act of the Scottish Parliament of 20th December
1567, were condemned as accomplices of Bothwell;[2]
so there can be no doubt that in the Frenchman
Paris we find here again the Nicolas Hubert called
Paris, through whom the enemies of Mary were now
enabled to produce those declarations, which, along
with her alleged letters and sonnets, became so
damaging to her while in life, and also since her
death in the controversy that has raged for nearly
three hundred years round her memory, and that
has found in them a chief ground for charging her
with a share in Darnley's murder. A main point of
contention in this controversy has been the question
as to when Paris can be assumed to have come into
the hands of the new government.[3] But while this
question is now solved by the document given

---

[1] Note T, Appendix.
[2] *The Acts of the Parliaments of Scotland*, iii. 5. Compare Anderson, *Collections*, iv. 152.
[3] " *When* Paris was first seized by the rebels, does not appear," is said by Whitaker; and this point, upon which he lays so much stress, recurs again in the question:—
" *When* then shall we seek for the time of seizing Paris? We cannot find it in the seizure of so many others of the murderers in the Shetland Isles."—*Mary Queen of Scots Vindicated*, i. 470, 471. The

older authors, Keith, Tytler, Guthrie, Gilbert Stuart, imagined, as Whitaker remarks, but incorrectly, Paris to have been detained in prison over two years, before his declarations were made; his stay in Denmark, on which light is here thrown, having been altogether unknown to him and them. Agnes Strickland (*Lives of the Queens of Scotland*, vi. 201) and Wiesener (*Marie Stuart et le Comte de Bothwell*, pp. 183, 483, 495) make him indeed first fall into the hands of Murray at a much later above, the dispute has taken another turn, for just as William Murray altogether disappears after having been surrendered to Clark, so it becomes a problem what was done with Paris during the long period which elapsed before his landing at Leith in the middle of June in the following year. That Paris did actually re-appear for the first time in Scotland at this date, the Earl of Murray is at all events himself a witness in the autumn of 1569. Elizabeth had then hastily sent the Earl a message requesting the postponement of the execution of Paris, and in the letter of excuse returned by him for not complying with her desire these words occur :—" As to that quhilk your Majestie writes of ane Paris, a Franchman, partaker with James sumetyme Earl Bothwel in the murther of the king my soverains fader, trew it is that the said Paris arrivit at Leyth about the middes of June last ; I at that time being in the north partes of this realme far distant."[1] The Earl continues :—" Upon it followed that at my returning, efter diligent and circumspect examination of him and lang tyme in that behaulf, upoun the xvi. day of August bypast he sufferit death by order of law, so that before the recept of your hieness letter be the space of 7 or

time, but the date is already assigned to January or February 1568.

[1] Letter of the Earl of Murray from Stirling, 5th September 1569; Laing, *History of Scotland*, ii. 269, 270. Hosack, who lays much weight upon the information given by me about the surrender of Paris by Denmark, and who has printed the document in reference to it that I had brought to light

and communicated to him (*Mary Stuart and her Accusers*, Preface, p. vii. and pp. 245, 246), remarks, not without ground in regard to the above-cited words of Murray about the arrival of Paris at Leith: —" We are not informed why he was sent away from Edinburgh, where it was usual to bring political offenders to trial, and where all the other murderers of Darnley, without exception, had been tried and executed."

8 days he wes execute. Otherwise your Majesties requisitioun towardis the deferring of his executioun by way of death suld have been maist willingly obeyed, bringand with it sa gude reason. But I trust his testimonie left sall be fund sa authentick as the credit thairof sall not seame doubtfull neyther to your hienes, neyther to thame quha be nature hes graitest cause to desire condigne punishment for the said murther." This belief that the testimony left behind by Paris must appear authentic to all was not, as is well known, afterwards realised. What still renders suspicious that famous testimony furnished by Paris on the 9th and 10th of August 1569, while imprisoned in Murray's castle at St. Andrews, is the fact that there had also been other declarations extorted from him. For the same day on which Paris was executed there followed him to death that Sir William Stuart who two years before had been sent to Denmark as herald to demand the surrender of Bothwell, and against whom it was now expressly stated as a chief accusation, that he had taken part in a plot against the life of the Regent, the Earl of Murray.[1]

What Bothwell felt on hearing of his latest

[1] The Scottish Diary already so often referred to, which in more recent times was first brought to light, reports :—" Upoun the fyft day of August 1569, Williame Stewart, sumtyme lyoun king of Armes, being suspectit for airt and pairt of the conspirand of my lord regentis slaughter, and brocht to the castell of Edinburgh out of Dunbartane, and als Pareis frencheman, being brocht out of Denmark, and ane of the slayaris of our souerane lordis fader, to the said castell of Edinburgh, wer baith tane owt of the said castell to Sanctandrois, thair to be puneist according to thair demerittis."—" Upoun the xvi. day of the said moneth, Williame Stewart being convictit for witcherie, wes brunt, and the said Pareis convictit for ane of the slayaris of the King, wes hangit in Sanctandrois."—*Diurnal of Remarkable Occurrents*, p. 146. May not one assume perhaps that William Stuart during his stay in Denmark had by Bothwell, through Paris, been won over to such a plot ?

associates being carried away to the wretched doom
threatened against himself is not indeed expressly
reported, but fortune quickly gave the Earl an
opportunity of manifesting his disposition towards
his countryman who had shown himself his bitterest
persecutor, first in Scotland and then in Denmark,
while engaged in the service of a foreign prince.
After executing his commission as plenipotentiary
for the Scottish Government, Clark remained in the
military service of the Danish King, and in the
winter of 1569, as a mark of favour, his Scottish
troops were granted quarters in Landskrone ;[1] but
in the autumn previous he drew down upon himself
the King's unconquerable displeasure, because at the
new siege of Varbjerg, which cost the lives of Daniel
Rantzau and Francis Brockenhuus, he took advantage of the King's embarrassment to demand a new
contract in lieu of the one formerly agreed upon
between them.   He obtained what he asked, but
it did not avail much ; the rupture was increased
by the way in which the commissariat was then
arranged, inasmuch as the commanders of the enlisted troops were obliged to furnish advances of
money now for one thing now for another, and there
might easily arise uncertainty regarding points that
were not sufficiently treated of in the orders given.
At the conclusion of the war, when the King disbanded the greater part of the foreign soldiers, and
Clark also came forward with his account, the King,

[1] In the Danish Archives there
is a Latin bond, signed in Copenhagen the 16th of March 1569 by
Clark along with his lieutenant
Andrew Armstrong, in which they
render thanks " pro quo quidem
regio erga nos favore," give a
pledge for proper behaviour towards the inhabitants and the
laws, and without any respect to
their pay that they shall again
leave the fortress free and in good
preservation.

now learning what the amount was — seventeen thousand dollars — made assertions so extravagant about his outlay, that Clark, in spite of daily renewed petitions and entreaties, soon saw that he would not be paid. Accordingly, before the peace was settled at Stettin, he requested his discharge in order to leave the kingdom, at the same time imprudently letting it be known, that even if he could not get his pay in Denmark he would nevertheless, in other places and by other ways, seek to obtain his due. Just at this period, when he had fallen into disfavour, and was seriously suspected of having an evil design against the King, Clark's own countrymen provided weapons to be used to his disadvantage. For it would appear that the party strife, which, on the death of Murray, again rent Scotland asunder, was at this time transplanted to her sons serving in Denmark, so that some of the Scottish captains in this country now denounced as traitors, not merely Captain Clark, but also Alexander Campbell, a relative of the Earl of Argyll, and Archibald Stuart, a relative of Lord Ochiltree.[1] Captain Aikman declared that Alexander Campbell had been in the Swedish camp, and afterwards had negotiated with some of Aikman's men about passing over to Sweden, and that he had

---

[1] " Alter e nobilissima comitum Argatheliæ, alter item ex æque nobili Domini de Uchiltre familia," it is said in the Earl of Lennox's letter to Frederick II. dated Edinburgh 18th July 1570, preserved in the Danish Archives. Of the accusers named in this letter Gawin Elphinstone was he who in the year 1568 had brought over to Clark the power of plenipotentiary. Captains Walter Aikman and Richard Skowgall are subsequently mentioned in the years 1571 and 1572 for their participation in the party war in Scotland, during which the last-named was mortally wounded at the siege of Merchiston.—A Diurnal of Remarkable Occurrents, pp. 137, 238, 259, 262, 263, 294, 296, 297.

in vain, through his lieutenant, Thomas Robinson, called upon Captain Clark to imprison Campbell, and subject him to punishment. Gawin Elphinstone at the same time produced a copy of a letter which he asserted had formerly been conveyed by Clark to the Earl of Murray, and which must have given no less offence to the Danish Government. This letter had been sent to Murray on the news reaching Denmark of the escape of Mary Stuart from the prison of Lochleven ; and in it Clark, after upbraiding the Earl of Murray for allowing the Queen an opportunity of flight—or, as the vehement Calvinist expresses it, that he had " given that unmerciful Jezebel too much liberty, and had not, according to the teaching of God's Word, given her to the dogs to devour her flesh and bones "—had presumed to add a peremptory order not to permit Axel Wiffert to bring more soldiers from Scotland to the service of Frederick II. before it was agreed on the Danish side to surrender the imprisoned Bothwell, whom " they retained as a great and precious relic." [1] Captain Clark was summoned to appear for judicial examination at Copenhagen, which took place on the 16th of June in presence of Peter Oxe, John

[1] The words are taken from the Danish translation of Clark's letter to the Earl of Murray, which is preserved in the Privy Archives, along with a duplicate of the Latin original. In the original letter the words about Mary are: " Doleo autem vestra clementia adeo incircumspecte tantam licentiam isti crudeli Jesabellæ permisisse, et non potius secundum præscriptum verbi Dei carnem ipsius et ossa canibus devoranda præbuisse ; " about Bothwell : " Reputant enim eum tanquam reliquias preciosas, existimantque vos eum multo redempturos precio." Notice of this remarkable letter was immediately communicated to Sir William Drury at Berwick, who, on 14th June 1568, was able from it to tell Cecil, that Clark's demand had as its object that the Danish ambassador " should be stayed, until they heard further from him."—*Calendar of State Papers, Foreign Series,* 1566-68, p. 500.

Friis, Björn Andersen of Steenholt—then the King's
commander of the Castle of Copenhagen—and many
others both noble and of common rank. As it is
expressly stated that the Scottish informers were
known at an earlier period while in their native
land as adherents of Bothwell,[1] so one is tempted
to believe that it was the Earl who had from
Malmoe first incited them to act, and had thus
become the special cause of the imprisonment of
these Scottish gentlemen. That Bothwell, at all
events, immediately joined their accusers, is evident
from a letter to Frederick II., in which Peter Oxe
and John Friis thus wrote to him on the 22d June
1570 from the Castle of Copenhagen :—" There
came here also to us yesterday some of the Scottish
captains, and gave us to understand that the Scottish
Earl, who is imprisoned in Malmoe, has had his own
messenger over here, and desires to tell us that he
would convict Captain Clark of three rascally actions,
the first of which he had done against your Royal
Majesty, the second against the King of France, and
the third against the King of Scotland ; and if he
did not succeed in making good this charge, then
would he be what he ought to be, all of which we
could not help making your Royal Majesty aware
of. And it seems to us best, with your Royal
Majesty's most gracious pleasure, that one or two of
the Scottish captains be despatched to Malmoe, a
step we do not wish to take before advising your

---

[1] Walter Aikman is characterised
in the Earl of Lennox's letter of
18th July 1570 as " notæ in Gallia
rapacitatis et domi omnium scelerum comitis Bothuellii admini-
ster." Thomas Buchanan also
speaks of " delatoribus illis quos,
esse audio nonnullos regiæ cædis
ministros," in his letter to
Frederick II., dated Copenhagen,
19th March 1571, preserved in
the Danish Privy Archives, and
first printed by Bergenhammer,
p. 355.

Majesty of it, in order that they may on the spot
make inquiry, by means of which the Earl, who is
a prisoner, might convict Captain Clark of such
treachery."[1] In his reply the King gave his consent,
and desired them "to send some of the Scottish
with some of the German captains to Malmoe to the
Earl, who is prisoner there, and learn by inquiry of him
what accusation he can bring against Captain Clark."[2]
Scottish letter-writers and journalists, in the year
1567, remarked the zeal with which the soldier despatched by Frederick II., as above-mentioned, threw
himself, during the rebellion against Mary and Bothwell, into the conflict with all the forces he could
command ; but this was, as yet, altogether unknown
to the Government in Denmark. After Bothwell's explanation of the events which attended or followed
the catastrophe on Carberry Hill, it became possible
to add to the two other heads of complaint against
Clark the following as a third :—" That he has
used the soldiers of your Royal Majesty in your
Majesty's employment against the Queen of Scotland." A court-martial to judge in the matter
met in the Castle of Copenhagen on the 28th of
June, consisting of the German captains, Jacob
Wins, Jürgen von Schweinitz, Jürgen von Minden,
and Edward Meffen ; and of the Scottish captains, Alexander Durham, Richard Skowgall, and

---

[1] Letter of Peter Oxe and John Friis to Frederick II., "Schreffuit paa E. M. s. Slott Kjöbnehaffn thennd 22 dag Junij aar 1570," in the Danish Archives. That in this letter, instead of "Alexander Cawall," we ought to read "Alexander Campbell," and instead of "Captain *Egmund*," "Captain Aikman," seems evident from a comparison with the letter of the Earl of Lennox of 18th July 1570. The letter is printed in Ryge, *Peder Oxes Liv og Levnets Beskrivelse ;* Copenhagen, 1765, 4to, pp. 248-9.

[2] The rough draft of the King's answer preserved in the Danish Privy Archives is dated from Frederiksburg, 24th June, A. 70.

Lorenzo Cagnioli, of whom the last named was undoubtedly a brother or relative of David Riccio's Italian countryman Timotheo Cagnioli, Mary's banker in Scotland.[1] The court desired at the outset, until Clark had made explanations about the heads of complaint, to restrict itself to the first, or his conduct towards Alexander Campbell. With respect to this the seven captains gave, as reported to the King, a verdict, in which they "have unanimously seen it right, and advise that we should take strict security from him so that he do not escape, since he has been so unfaithful to his oath and knew the traitor to your Majesty without wishing to punish him." In the letter in which Peter Oxe and John Friis reported to the King from Copenhagen the issue of the trial, they also add : "And we still keep him here in the castle until he provide proper security for himself, which we verily believe he will hardly be able to get."[2] And in vain did Clark then and afterwards emit a detailed statement in which he sought to excuse his conduct as complained of under the different heads that had at his desire been communicated to him in writing.[3] The King,

---

[1] The document drawn up in German, and attested by the seals of the seven captains, in which they declare their verdict, is "gegeben zu Coppenhagen Mitwochens post Johannis Baptistæ A°. 70" (*i.e.* the 28th of June 1570), and is contained in the Danish Privy Archives. An Alexander Durham, who was in the service of Darnley, had, after the death of the latter, got a pension from Mary, and on this account had been a long time imprisoned (Laing, *History of Scotland*, ii. 49 ; *Diurnal of Remarkable Occurrents*, p. 121),

just as Timotheo Cagnioli was. Lorenzo Cagnioli is found mentioned as being still present in Scotland in the year 1567 in a letter of Joseph Riccio to Joseph Lutyni.—Tytler, *History of Scotland*, vii. 367.

[2] Letter of Peter Oxe and John Friis to Frederick II., "Schriffuit. paa Eders May. S. slott Kiöbnehaffn thend 28 dag Junij, aar 1570," preserved in the Danish Archives. This letter is printed in Ryge, *Peder Oxes Liv og Levnets Beskrivelse*, pp. 249-250.

[3] Note U, Appendix.

who, at the close of the seven years' war, had come
to regard the Scottish soldiers with strange dislike,[1]
raised latterly so many difficulties every time the
Scottish Government or Elizabeth wished to be
surety for Clark, that this enemy of Bothwell had
to die a prisoner in Denmark.

The French minister in Denmark, Charles Dancay, remarks in one instance that he had learned
that the Earl of Murray, who, after permitting
Frederick II. to draw thousands of Scots from the
country to serve in his army, before his death expressed himself highly offended at the manner in
which nevertheless he had seen all his demands about
Bothwell disregarded by the King.[2] On the 23d of
January 1570, Murray, while riding through Linlithgow, the birthplace of Mary, was shot in open day
from the house of one of the adherents of the exiled
Queen, James Hamilton of Bothwellhaugh, and it
was not until after a bloody fight, and only by the
support of Elizabeth, that the Earl of Lennox was
enabled to succeed him as Regent. As the Scots,
who, at the close of the seven years' war had
returned about this period, not only disclosed the

[1] " Mais il a été d'une fort grand
rigueur enuers les Écossais," writes
Dancay on the 2d April 1571 from
Copenhagen to King Charles IX.,
adding: "Combien que durant
ceste guerre ilz ayent tres bien fait
leur debuoir, neantmoins le Roy de
Dannemarck leur est meruelleuse-
ment ennemy." The French minister mentions that the King has
forbidden the remainder of the
Scottish riflemen, who were then in
Jutland, but perishing with hunger, to come over to Zealand without a pass, that three hundred of
them had endeavoured to leave the
country for Germany, and that " les
aultres esperant trouer nauires au
port de Helseigneur pour retourner
en Écosse passèrent à pied quatre
grand lieues de mer sur la glace ou
plusieurs d'eux se perdirent." The
letter is contained in the collected
copy of Dancay's letters in the
Danish Archives.

[2] J'ay bien entendu que ledict
feu Regent d'Écosse se sentoit
grandement offensé de ce que le
Roy de Dannemarck ne s'y com-
portoit aultrement.—Letter of Dancay to Charles IX., dated 10th
June 1570, in Danish Archives.

secret of Clark's imprisonment in Denmark, but also
put in circulation a report of Bothwell's having been
set at liberty,[1] Lennox, as the father of the murdered Darnley, consequently felt himself still more
pressingly called on than his predecessor to apply
again to the Danish King. Elizabeth was not less
willing to support him than she was Murray on
former occasions by her representations to Frederick
II.,[2] and, in the name of both, an ambassador was
accordingly sent to Frederick upon whose prudence,
eloquence, and high character the utmost reliance
was placed. Resen is however altogether mistaken
when he speaks of this envoy as follows: " The
Queen of England and the King of Scotland have
caused the King to be visited by a distinguished
ambassador, the famous Mr. George Buchanan, the
former King's private tutor and historian of the
Scottish kingdom,"[3] and this mistake has not been
rectified by others, since of two authors who have
more recently treated of Bothwell's imprisonment,
the one, omitting the Christian name, confines himself to making the Scottish Government " send the
well-known historian, Buchanan, King James's tutor,

---

[1] " Verum quum nuper præter
omnium expectationem audiamus,
eum non modo carcere liberatum,
sed in bonorum etiam perniciem
incumbere, et accusatoribus etiam
pœnas, quas ipse meritus erat,
minari," it is said in a letter of the
Earl of Lennox to Frederick II.,
written in the name of James VI.,
and dated from Stirling 26 August
1570.—The Danish Archives.

[2] Compare letter of Elizabeth to
Frederick II., printed for the first
time by Laing in *History of Scotland*, ii. 304, 305. Clark received in

the letter this recommendation :
" Intelligat igitur Vestra Serenitas
Joannem Clerk præclare hic in
Anglia, nobis nostrisque diu esse
notum, nec vero quicquam unquam
in ejus moribus pravum aut fucat-
um vidisse quemquam, contraque
potius ea hominem virtue, fide,
integritate cognovimus atque audi-
vimus, ut nulla ratione nos dubi-
temus, quin ab audacissimo homine
Bodovellio comite, hæc innocenti
crimina afficta sint."

[3] Resen, *Kong Frederichs den
Andens Krønike*, p. 261.

as ambassador to Denmark,"[1] the other names the CHAP.
ambassador "The historian Thomas Buchanan."[2] XI.
The truth of the matter is in reality this, that Scot- 1570.
land's famous historian is undoubtedly named George
Buchanan, but it was by no means he who, in the
year 1570, arrived in Denmark as ambassador,[3] this
being, on the contrary, a relative of his, Thomas
Buchanan, a man also highly distinguished in
the times of the Scottish Reformation.[4] Thomas
Buchanan arrived in Copenhagen in the autumn of
1570, but in spite of repeated demands he firmly refused, during the absence of Frederick II., to deliver
the letters he had brought with him from his
Government and from Elizabeth.[5] At length, on
the return of the King, he was admitted to his presence in the castle of Copenhagen, where, on the
14th December 1570, in an elegant Latin oration,
he fully explained the object of his mission. In a
skilful representation he ascribed the murder of the
late Regent, the Earl of Murray, no less than that

[1] T. Becker, *Adelersborg*, in Danish *Folkekalender*. Tredie Aargang, p. 53.

[2] Worsaae, *Bothwell's Grav i Faareveile Kirke* (Illustreret Tidende), iii. 147.

[3] The confusion, which is also to be met with elsewhere (Wegener, *Om Anders Sörensen Vedel.* Kjöbenhavn, 1846, 4to, p. 199), has perhaps been occasioned by a portrait of George Buchanan which hung alongside of those of Copernicus and other celebrated men in the Museum of Uranienburg. But this portrait was only a gift from one of the Scottish ambassadors, who, at a later period, was sent to Denmark, Sir Peter Young, or "a Petro Junio," as the name is given by Gassendi in his *Tychonis Brahei*,

Equitis Dani, Astronomorum Coryphæi Vita. Parisiis, 1654, 4to, p. 123.

[4] Biographical notices of Thomas Buchanan, the nephew of the historian, are communicated by David Laing in *Proceedings of the Society of Antiquaries of Scotland*, vol. iv. (1861), part i. p. 85. He was provost of Kirkhill, and died on the 12th of April 1599.

[5] German account by the royal secretary, Elias Eysenberg, of his negotiations with Thomas Buchanan, dated "Kopenhagen, the 26th Nov. 1570," and the letter of Buchanan to the King about the same affair, Dat. Hafniæ, M. Vestræ, 30 Nouemb. die, anno 1570, both in the Danish Archives.

2 A

of Darnley, to one and the same party, and demanded
that Bothwell, as its chief head, should be punished
or surrendered.[1] By this oration, a written copy of
which he afterwards furnished by request, having
paved the way for his mission, the Scottish ambassador subsequently endeavoured by another narrative to make sure of the Danish Government's compliance. As at this period Mary had the hope, or
more correctly, was under the delusion, a delusion
fostered by the ruling party in Scotland and Elizabeth, of again being restored as Queen to her kingdom, Buchanan knew how, in accordance with this
delusion, sharply to distinguish between Mary, who
"altogether blindly" had been hurled into misery,
and her seducer, whose sudden attack upon the
Queen's person could now be no longer hidden from
the Danish Government. "That abominable traitor,"
Buchanan urged, "will never be able to deny that
he has openly practised violence towards Scotland's
exalted Queen, and by force dragged her away to the
strongest fortress intrusted to him in the kingdom,"
an inexpiable infamy in Buchanan's judgment, "as
that honourable and mighty princess, endowed with
God's greatest gifts, and for her distinguished vir-
tues and rare excellencies of mind and body to be
reckoned among the chiefest princes for centuries,

---

[1] Sed acie victi simile parricidium
commiserunt, comite Moraviæ, bonæ
memoriæ, Regis avunculo et regni
ejus regente interfecto, quale antea
commiserunt in Rege trucidando.
This "Oratio Mag^cl et Gen^al viri
Thomæ Buchanani Legati ac Ora-
toris Scotici coram ipsa Serenissa
Regia M^te amplissimisque regni
Senatoribus habita Hafniæ die 14
Decembris, die vero 16 hoc scripto
exhibita, anno 1570," is found, as
well as the answer by the Danish
Government of the 9th March 1571,
and the later Representation of the
19th March 1571, by Thomas
Buchanan, in the Privy Archives
of Denmark, from which these
documents have for the first time
been printed by Bergenhammer,
pp. 333-359.

would never have fallen, if those qualities had not CHAP.
XI. been debauched and destroyed by that monster in nature, through his spells, love-potions, enchant- 1571. ments, sorceries, and other evil arts."[1] Buchanan, before leaving Copenhagen, had by such means so far succeeded, that there was a greater disposition shown to meet the wishes of the Scottish Govern- ment than ever. For though again reminded of Bothwell's earlier acquittal by the Scots themselves, and though reiterated reference continued to be made to their former offer to let the charge against the Earl be prosecuted before the Courts in Den- mark, yet a prospect was now given them of being able to secure at last the required surrender of Both- well, provided that the Queen of England and the Scottish Government would, before the approaching Bartholomew's Day, or the 24th of August 1571, hand to the Danish King their sureties that Both- well's case would be tried and decided according to all the rules of justice and equity, that his surrender would never be urged to the injury of the King or his successors in the kingdom of Denmark and Nor- way, and finally that the Queen of England and the King of Scotland would, in future occurrences of the kind, bind themselves to reciprocity towards the Dano-Norwegian Government.[2] On the return of

---

[1] Scelus meo judicio inexpiable ; nam princeps illa illustrissima po- tentissimaque, summis Dei donis ornata, meritoque inter præcipuos multorum seculorum principes ob ipsius singulares virtutes rarissi- masque tum corporis tum animi dotes numeranda [numquam pec- casset], si hæ ab isto naturæ mon- stro, fascinationibus, filtris, incanta- tionibus ac veneficiis ceterisque malis artibus, corruptæ subversæ- que non essent.—Representation of Thomas Buchanan, "Dat. Hafniæ Majestatis Vestræ. 19 mensis Martii, anno Domini 1571."—The Danish Archives.

[2] De quo Regia ipsius Majestas ante diem Bartholomæi currentis anni certam declarationem exspec- tabit, ac re ipsa præstabit, ut expe- riantur Serenitates ipsorum eam

Thomas Buchanan to Scotland, Bothwell's fate thus
seemed settled. Again, however, the hand was
stretched out from a distance that had once already
saved him. Charles IX. had not only been made
aware by his minister in Denmark, Charles Dancay,
of the approaching surrender of Bothwell on St.
Bartholomew's Day,[1] but the French minister in
England, La Motte Fénélon, also reported to him
that the Regent, the Earl of Lennox, had stated
that the King of Denmark had at last fixed upon
this particular period for fulfilling his wish, and that
even Dancay in Denmark was said to agree to it.
" Therefore," wrote the French minister in England,
"the friends of Scotland's Queen humbly implore
your Majesty that you will never permit any such
thing, but as speedily as possible will prevent it,
since the return of Bothwell will entirely destroy
the good order which you have begun to establish in
that kingdom, and he himself will only be brought
completely to ruin the affairs and reputation of this
poor princess."[2]   " I am again," thus writes the
same minister some days later, " earnestly requested
to entreat your Majesty by all means to hinder the
return of the Earl of Bothwell; for it is admitted
that nothing in the world would become a greater

mutæ et auctæ conjunctionis, cum
ipsis et florentissimis Angliæ et
Scotiæ regnis, augendæ et dila-
tandæ cupidissimam esse.—Reply
of the Danish Government of 9th
March 1571, in Privy Archives.
    [1] Dancay's Report to the King
about Thomas Buchanan's mission,
dated "de Copenhaguen ce ij°
Auril 1571," in the Danish Archives.
    [2] Dont les amys de la Royne
d'Escose supplient très humblement
Vostre Majesté de ne vouloir per-

mettre telle chose, ains de la remé-
dier, le plus promptement que faire
se pourra, de tant que le retour du
dict Boudouel viendroit traverser
tout le bon ordre qu'avez com-
mancé de donner aulx choses du
dict royaulme, et luy mesmes seroit
conduict icy pour achever de ruyner
les affaires et la réputation de ceste
pauvre princesse.—Letter of 20th
June 1571; *Correspondance diplomatique de la Motte Fénélon*, iv.
147.

scandal to the reputation of this poor princess, or a greater confusion to her affairs, and to your own interests in this quarter."[1] Dancay received in Denmark new and decisive orders from his King to prevent Bothwell's surrender, and he knew how to enforce them.[2] The storm impending over Bothwell's head again passed away.

From the statements made above, and especially from the mode in which Bothwell assisted in effecting the ruin of Clark, it will be evident that the Earl was allowed no small liberty in Malmoe. An evidence of this liberty is found in a letter written in Copenhagen, 12th May 1569, and sent to Cecil by an Englishman, Peter Adrian, a native of the town of Rye, in Sussex, who was then serving as captain on board one of the Danish fleet. The writer explains that before Clark effected the surrender of Paris and William Murray, the last named, who was " once the Queen of Scotland's chamberlain,"[3] resided in Copenhagen in a merchant's house in which

[1] Je suys de rechef fort instantment sollicité de supplier Vostre Majesté d'empescher en toutes sortes le retour du Comte de Boudouel, car l'on estime que nul plus grand escandalle à la reputation de ceste pauvre princesse, ny nul plus grand destorbier à ses affaires et à ceulx de vostre service par deçà, ne se sçauroit venir de nulle aultre chose qu'on peult praticquer au monde.—Letter of 24th June 1571; *Correspondance diplomatique de la Motte Fénélon*, iv. 152.

[2] Letters of Dancay to King Charles IX., dated respectively Copenhagen, 15th July and 1st September 1571, and the corresponding letters of the same dates

to Catherine de Medici, in the Danish Archives. In the letter of Dancay to the King of 1st September 1571, he however allows himself this remark with respect to Mary's interest :—" Aussi tous ceux qui sont venuz en Danemarc pour poursuyvre ledict conte l'ont toujours excusée et rejecté toute la culpe sur ledict conte comme seul autheur et cause des calamitez advenues en Escose, tellement qu'il semble s'il estoit mort qu'la cause de ladicte Royne seroit d'autant plus facile et plus fauorisée d'un chascun."

[3] Letter of Peter Adrian to Cecil, dated Copenhagen, 16th May 1569. —*Calendar of State Papers, Foreign Series*, 1569-71, p. 70.

Adrian himself also resided, and where the latter, at the instigation of Clark, expressed so great an interest about the Earl of Bothwell, and pretended so much sympathy for his fate, that Murray was induced to write to the Earl in Malmoe regarding the friendly disposed Englishman he had met with, and that in consequence of this Bothwell himself wrote to the effect that Adrian should come along with him to Malmoe. Accordingly Adrian visited the Earl, and "remained with him four days, and lacked no cheer."[1] Bothwell, who all the time spoke with great freedom about his proceedings—freeing himself from any direct share in Darnley's murder, yet not denying that it was committed with his approval as well as with theirs who now made him so black, but who, should he once be at liberty, would be shown to be far blacker than he[2]—requested Adrian to repair to France with letters from him to Charles IX., Catherine de Medici, the Cardinal of Lorraine, a Scottish bishop (undoubtedly the Archbishop of Glasgow), and Monsieur de Martigues, adding that if he himself only succeeded by the help of France in getting out of Denmark, and had some French troops with him, he would land at Dumbarton and tread down all Mary's and his own enemies. According to the assertion of the writer, Bothwell was on the eve of penning the above-mentioned letters which Adrian had promised to Clark to transmit to Cecil, but the Earl had given up his intention of doing so, owing to tidings having come that a new breach had occurred between England and France—or more

---

[1] *Calendar of State Papers, Foreign Series*, p. 71.
[2] "That he murdered the King he denies, but denies not that it was with his consent.—*Ibid.* p. 72.

likely, as we venture to suppose, because in the
meanwhile it came to be suspected that he had to
do with an English spy.
To the conclusion, that for a length of time
Bothwell was not put in confinement for any audacious transaction, we are further led by taking into
account his relations during this period with Mary
Stuart. While the Queen, at the beginning of her
imprisonment in Lochleven, had in vain tried to write
to Bothwell before his arrival in Norway and Denmark,[1] she was able, a few hours after her eventful
escape on the 2d May 1568 from the mansion of
Lord George Seton at Niddrie, to intrust a message
to one of the Earl's friends, Alexander Hepburn of
Riccarton, who, in her name, was to endeavour to
take possession of Dunbar, and after that to carry
tidings from her to Bothwell in Denmark.[2] When,
after the loss of the battle of Langside and her
flight into England, Mary expressly declared
herself willing to be separated in a legal manner
from Bothwell,[3] and it became a main object with
the adherents of her cause, both in England and
Scotland, to bring about her marriage with Thomas
Howard, Duke of Norfolk, afterwards beheaded by

---

[1] She is said, while in Lochleven, according to the report of Sir Robert Melvil, that, when the latter, at one of his visits, talked with her in private, and had refused to undertake the care of a letter for Bothwell, to have thrown it into the fire.—Tytler, *History of Scotland*, vii. 135.

[2] Tytler, *History of Scotland*, vii. 175, 177.

[3] In an authorisation for the Bishop of Ross, Lord Herries, and the Prior of Kilwinning, dated from Mary's English prison at Bolton, 21st October 1568, she thus writes :—" Item, in cais ony thing beis proponit concerning the marriage of the erle Bothwell, and unlauchfulnes thairof, ze sall answer that we are content that the lawis be usit for separatioun thairof, sa far as the samin will permit. Item, anent the punisch-ment of the slauchter of my laitt husband, the executouris thairof to be punisht according to law and ressoun."—Labanoff, ii. 221.

Elizabeth, we find her friends carrying on negotiations about the matter with Bothwell in Malmoe. It is certain that Bothwell in the year 1569 there drew up an authorisation for Lord Robert Boyd, one of Mary's representatives at the Conference in England, in which he expressed himself willing to have his marriage with the Queen annulled.[1] It is likewise certain that the failure of Lord Boyd's mission, although he made his appearance in Scotland with the authority of both the Queen and the Earl, was entirely the result of the opposition of the Presbyterians, as Murray and a portion of the Scottish nobles whom the Regent had summoned to meet in a convent at Perth on the 25th July 1569, answered the Queen's proposal with the declaration that they would never agree to her separation from Bothwell.[2] Accordingly William Maitland, who had passed over to her side, could speak with biting scorn of the conduct of these same opponents, in formerly setting forth Mary's union to Bothwell as the ground of her deposition, and in now striving with no less zeal to maintain it.[3] Perhaps one of the reports which Buchanan sent home during his stay in Copenhagen, shows in the clearest manner that Bothwell's residence in Malmoe had hitherto been what one

[1] This authorisation from Bothwell was subsequently preserved by the descendants of Lord Boyd among the family papers, and is mentioned as still extant in the year 1746 (Chalmers, *Life of Mary Queen of Scots*, ii. 242). It is to be wished that one or other of the Scottish investigators may be able to bring it to light again.

[2] At the quhilk day it is said that it wes decreitit [be the] counsale, that ane honourable man should pas to the quene and counsale of Ingland with ane wreitting, declaring that my lord regent nor his counsale wald nather consent that the quenis grace of Scotland sould be separated fra the said erle Bothwile, nor zit that sho sould marie agane, nor wald ressaue hir auctoritie, realme nor honour.— *Diurnal of Remarkable Occurrents*, p. 145.

[3] Tytler, *History of Scotland*, vii. 235.

previously described as "an honourable imprisonment."[1] In a letter to William Cecil, Buchanan
called attention to the fact that, as he had got
reasons from men of high standing for supposing
that the Earl, when in Malmoe, had received letters
from Mary, so Bothwell also kept up a constant correspondence with the Queen when she was a prisoner
in England. So much was this the case, that there
was now occasion to keep a watchful eye upon a
certain Horsey, who had recently been sent off
"pairtlie be Bothwell and also be the cheifest of this
land," to investigate the course of affairs both in
England and Scotland, and that finally, likewise,
one of Bothwell's pages had two months before been
sent by him as a messenger to Mary, "which page is
a Danish borne, zit not easilie to be knowin by a Scott
be reasone he speketh perfyet Scottes."[2] Buchanan
therefore requested Cecil to take steps so that
these persons might not be able to reach Mary, but
might be seized and punished. It is also in perfect
agreement with this liberty allowed to Bothwell in
Malmoe, that Frederick II. not only assisted him
while there with money, but also took care that he
should be able to make his appearance in velvet and
silk clothes according to his rank.[3]

[1] Resen, *Kong Frederichs den Andens Krönike*, p. 229.

[2] Letter of Thomas Buchanan to Cecil, dated Copenhagen, 19th January 1571 ; Ellis, *Latter Years of James Hepburn*, p. 13.

[3] In the settlement of accounts by the king, "with our beloved Oluff Bagger, citizen in our market-town of Odense," it is said that the latter has "jointly supplied our beloved Bjoern Kaasz, our man, councillor, and officer in our Castle of Malmoe, according to his ex-cellency our High Steward's orders, English velvet and silk-stuff for lxxv dall. vj B, which we have conveyed for clothes to the Scottish Earl who is detained a prisoner in the same place." — From the draught of a settlement of accounts, dated "Hafnie, 2 Martii anno 69," in the Danish Archives. Sketches of Oluf Bagger, famous for his com-mercial activity and great building undertakings, are given by J.

CHAP.
XI.
1573.

It was in the year 1573 that there occurred for the first time a radical change in the treatment which Bothwell previously experienced in Denmark. The moving causes which led to it we have not been able to ascertain. It is possible that Buchanan, while seeking to place the early history of the Earl in a new light, may have prepared the way for the change by weakening his reputation with Frederick ;[1] but as for other causes, it is probable that unless the change was called forth by some alteration in Bothwell's personal affairs, we must seek for an explanation of it in the circumstances of other countries. Perhaps we may see in it one of the consequences of the French St. Bartholomew's night in the year 1572 ; that massacre in which five hundred Protestant nobles and ten thousand persons of lower rank were sacrificed, which destroyed in all Protestant countries the respect for the king who, from the windows of his own palace, made himself a spectator to the murder of his subjects, which called forth curses upon the name of the Guises, and everywhere lessened sympathy with the fortunes of Mary Stuart. Perhaps also the result of the party strife in Scotland may have decided the change. Although the Earl of Lennox had been surprised at Stirling on the 4th September 1571 by a party of the Queen's adherents, led by the Earl of Huntly and Lord Claude Hamilton, and shot by Captain Calder, yet the

Trützschler Hanck, *Kong Frederik II. og Oluf Bagger,* Odense 1837, by Vedel Simonsen, *Bidrag til Odense Byes ældre Historie.* Odense, 1842-44, iii. 72-143 ; and by C. T. Engelstoft, *Odense Byes Historie.* Odense, 1862, pp. 131, 147-152.

[1] " This ambassage was not without fruit, and put Bothwell out of all credit," writes Spottiswood, *History of the Church of Scotland,* p. 243.

enterprise came to nothing, and the third Regent, CHAP.
the Earl of Mar, having likewise died on the XL
28th October 1572, not without suspicion of being 1573.
poisoned, the Earl of Morton at length undertook
the government of Scotland in the name of James
VI., who was still in his minority. Supported by
Elizabeth, Morton succeeded in finally breaking the
power of the small party that still continued to
bear arms in the name of Mary, and at whose head
William Maitland and Kirkaldy of Grange sought
through many years to atone for the guilt of having
so largely contributed to the Queen's fall. Thomas
Buchanan, during his stay in Copenhagen, learned
that a main reason why Bothwell was not surrendered by Denmark was to be found in the attention with which the Danes followed party strife in
his country, but this strife was at last at an end,
after the Earl of Morton, supported by an English
detachment under Sir William Drury, was able on
the 25th April 1573 to begin the siege of Edinburgh Castle, and the brave garrison of which, or
the so-called " Castilians," were forced on the 20th
May following to surrender at discretion. Whether
in this or in other events the moving causes for the
severer treatment to which Bothwell was now subjected are to be sought for, the fact of the change
itself is at all events undoubted. " The King of
Denmark," so concludes Dancay, on the 28th June
1573, a letter from Copenhagen to Charles IX.,
" has hitherto treated the Earl of Bothwell very
well, but a few days ago he put him in a much
worse and closer prison."[1] Where this prison lay

[1] Le Roy de Dannemark auoit   tenu le Conte de Baudouel. Mais
jusques à present assez bien entre-   depuis peu de jours il l'a faict

Dancay in this letter does not state, but perhaps he may have disclosed its name in one of his letters of the year immediately following, which are now lost. It is at all events a countryman of his own, the celebrated French historian, James Augustus de Thou, who from his vast erudition for the first time gave publicity to the name of the prison in the far North where Bothwell is said to have ended his days. From his earliest youth De Thou had set before him as his life's work to continue Paolo Giovio's *Historiarum sui Temporis Libri* XLV. To the execution of this task he had directed all his studies, all his travels. After collecting materials for the 138 volumes of the work, he began in October 1593 to write it, and the 38th volume, in which he touches on Bothwell's history, was probably written a long time before the year 1603.[1] He names in this volume the old Dragsholm as the castle in Zealand to whose more rigorous prison Bothwell was transferred from Scania.[2] It was latterly called Adelsborg. This name first origin-

---

mettre en un fort mauluaise et estroite prison.—Letter of Dancay to Charles IX., dated Copenhagen, 28th June 1573, in the Danish Privy Archives.

[1] Düntzer, *Jacques August de Thous Leben, Schriften und Historische Kunst verglichen mit der der Alten*, Darmstadt, 1837, p. 56.

[2] In arctissima vincula Drachholmii trusus est.— Jac. Aug. Thuani, *Historiarum sui Temporis, Opera*, Offenbachi, 1609, fol. p. 804. It is remarkable that the authorities whence De Thou drew his information have also made him aware of the fact, that Bothwell after his flight from Scotland

had been "accusatus ab amicis cujusdam nobilis virginis Norvegicæ, quam ante plures annos pacto matrimonio violatam, alia superinducta deseruerat." Yet Mignet, Labanoff, and Teulet, who make Bothwell, so long as he lived, remain in Malmoe, have overlooked this passage in De Thou, which, by the fuller knowledge of the relations in the North it furnishes, forms a pendant to his sketch of the expedition against the inhabitants of Ditmarsh in the year 1559.—De Thou, *Bericht von den Vorfällen in Ditmarsen. Mit einem Vor-und Nachwort begleitet von E. C. Kruse*, in Kieler Blätter, Kiel, 1815-19, iv. 212-35, 407-26.

ated from the time when Dragsholm, after being CHAP.
escheated to the Crown, devolved to the family of $\underbrace{\qquad}_{}$
the famous Cort Adeler. Here, according to a con- 1573.
temporary Danish account,[1] the prison doors were
for the first time closed upon Bothwell on the 16th
of June 1573.

[1] " Anno 1573. Bleff den skot-
iske Greffue indseth paa Dragsholm," so states a note to " Der
xvi. Tag Junii " in one of Paul
Eber's Calendars which is now contained in the library of Karen
Brahe in Odense (*Calendarium
Historicum von dem ehrwürdigen
Herrn Paulo Ebero, von seinen
Sönen verdeutschet*, Witteberg, 4to,
p. 232). Only a part of the written
notes, which are added to this
copy of the *Eberskian Calendar*,
has formerly been printed from a
transcript of them which belonged
to Christen Testrup (in *Magazin
til den danske Adels Historie*.
Udgivet af det kongelige danske

Selskab for Fædrelandets Historie
og Sprog, Kjöbenhavn, 1824, i.
93-120), but they are now communicated from the original in a
more complete form under the
title of " Eiler Brockenhuus' Historiske Kalendaroptegnelser for
16de Aarhundrede, Udgivne af
Joh. Grundtvig, Kjöbenhavn, 1873."
The most of the notes were written
by Eiler Brockenhuus of Damsbo
and Nakkebölle, who died in the
year 1602, and who during his life
owned the Calendar, and this remark also holds good of the notes
about the state prisoners in Dragsholm.

CHAPTER XII.

THE changeful life whose early days were passed on " Bothwell Bank " beside the brown Clyde, or in Spynie Castle with the Bishop of Moray, was brought to as lonely and unnoticed a close behind the prison walls of Dragsholm. Here tradition still points out, in the part of the prison called Bothwell's cell, two iron bars in the wall to which the Earl's fetters are said to have been so fastened that he could move round with them.[1] An historical critic has, however, repeatedly shown of late how such traditions first arose at a period too recent for any one fully to believe the unauthenticated report. Yet it may be added that one in another country relates " that the King of Denmark caused cast him in a lothsome prisone, where none had access unto him, but onlie those who carried him such scurvie meat and drink as was allowed, which was given in at a little window."[2]

[1] *Prospekter af danske Herre-gaarde.* Udgivne af Fr. Richardt og T. Becker. Tredie Binds tredie og fjerde Hefte. Kjöbenhavn, 1847. It must only be a mistake which has led T. Becker elsewhere (in his sketch of Adelersborg in *Folke-kalender for Denmark.* Tredie Aargand, p. 53) incorrectly to state that Bothwell in Dragsholm "nevertheless got permission to go a hunting."

[2] *Historical Memoirs of the Reign of Mary Queen of Scots, and of a Portion of the Reign of King James the Sixth,* by Lord Herries, p. 96.

After Bothwell was incarcerated in Dragsholm CHAP. XII.
he soon ceased to be known to the world. But
seldom some brief intelligence about his latter days 1575.
found its way out, and, when not contradicted at the
time, passed into a wider circle. In the year 1575
the rumour got abroad that he was dead. Communications from Denmark in the spring brought to
·Scotland a story to this effect, and by the close of
the year a corresponding report was received in
France. In Scotland, however, it was not long
before this news was again contradicted, the Earl
of Morton having at midsummer written to Peter
Oxe forcibly reminding him of his still unfulfilled
promise regarding Bothwell, made to Thomas
Buchanan.[1] What is said to have given rise to the
foregoing incorrect intelligence is hinted at in a
passage in the journal of William Cecil. Among

[1] Letter of the Earl of Morton
to Peter Oxe, dated Edinburgh
26th June 1575, in the Danish
Archives. Morton's letter, which
he requested to be answered as
speedily as possible (" quam celer-
rime "), first arrived in Copenhagen
on the 29th of September, and on
the 24th of October, Peter Oxe
died at Fredericksburg. In the
account from Copenhagen, in which
Dancay, on the 24th November,
announces to King Charles IX.
that the kingdom of Denmark had
lost its famous High Steward,
these words subsequently occur:
" Le Comte de Baudouei écossais
est aussi décédé. Le Roi d'Escosse
aussi derechef a envoyé devers le
Roy de Dannemarck pour en faire
punition digne de ses faits"
(Nya Handlingar rörande Skandinaviens Historia, i. 116). The
connection in which the requisition
of the Scottish Government makes
its appearance with the early

report of Bothwell's death has led
Repp to explain the latter as an
expedient, by means of which the
Danish Government might possibly
get free of further importunity in
the matter. Repp remarks: " It
seems that the Danish authorities,
wearied by the Scottish and English demands on the one side, and
the French entreaties on the other,
willingly permitted the report to
be spread abroad that Bothwell
died in 1575 ; this would put an
end to a course of diplomacy which
was beginning to run unsmoothly."
The remark is contained in the
abstract of the above-mentioned
manuscript of Repp which, before
its transference to Captain Marryat,
was communicated by Ellis (The
Traveller's Handbook to Copenhagen and its Environs. By
Anglicanus. Copenhagen and London, 1853, p. 182 ; Latter Years
of James Hepburn Earl of Bothwell, p. 4).

CHAP.
XII.

1571-5.

other notes of this usually well-informed statesman we find under date 1575 the following passage :— " There came news out of Denmark, that the Erle Botheville and Captain Clarke were ded in prison ; howbeit, since that, the death of Captain Clarke is confirmed, and that Botheville is but great swollen, and not ded."[1] Such a mistake as that which is mentioned here by William Cecil would more easily receive credence from the fact that the walls behind which Bothwell had to spend the last years of his life were the same within which his countryman and foe was also confined. John Clark, after his condemnation in the Castle of Copenhagen, had been conveyed in the year 1571 to Dragsholm, and thus the two Scotsmen who had stood face to face with sword in hand on Carberry Hill were destined to end their days as prisoners under the same roof. In vain the Earl of Lennox, who, during the party conflict in Scotland, wished to avail himself of Clark's military skill, sought to ascribe to him a privileged character as Scottish ambassador in Denmark.[2] Equally in vain did the Earl of Morton in the year 1574 make a further attempt to procure his freedom, for though in order to get him released he then sent to Denmark a new guarantee for Clark,[3] yet Frederick declined to consider this guarantee sufficient.[4] In harmony with the notes of William

[1] Murdin, *State Papers relating to Affairs in the Reign of Queen Elizabeth*, p. 285.
[2] Letter of the Earl of Lennox to Frederick II. issued in name of James VI., and dated Leith, 5th July 1571, in the Danish Archives.
[3] Letter of Earl of Morton to Frederick II. issued in name of James VI., and dated Stirling 19th August 1574, in the Danish Archives.
[4] The King wished to have the guarantee so expressed, that, provided Clark or his adherents tried to procure compensation for themselves at the cost of the King's subjects, there should in it be expressly promised the King " facultas et potestas Scotorum naves et

Cecil, according to which Clark did not long survive this the last known mediation by Morton in his behalf, the Danish annotated Calendar represents Captain John Clark as dying in Dragsholm in 1575.[1] As for Bothwell there are not wanting statements which show that in his case death was some years longer in reaching its victim. Thus we have a Scottish statement according to which Bothwell's imprisonment lasted for ten years, a statement which is first met with in the History of Scotland by Bothwell's bitterest enemy George Buchanan, and subsequently repeated in the equally contemporary Memoirs of Sir James Melvil, as well as in the Church History of Archbishop Spottiswood, and in the Notes of Lord Herries. Resen's *History of Frederick II.* also alleges 1578 as the last year of Bothwell's long continued imprisonment,[2] and one of the notes in the Calendar of Eiler Brockenhuus of the sixteenth century states not only the year but the day of Bothwell's death, assigning the 14th of April 1578 as the date.[3]

It was in Dragsholm that Bothwell ended his days, and the foreign island that had furnished him

bona, in salo ac statione nostra, tantisper arrestandi detinendique, donec subditis de damnis istis illatis, ex æquo et bono, plane satisfiat."—The copy of the reply of Frederick ii.,dated Skanderborg, 18th October 1574, in the Danish Archives.

[1] Eiler Brockenhuus in his copy of *Eber's Kalendarium*, under date 8th August, has remarked, that " Anno 1571 bleff Johannes Capitanius indseth paa Dragsholm," and under that of 14th April, that " Anno 1575 döde Johannes Capitanius paa Dragsholm" (Eiler

Brockenhuus, *Historiske Kalenderantegnelser*, pp. 34, 36). By " Johannes Capitanius" is undoubtedly meant in these passages Captain John Clark ; for that the latter was lodged as a prisoner and died in Dragsholm is also remarked by Resen in his *Kong Frederichs den Andens Krönike*, S. 262.

[2] " Same time," writes Resen under date 1578, " died also the Scottish Earl Botuel in his protracted imprisonment in Dragsholm." — *Kong Frederichs den Andens Krönike*, p. 315.

[3] Note V, Appendix.

CHAP.
XII.

1573-8.

with a prison finally yielded him a grave. His mother, Agnes Sinclair, or "the Lady of Morham," had died in 1573, retaining to the last, as may be inferred from her will, a deep sympathy for her unhappy son ; his grand-uncle, the old Bishop of Moray, had also died in the same year at Spynie Castle, and events showed that in Bothwell's native land there was no living relative, either his sister or her son, that ever entertained a wish to recover his remains. The Earl's coffin was brought from Drags-holm to the nearest church at Faareveile.[1] This church, which stands away from the village, on the west bay of Isefjord, in a lonely and quiet spot, the haunt of gulls and sea-fowl, is said to be the last resting-place of him who once was the husband of Scotland's Queen.

As tradition still points out in Dragsholm the room which was Bothwell's prison, so among the coffins in Faareveile Church, it continues to indicate one without any inscription or adornment as the coffin of the famous Scotsman. To ascertain the truth of the legend, this coffin was opened on the 31st of May 1858, but without any positive mark being seen that the corpse found in it was really Bothwell's. It has been well remarked by one, that a manifest simplicity in the decoration of the coffin, and a great economy in the silk material of the grave clothes, "might make it readily thought to be the grave of a distinguished state-prisoner, on whose interment no more expense was bestowed than was absolutely necessary."[2] But this remark

---

[1] Eiler Brockenhuus, *Historiske Kalenderantegnelser*, p. 42; Resen, *Kong Frederichs den Andens Historie*, p. 315.

[2] Worsaae, *Bothwell's grav i Faareveile Kirke.* Illustreret Tidende, iii. 148.

is weakened by the obvious reflection that a whole CHAP.
series of state-prisoners have, during the period XII.
between the Reformation and the establishment 1582.
of the sovereign power in Denmark, been im-
mured in the adjoining Dragsholm. It has indeed
been said "that the head" of the corpse in .question
"had an unmistakable Scottish cast,"[1] but this
evidence loses its force, as it can be affirmed that
Bothwell was not the only Scotsman that was
buried in Faareveile Church.[2]

In regard to the mental condition of Bothwell
when he ended his life, only one report at all precise has come down to us. It is to the effect
that the Earl had lost his reason before he died.
This report was first communicated by George
Buchanan in his History of Scotland, which was
published in 1582, only a few years after Bothwell's death. As Buchanan in his History refers this

---

[1] This is adduced as the opinion
of the deceased anatomist Professor Ibsen, by Worsaae in his
Bothwell's grav i Faareveile Kirke.
Illustreret Tidende, iii. 148. The
English tourist, Captain Marryat,
likewise declares :—"I defy any
impartial Englishman to gaze on
this body without at once declaring it to be that of an ugly Scotch-
man" (*A Residence in Jutland,
the Danish Isles, and Copenhagen,*
i. 418). How much of the "ugliness" alleged here ought to be
ascribed to the fact of the body
having passed three hundred years
in the grave, it is certainly not so
easy to determine.

[2] The note of Eiler Brockenhuus
in his *Eberske Kalendarium* at
14th April, is to the effect under
the same date :—"Anno 1575,
döde Johannes Capitanius paa
Dragshollm och bleff begraffuen i

Faareueil Kircke ved Dragshollm.
Anno 1578, döde den Skotske
Greffue paa Drasholm. Bleff och
begraffuen i samme Kircke." The
cause why the fact has so long
been overlooked that both Clark
and Bothwell found their graves in
Faareveile Church, originates from
the incorrect mode in which the
note just cited was formerly given,
particularly in *Magazin til den
danske Adels Historie,* i. 115.
For there, as in the copy after
which it is printed, it reads not
"Johannes   Chapitanius," but
"Johannes Capelaen," and this
error in turn led to these words in
the note adduced being translated,
"The Chaplain of Drachsholm,"
by Repp (Ellis, *Traveller's Handbook to Copenhagen and its Environs,* p. 183 ; *Latter Years of
James Hepburn Earl of Bothwell,*
p. 4).

CHAP.
XII.

1578-87.

event to the year 1578, so he also expressly states, in connection with it, that the Earl died insane.[1] The same report is repeated by a whole series of contemporary writers : by a Catholic author, who, in 1587, immediately after the death of Mary, wrote a book about her execution ; by Sir James Melvil in his Memoirs ; by Archbishop John Spottiswood in his History of the Scottish Church ; by De Thou in his story of Bothwell's imprisonment in Dragsholm ; and lastly, in the Memoirs of Lord Herries,[2] so that we would not expect in this matter to meet with any contradiction. But just as almost every point

[1] Ac fere post decennium, ad sordes aliasque miserias accedente amentia, vita turpiter acta dignum habuit exitum.—Buchanan, *Rerum Scoticarum Historia*, p. 224. As one of the sources whence Buchanan may have drawn his knowledge of Bothwell's condition at his death, we may venture to instance the Scotsman William Lummisden. The latter, during the Northern Seven Years' War, served under Captain John Clark, and seems, after his leader's imprisonment, to have had personal entrance to Dragsholm. A letter to Frederick preserved in the Danish Archives, written by Morton in name of James VI., and dated Edinburgh, 8th October 1576, recommends Lummisden, who had done his imprisoned master so many services ("honesta illius in patronum suum difficillimis etiam temporibus officia"), and by the death of Clark, saw himself deprived of recompense for his perpetual journeys between the kingdoms ("totiesque inter duo regna repetitæ expeditionis fructum"), to obtain now the pay from the King which was still owing him for his share in the Seven Years' War. That the Scottish historian

knew Lummisden personally, and received explanations from him about other Danish circumstances, is proved by a letter from Buchanan, dated Stirling, 6th September 1576, which he then sent with Lummisden to Tycho Brahe (Georgii Buchanani, *Opera Omnia*, tom. ii., *Epistolæ*, p. 14).

[2] Qui in Dania captus amens obiit. *Narratio supplicii et mortis Mariæ Stuartæ, Reginæ Scotiæ, Dotalis Franciæ, decollatæ in Anglia decimo octavo Februarii*, 1587, *Stylo novo, in Castello Fodringhaye;* Jebb ii. 116. Kept in a strait prison, wherein he became mad and dyed miserably.—The *Memoirs of Sir James Melvil*, p. 85. He was put in a vile and loathsome prison, and falling in a frensie, made an ignominious and desperate end.—Spottiswood, *History of the Church of Scotland*, p. 213. Desperate of liberty he turned mad.—*Spottiswood*, l. c. p. 243. Accedente ad sordes aliasque miserias amentia.—Thuani, *Historiarum sui temporis Opera*, p. 804. Being overgrown with hair and filth, he went mad and died.—*Historical Memoirs* by Lord Herries, p. 96.

in Bothwell's career has become a subject of con- CHAP.
tention, so also has this about the state in which he XII.
died. In a defence of Mary Stuart published anony- 1588.
mously, but written by a Catholic, Robert Turner,
in 1588, and intended to counteract the unfavourable impression of the Queen's memory produced in
Germany by Buchanan's History, he is accused of
having purposely penned falsehood, when he states
that Bothwell died insane. Turner relates that
Frederick II., as Mary's near relative, more than
once during Bothwell's residence in Denmark, is
said to have endeavoured to find out the truth from
him about the Queen's complicity in the murder of
Darnley, and, when the Earl lay at the point of
death, to have adjured him by that higher tribunal
before which he was shortly to stand, freely to
testify regarding her innocence or guilt. In a style
of highly-coloured romance, Turner proceeds to tell
how Bothwell is reported then with a loud voice to
have acquitted Mary of all share in Darnley's
murder, ascribing the whole guilt to Murray and
Morton, and to have confirmed all this in a written
confession left behind him. And if, then, Turner
concludes, Bothwell has given forth such a declaration before he ended his life, he cannot have been
mad when he lay on his deathbed, and the alle-
gation to this effect is only a new invention of
Buchanan for the purpose of depriving the testimony left by Bothwell of any significance.[1]

The conclusion, however, is not so satisfactory as
this Catholic writer wishes to represent it. At best
it would only prove what is desired, if Bothwell

[1] Note W, Appendix.

never had been at the point of death before he
ended his days in Dragsholm. But it is clear that
during the lengthened imprisonment of the Earl in
Denmark, it might very well at an earlier occasion
have been assumed that he was dying, although he
afterwards recovered. And that the declaration or
"Testament" of Bothwell, to which Turner above
alludes, supposing that such a document ever existed,
must in fact be referred to the time when the Earl
still remained—but did not die—in Malmoe, is unmistakably evident from the way in which this
alleged declaration is spoken of by Mary herself. In
a letter from her of 1st June 1576, written in her
prison at Sheffield to her faithful ambassador in
France, the Archbishop of Glasgow, these words
occur:—" Notice has been given me that the Earl
of Bothwell is dead, and that before his departure,
he made an ample confession of all his faults, and
denounced himself as the originator and guilty
agent of the murder of the late King, my husband,
of which he most expressly acquits me, testifying
by his soul's salvation to my innocence ; if this is so,
then such a testimony will be of much importance
to me against the false aspersions of my enemies,
and I pray you therefore in every possible way to
investigate the truth hereof." Subsequently in the
letter the Queen gives the names of the Danes
before whom Bothwell was said to have made this
declaration, and among such are adduced the then
Bishop of Scania and several members of the Scanian
nobility.[1] The contemporary French or English

---

[1] Ceulx qui assistérent à la dicte
déclaration, depuis par eulx signée
et sellée, en forme de testament,
sont *Otto Braw du chasteau*
d'Elcembro, Paris Braw du
chasteau de Vascut, mons. Gullun-
starne de chasteau de Fulkenster,
l'évesque de Skonen, et quatre bail-

abstracts of the declaration which have come down to us,[1] equally refer this testimony, if it ever was made, not less decisively to one or other of the first years of Bothwell's imprisonment in Scania. These abstracts of Bothwell's so-called "Testament," in which he entirely acquits the Queen of all share in Darnley's death, but accuses as parties to it, besides himself, Murray, Morton, and others, agree so far with the abstracts procured by some one for the Queen, in that they name as the Danish witnesses before whom the dying Earl was said to have made his Declaration only such as were all inhabitants of Scania, and besides expressly indicate Malmoe as the place where the Earl was then in his last moments. As witnesses are adduced, although under the distortion of names usual with foreigners,[2] besides the Bishop of Scania and the four magistrates of Malmoe, Björn Kaas, lord of Malmoe Castle, Otto Brahe, lord of Helsingborg, Henry Brahe of Vidsköfle, and Morgens Gyldenstjerne of Fultofte. Of these Henry Brahe died 19th February 1587, and Björn Kaas 26th March 1581, but Otto Brahe,

lifz de la ville.—Letter of Mary to the Archbishop of Glasgow, dated from Sheffield, 1st June 1576, in Labanoff, iv. 330.

[1] Note X, Appendix.

[2] As a fitting pendant to these distortions of names it may be mentioned that Bothwell's seizure by Eric Rosenkrands is spoken of as accomplished "a magnifico viro, Erico *Rofisincrans,* S. T. subdito, Beronensis civitatis præfecto."— Murray's letter of 30th September 1567 in the Danish Archives. Nor is this distortion of Danish names greater than that to which the names of Scotsmen are subjected in contemporary copies of

Danish Records. Thus one finds in these "*Her van Sitoudt*" (Lord Seton), "*Her van Levensle*" (Lord Livingston), *Her van Lindsen* (Lord Lindsay), *Juncker Charnickill* (the laird of Carmichael), *Juncker Kaudenscraus* (the laird of Coldingknowes). These examples, amongst many more, are selected by P. A. Munch, and given in a paper in *Norske Samlinger*, udgivne af et historiske Samfund i Christiania. Christiania, 1852-1860, i. 490. The distortion of the Danish names in these foreign abstracts would therefore be by no means sufficient to deprive them of credit.

father of Tycho Brahe, had already deceased 9th March 1571, and the old Morgens Gyldenstjerne, who carried the principal Danish banner in the expedition of Christian II. against the Swedes in 1520, and afterwards in the years 1531-32 defended Akershus against his former king, had died 8th October 1569. The Declaration whence these abstracts are said to be derived could therefore have only been made in one of the very earliest years of Bothwell's imprisonment in Denmark, or during the period between January 1568 and October 1569.

This Declaration, or so-called " Testament" of Bothwell, which he is alleged when dying to have made in Malmoe, from which an excerpt reached the eye of Mary, and which, as one of her adherents also reports, was sent by Frederick II. to different princes of Christendom, and notably to Elizabeth,[1] has never in any form been discovered. In vain did Mary seek by writing to the Archbishop of Glasgow on the occasion already mentioned, to obtain the original document or an attested copy of it from Denmark. In her letter to him she had added these words: " If de Monceaux, who has formerly conducted negotiations in that country, would make a journey thither to institute more exact inquiries regarding it and bring back attestations, I would very willingly employ him for the purpose, and let him have money for his journey." In James Beaton's letter from Paris the reply is given: " We

---

[1] Lesquels propos ayant esté fidellement recueillis de la bouche de Bodvel, et raportez au Roy de Dannemarck, furent depuis envoyez à plusieurs princes chrétiens, nommement à la Royne Elisabeth.— Adam Blackwood, *Martyre de la Royne d'Escosse* (Edinbourg, 1587), from a reprint in Jebb, *De vita et rebus gestis Mariæ Scotorum Reginæ*, ii. 227.

received the news of the Earl of Bothwell's death a CHAP.
good space ago, since which time the Queen-mother XII.
here (as Mons. Lansac acquaints me) has written to 1577.
the King, her son's ambassador in Denmark, to
transmit hither a copy of the Testament in form ;
but this hath not hitherto been done. I would
think it very proper to send over into these parts
Mons. de Monceaux, and I know also he would willingly enough undertake the journey ; however, your
Majesty cannot but see that I am in no capacity to
afford him money necessary for such a journey."[1]
In a subsequent letter of 4th January 1577 the
Archbishop mentions how this pecuniary embarrassment had prevented the accomplishment of the
intended journey,[2] while Mary, about the same
time in another letter from Sheffield, wrote the
Archbishop on the 6th January 1577, that she also
gave up the idea of any such special mission as
might procure the " Testament" in question from
Denmark.[3] Perhaps in the meantime she was
informed that it was not Malmoe but Dragsholm
which had since 1573 become Bothwell's prison, and
perhaps this information taught her to judge otherwise about the worth of the whole report. Yet the

---

[1] Letter of James Beaton, Archbishop of Glasgow, to Mary of 30th
July 1576.—Keith, Appendix, p.
142.
[2] Monceaux n'a voulu entre-
prendre le voiage sans avoir argent,
contant. Les 500 livres qu'il a
receu par votre liberalité avoient
esté dependus a ce qu'il, avant
qu'ils etoient receus.—Letter of
the Archbishop of Glasgow to
Mary, written from Paris, 4th
January 1577; Ibid., Appendix,
p. 142.

[3] J'ay eu avis que le roi de
Dannemarcque a envoyé à cette
reine (Elisabeth) le testament du
feu comte de Bothwel, et qu'elle
l'a supprimé secrètement, le plus
qu'il luy a été possible. Il me
semble, que la voyage de Monceaux n'est plus necessaire pour ce
regard, puisque la Reine mère y a
envoyé, comme vous me mandez.—
Letter of Mary to the Archbishop
of Glasgow, from Sheffield, 6th
January 1577 ; Labanoff, iv. 340.

CHAP.
XII.
1838.

belief of "Bothwell's Testament" has continued to be cherished by many down to our own day; for so late as the year 1838 Lord Palmerston was induced to order the British minister at Copenhagen, Sir Henry Wynn, to institute researches regarding its existence; and although the latter gave with good reason little prospect that any such Declaration was to be found in Denmark, this only tended to produce the impression that something of the kind lay hid in one of the English Archives.[1] Even in the most recent times it is only very few of the writers who have endeavoured to throw light upon Mary's history that omit to base their representations on this supposed Declaration which Bothwell was alleged to have made during his detention in Malmoe.[2] They specially refer to the fact that a so-called "Testament" of Bothwell at the time when Frederick II. was still alive had actually been produced as criminal evidence in a celebrated trial in Scotland. When the country had experienced the rule of its four Regents, who rose to this dignity on the deposition of Mary, the young King James VI., after a lengthened minority, put himself at the head of the kingdom, and one of the first steps of

[1] Three years after the giving of this order by Lord Palmerston Lord Stanhope writes in an article in *The Quarterly Review* (vol. lxvii. p. 342): "Although this suggestion came from a quarter opposed to Lord Palmerston in politics, it was received by his Lordship with the utmost courtesy and readiness, and he wrote accordingly to Copenhagen: but the answer of Sir Henry Wynn gave little hope that a paper of that remote period could be now recovered. Perhaps, however, the document sent to Queen Elizabeth, whether original or copy, may yet lurk in some of the recesses of our own State Paper Office."

[2] Wiesener has indeed found himself forced to assume that the extracts from "the Testament" have received "interpolations," but nevertheless expresses himself as decidedly as any one, that "la déclaration première emanait d'une source étrangère et indépendante, la chancellerie danoise." — *Marie Stuart et le Comte de Bothwell*, p. 508.

his reign was to cause his mother's bitterest enemy, CHAP.
the Earl of Morton, the last of the Regents, to be XII.
himself prosecuted as an accomplice in Darnley's 1581.
murder. The judicial records of this affair have,
with the exception of the sentence of death, been
purposely destroyed, or through mischance gone
amissing, but only two days after Morton's execution, on the 2d June 1581, Sir John Forster, Elizabeth's commander of the middle Border regions,
stated in a letter of 4th June 1581 to her Secretary,
Sir Francis Walsingham, the five articles which had
in Scotland been produced against Morton in connection with the murder of Darnley, and among
them he expressly alleges that "the fyrst is lorde
Bothwell's Testament." [1] Meanwhile there is every
ground to assume that what is here meant is only
one of the unproved abstracts of the "Testament"
with which we are sufficiently familiar.[2] On the
other hand, the idea does not seem after all inad-

[1] The original letter of Sir John
Forster, which is dated "at my
howse nighe Alnewicke, the 4th of
June 1581," is still preserved in
the British Museum, in the Har-
leian Library, Num. 6999, Art. 97,
and has been printed by Chalmers
in his *Life of Mary Queen of Scots,*
ii. 97-98. In it, with respect to
Morton, it is said :—" And, there
was XXII. articles put against him,
but there was none that hurt him
except the murder of the king,
which was layde unto him by IV
or V sondrye witnesses. The fyrst
is the *lorde Bothwell's testament,*
o. s. v." The remark, added in
the preface to the copy of *Les
Affaires du Conte de Boduel,* published by the Bannatyne Club,
still holds good :—" Among the
MSS. presented to the library of
the College of Edinburgh by Drum-

mond of Hawthornden in 1626,
was one entitled *The Earl of Bothwell's Confession,* dated at Malmoe
Castle ; but this document, with
some other papers, has been un-
fortunately missing since sometime in the last century." [This
document has recently been recovered, and, through the kindness
of the *Senatus Academicus,* is allowed to be printed in the Appendix, Note Y.—*Translator.*]
[2] Sir John Forster concludes his
letter thus :—" *Postscript :* The
man, that brought me this newes,
came from Edenburghe, on Frydaye
last, at two of the clock, and then
the said Earl of Mortone was
standinge on the scaffold ; and yt is
thought, that the accusations that
were laid against him were verie
slender, and that he dyed very
stowtlye."—*Chalmers,* ii. 98.

missible that we meet here with only another of the forged documents of which the deadly conflict between Catholicism and Protestantism has been so especially fruitful in the British Isles.[1] Mary and her friends have always asserted that those lost letters and sonnets, which were said to establish the Queen's share in Darnley's death, had been forged or falsified by the Presbyterians; it is just as conceivable that conversely one or other among the Catholics first fabricated the abstracts, gradually copied and circulated, of an imaginary confession, in which the exiled Bothwell, in the far North, was alleged to have decided the whole controversy, and made any further investigation superfluous. We certainly cannot say—with Malcolm Laing—that those abstracts name purely fictitious persons in Denmark, for we have shown above what Danish noblemen may be intended by the bungled names, and it must be admitted that those abstracts could have come only from a source which was no stranger either to the earlier history of Bothwell, or to the conditions under which he lived in Scania, in regard to which it is specially to be noticed that the magistrates in Malmoe, in accordance with a previously fixed provision of Christian II., are correctly stated as four in number.[2] Neither will we lay too much weight upon the fact that the abstracts plainly enough proceed on the false supposition that Bothwell, after putting forth his confession in Malmoe, also died in the same place, it being quite possible

[1] Note Z, Appendix.

[2] Ordinances of Christian Second, Cap. 4, Kolderup-Rosenvinge, *Samling af gamle danske Love.* Kjöbenhavn, 1821-1840, 4to, iv. 76. Cronholm, *Skånes politiska Historia,* i. 314.

that this might only be founded upon an error of
the transcribers. Still less would we build any
objection upon the circumstance that, as Thomas
Buchanan maintained during his stay in Denmark,
Bothwell had by magic and love-potions been
able to fascinate the Queen, so, according to those
abstracts, the Earl in his confession has acknowledged the same thing about himself.[1] For in those
times of witches and trials for witchcraft, it was not
merely believed about others that they were able to
bewitch, but people had everywhere, and especially
in superstitious Scotland, the same belief regarding
themselves, although the crime which legislation ·
stamped as witchcraft could not in reality be committed should the person be conscious of the criminal
intentions with which the imagination was operated
upon for the purpose, and it is therefore possible
that Bothwell, who was held by his contemporaries
to be well versed in the black art,[2] might have con-

[1] Poursuit après, comme par enchantement, auquel, dès sa jeunesse à Paris et ailleurs, il s'éstoit beaucoup addoné il avoit tiré la Royne à l'aymer.—The abstract in Keith's *History of Church and State in Scotland*, Appendix, p. 144. Lykewise he sayd that all the frendship which he had of the Queene, he gatt always by witchcraft, and the in-ventions belanginge thereunto, specially by the use of sweete water.—The abstract in Teulet, *Lettres*, p. 244.

[2] Comme il en sçait bien le mes-tier, n'ayant faict plus grande pro-fession, du temps qu'il estoit aux escolles, que de lire et estudier en la négromancie et magic deffendue. --Account of La Motte-Fénélon to King Charles IX., dated from London, 29th November 1568 ;

Correspondance diplomatique de la Motte-Fénélon, i. 20. That Mary had not emancipated herself from the belief of the age in magic Knox shows when, relating the famous conversation she had with him after his return to Scotland, he states how she also declared "that it was said to hir that all which he did was by necromancye," and when he subsequently tells, how in the year 1563 she said to him that she could not endure Lord Ruthven, "for I know him to use enchantment" (*History of the Reformation in Scotland*, ii. 278, 373). When Knox in his sixtieth year succeeded in getting married to Margaret Stuart, a daughter of Andrew Stuart Lord Ochiltree, in her fifteenth year, this new mar-riage, which both from the bride's high rank and youthful age seemed

founded effect and cause. But there still remains
one consideration with which any belief in the confession which the Earl is alleged to have made does
not admit of being reconciled.

When on 19th June 1566 Mary gave birth
to James VI. in Edinburgh Castle, and Darnley
came to visit her and see the child, the Queen is
reported to have said in allusion to the common
talk that Darnley's conduct had occasioned :—" My
Lord, God hes given you and me a sone, begotten
by none but you."[1] At these words the King
blushing bent down and kissed the child, and the
Queen taking it in her arms, and uncovering its
face, added :—" And I am desyrous that all heer,
both ladies and others, bear witnes ; for he is so
much your owen son, that I fear it be the worse for
him heerafter."[2] During a long reign first in Scotland and subsequently also in England, these words
showed themselves to be truly prophetic, Darnley's
indecision and want of self-dependence reappearing
in James VI. side by side with a love of knowledge
and an aptitude for learning which seemed an inheritance from his mother. Only once did he succeed in a way that amazed his friends in overcoming
this peculiarity of his nature. After lengthened negotiations a marriage was at last fixed between Scotland's young King and " Lady Anne of Denmark."[3]

not very natural, gave the Catholics so much the more occasion to
ascribe to the Reformer magic art :
—" Quacumque iter faceret, secuin
aliquot mulieres circumducebat,
quibus ad explendam libidinem
uteretur, donec magicis artibus
allectam filiam comitis Ochiltriæ
pro uxore habuit. Erat enim
magus, ut in multis per totam

vitam apparuit " (*Davidis Came-
rarii de Scotorum fortitudine doc-
trina et pietate, ac de ortu et pro-
gressu hæresis in Regnis Scotiæ et
Angliæ Libri quatuor.* Parisiis,
1631, 4to, p. 277).
[1] *Historical Memoirs* by Lord
Herries, p. 79.
[2] *Ibid.*
[3] According to a " conversation

Instead of the connection which had been intended between Mary and Frederick II., a union was to take place between their children. The bride was upon the journey to Scotland, accompanied by a fleet of eleven war-ships, which bore the Admiral of the kingdom, Peter Munk of Estvadgaard. She had set sail from Copenhagen on the 5th September 1589, when a continuous storm of tempestuous weather forced the fleet to run to Norway. The same boisterous weather also long prevailed on the coasts of Scotland. One of Mary's maids of honour whom she loved best, Jane Kennedy, who had the previous year bound the handkerchief over the eyes of the Queen, when at Fotheringay Castle she laid her head on the fatal block, and who after returning home to Scotland had married a brother of James and Robert Melvil, Sir Andrew Melvil of Garvock, perished on this occasion, because in spite of the storm she persisted in crossing the river Forth to Edinburgh, whither the wish of the King had called her to be lady of honour to his expected bride. On both sides of the North Sea it was agreed that witchcraft had conjured forth the extraordinary weather; the Scottish witches confessed this on their part, and in Denmark their coadjutors were burnt, having been accused by Peter Munk of attempting " to bewitch and destroy the King's fleet."[1] But James VI. on this occasion cared for

CHAP.
XII.

1589.

between the Queen of Scotland and me, Mr. Somer, on our journey from Sheffield Castle to Wingfield Castle the 2d September 1584," Mary Stuart then told the just named Englishman, a son-in-law of Sir Ralph Sadler, that such a union was broached, " but as the

crown of Denmark went by election, her son was not sure of any influence longer than the reigning king lived, and therefore he had no great inclination in that direction." —*The State Papers and Letters of Sir Ralph Sadler*, ii. 389-90.
[1] The words are quoted from a

CHAP.
XII.

1589.

neither witchcraft nor storm; "like as Leander of yore hastened to Hero" he would himself over the tumultuous billows seek out his bride. After a perilous voyage James VI., on the 3d of November 1589, landed with five Scottish ships on the island of Flaekker in Norway, and, after an address in French by his Scottish chaplain, David Lindsay, was married on the 23d of the same month to the Princess, who as yet did not understand the Scottish tongue. Meanwhile the stormy autumn was followed by an early winter for whose severity contemporaries did not know language strong enough, and accordingly the King received an invitation from his mother-in-law, Queen-dowager Sophie, and from Christian IV., who was still in his minority, to pass the winter on Zealand. In sledges sent from Denmark the newly wedded pair journeyed thither through Baahouse across the frozen-over Gotha-Elf and the Swedish Landflig, which at that time alone separated Norway and Denmark, through Varbjerg, Halmstadt, and Helsingborg.

By nothing did the son of Mary during the quarter of a year he remained in Zealand attract greater notice from his contemporaries than by the

letter-patent, dated from Colding-house 22d July 1590, and given in *Danske Magazin*, Tredie Række, i. 52. Sir James Melvil (*Memoirs*, p. 180) remarks, after having related how his sister-in-law was drowned: —"This the Scottish witches confessed to His Majesty was procured by them;" and likewise with respect to the storm that continued to prevent the Princess Anne's arrival:—"Which storm of wind was alleged to be raised by the witches of Denmark, as by sundery of them was acknowledged, when they were for that cause burnt." About one of these unhappy Danish witches, Anne Coldings, more precise mention is made in the sentence passed upon her by Christian IV. and the Senate 5th August 1590, given in Kolderup-Rosenvinge *Udvalg af Gamle danske Domme*, Kjöbenhavn, 1842-48, 4to, pp. 226-9. Compare also Garde, *Dansk-norske Sömagts Historie*, 1535-1700, Kjöbenhavn, 1861, p. 108.

desire for information which led him to listen to every means of enlightenment, and by the love of knowledge which made him ask questions everywhere. The foreign legal proceedings and the whole system of foreign jurisprudence received so much attention from him that some have been disposed to attribute to this circumstance the close agreement which the statutes of his reign latterly have with the Danish ordinances.[1] In like manner the university to which, in memory of his interest in it, he gave the silver goblet that was lost during the British siege of Copenhagen in this century, saw him each day for three hours in succession a listener to its lectures.[2] Outside the university and beyond Copenhagen this desire for knowledge also led him to give attention to one man of science after another, and to one train of ideas after another. From Uranienburg, where he was the guest of Tycho Brahe, and from Kronborg, whence he wrote letters home,[3] his eye glancing across the Sound could rest on the towers of Malmoe Castle, beneath which the Earl that had been his father's murderer so long lay

CHAP.
XIL
1590.

---

[1] Barrington's *Observations on the more Ancient Statutes from Magna Charta to the Twenty-first of James I.* The fourth edition, London, 1725, 4to, p. 553. Barrington remarks that "it is remarkable also that three of the statutes of this reign for the punishment of criminals agree exactly with the Danish ordinances on the same head."

[2] Slange, *Geschichte Christian des Vierten, mit Anmerkungen von J. H. Schlegel.* Kopenhagen und Leipzig, 1757-71, 4to, i. 112.

[3] David Irving, *History of Scottish Poetry.* Edited by John Ait-

ken Carlyle, Edinburgh, 1861, p. 492. One of his letters, which is dated "from the Castell of Croneburg, quhaire we are drinking and dryuing our on the auld manner," alludes probably to the wedding feast at Kronborg, 19th April 1590, on occasion of the marriage of Duke Henry Julius of Brunswick-Wolfenbüttel with Elisabeth, another of the sisters of Christian iv. In Elsinore James also went to see the Scotsman, Thomas Kingo, grandfather of the bishop and poet Thomas Kingo.—N. M. Petersen, *Bidrag til den Danske Literaturs Historie.* Kjöbenhavn, 1853-61, iii. 634.

2 C

imprisoned. At Roskilde, where he visited not only the cathedral, but also old Niels Hemmingsen, he stood on the same firth on whose shore a few miles off the peaceful grave covered the remains of him who had been his mother's lover. Was it possible that in spite of his thirst for information, which was so manifest everywhere, he could forget the Earl of Bothwell alone? While yet a child he had been greatly moved when the abstract of Bothwell's "Testament" came under his notice [1]—could he restrain every inquiry about it now when he himself stood where the Earl had lived? United to the King of Denmark's daughter, surrounded by the *élite* of the kingdom, no information which he could wish would be withheld from him. Followed home by Danish war-ships, filled by countrymen of his consort, he could still behold in Holyrood, when he and she were crowned on the 17th May 1590, a complete representation of Denmark's nobility, including, among others, Eric Kaas of Vaargard, Steen Brahe of Knudstrup, George Brahe of Gunde-

---

[1] This is stated by James Beaton, Archbishop of Glasgow, on the 4th January 1577, to Mary in a letter printed by Keith, *History of Church and State in Scotland*, ii. 142, 143. The little James VI. was one day sitting and writing in Stirling Castle, where Sir William Murray of Tullibardine was present in the same apartment and reading the copy of Bothwell's Testament (la copie du dit testament) to another nobleman. The young king suddenly rose from the table at which he sat, and asked to see what it was Sir William held in his hands, which, after several refusals, he obtained. After having read it through word for word he silently returned it and sat down again to write. But the whole of the remainder of the day he was unusually gay, and when he was asked the occasion he replied, "Tullibardine, have I not good reason, after seeing so frequent and so many accusations and calumnies printed against Her Majesty the Queen, my mother, I have to-day seen so manifest an attestation of her innocency?" Archbishop Beaton, who wished to gladden his mother, then a prisoner in England, with this trait of her son, adds that the circumstance had been told him by a nobleman who himself heard it from Murray of Tullibardine.

strup,... Hannibal Gyldenstjerne of Restrup, all sons
of the men before whom at one time the Earl of
Bothwell in Malmoe was said to have written the
" Testament " in question.[1]   All these now stood
where Mary had formerly set the ducal crown on
his head, face to face with his sister's son, Francis
Earl of Bothwell, Scotland's new High Admiral,
and a member of the Government which had been
installed during the royal progress, side by side
with his countess, Margaret Bothwell, a daughter
of David, Earl of Angus, and now one of the ladies
that held the Queen's train at the coronation.
That in these circumstances James VI., who " better
than any one " knew his mother's history,[2] never
then nor afterward sought to bring to light any
such attestation of her innocence as that alleged,
never caused it to be communicated to any of the
historians whose works he followed with such
interest, either De Thou, Archbishop Spottiswood,
or Camden, is therefore the strongest proof against
its authenticity.

While the winter sojourn of James VI. in Denmark demolishes all belief in any such confession as

---

[1] Contemporary account of the
marriage of Princess Anne, sister
of Christian IV., with King James
the Sixth of Scotland, communicated by P. A. Munch in *Norske
Samlinger*, udgivne af et historisk
Samfund i Christiania, i. 450-512.
The above-mentioned nobleman
we find here, pp. 490-491, given in
the list of the accompanying
Danish gentlemen who were present at the coronation in Scotland.

[2] When the two first volumes of
De Thou's History were published
in Paris, Isaac Casaubon, whom

James VI. had invited to stay with
him, wrote thus to the author :—
" Rex ipse, quo nemo est hodie
callentior istarum rerum, singula
recenset, atque ad exactissimam
veritatis trutinam exigit, missurus
statim ad te, ut veram narrationem
tuæ historiæ inseras, falsam et
calumniarum   plenam   rejicias."
The letter, which Casaubon dated
from London, 27th March 1611,
is printed in the introduction to
the English edition of De Thou's
History (*Jac. Aug. Thuani, Hist.
sui temporis.* Londini, 1733, fol. i.
44).

the abstracts mentioned above are alleged to have had for their foundation, on the other hand it serves to confirm the account given of Bothwell's insanity. Among the Scotsmen in the retinue of the King who had wintered in Zealand, and whom it is impossible to fancy indifferent as to Bothwell's latest destiny, was Chancellor John Maitland, the younger brother by twenty years of Scotland's famous Secretary, William Maitland, so often named in this inquiry; and among the authors in Scotland that first wrote after their countrymen's return home was Sir James Melvil. In the Memoirs of the latter, in which he speaks of the rigorous imprisonment under which Bothwell "became mad, and died miserably," he also states that, during the whole time the Danish gentlemen who were present at the coronation of the King and Queen remained in Scotland and were entertained in many ways,[1] he was ordered "to bear them company."[2] With the testimony of foreign authorities,

---

[1] Thus, in reference to the 20th May 1590, the remark is made by Robert Chambers (*Domestic Annals of Scotland, from the Reformation to the Revolution.* Edinburgh and London. 1858, i. 200): "This evening, being a Sunday, the Danish nobles and gentlemen, who had conveyed the Queen to Scotland, received a formal entertainment from the magistrates of Edinburgh. A handsome alcoved room, which still exists, in the house of the master of the mint, in the Cowgate, was appropriated for the purpose." Sunday was in these old times the day which was commonly chosen for merry-makings and feasts, of which examples are adduced by Joseph Robertson in his Preface to *Inuentaires de la Royne Descosse,* p. lxxix.

[2] His Majesty at his landing was pleased to send to me to bear them company, which I did until their parting, to his Majesty's great contentment.—*The Memoirs of Sir James Melvil,* p. 182. With respect to the Danish embassy of the year 1585—consisting of Manderup Parsbjerg of Haxholm, Henry Belov of Spötterup, and Dr. Nicholas Theophilus—which was sent to Scotland with the first proposal about the marriage, Melvil remarks (*Memoirs,* p. 162) in like manner: "So soon as the Danish ambassadours arrived by ship in this country, His Majesty ordered me to entertain them, and bear them company." That Melvil had access to good Danish authorities is further evident from the fact that he was also ordered in the years 1593 and 1594 to receive and look after two

there finally agree the saddest annals of the human
ra'ce, the annals of those in whom disease has at last
devoured the very soul. Upon only too many
pages of these one may read what great terror and
anguish of mind, incessant excitement, or bitterly
disappointed expectations, can awaken.[1] What
passed in Bothwell's mind during his long imprisonment, in the lonesome moments in which the scenes
of former times again flitted across the mind, and
the unseen Judge spoke, no pen has been able to
transmit to us. But no statement was needed to
unfold what he must have suffered when at last he
saw the men who had followed him to Denmark
sent back in misery as new victims for the old
offence, and when the only thought that daily
pressed upon him was that the next morning might
see him also given up to an ignominious and
horrible death ; or with what feelings, during many
dark hours, he must have contrasted these anxious
years with the proud expectations that had lured
him to a career so different. Few men have more
heedlessly than he striven to attain the highest
pinnacle of honour and power, and few men have
more speedily than he been hurled down from the
giddy height.

other embassies which at these
periods were sent to Scotland by
those having charge of the Government during the minority of
Christian IV. (*The Memoirs of Sir
James Melvil*, pp. 203-204). The
one of these embassies consisted of
Steen Bilde of Bildesholm, and Professor Niels Krag, who were to procure Queen Anne the possessions
movable or immovable that by her
marriage had, on the Scottish side,
been expressly assured her ; the
other consisted of Steen Bilde

and Christian Barnekov of Birk-
holm, who were to be present at
the solemn baptism of Prince
Henry, the eldest son of James VI.
and Queen Anne. After the last-
mentioned embassy returned to
Denmark, Sir James Melvil was
still in the year 1595 in correspondence with Christian Barnekov.—
De la Gardiska Archivet. Lund.,
1831-43, v. 113-116.
[1] Prichard, *On Sindssygdom-
mene.* Oversat af H. Selmer. Kjöbenhavn, 1842, pp. 217-235.

APPENDIX.

Note A, p. 56. The passport given to Anne Throndssön by Queen Mary :—

"Noveritis nos recepisse ac per præsentes recipere in fidem tutelamque nostram Annam Trundtze, filiam Christophori Trundtze qui regi Danorum præfectus maris fuerat, omniaque ejus bona mobilia et immobilia, eique liberam fecimus ac dedimus potestatem habitandi et commorandi in nostro regno atque inde discendendi ac redeundi quovis ei e re sua visum erit." O. Nielsen on Passport issued by Mary Stuart for Anne Rostung the Scottish wife, in *Danske Samlinger*, 1st Bind. Kjöbenhavn, 1865-66, pp. 397-398. The passport, which is given from a manuscript in the Royal Archives of Denmark, concludes thus :—" Datum sub sigillo nostro ac manu nostra subscriptum decima septima die Februari anno regni nostri tricesimo primo. Maria R." The editor correctly assumed that there is here a misprint for "vicesimo primo." L. Daae (*Historisk Tidskrift*, udgivet af den norske historiske Forening. Andet Bind. Christiania, 1872, p. 344) thinks that Anne Throndssön is also referred to in the old Scottish song, which is entitled, "Lady Anne Bothwell's Lament," in which a young woman complains of being forsaken with her child by her husband or lover; but this idea is certainly untenable. The heroine in this ballad is Anne Bothwell, a daughter of Adam Bothwell, Bishop of Orkney, by whom Mary and Bothwell were married. This young lady had had, according to historical accounts, a passion for a son of the Earl of Mar, Alexander Erskine, who forsook her, and was afterwards killed by an explosion of gunpowder at Dunglass.—Aytoun, *Ballads of Scotland*. Second Edition. Edinburgh, 1858, ii. 49.

Note B, p. 57. Account of John Stuart and his son Francis Stuart.

Randolph's words to Cecil, as given in Chalmers, *Life of Mary Queen of Scots*, ii. 212. John Stuart had already died at Inverness about the close of 1563. His widow entered, in the year 1566, into a second marriage with John Sinclair of Caithness, and after the death of the latter, in 1573, into a third, with Archibald Douglas, a relative of the Earl of Morton. Bothwell's sister, during her first brief union to John Stuart, bore a son, Francis Stuart, to whom Mary became godmother, and of whom his maternal uncle at a later period assumed the office of guardian. Named, as it would seem after Mary's first husband, and by his father's early death specially commended to her care, Francis Stuart received, even in his childhood while the Queen was still at the head of the Government of Scotland, many proofs of her kindness, and was afterwards, in a testament made at Sheffield during her imprisonment, recommended as her brother's son and her own godson to the favourable regard of James VI. particularly in order that he might succeed to the Bothwell estates. James VI. consequently considered Francis Stuart as his cousin, and although belonging to an illegitimate branch of the family, created him, in 1581, Earl of Bothwell and Lord High Admiral of Scotland, having at the same time made over to him all the rest of his uncle's long forfeited possessions and offices. His character was notwithstanding too much like that of his uncle, and his political life was also as stormy as his. However ungrateful the new Earl of Bothwell afterwards showed himself towards James VI., he never in the least forgot the kindness with which Mary had followed him from his cradle. He told James VI. to his face that if he submitted to Elizabeth's prosecution against his imprisoned mother, he deserved to be hanged, and when the tidings of her execution reached Scotland, he exclaimed that a coat of mail was now the only mourning he should wear, and put forth all his efforts to set on foot a hostile attack upon England. Seven years afterwards he was obliged to seek refuge in the wild Highlands of the North, and subsequently to betake himself to the Orkneys, whence he at length continued his flight over the Shetland Isles to France. In 1600 the French Government compelled him to withdraw into Spain, whence he betook himself to Naples, and there, after he had gone over to Romanism, he ended his life in the year 1612, having, it is alleged, died of grief at the death by accident of the eldest son of James VI., Prince Henry Frederick. After Earl Francis Bothwell's forfeiture, the hereditary office of Lord High Admiral of Scotland was transferred to the younger family of Lennox (properly Aubigny) until the latter's extinction in the reign of Charles II., when it was finally

abolished.—*Vide* Chalmers, *Caledonia*, ii. 473-479. Robertson's
Preface to *Inuentaires*, pp. xl. xli.

Note C, p. 62. The Queen's "Maries."
" In the quhilk the quenis grace, and all hir Maries and ladies
wer all cled in men's apperrell."—*Diurnal of Remarkable Occurrents*,
p. 87. The Queen's " Maries," who, when little girls of the same
age with herself, had been chosen to accompany her to France,
were four in number—Mary Livingston, who married, in 1565,
John Sempill of Beltreis ; Mary Beaton, who married, in 1566;
Alexander Ogilvy of Boyne ; Mary Fleming, who, in 1567, married
William Maitland, laird of Lethington, her senior by eighteen
years ; and lastly, Mary Seton, who, after losing by death her lover,
Andrew Beaton, remained unmarried, and, having for fifteen years
shared the Queen's imprisonment, subsequently entered a convent
at Rheims, where she ended her days.—Robertson's Preface to
Inuentaires, pp. xlvi.-li. In the Scottish national song called " The
Queene's Maries," given in the Minstrelsy of the Scottish Border,
the names occur differently ; there Mary Hamilton names them
thus :—

> " Yestreen the Queen had four Maries,
> The nicht she'll hae but three.
> There was Marie Seaton, and Marie Beaton,
> And Marie Carmichael and me."

Note D, p. 100. Testimonies to Mary Stewart's rare beauty.
Brantôme, *Vies des Dames Illustres*, in *Œuvres du Seigneur de
Brantôme*, i. 129. Brantôme's statement that the Queen in her
Highland dress " resembled a true goddess," is accompanied with
these words :—" Ceux qui l'ont veue habillée le pourront ainsi
confesser en toute vérité ; et ceux, qui ne l'ont veue en pourront
avoir veu son portrait, estant ainsi habillée." The painting to
which he refers has long ago been lost, but of the Highland female
dress of this period there is a description by Bishop Lesley, who
calls it very becoming (*De rebus gestis Scotorum*, p. 58). In the
series of old writings about Mary, which Jebb collected together
and printed under the title, *De Vita et Rebus gestis serenissimœ
principis Mariæ, Scotorum Reginæ, Franciæ Dotariæ: Londini,
1725, fol., we find other testimonies from contemporaries agreeing
with Brantôme's in reference to her rare beauty. Thus F. Strada
states :—" Ipsam quatuor regnorum insignia ornavere ; sed forma

cui parem ea ætate fuisse nullam memorant, digna Europæ totius imperio habebatur." (Jebb, ii. 105.) In like manner Robert Turner testifies :—" Audivi a multis, iisque sane in hoc genere bene lynceis, quicquid viderant in Anglia, Gallia, Italia, Germania, Flandria pulchri et venusti, id totum, quantum et quantulum erat, præ hac confirmatione membrorum, hac venustate, hac maiestate, hac hujus Reginæ suavitate penitus sorduisse." (Jebb, i. 385.) Adam Blackwood speaks of her in such terms as these :—" Inter omnes suæ ætatis Reginas admirabili atque incomparabili corporis pulchritudine prædita." (Jebb, ii. 177.) Also in De Thou (*Historia sui temporis,* t. iv. : Londini, 1733, fol. p. 435) we meet still with the same testimony, where he describes the execution of the Queen :—" Etiam post tædiosi carceris molestiam pristinum oris decus ac pulchritudo, quo tot homines in sui amorem rapuerat, integre adhuc relucebant."

Note E, p. 128. Poems of Mary Stuart.

" Ellese mesloit d'estre poëte, et composoit des vers, d'ont j'en ay veu aucuns de beaux et très-bien faicts et nullement resemblans à ceux qu'on luy a mis à sus avoir fait sur l'amour du comte de Bouthe-ville ; ils sont trop grossiers et mal polis pour estre sortis d'elle. M. de Ronsard estoit bien de mon opinion en cela, ainsi que nous en discourrions un jour, que nous les lisions."—Brantôme, *Vies des Dames Illustres* in *Œuvres du Seigneur de Brantôme,* i. 112. Mary's " Quatrains à son Fils," which she composed for the instruction of James VI., by whom they were prized as a precious relic, and of which there were still to be found, in the year 1627, more than one copy, have latterly disappeared, and now we have only a few undisputed poems from Mary's hand, hardly more than six, consist-ing in all of scarcely three hundred lines. These poems have all been printed, although not in a collected form, but only scattered through various works. (Cited in Robertson's Preface to *Inuen-taires,* p. cxvii.) Here we shall only more particularly refer to the most easily accessible which the reader may find in Laing's *History of Scotland,* ii. 217-221, and in Labanoff, vii. 346. That the two lines of verse, which Mary Stuart wrote with a diamond on a pane of glass in Fotheringay Castle, and which she has got the name of composing (Ballard, *Memoirs of several Ladies of Great Britain who have been celebrated for their Writing and Learning :* Oxford, 1752, 4to, p. 161), were in reality only a reminiscence from a well-known collection of poetry in the Queen's time (*Songs and Sonnettes,* written by the honourable Lord Henry Howard, Earl of Surrey and others : London, 1557, 4to, p. 53) has been remarked by Warton (*History of English Poetry :* London, 1774-1781, 4to, iii. 56), and that the well-known stanzas beginning "Adieu, plaisant pays de France," which reappear in Schiller's "Grüsset mir freundlich mein Jugendland," are only a literary mystification of the journalist Anne-Gabriel Meusnier de Querlon, who first—as "tirée du manuscrit de Buckingham"—communicated this poem in his *Anthologie,* published in 1765, has been made clear by Édouard Fournier (*L'Esprit dans l'Histoire. Recherches et curiosités sur les mots historiques.* Troisième Edition. Paris, 1867, pp. 181-187).

Note F, p. 166. The accusation of Buchanan against Mary in reference to her conduct with Bothwell.

"Ubi vero Edinburgum rediit, non in suum Palatium, sed in privatam, in proximo Joannis Balfurij, domum diuertit. Illinc in alias ædes commigrauit, ubi conventus anniuersarius, qvem scaccarium vocant, tum habebatur. Hæ enim ædes erant laxiores, et hortorum aderat amœnitas, et juxta hortos pene solitudo. Sed erat et aliud, quod omnibus his magis inuitaret. Habitabat in propinquo David Camerius Bothuelij cliens : cujus posticum erat hortis ædium Reginæ propinquum. Per id posticum Bothuelius, quoties libitum erat commeabat. Cætera quis nescit? Nam et rem ipsam Regina cum multis aliis, tum proregi et matri ejus est confessa : sed culpam in Reresiam, profligatæ pudicitiæ mulierem conferebat, quæ inter pellices Bothuelij fuerat, ac tum in intimis Reginæ ministris erat. Ab hac (quæ ætate inclinata a meretricio quæstu ad Lenonium se contulerat) Regina, vt ipsa dicebat, prodita est. Nam Bothuelius per hortum in cubiculum Reginæ introductus, eam inuitam vi compressit. Sed quam inuitam Reresia prodiderit, tempus veritatis parens ostendit. Nam post paucos dies, Regina vim vi, ut reor ulcisci cupiens, destinat Reresiam (quæ et ipsa vires hominis antea erat experta) quæ eum ad se captiuum adduceret. Regina vna cum Margareta Caruodia, omnium secretorum conscia, eam e zona suspensam, per maceriem, in hortum propinquum demittuut. Sed nunquam in re militari omnia sic prouideri possunt, vt non aliquid incommodi interueniat. Ecce zona repente frangitur. Reresia mulier et ætate, et corpore grauis, cum magno strepitu cadit. Sed veterna miles, nihil tenebris, nihil altitudine marceriæ, nihil inexpectato casu perterrita, ad Bothuelij

cubiculum penetrat : foribus reclusis, hominem e lecto, e complexu
conjugis, semisomnum, seminudum adduxit ad Reginam.   Hunc
rerum gestarum ordinem, non modo maxima pars eorum qui cum
Regina erant, sunt fassi : Sed et Georgius Dalglesias, Bothuelij
cubicularius, paulo ante quam pœnas luit, denarrauit, quæ ejus
confessio in Actis continetur."—*De Maria Scot. Reg.* p. 6, 7.

Note G, p. 191.   Notices of recent works on Mary Stuart's
connection with Darnley's murder.

Since this historical inquiry was first published in 1863, there
has been an increase in the number both of those who with respect
to the two questions treated of in this work have taken part against
Mary and of those who have acquitted her.   To the class of her
accusers have been added James Anthony Froude in his *History
of England from the Fall of Wolsey to the death of Elizabeth*, and
John Hill Burton in his *History of Scotland.*   By Froude, who
has set himself the task of clearing Henry VIII. and Elizabeth of
all charges of cruelty, and of finding in their whole acting only
sacrifices for the social welfare, there is shown, where he speaks of
Mary, a hastiness in the use of his authorities which has led to a
series of positive mistakes.   To many of these mistakes attention
was directed in 1868 in an article on *Marie Stuart et ses derniers
Historiens* by L. Wiesener in *Revue des Questions Historiques,
Deuxième Année,* iv. 385-436.   *Troisième Année,* v. 49-106, 353-
425.   Thus with Froude we meet with one of Mary's half-brothers
represented as " the Abbot of St. Cross," because he has failed to
notice that Sancte-Croix was the French translation of Holyrood ;
we have Whittingham Castle in East Lothian, where Archibald
Douglas resided, spoken of as " the hostelry " in which Bothwell
and Maitland met with Morton ; we find Darnley raving about
wishing to retire " to the Scilly Isles," although the expression " au-
de-là des mers " in the French letter referred to, as in all records of
that period, only has the meaning of the Continent ; and when by
the side of like mistakes we too often stumble upon the bad custom,
adopted for the purpose of making the representation more vivid,
of introducing the historical personages speaking in such a manner
that the same inverted commas in Froude embrace both utterances
which are sanctioned by the authorities, and utterances which
originate entirely from the author's fancy, we can by no means
regard as groundless the admonition with which the French critic
cautions against any such levity : " Si l'on n'y prenait garde, elle

ferait déchoir l'Angleterre du rang où l'avait portée le fort et droit génie de tant générations d'historiens." Wiesener's judgment of the way in which the history of Mary Stuart had been treated by Burton was not much more favourable, but to the complaints which he made, the new edition of Burton's great and meritorious work published in the year 1873 in many respects gives no longer the same occasion. Wiesener himself had, before he produced his critique of the sketches of Froude and Burton, given to the public a new work (*Marie Stuart et le Comte de Bothwell :* Paris, 1863) which in all respects acquitted Mary of guilt, but this representation was equally unable to gain universal acceptance (see *Historische Zeitschrift, herausg. von H. v. Sybel,* xiv. 521-524) ; latterly Alexander M'Neil Caird (*Mary Stuart, her Guilt or Innocence:* second edition ; Edinburgh, 1866), Jules Gauthier (*Histoire de Marie Stuart:* Paris, 1869, t. i.-iii.), and John Hosack (*Mary Queen of Scots and her Accusers:* Edinburgh, 1869) have taken the same side as he has. Gauthier attaches peculiar importance to a report which he has succeeded in bringing to light from the Archives of Simancas, according to which Elizabeth had herself in 1568, in presence of the Spanish Ambassador, spoken of the letters ascribed to Mary Stuart as false ; but regarding this it ought to be remarked that the statement of Elizabeth in question is older than the opening of the conference in England, and the production of those documents before the commissioners at Westminster, that it is found, as Gauthier himself alleges, previously in an account from Guzman da Silva of the 21st July 1568 (Dixome que *no era verdad,* aunque Ledington avia tratado esto, y que si ella le viese, le divia algunas palabras que no le harian buen gusto). Beyond comparison the chief of the most recent apologies for Mary is Hosack's, who has, for the first time, made public the general view of the preceding relations of Mary Stuart in Scotland, or the so-called *Book of Articles* which Murray communicated along with the alleged letters of his sister to the English Commissioners at Westminster (Hosack, *Appendix,* p. 522-548). It is manifest that Buchanan, if he did not actually take part in the composition of the text, has certainly borrowed from it the most of the touches for his subsequent pamphlet. Malcolm Laing, who had never himself seen the document now brought to light, has however erred in so far as he seeks to maintain that it was "undoubtedly the same " with the pamphlet of Buchanan (*History of Scotland,* i. 241) ; the better instructed Camden (*Annales rerum*

Anglicarum et Hibernicarum regnante Elizabetha, p. 144) having
with greater justice distinguished between both.   A new complaint
is met with in this charge of Murray against his sister, in so far as
it also maintains against her that in her testament made in 1566
she had chiefly favoured Bothwell, and, on the contrary, had not
granted Darnley the least part of her possessions (she disponit also
hir haill movables to uthers beside hir husband)—an accusation
which can now be most successfully disproved by the aid of those
autograph testamentary provisions of hers already appealed to,
which were found in the year 1854.

Note H, p. 195. Darnley's bed in the house of the Kirk-of-Field.
" Premièrement ung lict de veloux viollet à double pante, passe-
mente d'or et d'argent." So it is described in the inventory of
Servais de Condé, and " Decharge des meubles que j'avoye faict
porter au logis du feu Roy, lesquelz meubles ont esté perdu sans
en rien recouver," in *Les Inuentaires de la Royne Descosse,
Douairière de la France,* pp. 177-178.   This description of the bed
is hardly in accordance with the articles of complaint against
Mary which Murray and her other enemies laid before the Commissioners in England, and one of which (Hosack, p. 536) alleges
that the Queen had before the murder of Darnley caused certain
articles of value to be brought to Holyrood, namely, some tapestries
and a bed in the room of which " ane uther wors" had been set
up.   They refer to a declaration by Thomas Nelson, the only one
of Darnley's servants who survived the catastrophe, according to
which the Queen had caused " a new bed of blak figurat welwet "
to be removed from Darnley's sick-chamber, as she was afraid it
might suffer damage from the baths, and in its room had had " ane
auld purple bed " substituted.   But as the sole bed of black figured
velvet, which was found in Holyrood, could only be improperly
designated " ane new bed," as it had previously come into the
Queen's possession in the year 1562, so Darnley's bed, which was
destroyed by the catastrophe at the Kirk-of-Field, could by no
means be justly represented as an old bed, but was a richly got-up
present from the Queen to him in the previous year, as is unmistakably evident from the official inventory lists furnished by
Servais de Condé.   Confidence in the whole history of this
exchange might besides have been previously weakened, if it had
been noticed that Buchanan, who is assumed to have assisted in the
drawing up of the articles of complaint communicated to the

English, has afterwards in his *Rerum Scot. Hist.*, p. 214, made the Queen's bed, and not the King's, to have been exchanged. Nearly three hundred years nevertheless required to pass away before the entire accusation received a correct elucidation by the discovery of the inventories of Servais de Condé of all the furniture lost in the catastrophe of February 1567,—a discovery which was fortunately made during the examination of some juridical documents belonging to the beginning of the sixteenth century. Not without reason did Sir James Simpson immediately after bring forward in a discourse this discovery as one of the most remarkable examples of how " disputed points in Scottish history have occasionally been decided by manuscript discoveries which were altogether accidental " (*Archæology, its past and its future work :* Edinburgh, 1861, p. 44). But even if such an historical elucidation and correction of the facts of the case had not been forthcoming, it may, from a purely psychological point of view, awaken surprise that the command ascribed to Mary already referred to,— or, indeed, even the circumstance that one of her ladies, Margaret Carwod, is said, according to the declaration of Paris, one day to have caused the latter to bring back a black counterpane from the Queen's own room in Darnley's dwelling—could have been represented even by many more recent authors, and still by Teulet (*Lettres*, p. 88), as something so aggravating. I should like to know if indeed any wife, not to say a magnificent Queen, who was about to murder her husband, would, in order to preserve from injury some article of furniture, make light of all else ? " Where shall we find," as Lord Stanhope well remarks in a review of Tytler's *History of Scotland* (*Quarterly Review*, vol. lxvii. p. 339), —" Where shall we find another case of a Queen exclaiming : Strangle my husband in his bed, but spare, oh spare, the curtains and the coverlet !"

Note I, p. 236. The particular place where Mary was seized by Bothwell.

The act by which Bothwell, on the 20th December 1567, was outlawed states that he had surprised the Queen " in via sua inter Linlytgow et oppidum Edinburghi prope pontes vulgo vocatos *foull brigges.*" (*The Acts of the Parliaments of Scotland*, iii. 6.) The name of the place mentioned has by some in more recent times been identified with Fountainbridge, now a sort of suburb to the west of old Edinburgh, having the suburban villages of Greenhill

and Merchiston to the south. This is the opinion of Burton
(*History of Scotland*, second edition, iv. 216). It is not, however,
Buchanan alone who makes Bothwell meet the Queen " ad *Almonis
pontem* " (*Rerum Scot. Hist.*, p. 217), but previously in an order
of amnesty issued 1st October 1567, in favour of one Andrew
Reidpeth,—who had been among Bothwell's followers at the seizure,
and subsequently in his service, took part in the defence of Dunbar
Castle,—it is likewise said that the Queen had been made prisoner
"prope aquam de *Awmond*" (Hosack, *Mary Queen of Scots and her
Accusers*, p. 567). Robert Chambers (*Domestic Annals of Scotland*,
second edit. 1859, i. 42) thinks with better reason that he finds
the place where the Queen was seized on the road from Linlithgow
to Edinburgh two miles from this, and in the vicinity of which one
bridge passes over the Almond and another over Gogar-burn. Of
the two contemporary diaries which have recorded the events, the
one makes the seizure occur "at ane place callit the *briggis*"
(*Diurnal of Remarkable Occurrents*, p. 109), the other (*The Diary
of Robert Birrel: Fragments of Scottish History*, p. 8) "at the
bridge of *Craumont.*"

Note K, p. 241. Account given in contemporary public documents of the abduction of the Queen.

In " A Declaration in name of Scotland's nobles," dated 11th
June 1567, there is spoken of " the ravishing and detentioune of
the Quenis majestics persoune." In " a Proclamation by the
Lords of the Privy Council and the nobles," dated the 12th June
1567, it is said :—" James Erle Bothwell put violent handes on
our Soveraine Ladies maist nobill persoune." In " the bond of
union of the nobles of Scotland," dated 15th June 1567, the
language is used :—" He ambesett hir Majesties way, tuke and
ravishit hir maist nobill person." Further speaks " an Act and
Proclamation about seizing the Earl of Bothwell," dated the 26th
June 1567, of " Hir Hieness awin persoun tressonabille ravischit."
In " the answer from the Lords of Scotland to Sir Nicholas
Throckmorton," dated the 11th July 1567, the words occur :—
" How shamefully the Queen our Sovereign was led captive, and by
fear, force, and (as by many conjectures may be well suspected)
other extraordinary and more unlawful means compelled to be the
bed-fellow to another wife's husband." In " an Act of prohibition
against paying rents to the Bishop of Murray, and about arresting
him for his support of Bothwell," dated 21st July 1567, it is finally

said of the latter :—" Efter he had alswa tresonabilie revesit hir
Majesties maist nobill persoun, and led hir captive to Dunbar."
Anderson's *Collections*, i. 130, 131, 136, 139, 142.—*Keith*, i.
418. These various statements hardly agree with the story told by
Buchanan (*Rerum Scot. Hist.*, p. 217) :—" Interea Sterlini collecta
sincerior pars nobilitatis ad Reginam mittunt, qui rogarent;
spontene, an invita, teneretur; Nam si invita illic esset, se,
coacto exercitu, eam liberaturos. Illa, nuncio non sine risu
recepto, respondit; Se invitam eo adductam, sed ita humaniter
tractari, ut de priore injuria non habeat quod multum queratur."

Note L, p. 291. Bothwell's own account of his life written in
Denmark.

Suhm had previously stated with accuracy the title of this
manuscript which is now found in the Royal Library of Stockholm :
—" Les Affaires du Conte de Boduel, l'an 1568, nec non Caroli
Dantzæi, Galliarum Regis Legati Literæ ab anno 1575 ad annum
1586, ad Regem, Reginam, Proceresque Galliæ, datæ durante
legatione in Dania." The title-page has this superscription :—
" Ex donatione excellentissimi viri Dni Claudii Plumii J. U. D. et
in Regia Acad. Hafniensi Prof. anno Messiæ Regis Æterni
mdxliv die xviii Augusti," and the manuscript is supposed to have
come to Sweden at the time when the Library of the Royal
Historiographer Stephanius was sold to the Swedish Chancellor, M.
G. de la Gardie. See Molbech, *Danske Haandskrifter fornemlig
af historisk Inhold, i det Kongelige Bibliothek i Stockholm.
Historisk Tidsskrift*, iv., 143. Werlauff, *Historiske Efterretninger
om det store kongelige Bibliothek*, Kjöbenhavn, 1844, p. 19. The
portion of Dancay's correspondence likewise preserved in this
manuscript has been published as the 11th part of *Handlingar
rörande Skandinaviens Historia* (or *Nya Handlingar rörande
Skandinaviens Historia*, 1st part), with the special title :—" *Correspondance de Charles Dantzai, Ministre de France à la Cour de
Dannemarc*, Stockholm, 1824, while the portion of Dancay's
correspondence which is preserved in the Danish Privy Archives
still awaits publication.

Note M, p. 301. The exaction of " Ox and Sheep Silver " in
Shetland.

The origin of this exaction is involved in obscurity, but Schiern is
wrong in representing it as a separate tax imposed by government

2 D

and as levied also in Orkney, the fact being that it is simply a part
of the *cumulo* duties payable to the Earl of Zetland as owner of the
ancient lordship.   As such, Gifford, writing in the year 1733, expressly says that it was paid that year in money.   In the year
1812, the then Lord Dundas, predecessor of the subsequent Earls
of Zetland, obtained a private Act of Parliament empowering him to
disentail.   In the schedule attached to the Act the revenues of
lordship are specified, consisting of, I. "Feir and Umboth duties,"
and II. "Scatt, wattle, sheep and ox money," the respective
amounts from which in each parish being also given.   Following
upon the Act of disentail, these duties have to a large extent been
bought up by the landowners, and are therefore extinguished.
Those not so bought up are still levied.   There is therefore no doubt
that the "ox and sheep silver" was levied directly in the islands of
Shetland, the fact being that no such exactions imposed were ever
known to have been removed.   For the information contained in this
note I am indebted to the kindness of Colonel Balfour of Balfour
Castle, Orkney, and Gilbert Goudie, Esq., Edinburgh.—*Translator.*

Note N, page 309.   The pursuit of Bothwell in Shetland and
the fate of some of his companions.

"Ye Laird of Grange with ye Constabill of Dunde is landit in
Schytland, and hes tain ye pryncepall man of ye cuntre, and hes
takin ane of the lord Bothelles shippis."—Letter of David Sinclair
to the Earl of Bedford, 15th September 1567.   Ellis, *Latter Years
of James Hepburn Earl of Bothwell*, p. 10.   "Leaving his ship
behind him, which Grange took, and therein the Laird of Tallow,
John Hepburn of Bantoun, Dalgleesch, and divers other of the
Earl's servants."—*Memoirs of Sir James Melvil*, p. 85.   Melvil's
account of what occurred in Shetland is, however, far from correct.
For instance, it is undoubted that of Bothwell's servants, both
George Dalgleish and William Powrie had two months previously
fallen into his enemies' hands, the first examination of them, which
is still extant (Laing, *History of Scotland*, ii. 243-251), having been
held on the 23d and 26th of June 1567.   Then as regards John Hay,
laird of Talla, we know that having, with one of his servants, James
Ross, hired a fishing-boat to convey him back to Scotland, he was
on the 11th July betrayed to Lindsay, and by him was brought a
prisoner to Edinburgh Castle, where he was examined on the 13th
of September.   "This Johne Hay," expressly says an original
authority (*Diurnal*, p. 121), "past to Orknay with James Erle

Bothwill, and quhen the schippis send be the Regent and Lordis to Orknay and Zetland for (in order to) invaid the said erle and his schippis, the said Johne, and James Ross, ane servant man, conducit ane fischeing boit of Pittinweme to transport thame to Lowthiane, quhilk bote come to Pittinweme, and causit shaw to the Lord Lindsay, that sik ane man and servant wes come thair with thame." The only one of the witnesses against Bothwell mentioned by Melvil, whom the enemies of the former succeeded in bringing back from their expedition to the Shetland Isles, is therefore John Hepburn, laird of Bolton. In the confession, which the latter before his execution made to the priest (Laing, *History of Scotland*, ii. 263), he himself also says, that he saw in it the Providence of God, that "I had schippis providit to flie, but coulde not escape," which most precisely intimates that he also had been taken on land, not on sea.

Note O, page 310. Intercourse between the kings of Denmark and those of Scotland.

P. W. Becker, *De rebus inter Joannem et Christianum II., Daniæ Reges, ac Ludovicum XII. et Jacobum IV., Galliæ Scotiæque Reges, actis.* Hafniæ, 1835, p. 35. In the beginning of the year 1558, Christian III. was invited by Mary and the Dauphin to come to Paris in order to be personally present at his relative's approaching marriage, but in consequence of his then impaired health, the King had himself represented on the occasion by a Danish Ambassador (Stephanii, *Historiæ Daniæ libri duo, regnante Christiano Tertio;* Soræ, 1650, 4to, p. 102). The branch of the Oldenburgh royal race, which was expelled by the dethronement of Christian II., also sought during their exile like that remaining to cultivate connection with the royal family in Scotland. The idea that one of the exiled king's daughters might marry the father of Mary, James V., and bring the latter the whole of Norway as dowry, was cherished by the Emperor Charles v. (Tytler, *History of Scotland,* v. 196.) To the importance of the bond which subsisted between the Duchess Christine of Lorraine, the most renowned daughter of Christian II., and Mary, "propter conjunctionem sanguinis, quæ est inter ipsam et Reginam Scotiæ," Languet believed that he ought to call the attention of the Elector of Saxony in a letter from Paris of 17th November 1565 (*Epistolæ ad Joachimum Camerarium;* Lipsiæ et Frankfurti, 1685, p. 231). Duchess Christine also visited Mary before the latter, in the year 1561, retired from

France (*Négotiations, Lettres, et Pièces diverses, relatives au Règne de François II., tirées du portefeuille de Sebastien de l'Aubespine, Evêque de Limoges.* Par Louis Paris. Paris, 1841, 4to, p. 752).

Note P, page 312. Royal Danish suitors for Mary's hand. William of Orange wrote from Breda, in April 1561, to the Elector of Saxony, that he had got secret intelligence from the Court in Paris, " das der Kunig von Dennemark neulich seine Bothschaf das gehabt und um des verstorbnen Kunigs Wittwe hab lassen werben mit vielem erbieten." (*Archives ou correspondance inédite de la Maison d'Orange Nassau.* Recueil publié par G. Groen van Prinstern. Première Série. Leide, 1835-1847, i. 57.) In the same year, Languet wrote from Paris on the 9th October 1561 : —" Audio ex iis, qui e Scotia veniunt, Scotos non abhorrere a conjugio Danico." (Huberti Langueti *Epistolæ secretæ ad principem suum Augustum, Sax. ducem et S. R. I. Septemvirum.* Primus e museo ed. J. P. Ludovicus. Halæ, 1699, 4to, p. 146.) The project of marriage referred to had certainly been intrusted to the ambassadors, whose mission both to Mary, who was still remaining a widow in France, and to the Government in Scotland, is found mentioned, along with the statement of another commission, by Resen in 1561. (*Kong Frederichs den Andens Krönike,* p. 53.) The subsequent negotiations in the same matter, in course of which the sister of Frederick II., Anne Electress of Saxony, sent a portrait of Mary to Denmark, and which continued till the union of the Scottish Queen with Darnley, are more particularly noticed in the communications of G. Droysen in the so-called " dänische Bücher " in Weber, *Archiv für die sächsische Geschichte* (Fünfter Band) Leipzig, 1867, pp. 7-8 ; and in F. Krarup, *Oplysninger om Kong Frederik den Andens Ægteskabs-Forhandlinger ;* Kjöbeuhavn, 1872, pp. 27-30. Much earlier, while Mary was but a child, before she was betrothed, in 1548, to the Dauphin, her hand had been offered in marriage during the reign of Christian III. by a French diplomatist to the King's young son (Ribier, *Lettres et Memoires d'Estat des Rois, Princes, Ambassadeurs et autres Ministres sour les règnes de François I., Henry II. et François II.* Paris, 1676, fol. i. 606-607.)

Note Q, p. 319. By whom Bothwell was detected in Bergen. " Being detected by some Scottish merchants."—*Spottiswood,* p. 213. " Where he was knowen by some Scots merchants, that acquented the Earle of Murray at their returne."—Herries, *Histori-cal Memoirs*, p. 96. " Cognitus tandem partim vultus serenitate partim indicio mercatorum."—*Maria Stuarta, Regina Scotiæ, Dotaria Franciæ, Hæres Angliæ et Hyberniæ, Martyr ecclesiæ, innocens a cœde Darnleiana*. Vindice Oberto Barnestapalio (Roberto Turnero). In-golstadii, 1588, Jebb, i. 415. In these instances, however, Norway is confounded with Denmark. A proof of the residence of many Scottish merchants in Bergen is furnished in a letter by Frederick II., of 27th December 1567, in which, in consequence of the great conflagration of the city in the previous year, he grants the same the tithe-money which was exacted for the English and Scots that died in Bergen. (Absalon Pederssön, *Dagbog*, p. 283.) Another proof of the intercourse between the two countries we have in the importation at that period of horses from Norway to Scotland. (James Paterson, *James the Fifth, or the " Gudeman of Ballangeich*," *his poetry and adventures ;* Edinburgh, 1861, p. 264.) During the stormy epoch in the history of Scotland in the seventeenth and eighteenth centuries, Bergen afterwards saw more than once Scottish exiles as guests. Thus, in 1646, James Graham, Marquis of Montrose, came to Bergen in a Norwegian ship, whence he journeyed overland to Christiania to King Christian the Fifth (Mark Napier, *Memoirs of the Marquis of Montrose ;* Edinburgh, 1856, ii. 643, 656. Mikel Hofnagel, *Optegnelser i Norsk Magasin* (udg. N. Nicolaysen); Christiania, 1860-1870, ii. 212), and in the year 1746, thirteen, mostly leading Jacobites who had escaped after the battle of Culloden, arrived in Bergen on board the vessel of a foreign skipper, which they had taken possession of. (L. Daae, *Christopher Throndssön Rustung hans sön Enno og hans Datter Skot-tefruen*, i Historisk Tidsskrift, udgivet af den norske historiske Forening, i. 160-161.)

Note R, p. 344. The memoirs written by Bothwell during his imprisonment in Denmark.

Of the memoirs named there are two contemporary transcripts. One of these, which was formerly found at Drottningholm, and which, as already stated, is now preserved in the Royal Library in Stockholm, has this attestation by Dancay attached to it : " Je receus cette instruction au chasteau de Malmeu, le xiiiᵉ. jour de janvier, l'an 1568, du Sieur Jacques de Boduel, conte de Boduel, duc des isles de Orquenay, Mary de la Royne d'Escosse, etc. ; et l'ay présenté à Helsingbourg au sieur Peter Oxe, présent le sieur Jehan Friz,

Chancellier, le xvi. de janvier. Surquoy je receus d'eux mesmes la response au chasteau de Copenhagen le xxi. du dict mois." This duplicate has therefore been a copy which Dancay reserved to himself, since in Helsingborg he delivered the original memoirs to Peter Oxe. It was printed for the first time by the Bannatyne Club. The other contemporary transcript which is preserved among the family papers of d'Esneval in the Castle of Pavilly in Normandy, has marginal notes which, in a couple of words consecutively state the contents of the text, and conclude with this addition : " Le dict conte a luy mesmes écris les annotations qui sont en la marge." It has, therefore, without doubt been sent by Bothwell himself to France, where it was probably on account of his own explanations afterwards given up to Baron d'Esneval, Lord of Courcelles, when the latter went in the year 1585 as French Ambassador to Scotland. This copy was first made use of by Prince Labanoff in his *Pièces et Documents relatifs au Comte de Bothwell.* With some few variations both copies have nearly a perfectly harmonious text, which has been cited in this work after the printed copy in Teulet, *Lettres,* pp. 155-189.

Note S, p. 344. Attempts made by the Danish Government to regain possession of the Islands of Orkney and Shetland.

The last book of Torfæus's *Orcades* (p. 207-228) is merely a statement "De indefessis potentissimorum Regum Daniæ Norwegiæque studiis jus suum in Orcades adjacentemque Hetlandiam pacifice repetendi." At the close of the reign of Christian iv., who, notwithstanding his own adverse circumstances endeavoured with both money and men to aid Charles i. during the civil war in England, this object was believed in Denmark to be so nearly gained, that according to Torfæus it was said to be a question as to which of the members of Council should have the management of these islands. During the naval war against England in which Frederick iii., along with the Dutch, took part in the years 1666-7, it is also said to have been intended that Vice-Admiral Nicolaus Heldt should attempt the conquest of the Orkney Isles, and at the Peace of Breda an express reservation was still made by the Danish Ambassadors protecting their rights in this matter (*Samlinger til Denmarks Historie under Kong Frederik den Tredie,* Udgivne af P. W. Becker ; Kjöbenhavn, 1847-57, ii. 152, 195-96, 408). The publication itself of Torfæus's *Orcades* at the close of the century may be considered as a reservation from the Dano-

Norwegian side, since Torfæus in the dedications of his work to Christian expressly designates the islands as "provinciam Tuam." The king's ministers, on account of the pointed way in which the right of redemption of the islands was insisted upon, would not give their consent to the printing of the work, but Christian v. himself subsequently commanded that "the claims (in question) so far from being deemed forbidden, the book must, on the contrary, by no means see the light, unless they were fully detailed" (Eriksen, *Thormod Torfesens Biographi.* Minerva for December Maaned 1787, p. 307). Finally, in the middle of the eighteenth century Frederick v. once more repeated the demand for the restoration to Denmark of the Orkney and Shetland Isles (*Historisch-genealogische Nachrichten von den vornehmsten Begebenheiten welche sich an den europäischen Höfen zugetragen.* Leipzig, 1741-1752, cxl. 695).

Note T, p. 358. Clark's acknowledgment of the surrender to him of William Murray and Paris in Denmark.

As this remarkable document has not hitherto been printed, we give it here from the contemporary copy in the Danish Archives : " Ego Johannes Klarck, Scoticorum cohortium Capitaneus, profiteor hoc meo chirographo accepisse me a Nobili ac præstanti Dño, D. Petro Oxe de Gislefeldt, Regni Danici Magistro curiæ, duos viros, utpote Vilhelmum Murranum et Paridem Gallum, qui dicuntur proditores necnon interfectores Sereniss : Regis Scotorum piiss : memoriæ Henrici etc : quos præfatos me obligo sisturum judices Regni Scotici, ibi examinandos ac puniendos, si sontes reique fuerint, liberosque pronunciatos demissurum, hac tamen lege, ut eis concedetur (sic) tempus unius mensis, amicos ac propinquos suos sollicitandos (sic) si quos habuerint, qui eos de crimine, quo sunt inusti, purgare possint aut velint. Hæc ita firma atque vera esse, sigillo meo proprio atque nativo muniendum volui. Datum Roschildiæ 30 Octobris, Ao. 1568." This document, agreeing most completely as it does with the fact, elsewhere mentioned, that Clark was also able in a letter from Roskilde of 20th November 1568, himself to report to Cecil the surrender of "both Bothwell's servants" (*Calendar of State Papers,* Foreign Series, 1566-68, p. 575), best discovers with how great injustice it has formerly been asserted by one, that "the papers found in the Danish Archives contain nothing besides which can throw the least light on Mary's history" (*Bergenhammer,* p. 226). Only lack of more pro-

found knowledge of that on which the critical investigation of Mary
Stuart's history specially depends, can have overlooked the significance of a contribution as that just given.

Note U, p. 366. Answers of Clark to the charges brought
against him in Denmark.

His written declaration, in reference to the complaints communicated to him 1st July, is preserved in the Danish Archives.
With respect to the accusation of Aikman, its main contention is
that the latter had allowed day after day to elapse without producing witnesses, while Aikman and Campbell, who had long been
personal enemies, were, subsequently to the date of the first-mentioned charge, reconciled, and had exchanged gifts as a sign of
friendship. The letter to the Regent in Scotland complained of,
Clark acknowledges to be from himself, but he assumes that by
writing it he cannot have erred, considering that he had received
full power to negotiate about Bothwell's surrender. In respect to
the third charge, viz., his conduct in Scotland in the year 1567,
he maintains that Mary, when at that unquiet period she departed
from Edinburgh, had in vain summoned him to enter her service,
in which case she would send Frederick II. as much money back
as Clark had brought with him from Denmark ; that he had certainly with good counsel and plans assisted the rebels against
the Queen " and the traitor who called himself her husband," but
that at Carberry he had nevertheless been followed only by four
Swedes, the other soldiers having been enlisted by him twelve days
later ; and that if any one could prove that at the time the
Queen was made prisoner he had given away or lent any of the
money intrusted to him, " he would submit to lose both life and
honour."

Note V, p. 385. The date of Bothwell's death.

Eiler Brockenhuus' *Historiske Kalenderantegnelser*, p. 42. Against
the weight of this and other statements which make Bothwell's
imprisonment last for ten years, and refer his death to the year
1578, J. Grundtvig has brought forward a new testimony, which
however does not possess the value he wishes to attach to it. The
accounts themselves for Dragsholm are now wanting, but if we take
the "short abstracts" of the feudal accounts by themselves, it is
found that the abstracts relating to the yearly accounts for 1573-
1574, 1574-1575, and 1575-1576, state that the expenses for

Dragsholm, among various not always specified purposes, were also for "the Scottish Earl." The abstracts of the following year's accounts on the contrary present no longer under the heading of accounts for Dragsholm this laconic statement, and from this it is concluded that Bothwell must by that time have been dead. But the abstract relating to the accounts for the year 1571-1572 mentions also that the expenses of Dragsholm, among different other purposes, had been for "Captain Klerck, who was there kept a prisoner." The abstract of the next year's accounts, however, contains under the heading of accounts for Dragsholm no such statement, and yet it is acknowledged on all hands that Captain Clark for some years after this date still "remained there a prisoner." If then in this case it is altogether impossible to draw any conclusion from silence on the part of the abstract of accounts as to death having occurred during the year, a similar conclusion can with no certainty be inferred from corresponding silence in the other abstracts of accounts.

Note W, p. 389. Turner's account of the death of Bothwell.

Carcerem Bothuelli vide Reginæ theatrum, et ipsam mortem testem innocentiæ. Siquidem Rex Daniæ pro communione sanguinis et familiæ, quae illi perpetua est cum regibus Scotis, cum sæpenumero minis illecebrisque conatus fuerit exprimere e Bothuello veritatem, tum in mortis articulo aggressus hominem, per Dei paulo post futuri judicis obtestationem, ut liberam iam tandem vocem mitteret indicem innocentiæ, aut sceleris Reginæ indicem. Post multum variumque sermonem de multa variaque re, quem cum Rege habuit, libera altaque voce ita sibi Deum propitium precabatur, ut Regina cædis Darleianæ nec conscia, nec præscia. Regi de percussore pergenti quærere, Murranius spurius, inquit, orsus est, Murtonius duxit, ego cædis hujus telam pertexui. Literas relinquit scriptas, modum præscriptum, locum notatum, conjuratorum numerum, fidem datam, alias res indices cædis et authorum. Moritur Bothuellus, vivit Danus princeps vestrarum partium testis. Bothuellium amentia perditum exhalasse scribit Buchananus, scilicet ut populus credat has voces fuisse insaniæ, non veritatis. *Maria Stuarta regina Scotiæ, Dotaria Franciæ Hæres Angliæ et Hyberniæ, martyr ecclesiæ, innocens a cæde Darnleiana.* Vindice Oberto Barnestapalio. Ingolstadii, 1588, from a reprint by Jebb *De vita et rebus gestis Mariæ Scotorum Reginæ,* i. 415. The ascription of Turner's Dedication to "D.

Gulielmo Alano, S. R. E. Cardinali" shows that he executed the
work "Venetiis, idibus Februarii 1588."

Note X, p. 391. Bothwell's dying declaration or so-called
"Testament."

The French abstracts of this document have come to us from the
Scots College or le Collège des Écossais, which was founded in the
University of Paris in 1333, by James Bishop of Moray. It was
united in 1639 with a seminary for Scots Catholic priests that had
been established by the Archbishop of Glasgow, James Beaton, for
many years Mary's Ambassador in France, who died in 1603.
The college, which at first stood in Rue des Amandiers, was removed in 1665 to Rue des Fossés-Saint-Victor, where in the chapel
is preserved in a gilt urn the brain of James II., the last of the
Stuart kings of Great Britain. Along with very many other
colleges and seminaries the Scots College was also abolished during
the Revolution in 1792, but was re-established under the Imperial
Government, united with the Irish College, and placed under the
superintendence of the French University, and has still its domicile
in Rue du Cheval Vert or Rue des Irlandais (Belin et Pujol,
Histoire civile, morale, et monumentale de Paris, Paris, 1843, pp. 134,
358). Among the many documents belonging to the history of
Mary which were preserved in the Scots College from the period of
Beaton's long-continued embassy, but which latterly went amissing,
was a contemporary abstract of the declaration ascribed to Bothwell. This abstract, however, was one of those contributed by
the college, which Keith was able to make use of, and which was
long ago reprinted in his *History of State and Church in Scotland*,
Appendix, p. 144. It begins thus:—"Le Comte de Bothuel,
malade à l'extrémité, au château de Malmay, a vérifié ce qui s'ensuit.
L'Evesque de Scone, avec quatre grands Seigneurs, à sçavoir : les
Seigneurs Berin Gowes, du château de Malmay, Otto Braw, du
château d'Ottenbrocht, Paris Braw, du château de Vescut, et
M. Gullunstarne, du château de Fulcenstrie, avec les quatre
baillifs de la ville, prièrent ledict Comte de déclarer librement
ce qu'il sçavoit de la mort du feu Roy Henry et des autheurs
d'icelle, comme il vouloit répondre devant Dieu et au jour
du jugement, là où toutes choses, tant cachées soyent-elles,
seront manifestées." In the British Museum are two contemporary abstracts of the Declaration, written in the English language,
both in the Cottonian Collection, Manuscr. Caligula, D. H. fol. 519,

and in Manuscr. Titus, c. vii. fol. 39. Somewhat different in the editing, they agree in their contents with the French abstract. The beginning is as follows:—" The confession of my Lord Bothwell before y dyed in presence of dyvers lords of Denmarke, being maire lang in latin and danisk. The lords present weare these: Baron Gowes of Malmye Castle, Otto Brawe of Elsinbroncho Castell, Monsieur Gullionestarne of Fowltostie Castell, tho bishop of Skone and four baylies of the towne, who desired him that he would declare his conscience and say nothinge but the truth concernand the Kiuge and Queene of Scotland with the childe." The abstract contained in the English manuscripts has been printed by Miss Agnes Strickland in her *Letters of Mary Queen of Scots and documents connected with her personal history*; London, 1843, iii. 123-125; more accurately by Prince Labanoff in his *Pièces et documents relatifs au Comte de Bothwell*, pp. 47-49, and by Tculet in his *Lettres*, pp. 243-245.

Note Y, page 395. The testament and latter will of the Lord Boduell.

[Two MSS. with this title, differing somewhat in their spelling and handwriting, are now in the library of the University of Edinburgh. How they came into the hands of Drummond is not known, but the probability is that he obtained possession of them through some friend who had been in the court of James VI. It would appear from the fact that two other MSS. of the same document, almost identical with the two in the University Library, are still extant in the British Museum, that numerous copies, all derived from the same original, existed at one time in the country. The reader who is desirous of seeing how very much alike all these MSS. of Bothwell's so-called testament are, may compare the one printed verbatim in this note with that given by Miss Strickland from the MSS. in the British Museum, *Letters of Mary Queen of Scots*, vol. i. pp. 304-6. The two MSS. now in the library of the University of Edinburgh were recovered, along with some others, in 1875. They had been taken home for some purpose by a former librarian, and he having died suddenly while they were in his possession, they fell into the hands of one of his relations, who, on learning subsequently their nature, restored them to the present librarian, John Small, M.A.—*Translator*.]

" The confessione of the Lord Bothuell, before he dyed, in the presence of 4 Lords of Denmarke uith many uthers in Malmye

Castle, under the King of Denmarks jurisdictiono; being more at length in the Latine and Danes tongue written. And these be their names, Berreis Cowes of Malmy Castle, Otta Braw of Alffenbrowghe Castle, Pieris Braw of Veseull Castle, Mouns. Gulliam Starne of Sentoftira Castle. With the Bishope of Skone and four Baylyves of the Toune, desyreing him that he would declare his confession, and say nothing but the truth, concerning the King and Queene and childe hir sone.

"Secondly, he did take it upon him with his death, That the Queen did never knou nor consent to the death of the King; but he and his freinds by his appoyntment and devyse; and likuyse divers uther Lords consenting therunto, which uas not there at that present deide doing. And thes be ther names, The Lord Mortoun nou regent, The Lord James, The Erle of Glencairne, The Erle of Argyle, The Lord Robert, The Lord Lethingtoune, The Lord Boyde, The Laird of Grange, The Lord Erle Huntley, The Erle of Crawfourd, The Laird of Buckleuche, The Lord of Pharnyharst (Fernyhurst) uith many others.

"Thridly, he did confesse, that all the freindship he had at the Queens hands, was by means of witchcraft, and all inventions that belong therto, to make hir to love him: and he did find the means to put his maryed uif away. He did confesse that after the mariage he did seek all the means possible to destroy the young child: And also he sought all the means he could to destroy many Lords of Scotland, and that by treason.

"Fourthly, he confessed that he had deceived many Gentlewomen both of France and England, uith many other uilde facts uhich he said uare too long to rehearse, asking God forgivenes therfore: And likuyse did confesse, that he had taken auay tuo Ladys Daughters out of Denmark into Scotland, and made them both beleive he would marry ȳm, and did defloure yem of their virginitie, and likuyse many Gentlewomen of Scotland.

"Fifthly, he confessed that he had deceived tuo of the Borrou maister's daughters of Hokirks,[1] with many moe deids in that place; uhich he said uould be too long to declare at length: But these expressed and all his offences he did since his birth, he did aske forgivenes, and did forgive all the uorld, and uas sorrowful for his offences, and did receive the sacrament, that this uas good and true. And therafter dyed.

[1] Lübeck, according to the copy printed by Miss Strickland.

Note Z, p. 396. Alleged forged documents produced during the conflict between Protestantism and Catholicism.

As a pendant to the statement in the text on this subject, we may certainly adduce from contemporary Continental literature the so-called " Discours du Roy Henry troisiesme à un personnage d'honneur et de qualité estant près de sa Majesté sur les causes et les motifs de la St. Barthélemy." It professes to be an account of how Henry of Anjou, two days after having arrived as King of Poland in the year 1573, in the, to him, altogether foreign city of Cracow, being tormented by agony of mind, is said, during a sleepless night in the palace to have called an unnamed confidant of his, to whom he confessed that the frightful images of St. Bartholomew's night would not allow him to sleep, and then by a discourse as to how everything on that occasion took place, to have sought ease to his mind. Against the genuineness of this account, which Sismondi, Michelet, and Henri Martin accepted as authentic, Mackintosh (*History of England*, London, 1830-1836, iii. 230) in the first instance, and more recently Ranke (*Französische Geschichte, vornehmlich im sechszehnten und siebzehnten Jahrhundert*, Stuttgart und Tübingen, 1852-1861, i. 330) have with reason declared themselves.

INDEX.

2 E